SHADOWS OF THE PAST

"Upset husbands do weird things. Could be he's the one responsible for the trouble you've been having, the marks on Alex, the problems at work."

"It's not like that! He wouldn't do those things! It's someone from before."

"Before?" Nick forced himself to sound only vaguely interested. "Before what? Before you were married?"

Kate began to walk around the room. "I don't know what I meant . . . Just that it wasn't Paul. He wouldn't hurt his own child."

"What is it you're afraid of, Kate? If there's something in your past you're ashamed of or afraid of, you're not going to be able to keep it locked away, you know. We'll find out."

She wouldn't even look at him.

He tried again. "Is there someone from your past who might have a grudge against you? An old lover, perhaps?"

"No!" Kate said at once.

The response was so sharp that both police officers focused on Kate's face, which was moist with perspiration. She stopped pacing. "No one," she repeated, and sensed that she had screwed up. *They know!* she thought, beginning to panic, then changed her mind. *No, they suspect. But they'll start probing.* And a voice deep in her brain, much more urgent this time, whispered, *Run, Kate, while you have time . . .*

Praise for *When The Wind Blows*

"A real corker. Fox uses misdirection with the skill of a master magician, keeping us looking in one direction while he does something sneaky with the other hand . . . sit back and enjoy the show."

—*Booklist*

Praise for *All Fall Down*

"Page turner of the Week. A supercharged first novel."

—*People Magazine*

"This one scared me."

—*New York Times Book Review*

"Breathtaking. Brimming with suspense."

—*Publishers Weekly*

CRADLE
AND ALL

Zachary Alan Fox

PINNACLE BOOKS
KENSINGTON PUBLISHING CORP

http://www.pinnaclebooks.com

For Ken and Mendy.
And for Caleb.

July 9

Do I let you read this, Kate? Katie? Katherine?
*I've pondered that for years. Do I let Kate Katie Katherine,
or whatever you're calling yourself now, see why her life has
become a living hell?*
Or not?
Of course I do. Or it all becomes as pointless as life itself.
But only after.
After . . .
*This is how we'll do it, then: I'll keep this lively little journal,
noting down our feelings, you and I, and when it's over, when
you're writhing on the floor pleading with someone to kill you
because you haven't the guts to do it yourself, we'll read it
together so you can understand why it had to happen exactly
the way it did.*

1

Your baby is going to die.

The first threat scrolled across Kate's computer screen as she hurried to finish a medical form for a Korean woman having a cesarean in the maternity wing. The office door was open, as always, and the bedlam from the emergency room forty feet away swirled noisily around her, doctors and nurses rushing an appendectomy to the OR, an ambulance pulling up outside as its siren groaned down, Jerry Springer on the waiting-room TV breaking up a fight among half a dozen guests, while a middle-aged drunk with a bloody face and a broken arm was screaming obscenities at the television and the cops and anyone nearby as he was handcuffed to a chair.

What did that say?

Kate blinked, shook her head, and looked again at her monitor. It wasn't there. *I imagined it, didn't I? Must have. Nerves.* And guilt, she supposed with an annoyed sigh. Well, why not, working in a madhouse like this, while Alex, her eight-month-old son, was at the sitter's? Of course she worried about him. She spent half the day wondering how Alex was doing, but . . .

"Kate!"

Patty Mars, an admitting clerk and Kate's closest friend at work, burst into the office, her feet sliding on the tile floor. "Didn't you hear the page? We've got an abuse case for you. A five-year-old girl, banged up pretty badly. How's your Spanish?"

"As bad as yesterday," Kate said, getting to her feet. As the only day-shift social worker she was responsible for a

myriad of duties, including interviewing the parents of any
child who hospital personnel thought might be the victim of
abuse or neglect. California law required that all such cases be
reported to the authorities. It was Kate's responsibility to make
that determination. And the most depressing aspect of her job

Kate began to follow Patty down the hallway, past scurrying
nurses and orderlies and half a dozen beds of moaning patients
waiting to be seen, when she stopped suddenly as an infant
was hurriedly wheeled past on a gurney heading toward the
elevators.

"What?" Patty asked impatiently, looking back without
stopping.

"The jumpsuit that baby had on. It was just like Alex's."

"So?" She grabbed Kate's arm, jerking her forward.

"But I *made* Alex's jumpsuit; I didn't buy it. I got the
material at Fabric City last month. It was the end of the bolt."

Patty looked at her with impatience. "That wasn't Alex
Kate. He was Hispanic or Asian. Jesus!"

"I know. But . . . Oh, never mind." They hurried into the
ER, and to a screened-in area where Dr. Joel Symonds, just
out of his residency, was hovering over a tiny, dark-skinned girl
sitting stiffly on the edge of a bed. She had obvious abrasions to
her arms and legs, and looked frightened to death of the medical
equipment and noise and strange people hovering around her
Symonds didn't look up, seeming to sense Kate next to him
as Patty hurriedly veered off for her own office. "Probably
nothing broken, but we'll take an X ray just to be sure." He
smiled at the girl and laid a hand on her shoulder. "Anna
Delgado, I'd like you to meet the prettiest lady in the hospital—
Kate McDonald. She's here to help you. She'll want to talk to
you later, and I want you to be nice to her. OK?"

Patty was already at the door. Kate yelled out, "Come by
on your break," and Patty waved an acknowledgment without
turning around. Bending down to be level with the young girl's
face, Kate smiled. "Happy to meet you, Anna. My, you're
pretty, aren't you? How old are you?"

The little girl stared at her with wide eyes but said nothing.
Kate tried again. *"¿Habla usted inglés, Anna?"*

The girl's face was frozen shut. Only her eyes moved, darting fearfully about the room.

Symonds's tone became grave. "She's been beaten pretty badly. Look." He gently settled the girl onto her back, then turned her over and pulled down her shorts. Her buttocks were red with welts.

Kate silently gasped. *Your baby is going to die.*

"Makes you wonder, doesn't it?" Symonds went on. "What kind of person would do that to a forty-pound child?"

"You'd be surprised," Kate said in an undertone. "I've seen it in families from Beverly Hills to East L.A. You never get used to it, though."

Kate helped the girl sit up again. "Did your mommy or daddy do this to you, Anna? *Madre o padre?*"

The girl closed her eyes, drew her elbows in tightly to her body, and began to tremble.

"I've got to get her to X ray," Symonds said. "I think her right femur may have a hairline fracture. The mother's in the waiting room. There's no question of abuse, only who's responsible. Good luck with her. She hasn't been very cooperative so far."

When Kate entered the waiting room the drunk and the two policemen had disappeared, no doubt to the locked police ward down the hall. A dozen people slumped in ripped Naugahyde chairs, mostly ignoring Jerry Springer's guests shouting furiously from the television bolted to the ceiling, staring instead at their feet, or weeping silently, or holding pained parts of their body. Anna's mother, wearing a blouse and dark slacks, was in the middle of the room, gazing into space. She jumped when Kate said, "Mrs. Delgado, I'm Kate McDonald, a social worker for Midtown Memorial Hospital. Do you mind if I ask you a few questions?"

The woman was about thirty-five, short and stocky, with thick black hair swept up under a blue and red scarf. Mayan, Kate thought, from southern Mexico or Guatemala. She looked frightened, and her eyes darted to the door as though she were going to bolt any minute.

"Anna," the woman demanded. *"¿Donde está ella?* I need to take her home. Now."

"Anna is having an X ray. You'll be able to see her in a moment. I just need to fill out some forms first." Kate smiled, hoping to disarm the woman; many of Midtown Memorial's patients didn't understand English, but all of them understood forms. Kate didn't mention that they would be faxed to the LAPD as soon as they were completed.

The woman looked again toward the door.

"Por favor, señora." Normally Kate interviewed people in her office, but she sensed that if she tried to take Nora Delgado deeper into the hospital the woman would disappear. Instead she lightly put her fingers on Mrs. Delgado's arm, knowing that touch often encouraged trust, and smiled. *"Por favor.* Only a few minutes. *Cinco minutos."*

Still the woman hesitated. Kate tried a new approach. *"No migre, señora.* No deportation. Please! *Cinco minutos."*

The woman's face eased somewhat. Kate again lightly touched her arm, encouraging her to stand, and pointed to the semiprivate desk ten feet away. Patty Mars was at the adjacent cubicle, getting insurance information from a woman with a bandaged eye. With a final desperate glance at the entrance door, Mrs. Delgado followed Kate.

"Now," Kate said after they were seated, "your name is Nora Delgado?"

The woman's hands began twisting in her lap. *"Sí."* She bent forward. "Anna. She is OK?"

"We're having her X-rayed. She may have a broken or fractured leg. Do you know how this happened?"

The woman's eyes moved briefly away. "She fall down. In the *cocina,* the kitchen."

Kate didn't believe her but made a note. "And the marks on her bottom?"

Mrs. Delgado frowned with incomprehension.

"Her—" Kate tried to remember the word. *"Las nalgas.* She has been hurt."

"No, no." The woman's face flushed and her voice shook. "She fall. From running."

Kate stared into her face. "She was beaten, hit." She mimicked with her hand.

Mrs. Delgado twisted around as if to stand up, but decided to remain seated. "Anna run in the kitchen. She fall down. Hurt herself. No hit."

Kate's attention was suddenly drawn to the woman's neck. She bent forward to look more closely. "How did you get those scars? Did your husband—"

"No! No!" The woman shot out of her chair and spun around. Everyone in the waiting room was watching them now. "I want Anna!" She took a step away from the cubicle. "Anna!" She began to scream.

"She has to be treated—"

"No!" Mrs. Delgado whirled back to Kate, facing her angrily. "I want her. Bring her. I take her home."

"We have to care for her. She's been hurt. If you're afraid of your husband we can—"

But the woman turned and hurried toward the door to the ER. "Mrs. Delgado, you can't go in there."

Howling fiercely, she burst through the swinging doors and out of Kate's sight. One of Jerry Springer's guests was on her feet, screaming, "Y'all never cared about nothin' 'cepting yourself," but no one was watching; they were all staring instead toward the ER, where they could hear Mrs. Delgado's muted voice, and catch fleeting glimpses of the turmoil inside as the doors swung back and forth.

Kate grabbed the phone and dialed eight. "Security," a bored voice answered.

"The ER," she shouted. "Stat. And get someone who speaks Spanish."

A guard was right outside the exterior door. He burst in just as another ambulance, siren screaming, drew up to the Emergency entrance, and again everyone in the waiting room stared with mute fascination as the guard raced past them, followed by Kate, and pushed through the still-swinging doors.

Mrs. Delgado was screaming at Dr. Mohammed Kamel, the large, bearded head of the emergency room, tearing at his blue tunic with her thick fingers, pulling it from his body as he attempted to defend himself.

"I want my daughter!" the woman screamed. "What did you do to her?"

Kamel was muttering in Pakistani and trying to defend himself, while a nurse unsuccessfully tried to pull Mrs. Delgado away from him. The security guard seized one of the woman's arms just as another guard rushed into the ER and grabbed the other.

They managed to drag the woman away from Kamel, whose arms had been bloodied from her fingernails. As they hurried her toward a locked office nearby, one of the guards turned to Kate. "There're two cops in the jail OR. Better get them. And tell them to hurry."

"Medicine and social work," Kate muttered as she maneuvered around a gurney being rushed inside by ambulance attendants screaming, "Gunshot!" She began to race down the hall. "The 'helping professions,' making the world a better place for all of us."

And just another day in Bedlam . . .

2

Which always made coming home that much more relaxing, even though she knew her in-laws would be there today. "Oh, no, Helen. You really shouldn't have gone to all this trouble."

Really shouldn't have! Kate thought with a sigh as she looked at the standing rib roast Helen had just taken out of the oven. But she would never say anything to upset her mother- and father-in-law, especially on her and Paul's fourth anniversary. Helen and Tommy had both recently retired from teaching jobs, and most of their pleasure in life came now from doing things for their son and his wife, as well as playing attentive grandparents to eight-month-old Alex. They were, Kate had come to appreciate over the years, extraordinarily caring people, and the fact that they sometimes involved themselves in her life more than she would have liked was a minor inconvenience.

Kate was tasting Helen's gravy when she heard the front door open, and seconds later Paul, looking disheveled in the July heat, burst into the kitchen holding a dozen pink roses to add to those he had brought home on each of the previous three nights.

"I'd hate to see your house on your fiftieth anniversary," Tommy joked, giving his son a hug while Kate found a vase for the flowers.

"Hey, it's a tradition," Paul said happily. "But maybe we'll top out at ten dozen. Six more years. This place will start to look like a funeral home by then."

"Not a chance," Kate said, kissing her husband on the lips. "You promised: a dozen for each year, and if that means fifty dozen someday, so be it."

Paul laughed and stripped off his tie. At thirty-two he was two years younger than Kate, though he managed—at work, anyway—to affect the quiet dignity of most of his older colleagues in the district attorney's office, where he was one of the vast army of bottom-rungers, with only three years' service. At home he was the most energetic and exuberant person Kate had ever encountered. With his long-distance running and basketball and ever-changing enthusiasms for this or that hobby or game or social cause, Kate sometimes felt exhausted just looking at him.

"Where's the big kid?" Paul asked at once. "Not asleep, is he? My God, all he does is sleep. When I was his age I was already reading law books. Right, Mom?"

"You were never his age, Paul. You started life as a 'terrible two' and the next thing I knew you were eighteen and leaving for college. Let the poor child sleep if he wants to."

As though on cue Alex started crying from the upstairs nursery, a word Kate still had trouble uttering with a straight face. Having recently moved into their 3,500-square-foot Brentwood home after living in a two-bedroom bungalow in the Valley since marriage, she wasn't used to "nurseries" and "sewing rooms" and, God help her, a "conservatory." Sometimes she thought she was caught in a real-life game of Clue. *Professor Plum, in the conservatory, with the candlestick.*

Paul ducked out of the kitchen, and moments later they heard his rapid tread on the stairs as he hurried down with Alex held high above his head, arms flapping weakly like a bird in distress. "It's Alex the Wonder Baby, going for a flight to the moon." He swooped the baby around and around near the ceiling and made airplane sounds.

Alex seemed caught between giggling and crying, settling finally on the latter.

"Hungry," Helen said with grandmotherly wisdom.

As Paul passed his son to a waiting Grandpa, Kate asked, "Have you seen that blue and red jumpsuit I made for him?"

Paul shrugged and brushed his longish blond hair from his forehead—like a young Robert Redford, Kate thought every time he did that, and never told him it was one of the things that attracted her to him. "No, I haven't seen it for a while. It's probably in the wash."

"Probably," Kate agreed.

After several moments of cooing and chin tickling, Kate took the increasingly demanding Alex to the semidarkened nursery, and sat in a rocking chair to nurse him. Her breasts were sore and the nipples painful to the touch. It was time to switch to milk and juice; eight months of this was enough, especially extracting mother's milk with the breast pump and storing it in a refrigerator so Alex could be fed when she was at work.

Something's not right. Someone's been in this room. Now where in the world did *that* idea come from? She looked around the room and saw nothing out of place. Still . . . *Oh, stop it! Don't be a fool. No one's been in here. My goodness!*

Your baby is going to die.

God, she was getting neurotic, sensing strangers in her home and seeing nonexistent threats on a computer, of all places. High-tech hysteria, from too many hours in front of a monitor, as well as eight hours a day spent dealing with others' tragedies. Maybe she ought to find a more peaceful place to work. Midtown Memorial Hospital, just off Sunset ("A Celebration of Wellness in Central Hollywood") was a microcosm of the worst of L.A. life: daily shootings, wife beatings, gory attention-grabbing suicides (jumping off the roof of a Sunset Strip hotel, self-immolation in the Paramount back lot, a bullet in the brain while sitting on Rudolph Valentino's grave), as well as gang rapes that left the victim bloodied, senseless, and, increasingly, dead. On the other hand, it was this seamy slice of life that was responsible for Paul's job in the DA's office, and which was paying for their house.

"Hey, you two about done in there?" It was Helen, anxious to put her anniversary dinner on the table. Kate wondered what sort of dessert the woman had concocted this time. With all day to cook she had been coming up with unbelievable—and unbelievably fattening—dishes that Kate never would have attempted, but also never could resist. Besides, it was nice to forget about diets and sensible eating once in a while.

She looked down at her child. "How about it, Alexander the Great? Had enough?"

The baby made a slurping noise. "Give us a few more minutes," Kate yelled. "The more he has now the less he'll need later." Or so the theory went. Must have been a man who thought that one up.

They ate on the patio, under a white latticed roof ablaze with bright purple bougainvillea. Nature cooperated by spreading a layer of low clouds over the Pacific that reflected the setting sun in a garish Cecil B. DeMille sky that dripped blood over the California coastline. "We ought to have Charlton Heston dressed up as Moses to do the serving," Tommy said, looking at the Technicolor clouds. Then he reconsidered, "Maybe not. Last time I saw him he was carrying these two tablets listing all the things folks couldn't do anymore. Took all the fun out of life."

As always when Helen took care of things, dinner was perfect, the only sour note coming when Kate said, "I had the weirdest sensation at work today. I was staring into my computer monitor when I thought I saw a message that said, 'Your baby is going to die.' "

Everyone's head bobbed up at the same time. "What?" Paul said. He stopped chewing.

"It seemed to scroll across the screen, but when I looked back it was gone."

Tommy smiled at her as a blue jay, its long tail proudly erect, landed on a railing next to them and eyed the food on the table. "Maybe it's postpartum blues. I saw a TV show on that once, women acting weird after a baby is born."

"Oh, don't be foolish," his wife said. "You don't have postpartum blues eight months later. Kate was just imagining things. It's that terrible place you work. You ought to find a job in a nicer part of town."

"Oh, Hollywood's not that bad," she lied.

"I don't understand," Paul said. His voice was concerned. "Did you actually see it or just imagine it?"

Kate shrugged and felt a little foolish. She probably shouldn't have brought it up. "Imagined it, I guess. But it seemed real at the time." She suppressed an unexpected shudder, a chill that trickled along her spine as though someone were dragging an ice cube down her back.

"Have you been worrying about Alex?"

"No. Not at all."

Helen asked, "He doesn't have any problems, does he? He's healthy?"

"It's nothing like that, Helen. Just the pressure of spending all day with other people's problems, I'm sure."

"You haven't had any more trouble with Zamora, have you?" her husband asked. "I talked to Glazier last week about her. He said he'd look into it."

Paul was on Midtown's board of directors, a largely ceremonial position that allowed him to demonstrate public-spiritedness, but also made him aware of hospital politics and the difficulties of running a huge urban health care facility. That, coupled with Kate's pillow talk, made him familiar with the problems she and other employees had encountered with Judith Zamora, a hospital administrator. Paul had brought it up with Dr. Elton Glazier, the hospital president, who had seemed concerned and said he'd check it out and let Paul know what he'd found.

"Troubles with the Monster of Midtown?" Kate asked with excessive sweetness. "Why certainly not. How could anyone have problems with a person of such a helpful, gentle, and easygoing disposition?"

"Shoot," Tommy said, waving his fork in the air, "I never did understand all this nonsense about getting along with your boss, or enjoying your work, or not being 'fulfilled,' whatever that means. You're not supposed to like your job. If you were it wouldn't be called *work;* it'd be called *fun.*"

Paul smiled as he lifted a forkful of bacon-covered string beans. "That's either the most profound thing you've ever said, or something really stupid, Pop."

Tommy patted Kate's hand and tilted his head across the table toward his wife. "Helen and I put up with dictatorial principals and incompetent administrators for forty years."

" 'Incompetent administrators' is a redundancy," Helen said in a tone so snappish it startled Kate.

Tommy was annoyed at being interrupted. "Having trouble with a boss is just part of life. Could be worse, you know. You could be in the post office. When people there get upset they don't bitch and moan; they whip out an Uzi and start firing. It's given 'disgruntled' a whole new meaning."

"And the victims end up in the ER while I have to interview the next of kin," Kate said.

Paul looked up. "Has anyone ever heard of a 'gruntled' employee? Maybe that's what I am."

Helen suddenly came to her feet. "Enough of guns and death already. Who's ready for a chocolate soufflé with hot fudge sauce, fresh iced raspberries, and a giant mound of home-made whipped cream? Surely someone here can appreciate the finer things in life."

Five minutes after Tommy and Helen went home to Sherman Oaks, the doorbell rang and Lilliana Elizabeth Quinlin, Kate's next-door neighbor, smiled wanly, said, "Happy anniversary," and handed Kate a potted orange and purple orchid. "Grown at home, hon. I learned my lesson last year when I gave you a rose and it died of embarrassment among Paul's thirty-six sexy rivals. This time I thought I'd better try something a little more exotic."

Kate laughed and held the door open. "Come on in, Lilliana. Paul's upstairs taking a shower." She took the fragile-looking flower and led the way to the family room with its wall of French doors overlooking the fenced-in pool, now lit up with accent lights.

"I won't stay long," her friend said, sitting down on the butter-soft green leather couch that Kate had just bought. "I realize Paul's never thrilled to find me here."

"Oh, that's not true and you know it."

"Oh, that *is* true," she replied happily. "Don't try to gloss it over with kind words. Some men just react to me that way. Most men, I guess. I've never figured out why."

About forty years old, thin almost to the point of emaciation, with short black hair and a hard but pretty face, Lilliana had moved into her sprawling house next door shortly after her marriage to Hans, a man more than ten years her senior, who did something obscure in investments, though Lilliana claimed not to know anything about it. It must have been rewarding, though, since it allowed her to spend her days gardening, playing tennis, or working out at a local health club. Paul, who disliked few people, had felt uncomfortable around Lilliana from the first. The Queen of Clean, he called her, because of the way she compulsively scrubbed her house from top to bottom. Sometimes they'd see her at midnight through the windows, scouring kitchen walls or vacuuming the living room. But Kate liked her, especially liked how her dry sense of humor could turn the day's misadventures from annoyances to something to laugh about.

"Four years!" Lilliana announced as though it were an achievement of unparalleled proportions. "I don't know how you and Paul manage it. My three marriages together don't add up to four years."

"That's a fib, Lilliana."

"OK. So they add up to—let me see." She leaned back and closed her dark eyes as though the calculations were difficult and she had to call upon some higher powers of computation. "Hank the Bank, as he's affectionately known, lasted eight dreary years, though the alimony lasted ten. Walt the Weasel was worn out after only two years and two months, poor dear, and slunk back to his mousy-looking first wife, who foolishly took him in. And Hans—what should I call him? Hans the Secret Mafiosi? Hans the Hunnish Philanderer? Well, Hans hasn't put in even two years yet. Not until September. I may not let him make it."

"Come on, Lilliana. Hans is not as bad as you make him out to be. I like him."

"Honey," she said, putting her feet up on the coffee table, "all men are just as bad as they want to be. And Hans wants it a lot. Why do you think he's always 'working late' or 'with a client' until eleven or twelve every night? It's funny how all his clients seem to tire him out so much he's never in the mood for his wife."

Fearing another recitation of Lilliana's supposedly nonexistent sex life, Kate said, "We had another gang victim end up in the ER today. A boy of about fifteen, shot nine times at Hollywood High because he had the wrong sneakers on."

So they chatted about the deterioration of life in Los Angeles for ten minutes until Lilliana got up to leave. "I don't want to push my luck with Paul. He's already convinced that I'm over here more than I'm at home. Something my own husband would never notice, by the way."

Ten minutes later Kate was heading up the stairs when the phone rang. She took it in the large master bedroom that she had been decorating in a frilly "country" fashion, though Paul had asked, "What country? Eighteenth-century France?" A cheerful voice on the other end of the line said, "Happy anniversary, hon."

"Oh, Mom. Thank you so much." Kate brightened at her mother's voice. Her father had died four years ago, and her mother, still in the same house in St. Louis she had lived in for half a century, didn't want to travel all the way to Los Angeles, so Kate saw her only once every year or so when she and Paul went east.

They talked for fifteen minutes, mostly about Alex, whom her mother had yet to see. "I've been going through your old baby books, Katie. You looked just like those pictures of Alex you sent. He has the same square jaw."

"And Paul's eyes."

"Your hair, though. I hope he doesn't have your temper, too." The older woman's voice instantly shot up. "I didn't mean it like that, honey. I just meant babies can be so demanding."

"I know, Mom. Alex is a dream. He sleeps right through the night, and almost never cries, except when he's hungry."

"Well, you certainly weren't like that. . . ." And so it went for another few minutes until her mother said she was planning to go to bed. After saying good-bye, Kate glanced in the closet, where she had stashed her anniversary gift for Paul—a leather briefcase from Coach that cost more than she had ever spent on a gift in her life, then jumped when a hand clamped itself on her bare neck. She spun around, her heart pounding, to see her husband standing in the nude, his hair still wet from the shower. "Happy number four, Katie, my love," he said, pulling her off her feet and against his body. "It's nine o'clock. Time to start the real celebration."

She broke free and began to unbutton her blouse. "What took you so long?"

3

"Oh, no, please," Kate muttered as she awoke to Alex's crying. She opened her eyes onto the digital clock—2:17—then closed them again and tried to will herself back to sleep. *This isn't happening. I'm dreaming it.*

The crying got louder and louder until Paul said, "You'd better get up."

Kate burrowed her head into the pillow. Hadn't she just told her mother how Alex always slept through the night? "You do it," she finally muttered.

"Sorry, Katie. Would if I could, but it's you he wants."

She flipped on the bedside light. "I don't think he's hungry, Paul. He hasn't woken up during the night in months."

"You want me to—"

"No, no, I'll handle it." *Whatever it is.* She swung her feet to the floor, felt around for her slippers, then gave up. "God, I hope I'll be able to get back to sleep." But she heard Paul's soft snoring coming from behind her.

"Oh, well . . ."

Barefoot and half-asleep, she walked into the nursery, where Alex was still crying, switched on the Big Bird lamp, and began screaming at once.

Paul, without any clothes on, was next to her in an instant. "My God," he said, as a rat raced across his bare feet.

Kate snatched Alex from the crib. His fingers and toes were bloody, and his screaming was getting louder and more out of control. "How did they get in here?" she asked. Her body was shaking uncontrollably, and she could sense herself becoming hysterical as at least a dozen rats scurried around the nursery floor.

Without hesitation Paul emptied a plastic bucket that held toys and plopped it down over one of the rats. Quickly turning the bucket upright, he forced the rat inside with a pillow from the crib. Holding the pillow, stained with Alex's blood, on top of the bucket, he reached down and grabbed another darting rat with his bare hand, then moved the pillow enough to drop it inside.

"Wait here. Don't move." Paul raced into the hallway with the bucket.

"My God," Kate screamed. "They're everywhere. There's more behind the dresser."

Paul ran toward the stairs, but the pillow fell or was pushed from the bucket. When he swooped down to retrieve it one of the rats reared up and bit his finger. Swearing savagely, he dropped the bucket to the floor and the rats raced back along the hallway toward the nursery.

"Shut the door!" he screamed. "They're coming back that way."

The door slammed and the rats veered away, heading instead for the lighted bedroom Kate and Paul had just come from.

"Jesus," Paul muttered, and ran down the hall in time to see the rats scurry under the king-size bed. He dropped to his knees, yanked up the sheets, and saw the rodents' heads not two feet away, bloody black noses twitching, and tiny eyes staring hatefully at him.

"Get out of here, damn you!" Paul grabbed a shoe and swiped at them, but instead of retreating, they burst from under the bed right at him. Instinctively he lurched back, but the rats shot forward, intent on attack, and bit his bare ankle and foot. Losing his balance, he tumbled awkwardly onto his back, feeling suddenly vulnerable in his nakedness. The rats raced between his legs, leaping onto his stomach and chest, razor-sharp toenails digging into his flesh and leaving a trail of scratches on his neck and face as they headed toward the dimly lit bathroom five feet away. Paul could hear them run into something and knock it over—a can of cleanser probably. Rolling onto his stomach he quickly lunged forward, grabbed the door by the bottom, and pulled it shut.

From somewhere beyond the bedroom he could hear Alex's wailing above the sound of Kate choking on her tears. Hurrying into the hallway he found them sitting on the floor outside the closed door of the nursery. "Hang on. I've got them trapped."

"There must be ten more in the nursery. But we've got to get to the hospital. Alex's fingers and toes . . ."

Paul looked at the baby, then down at his own bloody ankle. "I'd better kill the ones in the bathroom so they can do a rabies test. If not we'll both have to get the shots, and they're not fun."

"God." Kate felt as if her knees were going to give way, and she slumped against the wall.

"It won't take long." Paul shut the bedroom door and thought, What am I going to kill them with?

Still naked, he went through the house to the garage and flipped on the light. There wasn't much to choose from. It would have to be a shovel. Something about arming himself with a shovel made him shiver—a primitive weapon against a primitive enemy.

The rats seemed to be waiting for him in a corner of the bathroom under the sink, making angry hissing sounds and darting their heads quickly back and forth, as if prepared to make a final stand. Aware of his nakedness, Paul stepped forward, holding the shovel like a spear. "Don't move, you filthy little bastards. Just stand there." He raised the shovel.

Five minutes later, dressed in Dockers and a T-shirt, he found Kate cowering in the hallway, her back against the wall and Alex pressed protectively against her chest. "Go ahead and get dressed. I'll watch Alex."

As Kate handed him the baby he said, "Don't go in the bathroom. Use the one in the hall."

"Is the ER always this crazy at three A.M.?" Kate could hear the tension in Paul's voice as he looked around at the half dozen patients being attended to in the overly bright room with its banks of fluorescent lights and harsh white walls. The waiting room beyond held at least another twenty people, patients, friends, family. There was noise and confusion everywhere, doctors yelling, nurses arguing, patients moaning. A uniformed armed guard stood just inside the door, the walkie-talkie on his belt sputtering static and short bursts of incomprehensible words, while another waited outside the ER entrance, and others patrolled the parking lot and main entrance.

"Weekend nights," Dr. Joel Symonds said pleasantly, bandaging Alex's fingers. "What do you expect? This is Hollyweird. Friday and Saturday are OD nights—ecstasy, crack, smack, and crank. Sunday through Thursday are our officially designated gang-shooting nights. There's always something going on, but if you come in on weekends I can guarantee you more fun than a year's worth of *ER* episodes."

"Joel," Kate said softly. She wasn't in the mood for this. It was her baby who was injured. Alex had finally stopped crying, but he looked miserable as all these unfamiliar faces loomed over him, ministering to his wounds.

"Hey, Mom, relax. He'll be OK. A little nibbling on the fingers and toes never hurt anyone. I do it myself sometimes. It's no big deal. Isn't that right, Alex, my friend?" He tickled the boy's belly.

"As long as it's not rabies," Paul reminded him.

"Well, there is that. Animal Control can tell from the corpus delicti. Only takes twenty-four hours, I think. I wouldn't worry. I've never heard of a case of rabies in L.A. as long as I've been here."

"Four years," Kate said numbly. How did she remember that?

Symonds smiled. "Yeah. A newcomer. But every doctor in the ER came from somewhere outside L.A. This is the crossroads of the world." He began to wrap the boy's toes in gauze. "You'll be able to take this off tomorrow. Leave the fingers wrapped until Tuesday, though. How did rats get in a crib anyway? And in Brentwood, no less. You're ruining my image of the good life."

"California's dirty little secret," Paul told him. "They live in the tops of palm trees. They don't usually come in a house, though."

Symonds straightened and looked from Paul to Kate. "These

nasty little fellows of yours scooted down a fifty-foot palm, came inside, waltzed upstairs, then went casually down to the nursery, and somehow climbed up and into the crib?''

"Yeah," Paul said, sounding suddenly defensive.

"You keep the nursery door closed?"

"No," Kate said. "I want to hear Alex if he cries."

"Good idea. But maybe you ought to get one of those baby-minder microphones and leave the door closed from now on." Symonds picked the child up. "Hefty little fellow, aren't you? Maybe we'll give you a course in self-defense. The boys against the rats." He passed Alex to Kate. "He's OK, but keep an eye on him. It isn't too many kids who end up as the entree on a rodent menu. It's damn weird, when you think about it."

4

"Rats?" Patty Mars said at work Monday morning. Her face screwed up in revulsion. "You've got to be kidding. Where you live?"

"I was surprised, too. I guess they nest in palm trees and create nasty little rat families." Kate was amazed at how calm she could be about it now. A little over forty-eight hours ago she was so frightened she couldn't keep her body from shaking uncontrollably. Paul wouldn't even let her hold Alex until they got home from the hospital, so afraid was he that she was going to drop him.

"But they were in your *house,* not a tree. And biting Alex. God, that's creepy. Can you imagine lying there while those sharp teeth are chewing the flesh on your fingers?" She shivered and added, "Yuk."

Patty was a year older than Kate, and her only real friend at the hospital, though her lifestyle was as far from Kate's as it could be. At five-foot-five and 130 pounds she was far from svelte, but it didn't stop men from being drawn to her like bees to clover. Her blond hair, pretty face, and busty physique certainly added to her appeal, though Patty insisted it was her bubbly personality men were attracted to. "That, and the fact that I like sex more than the preliminaries. I don't know why everyone acts like it's so damn weird. I mean, who really cares about candlelight dinners and long walks on the beach? Let's get down to business. Right?"

She hovered next to Kate's open door, knowing she had to get back to her admitting desk in the ER before she was missed. "And the rabies test was negative?"

"Thank God," Kate said. "I'm not sure an eight-month-old can survive rabies."

Frankie Yorba, a muscular ER orderly, strolled by and said, "Hey, Patty Mars Bars. Out of your area but lookin' good, babe. Let's do it tonight."

"Go lift some weights, Frankie."

Yorba laughed as he disappeared toward the operating room. "Can't stay away from me, can you?"

A different male voice said, "How's the little guy doing?"

Joel Symonds, in his green operating room scrubs, walked in past Patty and pulled the paper cap from his head. "Fine," Kate told him. "But I'm afraid he's going to get too used to me being around every time he opens his eyes. I didn't let him out of my sight over the weekend. It's going to make it difficult for the baby-sitter."

"Well, it's understandable," he said. "But in a few days you'll both forget this ever happened. Who's watching him now?"

"The sitter. Mrs. Alamada. She lives on Las Palmas."

"You trust her?" He wiped an arm across a sweaty forehead, then stared at her.

Kate was startled by the question, and had a sudden image of Alex's bloodied fingers and toes. "Trust her?" What did he mean by that? "Of course I—" She stopped as Symonds was paged stat to the ER. Simultaneously, the phone rang and she snatched at it, listening just a moment, then saying, "They're on the way." Kate put the receiver down. "Auto accident. Two incoming. One's pretty bad."

Symonds had already disappeared. Patty muttered, "Shit," and started to leave also. Kate yelled, "Come by at lunch and we'll share a salad I made."

Patty rolled her eyes. "Yeah, right. Salads! I'll bring some Reese's Peanut Butter Cups and Snickers bars. Gotta keep my energy up."

Alone for the first time since coming in, Kate flipped on her computer. As it slowly came to life with a series of beeps she looked around the office. She had brightened its determined bureaucratic dullness with a half dozen watercolors on the walls, and photos of Paul and Alex on her desk. After being in the job for a month she asked higher-ups to carpet the office to soften its appearance to the often overwrought people she was required to see during the day. The administrator she asked recoiled in horror: only vice presidents and up are permitted carpets, he insisted with a gravity she had thought hysterical. So Kate bought sixteen yards of a deep-pile beige carpet with her own money, and one afternoon she and Frankie Yorba installed it, Frankie lifting the desk and file cabinets and Kate hurriedly shoving the carpet underneath, then securing the edges with double-sided carpet tape.

That was when Kate first began to wonder about Frankie. In his late twenties, with the trendy, perfectly barbered goatee of a Hollywood hanger-on, and an accent he could turn on and off at will, he had always struck Kate as too artificial, too carefully manufactured to take seriously. But he had never bothered her as he sometimes did Patty, so she didn't hesitate to ask for his help. When he had touched her on the seat while they were on their hands and knees taping, Kate ignored it. Maybe it was accidental. But when it happened again, this time his fingers lingering and following the curve of her butt, she spun around, an angry look on her face. Frankie smiled and held up his hands. "Hey, sorry. You was moving in my direction. I didn't want you to bump into me, is all."

Kate didn't believe him, but didn't want a scene either. She had kept her voice level. "You have to be careful about that sort of thing. Someone could charge you with sexual harassment."

Frankie laughed and stripped off a long piece of tape. "Touching your butt? Naw, you'd know it if I was getting sexual. Believe me. And I ain't a butt man, anyway, if you know what I mean." He stared at her bosom.

Ever since, Kate had kept her distance from the young man, though it was inevitable that work would throw them together on occasion. Almost always he would grin, and his gaze would settle on her breasts. A few times he had asked her to coffee or tried to get personal, but he seemed to have given up last year when she finally got angry with him. Now, Kate thought, every time he looked at her he seemed to be laughing at some private joke.

The computer came alive with the report Kate was only half-finished with when she had gone home Friday. As she bent over the keyboard the words *ALEX IS DYING* seemed to scroll across the monitor in three-inch letters, then disappeared in a storm of red dots that briefly filled the screen.

She felt a moment of dizziness and put a hand to her head. "My God." Her eyes squeezed closed and her heart pounded against her ribs. *I didn't imagine it,* she thought. *I didn't!* Her eyes snapped open. The half-completed hospital form stared at her from the screen. No threats. No red dots. *I saw it! I know I did!*

She began to get angry. Who was doing this? It clearly wasn't a joke; it was meant to disturb her. But why? She didn't have any enemies.

Feeling stupid, she picked up the phone and called Mrs. Alamada. "Of course he's all right," the woman said. "His toes don't even bother him. Sometimes he puts a finger in his mouth, though, and the bandage tastes funny and he cries."

"Does he have his binky—his pacifier?"

"Sure. Got it right now. Happy as can be."

Kate put the phone down and rested her forehead on her hand. Worrying about Alex was starting to affect her physically. She had been feeling more and more dizzy and tense lately, her heart suddenly speeding up for no reason. It was almost like having a panic attack, except there was never anything she could point to that had frightened her, only vague and ill-defined concerns about Alex. Maybe Helen was right and it was time to find a calmer place to work. Were there any calm hospitals nowadays? Sure . . . rural Montana, maybe. Or Jupiter. Barring that, she'd better learn to make do with the job she had. Especially since her husband was on Midtown's board. Going to another hospital would make him look foolish.

At noon Patty came by with a cheese sandwich from the cafeteria. "Sure you don't want to split this with me? It's better than— God, what is that you have there? It looks like the stuff my mother used to make for lunch—lettuce and—ugh, is it beans?'' Her eyes squinted as she peered into Kate's plate.

"It's a three-bean salad. And *my* mother showed me how to make it. So there.''

Patty laughed. "You might be younger than me, but sometimes you act like a spinster from the forties. Three-bean salads and nights at home in front of the fireplace. Jeez, girl, put a little excitement in your life.''

"I'm married, Patty. I don't need excitement.''

The other woman laughed. "That's exactly what I mean. Just because you're tied to Mr. Right doesn't mean there can't be a few Mr. OKs in your life, too. Or better than OKs. Look at Symonds. He never misses a chance to come in here and drool over you. How can you pass up an opportunity like that? The guy's going to make four hundred thousand a year by the time he's forty, if he ever gets out of ER work. And he's got a belly hard as a washboard and arms like a gymnast. We can only hope about the rest.''

"Patty, lay off, OK? I'm happy. I don't need a Mr. OK. I've got Mr. Super.''

"Yeah, well, why are you working in a hospital, then? I'm here to meet men with bucks. Did I tell you I'm going out with Lavkin tonight?''

"The ob-gyn?''

"Yeah. An expert on women's plumbing. Ought to be fun. For once I'll be able to tell an obstetrician to 'Push, push, push.' '' She laughed infectiously.

"Sometimes I worry about you,'' Kate said, laughing along with her friend. "All these men of yours—don't you worry about ending up with some creep you can't get rid of?''

The other woman shrugged as she chewed her sandwich. "Yeah, it happens from time to time. Miles Ramsey—''

"In Respiratory Therapy?'' Kate was surprised.

"Yeah. Nice-looking boy. Emphasis on *boy.* We went out two or three times but just didn't hit it off. Or *I* didn't. Something too off-kilter about him. Like an unmade bed, you know—you just want to straighten things out. Except I'm not the straightening kind. Let someone else take care of it.''

"Has he been bothering you?"

"Not 'bothering' exactly. He's really quite sweet. Just calls, sends me flowers, every once in a while zaps me an e-mail saying how much he adores me and wants to spend the rest of his life with me, blah, blah, blah. Not likely, Miles. Too many other fish to fry right now, especially doctors. I'm only up to the *L*'s in the hospital phone book."

Kate felt a shiver of apprehension. "I hope you're careful with your dates. I mean, you make them wear a condom, don't you? You've seen enough AIDS cases come in here to take precautions."

"Condoms? Oh, sure, Katie. Every single time, absolutely without exception. Except when we're in a hurry. Then sometimes we forget. Or don't have time. Or don't care. Who wants to stop and rip apart a little foil envelope? Anyway, have you ever met a man who wants to wear a rubber? They all say the same thing: Why go wading with boots on?"

Patty put her sandwich down and wiped her hands. "Anyway, I can handle myself, believe me. Last week some weirdo called me here at work. It was supposed to scare me, I guess, but I didn't even let him finish. I just started screaming bloody hell at him and he hung up. I think he didn't know what to do when I didn't play the hysterical female like he expected."

"What'd he say?" Kate tried to keep her voice calm, thinking of the threats on her computer.

She leaned toward Kate and made her voice go spooky. " 'You are going to die,' or something stupid like that. Not very original. And he disguised his voice, trying to sound evil! But as soon as I heard the word *die* I let him have it. Dumbshit didn't know what to do and hung up." She laughed and stuffed the remainder of the sandwich in her mouth. "Anyway, he never called back. Maybe he got the wrong number. He was probably trying to call his ex-wife. He's right, of course. I'm going to die."

"What?"

Patty smiled and grasped the napkin, wadding it up. "We all are, right? It's just a matter of when. My time won't come for a long while yet."

Kate pushed her salad away. Suddenly she wasn't in the mood for food.

"You OK? You haven't looked real good lately. Something bothering you? Besides rats, I mean."

"Just dizzy and a little sick to my stomach. Flu, maybe. Why not? We see sick people all day, every day. You've got to expect to come down with something from time to time."

"Yeah, but . . ." Patty had been glancing at the door. She winced and dropped her voice. "Oh, God, the wicked witch of the sixth floor is trotting this way. There's a rumor going around that she has cloven hooves and a tail. You want me to ask her if it's true?"

Kate looked up to see Judith Zamora, her supervisor, heading toward them with her typical no-nonsense walk, *clop-clop-clop* on high heels that would have given Kate shinsplints. For reasons Kate could never figure out, Zamora disliked her and always had. The woman stopped in front of Kate's desk. "The mailroom called me and—"

"We're on lunch," Patty said.

"What?" Zamora's dark eyes swung around and honed in like gun sights on Patty. With her high cheekbones, black hair, and dark eyes she had a Gypsy look, but Kate assumed she was from Spain, since someone said she spoke Castilian without an accent. Kate could imagine her as a flamenco dancer in a seedy Barcelona nightclub, pounding the wooden floor and clapping her hands above her head as she scowled at the patrons.

"Lunch," Patty repeated. "See?" With two fingers she held up the wrapper from her sandwich. "Our own time."

Zamora turned from Patty as though she didn't exist, and stared at Kate. "The mailroom said a pornographic magazine arrived here for you."

Kate's jaw dropped while Patty sputtered, "Say *what?*"

"This obviously has to stop. I can't imagine what you were thinking. Whatever you do in your own time, of course . . ." There was a sheen of sweat on the woman's forehead that glistened harshly in the overhead light.

"But I didn't send for it," Kate said, as her mind began to slip. Her heart started beating rapidly and she felt suddenly out of breath. "Honestly. Why would I want something like that sent to work? Maybe someone's trying to embarrass me." And her mind slipped again, an ancient memory unexpectedly surfacing: *Their faces are swimming with sweat—yelling at her—all of them, surging forward and screaming with hatred. A man has her by the arm, forcing his way through the crowd while her heart beats with a fear she's never felt before. Her body's cold, so drenched with perspiration her blouse sticks to her skin. She knows she's going to die now. . . .* Then her head jerked abruptly as she became aware of Zamora's angry glare. "I'm sorry. What did you say?"

The sweat was still on the woman's face, a drop falling to her upper lip, which quivered with emotion. "I said it's a strange way to embarrass someone."

Kate felt the dizziness in her head again, and forced herself to answer, but couldn't look at the woman. "It worked, didn't it? That's why you're here. And why I'm embarrassed."

"What's to be embarrassed about?" Patty demanded. "People without their clothes on. It's legal. Haven't you ever heard of the Supreme Court?"

Zamora gave her a withering look. "It is not legal at work. Anything that makes the workplace hostile or uncomfortable is considered sexual harassment. We could get sued."

"What if that *anything* is an overbearing, officious, tight-ass supervisor with horns and a tail?" Patty's eyebrows went up. "Can you get sued for that?"

Zamora held her temper with difficulty. "If you worked for me I'd have you out of here in a minute."

"Honey, if I worked for you I'd be in jail for homicide."

The other woman spun on Kate, her anger escalating. "I've told the mailroom to report to me if you receive anything else of this sort. And to send it back to the mailer."

Patty jumped in at once. "You can't do that. It's interfering with the mail, a federal offense."

"Patty, please." Kate closed her eyes, wishing her friend would shut up.

"But you heard her. She admitted to it. I'll call the FBI." Her eyes shone with glee.

Kate leaned forward and rested her elbows on the desk. "Someone must be trying to make me look stupid, or anger me, or—" *Or frighten me.* She thought of the computer messages. *I did see them. I'm sure!* Was it the same person? It had to be.

Zamora seemed not to hear her. "If you want to sit around and watch people copulate, do it at home and on your own time. But keep your private life private!" She wheeled around and marched out.

"Copulate?" Patty said wonderingly, as Zamora's high heels clicked into the distance. "She actually said *copulate?*"

"You don't always help things," Kate told her wearily.

"Oh, come on. I just said what you're thinking and can't say because you work for the bitch. You ought to thank me. It's true, isn't it?" She bent forward over the desk so Kate would have to look at her, adding, "And I looked at her feet: no toes!"

Kate laughed. "Yes, everything you said is true. And I wish I had the guts to say it."

"I'll tell you what. You can insult *my* boss sometime. If I can figure out who the hell it is. In the meantime, come outside with me. I need a cigarette. I love smoking restrictions. It's the only way to meet administrators. Those that still smoke, anyway. I'm going out with the VP of planning next Saturday. Lovely man, and divorced. Or almost. Or thinking about it. Something like that. He wasn't real clear."

Kate stood up. "Maybe I'll have a cigarette, too. I usually smoke one every decade, and the nineties are almost over."

Ten minutes later, when they wandered back inside, Frankie Yorba was coming out of Kate's office. "Something I can do for you?" Kate asked, annoyed at finding him in her private area.

He smiled. "Just looking for Doc Symonds. Hey, Patty, how's it going? You never talk to me anymore."

"Going fine, Frankie. You're straying a little far from home, though."

"On a hunt, gotta find the doc."

"You ever think to page him?"

"Hey, paging! Good thinking. I'll do that."

"Jesus," Patty said when he was gone. "What a body that boy has. And an IQ almost as large as his chest size."

"He seems to like you," Kate said teasingly.

"He asked me out a few times. I told him I don't rob cribs. Pissed him off, but better than telling him I can't date bodybuilders. My own narcissism is bad enough; I don't have time for theirs." She plopped down in the visitor's chair as Kate sat behind the desk. "What do you think he was really doing in your office?"

"What do you mean?"

"If he was looking for Symonds he wouldn't have to go inside, would he? The door was open. All he had to do was look. Even Frankie could figure that out."

"Then why—"

"I don't know, but if I had to guess who around here was sending women pornography, Frankie would top my list."

5

"Oh, come on, Lilliana. Hans can't be that bad." Kate sighed and ran a hand through her hair.

"Can't he? Do you know what time he got back last night after 'meeting with clients'? Two o'clock! He sneaked into bed like a four-year-old, thinking I wouldn't know what time it was. How stupid does he think I am?"

Kate hadn't been home ten minutes before Lilliana showed up on the doorstep with her usual litany of husband complaints. *I need to be more assertive,* she thought; *I need to learn to say no.* But Lilliana didn't give her the chance, brushing past Kate as though she weren't there and heading straight for the liquor cabinet, where she poured two inches of scotch and, after a moment's hesitation, added an ice cube. Kate, feeling the tension of the day, poured herself a glass of Chablis from a bottle that had been cooling for two weeks in the refrigerator. She couldn't remember the last time she'd had a drink before dinner.

"He reeked of Giorgio, of all things. I should know; I have a cabinet full of the stuff."

"Maybe that's why he smelled like it."

Lilliana gave her a withering look. "Don't be naive. I haven't worn Giorgio in years. That's why it's sitting in a drawer somewhere. It's probably fermented into cognac by now."

Kate sipped her wine and tried to smile for her friend, but there was a tension headache pounding in the back of her neck, and she felt dizzy and vaguely nauseated again. She must be coming down with something. Sitting in the large living room that still wasn't completely furnished, she could see Lilliana's sprawling two-story house across the cul-de-sac. Water from a lawn sprinkler just outside splattered against the large picture window, the drops running down in nervous little rivulets, to be replaced almost at once by another splattering, over and over and over. There was something comforting about the mindless repetition, the cotton-soft plonking of water on glass, the erratic little streams racing toward the sill. Alex was asleep in his playpen next to Kate, who still felt guilty about the rat bites. Lilliana caught her staring at the baby. "You're going to spoil him with all this attention, you know. Do you think your baby-sitter is this attentive?"

"I don't care if I spoil him," Kate said, leaning over and smiling at the child. "He's my heart and soul. I'll spoil him all his life."

"Oh, God. Spare me the motherly melodramatics." Lilliana was starting to slur her words. "You are so . . . soap opera-ish sometimes. *All My Children, Days of Our Lives*, and *As Kate Mothers.*"

Kate chose not to get angry. Her friend had never had children and was ignorant of what it meant to be a parent. And probably, despite what she said now, jealous of Kate. How else to explain Lilliana's nasty comments every time the question of child rearing—or happy marriages—came up? *We hate what we can't have,* Kate thought, in a surprisingly philosophical mood. *It must be the wine,* she decided with a giggle she kept to herself.

"What did the doctor say about any permanent damage?" Lilliana asked, evidently deciding to show some neighborly concern for once.

Kate stood up, felt a sudden spiraling of dizziness just behind her eyes, and rearranged the blanket covering Alex, who was beginning to stir awake. "There's nothing serious. In a couple of weeks we won't even be able to tell it happened."

"Maybe you should get an alarm system. They have these microwave detectors that would let you know if more rats got into the house."

"Paul already suggested it. But I think we'd probably set it off every time we got up to go to the bathroom or look in on Alex." Kate moved back from the playpen and sat down heavily on the flowered couch.

Her friend squinted at her through eyes going blurry with alcohol. "Are you all right? You don't seem well today. Are you coming down with the flu?"

"Just a little woozy lately," Kate said, her hand going unconsciously to her forehead. "Probably something I ate."

Alex began to stir some more, and with an effort pushed onto his back, then somehow seemed to sense that his mother was nearby and began to cry.

"Dinner," Kate said, and stood again, picking up the baby.

Lilliana also came to her feet, a little uncertainly, and said, "I guess I ought to go home. Hans and I are supposed to go to dinner and a show tonight. His half-assed attempt to keep the home fires lit, if not actually burning." Her eyes narrowed with emotion as she stared through the water-flecked window at her house across the way. "You don't know how good you have it, you and Paul. Don't screw it up." Then, as though appalled at this moment of self-revelation, she walked out the door.

Holding Alex with one arm, Kate undid the top button of her blouse and the left side of her nursing bra. As she sat down, Alex pressing against her breast, she could see Lilliana, distorted into fun-house shape by the watery glass, disappear into her house, slamming the door behind her.

Paul got home at six-thirty. Rather than immediately carrying his briefcase upstairs to the den as he usually did, he dropped it on the dining room table, put his head back, and roared, *"Christ!"*

Kate came in from the family room, holding Alex. "Daddy's home, honey. Do you want to say hello to Daddy?"

Alex smiled from his pudgy red face, and Paul seemed to relax at once. "Hi, pal. Have a nice day with Mrs. Alamada today?" He lifted the boy from Kate and held him just inches from his face. "Say something intelligent, kiddo. You ought to be beyond the goo-goo, da-da stage. Say 'The American judicial system is in a state of complete collapse!' "

But all Alex could manage was a laugh that became a bubble

of spittle. "Go ahead and mess up my suit," Paul said with mock anger. "It would be the perfect end to my day."

Kate took Alex from her husband, and asked with disingenuous surprise, "Bad day in court?"

"Bad day with the damn parole board. There aren't enough cells in California to keep even a third of the convicted criminals actually in jail. So they parole most first and second offenders after only a fraction of the sentence the jury thinks they handed out in the interest of justice, so-called." He took off his suit coat and loosened his tie. "Do you remember Leo Petrosian?"

"Sounds familiar, but that's all. Nothing specific."

Paul went into the kitchen and came back with a Budweiser. "Skinny little Armenian guy, came to this country as an orphan when he was thirteen, and in trouble ever since. A wild man who probably should have been put in a mental hospital rather than a foster home when he immigrated. Two years ago he stuck up a dry cleaner in the Silverlake area, and got mad when there was only thirty-eight dollars in the till. So he started screaming in Armenian and shooting off his Tek 9, blowing out windows, assassinating bottles of fourteen-year-old scotch, and wounding the owner in the arm." He swilled half the beer. "I got him seven-to-nine in Tehachipi and forgot about it. One more L.A. lowlife off the streets, not that anyone would notice. Until today. I got a dozen white roses delivered to the office this afternoon, with a note from Petrosian: 'Coming at you, Prosecutor.'"

Kate suppressed a shiver. "What does that mean?"

"When he was convicted he turned to me in court and said something like, 'Better watch your back when I get out, because I'm going to be coming at you.' Jimmy Cagney or Edward G. Robinson stuff, like he'd been watching too many old movies as a kid in Armenia, and thought that was how macho American hoods were supposed to talk."

"And he served only two years?"

"I called the parole people. They said he was a model prisoner and that's why they let him out so early. You've got to understand that 'model prisoner' in California means he didn't belong to a gang like the Aryan Brotherhood, or stab someone in a fight, or cut the warden's dick off. They've got to prioritize when it comes to early-outs, and good ol' Leo—a hundred and thirty-eight pounds of newly reformed gangster—was at the top of their list.'' He finished the beer, banged it down on the table, and jabbed a finger into Alex's tummy. "Hey, how're the injuries, little fellow? Feeling OK?"

Kate frowned. "But what's this man going to do? Is he going to try to hurt you?"

Paul waved a hand while making faces at Alex. "After a public threat and following up with a note two years later? Not a chance. Anything happens to me and Petrosian's the first person they'll look for. He's already got two strikes; the next is life. No, little Leo's trying to get under my skin, wants me to worry and lose sleep, and think about the terrible thing I've done to him. But it ain't going to happen. I figure I'm the safest guy in town now, with Leo knowing what awaits him if he goes down again."

"But—"

"Kate, stop worrying. OK? Nothing's going to happen. Now, how's my bud doing with his toesies?" He nuzzled the boy's stomach, making him laugh.

Kate took a silent breath. "He's doing fine. The bandages on his fingers can come off in the morning. I'll do it before taking him to the sitter's."

Paul stood and walked behind Kate's chair. He began to massage her neck, his hands slipping after a moment down to her breasts. "We're not through celebrating our anniversary, are we?"

She smiled up at him. "Not a chance."

His hands moved up, gently cupping her face, his thumbs massaging her cheeks, and sending an erotic shudder through her. "Race you upstairs."

"Let me put Alex in the playpen."

Kate took Alex from the high chair and carried him into the living room. Bending over, she set him down in front of two of his favorite stuffed animals. Then her eye noticed something unusual, and she moved aside one of the animals to see a pink plastic rattle. Her hand trembling, she picked it up. For a long moment she stared disbelievingly at it.

"What's that?"

Kate jumped. Paul was nude already. He had his hand on her hip but his face was curious. "Did you buy that for Alex? Why pink?"

Kate's first frantic impulse had been to hide it behind her back. But Paul reached around and took it from her. "It doesn't look new. How long has he had it?"

Kate tried to make her voice stay calm. "I don't know. I never saw it before. At least I don't remember."

Paul shook it, the rattling noise drawing Alex's attention. "My folks, probably. Unless it was among the two tons of gifts you got at baby showers." He shrugged and tossed it toward Alex, then turned Kate around. She was ashen, her hands shaking as she gripped the edge of the playpen. "Hey, you feeling all right?"

"Yes, fine. A little dizzy, maybe."

"Not too dizzy for—"

"No. I'm fine. Really." She looked at his nakedness, his desire obviously aroused.

Putting an arm on her shoulder, Paul turned her around so they were both facing the stairs. "Allow me to point the way."

Darkness surrounded her, limitless, thick and hot, as though the night air had turned liquid. Vaguely Kate could make out a pinpoint of light shimmering somewhere in the distance. She concentrated her eyes and mind on it—what was it?—and realized she was staring at Lilliana's porch light. How could she see that from the bedroom? Her head felt heavy, and her body tingled. *Sick? Am I sick?* Then she shuddered and realized she wasn't in bed—she was standing in the living room. *What am I doing here at*—she looked abruptly at the digital clock on a table—*2:14 A.M.?* Shivering, she wrapped her arms around herself and realized she was naked. *My God, I'm sleepwalking. I thought I was over that years ago.* Her eyes closed and she felt herself begin to lose her balance. Putting a hand out to steady herself against a chair, she thought, *It's coming back, isn't it? It's happening again.*

She began to shake.

Dear God, no. Don't do this to me.

6

Chuck, the barrel-chested guard at the ER entrance, muttered, "Big troubles, Katie," under his breath as she hurried up to the door the next morning. She turned and said, "What?"

He opened the door for her. "It's Patty. Someone left a dead cat on her desk."

"My God!" Kate could see a crowd of people milling around Patty's admitting desk. A policeman was holding a paper bag, presumably with the remains of the cat inside.

Kate started at once for Patty's desk but Chuck said, "Better not. Dr. Kamel's having a hissy fit, wants everyone to pretend this never happened." Kamel's voice could be heard as he wove through the crowd. "Please, people. Back to work. Everyone—"

Joel Symonds suddenly joined her just inside the door. "Pretty sick, isn't it? The cat was eviscerated, its sex organs removed."

"You're kidding!" The air seemed suddenly cold, and she felt a shiver go through her body. "Does she have any idea who did it?"

"No, there was no note or anything like that. Just a cat. And its guts, lying on her desk."

Kamel was striding about in front of them, waving his arms. "Please, out of the waiting room. Everyone! We have work to do."

Kate and Symonds joined the throng moving reluctantly away from the admitting area as Kamel swept past them, clapping his huge, thick-fingered hands and shouting, "Quickly, quickly, quickly . . ."

"He was in the Pakistani army, you know," Symonds muttered as the room began to empty. "One of their best doctors. One of ours, too. Unfortunately he never understood the difference between military and civilian life."

Kate started to say something, but they were interrupted by the PA calling the trauma team to the ER stat as a medevac helicopter prepared to land on the roof. Instantly everyone was in motion. Symonds said, "Maybe I'll see you on break," and took off at a run, Kamel and a half dozen nurses following. Suddenly the waiting room was empty.

Kate turned around and walked back to the admitting desk. Patty was sitting dejectedly, her forehead propped on her hand. "Is there anything more you need from her?" she asked the policeman.

"I guess I can wrap it up. If we get any leads we'll call." He didn't sound optimistic.

Patty looked up at her. "Did they tell you it was my cat?"

"You mean your cat from home? Your daughter's cat? But how—"

"Not how. Who?" She slumped down in the chair, tears coming to her eyes. "What am I going to say to Tammy? She's had that cat for eight years."

"My God." Kate put her hand on her friend's shoulder. "Come on, girl, let's go down to the cafeteria and pig out on pie and latte for a couple of hours. Let someone else worry about the admits. We've both had enough of real life for a while."

Once again feeling exhausted and slightly ill after work, Kate sighed with more displeasure than she cared to admit as she pulled into her driveway and saw Lilliana Quinlin coming from the McDonalds' backyard. She killed the engine but for some reason didn't move, as though trapped in the car as her neighbor approached.

"I thought I heard you out by the pool," Lilliana said through the open window. She was dressed in brief white shorts and a flowered silk blouse. Together they probably cost five hundred dollars.

"Lilliana, I work. I don't spend weekdays out by the pool."

"But it's almost five. I just assumed ... Well, I did hear someone talking. I thought it was you."

"And who did it turn out to be?" Kate asked, wondering what the woman was really doing in her backyard.

"Nobody!" Lilliana said cheerfully, then twirled her fingers near her head. "Age, my dear. I'm getting old, a fact my darling Hans made plain last night at dinner. So romantic, he is. He always knows the perfect thing to say."

Kate pushed on the door and stepped out onto the driveway. "Well, come on in and tell me all about it." As though she had a choice in the matter; when Lilliana wanted to visit she visited. Kate reached into the back of the Mustang and took Alex out of his car seat.

"His bandages are off," the other woman said with interest. "And there're no scars?" She lifted one of Alex's hands and made cooing sounds as she inspected his fingers. "Well ... maybe they'll disappear with time. They're not very big. And I don't suppose boys care about scars anyway, do they?"

"There aren't going to be any scars," Kate said with annoyance. "The doctors promised."

"Well, there you are," Lilliana replied, and Kate thought, Does that comment actually mean anything, or am I just losing the ability to reason?

Holding Alex with one arm, Kate unlocked the door, then told Lilliana she was going to change him before seeing if he'd take a nap. As her neighbor veered off for the living room Kate headed upstairs. When she returned five minutes later Lilliana was sitting on the couch, her feet tucked up beneath her like a teenager, and staring glassy-eyed through the window toward her own house. She had a half-empty tumbler of wine in her hand. "Aren't you going to have a drink?" she asked as Kate settled down on the other end of the couch.

"I don't think so. I haven't been feeling well lately. And alcohol just makes it worse."

"Don't feel well how? Are you still dizzy?"

Kate waved a hand weakly. "I guess that's the word. Maybe *weird* is a better word. I even found myself sleepwalking last night. That hasn't happened in years. It's a strange feeling to wake up and not know where you are."

"Nerves," Lilliana said with certainty. "You're upset about something."

"No, I don't think it's that." Kate tried hurriedly to think of a way to change the subject.

"You and Paul getting along? I've always heard being married to an attorney is worse than being married to a shrink." She gave a theatrical shudder, as though either thought were too appalling to consider.

"Of course, we're getting along fine. Better than I ever would have hoped." Uh-oh, Kate thought too late, that's the sort of comment that usually brings out the worst of Lilliana's barbed comments. Envy, with Lilliana, was never far from the surface. Or was it just impatience that anyone could actually be happily married?

But the other woman merely said, "Maybe you ought to see a neurologist. There might be something wrong upstairs."

"A brain tumor?" Kate asked with raised eyebrows. She didn't know if she should be angry or amused.

"That's not the only thing it could be. But if you're dizzy and it's not nerves there's a cause, isn't there? A physical cause? Come on, Kate, that's just common sense."

"I suppose."

"Isn't there a neurologist at Midtown?"

"I'm sure there is. I don't know any of them, though."

"What about your work? Is something interesting going on there? A clandestine love affair with an ER doctor maybe? Someone to ring your mental bell a little and make you all woozy in the head?"

"You know better than that."

"Of course, Kate the chaste. Oh, lordy." Lilliana's eyes darkened as she glanced at her house. "Siegfried, my very own Teutonic knight, is home early from the wars. How my heart does pound with desire!"

Kate looked out and saw Hans Quinlin, broad-shouldered and handsome at fifty-five or so, step from his silver Jaguar, a Gucci briefcase in his hand, and head inside.

"That must mean his girlfriend is tied up tonight. And with Hans, honey, that's literal. His sexual interests run to the unusual, to say the least. Which is probably why he's been married four times."

"Please, Lilliana." Hans seemed, to Kate's eyes, a devoted, if extremely busy, husband who never had anything but compliments for his wife.

Lilliana's own life before moving to Brentwood was obscure to Kate, and because of the other woman's penchant for self-dramatization, she never knew how much to believe. She knew Lilliana lived in London for a while, and had been a literature professor in New England until she queried her students one September morn and could not find even one who could identify John Keats or William Blake. She walked out of class that day and never returned, even to empty her office. She seemed to have a good deal of money, though, either from an inheritance or one of her ex-husbands. The only time Kate had asked about her past Lilliana slumped back on the couch, one arm flopping against her forehead like a 1930s film queen, and intoned in a deep, low rumble, "I had a great *tragedy* in my young life," and then giggled and said, "*Bor*ing, dear. There is little to tell, beyond *veni, vidi, vici.*"

"Pardon?"

"Julius Caesar. I came, I saw, I conquered."

Lilliana turned sharply from the window. "Oh, don't get upset with me, Kate. I'm not going to bore you with the sad tale of my sex life. Such as it is. What is there to tell anyway? My loving and energetic Hun manages to play golf five times a week but can find time for me only once a month. It's uncanny how precise and *Germanic* the timing is, almost like clockwork. I suppose his secretary, the luscious young Tina, calls him and says, 'It's the sixteenth. Don't forget to screw your wife.' Thank God for the pool man and the UPS driver. Don't you just love those shorts they wear?"

Kate got up and poured herself some wine.

"I'm embarrassing you. I didn't mean to. Honestly. It's *your* wine so it's all your fault, you see. I guess it's not just men who can be messed up, is it? We all fall from grace." She laughed, drained her glass, and veered suddenly off in another direction. "Are you still breast-feeding or have you weaned the little one yet? I'll bet Paul's after you to give it up, isn't he? You know how men are: 'Those boobs are mine.' "

"He's never mentioned it. We both feel breast milk is healthier." God, I sound like a self-righteous prig, Kate thought. "Anyway, I've already started to wean Alex. In another week he should be completely on bottles."

But Lilliana had already lost interest and reverted to her earlier conversation. "Can you believe Hans wanted to videotape us having sex last year? *Us?* I just laughed and said, Whatever for, dear? It'd be like watching some ancient sitcom you can't stand."

"Maybe you two ought to take a vacation together this summer," Kate said, trying to encourage Lilliana toward a new area of conversation. "Why not go to Mexico? Or the Caribbean? Just spend some time together in a romantic location."

"Hans's idea of a vacation is to go to New York and talk to clients. Which means I spend my time in the hotel room trying to seduce Puerto Rican bellhops, or shopping for hours. With *my* money, I might add. He's the one who married 'up,' as they say. Anyway, you and Paul are the exotic-vacation sort. Lying on a black-sand beach in some lush tropical paradise, rubbing coconut oil on each other's quivering body parts. I'm afraid Hans and I are far beyond that now. God, what a way for someone only forty to talk!" She stood up suddenly. "I may as well get over there and see what brings my warrior home so early. Perhaps he has *amore* on his mind. Open your window wide, Kate, and listen for the sounds of passion. This may be . . . historic!"

At dinner that night Paul had little sympathy for Patty Mars and her dead cat. "From what you've said, she brings on her own troubles." He poked with interest at the moo shu pork and orange chicken that had been delivered by the Wok Inn because neither of them was in the mood to cook. "It's got to be an ex-lover. Right? Someone she dumped? One of the many.

The law of averages says at least one would be mightily pissed off.''

"I don't think that's fair, Paul. She didn't ask someone to kill her cat and drop it on her desk."

"It's not a question of asking, my love. It's how her behavior is going to be perceived by some of the men in her life. Given the numbers, some of them have to be weird. Live by the sword and die by the sword."

"Is that why Leo Petrosian is harassing you? Because you're not careful about how you're *perceived?*"

"Not fair. I was doing my job. If it'd been any other prosecutor Petrosian would be equally upset. Or worse. At least I don't gloat at the defendant after sentencing, like some of my colleagues. Anyway''—he speared a piece of chicken—"Leo sent me a get-well card today. Sweet guy, huh? He really cares for me."

Kate ate some egg rice. It was the only thing that had appealed to her once all the little white boxes had been opened for inspection. Even the tea tasted funny today. "What is this Petrosian going to do, Paul? Just send you threats every day? Don't you think he might try something?"

"Hon, everyone in the office has been threatened. The law of averages again. I filed a report on him yesterday with Clovis, and she told me that I was number twenty-six to be threatened by an ex-felon this year. And that's only those who've taken the trouble to write it up. Most people in the office just ignore it. It's part of the job, like sleazy defense lawyers and senile judges who forget what case they're presiding over. Could you pass me the rumaki, please?"

"Most people don't get their cats eviscerated and delivered to them at work, either, I suppose."

"Look, I feel sorry for your friend. But there's a reason why this happened to Patty and not to you or someone else. It's this lifestyle she's taken up."

"I was threatened, too."

"Meaning what?" He put the rumaki down and looked at her.

"On my computer at work. It's happened twice now."

He said nothing, but she could see his mind working, wondering if it was real.

"Threats to *Alex*, Paul. He was even named once."

Paul started to say something, then hesitated and frowned. "I don't know how to say this without sounding insensitive, but . . ."

"But did I really see it? Or am I imagining things? Or perhaps I'm not feeling well lately and only thought I saw it."

He shrugged and put the remainder of the rumaki in his mouth. "Well, you're obviously not feeling well. You haven't eaten anything."

Kate looked at her plate. After a moment she said, "I had a big lunch. Patty and I. I wanted to cheer her up, so we went out." Kate had sat alone at her desk during lunch. She had no idea if Patty had even eaten. She hadn't seen her since early morning.

"OK," he said. "Let's assume you did see the threats."

"No, Paul. *Assuming* turns this into a theory. Try again." Despite her normal desire to avoid conflict, she found herself pushing him in a way that was bound to end up in an argument, and she wasn't sure why, only that she was getting angrier by the minute.

"OK," he replied after a moment. "You saw them. Threats on your computer. Now . . . why would anyone do such a thing?"

"Paul, do you really think I have an answer to that?"

"Then why are we talking about it?"

"I'm not. You are. You brought all this up. To prove what a slut Patty is."

"That's not it at all."

"That's exactly it. Tell me something: is Patty's behavior any different than, say, that of a dozen men in your office?"

He stared at her a minute. "Probably not."

"Then maybe she's not so bad after all. The difference is that she's a woman."

He looked at her a moment, then smiled grimly and raised his hands in defeat. "Good trial technique, Counselor. My case is thrown out of court even before I can cross-examine."

"What's your final word, then?" she demanded. "Final two words. And get it right the first time."

"I'm wrong."

Kate smiled and clasped his hand. "Perfect. And no more talk about Patty's terrible behavior."

"I accept the terms of probation."

"Who says the American justice system doesn't work?" She felt a sudden surge of warmth toward her husband and squeezed his hand. Just then Alex started crying. Kate sat back in her chair and smiled. "Guess what else you get to do, Pop? There's pureed carrots and steamed tomatoes in the refrigerator. Warm them up on the stove. Not too hot, now."

July 13

Liar, liar, liar!
You've always had trouble with the truth, haven't you, Katie Kate? You, with your right-brain alternate view of reality, keeping secrets and convincing yourself that it's not a lie, it's . . . well, what do you tell yourself, Crazy Kate? How do you rationalize all the things you've not told Paul? Do you say it can't be a lie because it's not something you've done, it's something UN-done?
How clever we can be in finding excuses for the inexcusable. You, my dear, are a past master at fooling yourself almost as well as you fool others.
But I seethe when you're not honest. I feel such a pure, liberating hatred that my whole body shakes. A hatred that can express itself in a million ways—or one.

7

Where am I? Kate's heart pounded and the breath caught in her throat. In the odd manner of dreams she tried to run and couldn't, though she felt her legs hurriedly propelling her forward through the darkness. Terrified, she tried to scream but nothing came out. Panic rose as her mouth stretched wide, yelling, *Help, help* . . . though no one could hear. Then her eyes opened and she thought, *Who's after me?*

Suddenly she felt the air, cool and bracing against her naked shoulders, and realized she was in her flimsy nightgown and standing in the hallway outside her own bedroom. *Sleepwalking again.* A shudder ran along her spine. *Why am I doing this? What's happening to me?* There had been a time years ago when sleepwalking was a nightly occurrence. Nerves, her doctor had said, and put her on a regimen of tranquilizers—Halcion, though she knew it supposedly made some people psychotic— at bedtime. Within six months the sleepwalking had ceased, but the terrible dreams—running, running, as a faceless man chased her—remained, and she would wake up breathless, her legs sore, and sweat swimming along her torso.

The door to the bedroom was closed. I must have done that in my sleep, she thought. Trying not to make any noise, she turned the handle and let herself back inside. Paul wasn't in bed, but she could see a light from under the bathroom door. Letting herself gently down on the mattress, she waited for him to return. No more dreams, she prayed. No more sleepwalking.

Help me!

Ten minutes later she was asleep.

* * *

Alex was sobbing. Not the loud shrieks of a few nights ago, but a gentle moan that drifted down the hallway like smoke and gathered around Kate's ears. She sighed and looked at the clock. Just after two o'clock. Would she ever get any sleep tonight?

Groggy with exhaustion, she slipped out of bed, strode down to the nursery, and turned on the low-voltage lamp that threw a dim illumination over the crib. Alex was on top of his covers, tossing uncomfortably. "What's wrong, honey, not feeling well tonight? You got what Mommy's got?" She reached down, picked him up, and could tell at once that he had a fever. Not just a fever, she thought: he was burning up. It must be at least 102 degrees.

There was a rectal thermometer in the closet, but she wasn't sure Alex would stay still long enough for it to register. Clasping the boy to her shoulder and murmuring comfortingly, she went to the closet, careful not to step on the baseball-size blood spot on the carpet where Paul had killed one of the rats, and began to rummage through baby materials on a shelf. Finally finding the thermometer she crossed to the rocking chair and sat down with Alex on her lap. "You're so hot," she murmured, pulling down his pajama bottoms and opening his diaper. "But I don't think you have what I have, honey. I don't have a fever, just a weird head and sick tummy. How's your cute little tummy?" She tickled his stomach, but instead of giggling, as he normally did, he began to wail louder. "Hey, calm down. Don't wake up Dad. He's got court tomorrow. We don't want a sleepy prosecutor, do we? Remember what he said about the state of justice in America? Pop's got to be on his toes."

Rolling the boy over, Kate inserted the thermometer. At once his crying increased. "I know you don't like this, hon. Almost as much as I hate doing it." Alex squirmed on her lap. Kate held him awkwardly with her left arm and tried to keep the thermometer steady with her right. "Relax!" she whispered. "You wouldn't want this to break in your butt. Then we'd really have a problem."

She glanced at her watch and tried to keep the thermometer inserted for three minutes, but had to remove it after two. "All right, let's see what you've got." She held the small instrument up but couldn't read it in the dark. Hefting the baby to her shoulder, she walked to the door, where the overhead light switch was, and flipped it on. "Oh, my God!"

Still holding the boy with one arm, she raced down to the bedroom and flicked on the light. Paul sat up at once and blinked in confusion. "What—"

"Alex has a fever of a hundred and four. We've got to get him to the hospital right now!"

"Jesus!"

"Get dressed. No. Watch Alex while I get dressed." She put the child down on the bed and hurried to the closet.

"Can't we just give him some Tylenol and stick him in a cool bath for a while? That's what my mother always did." He was rubbing his eyes and trying to force himself awake.

"Not for a fever of a hundred and four, Paul. We don't know what caused it. It could lead to seizures or even brain damage if it gets any worse." She pulled on her slacks and grabbed a blouse without looking at it. "Damn it, where are my shoes?" She saw them on the floor of the closet and scooped them up with one hand. "Hurry and get dressed. I'll get a diaper on Alex."

While Paul pulled on his slacks, Kate took a cold washcloth from the bathroom and draped it over Alex's head; then she hurriedly put a diaper on him. "You poor baby. I feel so sorry for you. But you're going to be OK, Alex. Mommy promises."

Paul finished dressing and took the child. "He's really burning up, isn't he? How could it come on so quickly?"

"Who knows? Babies get things, I guess." And a strange memory, a remark someone had made to her years ago, crossed her mind—*Babies get sick, don't they, and die?*—but she forced it away with an angry shake of her head, and a muttered, "Damn it! Damn it, no!" She took Alex from Paul's arms. "You drive!"

* * *

Joel Symonds wasn't in the ER tonight, but another doctor Kate only vaguely knew—Monica Packard—took Alex at once and began an IV. "You don't have any idea when this started?"

"Late tonight," Kate said. "I put him to sleep at nine, and looked in at ten-thirty before going to bed."

Dr. Packard drew the curtains around the hospital crib on the extreme edge of the ER while a nurse patted Alex with a cold compress. "Did you feel him then?"

"No. Only looked at him. But he was sleeping soundly."

Packard looked up at another nurse hovering nearby. "I want a complete blood test. Call the lab. I need the results stat."

A man was moaning somewhere out of their sight. Kate had a vague recollection of seeing him bandaged and handcuffed to a bed as they rushed Alex inside.

The doctor pulled Alex's diaper off. "I'm sure we can get the fever down, but I'm concerned about anything that comes on this fast. It doesn't seem like influenza, but it's possible. We had a case of Type-A Asian a few days ago. It's not the sort of thing you want a child this age to come in contact with. But I think it's more likely to be some sort of infection."

A woman appeared to draw Alex's blood. He was writhing so much a nurse had to hold him tightly so he didn't hurt himself while the needle was inserted. Dr. Packard took Kate by the elbow and led her and Paul away so they wouldn't have to watch the blood being drawn. "Why don't you two go out in the waiting room for a while? We should get a preliminary on the blood test pretty soon."

The nurse who had been holding Alex called suddenly from behind them. "Dr. Packard?" Her voice was concerned, and Kate spun around at once.

"Go ahead," the doctor said, pushing gently on her shoulder. "I'll come for you when we know something. You shouldn't be back here anyway." She turned and headed quickly toward Alex just as the doors banged open and a woman with bloodied hands and cheeks was wheeled inside by EMTs. Kate and Paul were almost to the waiting room when Packard's voice called them back.

Alex was on his stomach. In a voice that seemed steadied only by a great effort, the doctor said, "How do you think this happened?"

Black-and-blue marks about a half-inch wide almost completely circled the child's arms just above the elbow. Another fainter set encircled his legs above the knees. Kate almost shrieked. "What is it?"

Packard turned Alex over. "Strange, isn't it? You can see a little redness on the front here, but not like it is on the back."

Paul said, "I don't understand. Is this from his fever?"

"Didn't either of you notice anything before you brought him in here? What about when you changed him?"

"No," Paul said, and looked at Kate for confirmation. Her eyes had gone wild and her voice rose almost to a scream. "Of course not. I would have told you." Her gaze flew from Paul to Dr. Packard.

"You didn't notice his arms and legs at all tonight?"

"I gave him a bath about seven. If there had been anything I would have seen it."

"And you took his temperature rectally?"

"It was dark. I didn't notice anything."

"Then this happened to him sometime after seven o'clock?"

Paul seemed confused but also vaguely upset by the doctor's manner. "I don't understand. What do you mean 'happened' to him? Is this part of his influenza? What 'happened'?"

"She's saying this was intentional," Kate almost shouted. She could feel the pulse in her forehead begin to jump. "She's saying one of us did this to Alex on purpose."

"To hurt him? Are you crazy?" He stared at the doctor in disbelief. "You think we tried to hurt our child?"

"Check his temperature again," Packard told one of the nurses. The woman took an ear thermometer off a table and had the results in seconds. "One oh one."

Kate visibly relaxed. "Thank God."

But Paul's anger was mounting by the second. "Wait a

minute. You're accusing me—or Kate—of assault, or attempted murder, or what? What the hell are you trying to say?''

The doctor gently rolled the boy over on his stomach again. ''I'm not accusing anybody of anything. Look at these marks. If I had to guess I'd say they were made by a ligature. The reason they're more serious on this side is that a knot was probably tied right here.'' She pointed to the most discolored skin. ''It looks like the ligature was deliberately twisted so the knot would dig into the flesh. It must have been painful. Didn't you hear anything during the night?'' Her eyes were on Paul. After a moment she glanced at Kate, whose knees suddenly went wobbly; she could feel herself becoming faint, and shook her head to maintain consciousness.

Paul was furious. ''That's crazy. Someone tied a—a what? A piece of string? A leather strap?—around his arms and legs? There must be some other cause. That's possible, too, isn't it?''

It wasn't Paul's courtroom voice, Kate sensed through the fog of emotion her mind had become. He wasn't interrogating; he wasn't the hotshot DA. He was frightened and disbelieving.

''Of course it could be something else,'' Packard said, and didn't notice Kate close her eyes, her lips barely moving as she said to herself, *Please don't do this to me!*

''But,'' Packard went on, ''I can't imagine what it might be.''

''I don't believe this is happening,'' Paul said. ''I'm being accused of harming my own child—''

''Don't, Paul,'' Kate pleaded. She reached out and touched his shoulder, afraid he was going to lose his temper.

''Do you know I'm a deputy district attorney?'' he demanded angrily.

Packard took a chart off the bedside table and flicked it open. ''Then you'll understand that I have no choice but to notify the police about this.''

''What?'' Paul instinctively took a step forward as if he was going to hit her.

''Paul, no!'' Alarmed, Kate grabbed his arm.

''This is the second instance of possible abuse or neglect in less than a week,'' the doctor said. ''You, more than most people, should realize we have no choice. In truth, the first case should have been reported. I guess whoever handled it let it go because your wife works here. But this time we can't ignore—"

"*Abuse?* Because Alex was bitten by rats? And now he has a fever!"

"Not the fever. That could be caused by anything. I'm talking about the marks on the arms and legs. That was not accidental. Someone tried to inflict pain on this child. Someone tried to hurt him. And succeeded."

"And you're accusing . . ." Paul's voice boomed around the ER.

The doctor looked at him calmly. "Do you want me to call security?"

"Goddamn you, I'm on the board of this hospital! You can't treat me like this."

"I really don't care who you are, Mr. McDonald. But I do care about Alex. This child was deliberately injured tonight, and I'm notifying the police."

"Jesus!" Paul spun away from her. "Do what you want. This is crazy, it's madness. Alex is sick, that's all. The police aren't going to do anything."

"Probably not. But our responsibility is to make a report. Like I said, you should know this better than anyone. It's your department that decides whether or not to prosecute."

Paul rubbed the perspiration off his forehead. "How long is Alex going to have to stay here?"

Dr. Packard looked from Paul to Kate. "Let's wait for the initial lab results. If there's nothing serious you should be out of here before morning. You'll have to keep him on Tylenol for forty-eight hours, though. Give me a call in a couple of days. The other lab tests should be back by then. You can have a seat out in the waiting room. I'll come and get you when it's time to take him home."

The sun was coming up behind them when Kate drove back to Brentwood, Paul in the passenger seat next to her, Alex strapped in his child seat in the rear. Paul was still fuming, but at the law now, not the hospital. "It's goddamn asinine! They leave it up to doctors or nurses or even teachers to decide what constitutes abuse because there're no guidelines. So is a kid with a stubbed toe abused? How about a scab on a knee? Or a fever? If another doctor had been in the ER tonight he might have said, Hey, look at these funny marks on his arms, and thought nothing of it. I mean the skin wasn't even broken. But that hard-ass Packard looks at it and screams *abuse!*" He turned around to look at Alex. "Feeling better, kiddo? Jeez, he still seems listless, Katie. It must be the medicine."

The air around her was stiff and frigid against her skin, as though she had walked into a room full of dry ice. She wanted to turn on the heater but knew it was she who was cold, and not the temperature. She said, "Are you going in to work today? Maybe you could take the day off and stay home with us."

"I can't! Christ, I'm due in court in three hours."

You're lying, Kate thought suddenly, and then wondered, *Why did I think that? My God, don't do that, don't turn on Paul now.* Her eyes went briefly to him as she continued to steer.

Paul asked, "You're going to stay home, aren't you?"

"Of course." The sun caught the rearview mirror, creating a burst of white light that made her squint.

Paul turned again to look at Alex's arms. "What do you think those marks are? And don't tell me ligatures. Jesus!"

"I don't know, Paul." She stopped at a red light on Wilshire. Her hands tightened on the steering wheel, and she shook her head to keep from falling asleep. Vaguely she remembered sleepwalking during the night. How long had that lasted? Five minutes? An hour? It was funny she hadn't heard Alex then. She had been near the nursery door.

"And you didn't see them earlier tonight?"

"How many times am I going to have to answer that question? They weren't there!" The light turned green and the Mustang jumped ahead. There were only a few other cars on the street. The exclusive stores and upscale office buildings looked harsh and alien without people to soften them, like a model train outfit or a vacant movie set.

"Sorry. I'm just trying to figure out what the hell's happening."

Me too, Kate thought as her fingers tightened again on the steering wheel. *Like why the hell have I been so sick lately? Why am I sleepwalking? How did so many rats find their way into the nursery? And why do I suddenly feel you're hiding something from me? It's my nerves,* she thought; *I'm becoming antsy and suspicious of everyone.*

Finally Kate pulled into the driveway. Across the way Hans Quinlin was unlocking his Jaguar and stowing his briefcase in the back. He stopped what he was doing and waved at the McDonalds as Kate killed the engine.

Paul smiled and waved back, but his voice was cold with sarcasm. "I wonder why he goes to work so early. And what kind of investments he handles. Investment in what? And for whom? I ought to do a background check on him someday." He leaned over the front seat. "Come on, Alexander. Pop's going to feed you breakfast. First time for that, huh, kid?"

Kate hadn't gotten out of the car.

"Hey, hon, you going to spend the day in the driveway?"

But Kate didn't hear him; her mind had jumped back to last night: *If you were in the bathroom all that time, why didn't I hear you? I didn't even hear the toilet flush.*

"Kate!"

"Yes." Her fingers came down on the door handle. *I must have gone right back to sleep,* she told herself; *that's why I didn't hear you.*

8

The alarm began buzzing at 9:30, the high-pitched tone hitting Kate's brain like a jolt of electricity. She rolled over automatically and switched it off. Less than three hours' sleep. Fighting a desire to close her eyes for just a few more minutes, she sat up, rubbed her face to force wakefulness, and suddenly remembered everything that had happened just hours before.

A sinking feeling grew in her stomach as she fell back on the bed. Would Packard actually file an abuse report with the police? Well, damn it, let her. Nothing would come of it. It was stupid. Alex just had some sort of reaction to an insect bite, or perhaps the rat bites. It wasn't done intentionally. They had no evidence, no *proof!*

Paul had still been fuming when he got ready for work at 7:00. "A few red marks! What's it going to do for my reputation at the office when they find out my wife and I are suspected of child abuse? God, this law is idiotic, an overreaction to real abuse. So the police have to spend time investigating innocent people while twelve-year-olds are forced into prostitution."

Walking toward the nursery Kate shivered and put a hand on the wall to steady herself. She had been feeling stranger and stranger lately, an eerie light-headedness that seemed to bring with it a racing heart and wobbly knees. Maybe she ought to have one of the ER doctors take a look at her. She had to be coming down with something. It didn't seem like the flu, though; she would be feeling fine; then her heart would suddenly start palpitating and she'd think she was going to faint.

Standing still to let the feeling pass, she shook her head, then continued down to the nursery. Alex was asleep, one arm under his head, another grasping a small stuffed Big Bird he had become attached to. Kate felt a rush of love as she looked at him. *How marvelous babies are, how innocent when they come into the world. The real harm we do to children,* she knew from years as a social worker, *is invisible because it's mental, not physical. How do we destroy you so? What happens to your innocence as you grow?* She laid her fingertips on his forehead and he squirmed slightly. No fever, thank God. There was a bottle of infant Tylenol on the changing table. Every four hours, the doctor said. She filled the dropper halfway, then lifted her child from the crib. "Sorry, honey, but you have to wake up for just a minute. Then you can go back to sleep."

Alex moaned uncomfortably as his eyes reluctantly opened. Kate smiled, felt her heart swell. "Good morning, beautiful. I don't want to get up either. This won't take long."

She held him on her lap and administered the medicine. Alex made a face, coughed, but kept it down. "Might as well change you while you're up."

Gently placing him on top of the changing table, she opened the top drawer, and froze. Alex's blue and red jumpsuit was stuffed behind a pile of diapers. It hadn't been there the last time she looked, she was certain. Or was she certain? The last time she had opened this drawer was in the middle of the night when Alex was crying from his fever. But what about earlier in the day? If it had been there she certainly would have seen it. Paul must have found it. That had to be what happened; Paul found the jumpsuit and put it here instead of in the dresser.

Taking out a diaper she changed Alex, trying not to look at the marks on his legs and arms, then put him back in the crib. "Pleasant dreams, hon. Try to get at least four hours so Mom can sleep, too. OK?"

But Kate was in her nightgown and bathrobe, having a cup of coffee in the kitchen at 11:00 when Lilliana rang the doorbell. "I didn't wake you, did I? You look like you just got out of bed."

"No, no. Come on in. I tried to sleep but those nice folks at MCI called to see if I wanted to change my long-distance carrier.'' Kate stifled a yawn so her sleeplessness wouldn't be so apparent.

''How lucky for you!'' Lilliana said as they sat at the kitchen table. ''I love talking to telemarketers. They're so much more articulate than Hans.''

''Oh, Lilliana, he's not that bad, and you know it.''

''A fat lot you know. He grunts in German, claims to dream in Polish, and screws in Italian, meaning after five minutes he's off brewing up some cappuccino and looking at *TV Guide* to see if there's a soccer game on. Are you going to offer me any of your dull American coffee or not? A bagel would be nice, too. And some cream cheese. I'm starving.''

''No bagels, Lilliana. Sorry. There's coffee on the counter. But I don't know how you can eat like you do and not balloon up. If I ate that way I'd weigh two hundred pounds.''

Lilliana, who probably weighed about one hundred, said, ''The marvel of genes, my dear. My mother and father were rail thin. I looked like an exclamation point until I got a boob job.''

''You didn't! I never would have guessed.''

Lilliana sat at the table and looked down at her bust. ''Sometimes I think it's a bit much. Oddly, Hans seems not to care one way or another. The meter reader does, though. I was sunbathing when he came in the backyard yesterday, and I thought the poor boy was going to faint.''

''Weren't you wearing a swimsuit?''

''Of course not. That's what *sunbathing* means—au naturel, in the buff, without clothes, buck naked, starko. No, I just quietly read my Wordsworth and pretended not to notice. Given the amount of time he was there I must have a difficult meter to read. Perhaps I'll ask Hans about that. He's such a store of interesting but useless information. What are you doing home, by the way? I thought you were one of those neurotic people who never took a day off.''

Kate told her about Alex's temperature, and the rush to the hospital.

''Good God,'' the other woman said. ''First rats, now an infection. What a week for the poor kid.''

Kate hesitated, then mentioned the marks on Alex's legs and arms. "Red splotches," she said. "Although on the backside they were more black and blue."

Lilliana looked at Kate over her coffee cup. "And you don't know what caused them?"

"We haven't any idea."

"Did it look like someone tried to hurt him? What about that woman who watches Alex during the day? Maybe she got upset at his crying and smacked him. I've heard about that happening. Especially at day care."

"No," Kate said at once. "Mrs. Alamada would never do anything like that. She's been baby-sitting for thirty years. I know a lot of people who have used her. Everyone loves her."

"What do you know about her husband? He might be some kind of weirdo who likes to inflict pain."

"Her husband's been dead for years. She lives by herself. Anyway, I gave Alex a bath last evening. The marks weren't on him then."

"And you didn't have any visitors?"

"No."

"Kind of narrows it down, doesn't it?"

"What does that mean?"

"Well, you didn't do it."

"Paul? Is that what you're saying?" Her voice became shrill.

Lilliana put her cup down. "No. All I meant was there were two people in the house last night, and you didn't do it."

"How can you say such a thing?" The hand holding her cup began to shake and she put it down on the tabletop, spilling a few drops.

Lilliana stared at her without emotion. "What's the alternate explanation?"

"Some natural cause, according to the doctor," she lied. "Blood vessels contracting. Or sleeping funny like babies do, arms and legs askew. Or reaction to an insect bite."

Lilliana shrugged. "Well, what do I know? I never had kids, so I don't know anything about how they sleep, or infections, or anything else. Maybe if I had—"

But Alex suddenly began to cry from upstairs, interrupting them.

"Hold on," Kate said. "I'll be right back. He probably wants to be changed."

"Bring him down. Maybe we can grill him and find out what happened last night. *Something* caused those marks."

Lilliana was pouring a third cup of coffee when Kate returned—in slacks and a blouse this time—with Alex. "Here he is," she said happily and nuzzled her son's face. "The man of the hour. How would you like some grape juice, young sir? Sound good?" She put him in a high chair.

"Finally weaning him, huh? Was that Paul's idea?"

Kate took a bottle of juice out of the refrigerator and put it in a pan of water on the stove.

"Why not use the microwave? It's faster."

"Too hot. This is better. And he likes it warmed up instead of cold."

Lilliana picked up Alex's arm and looked at the marks. "Much ado about nothing. I get more banged up than that gardening."

"It looked worse last night. And his fever was a hundred and four."

"Well, I guess that could be serious. Is he on antibiotics?"

Kate looked at the clock. "Just Tylenol for the fever."

"He seems OK now, though, doesn't he? How about it, little man? You feeling better?"

Alex made gurgling sounds.

"I guess that means yes." When Kate sat down Lilliana said, "I took your advice last night and told Hans we should take a vacation this summer. Some romantic place for just the two of us, I said. He agreed at once."

"That's wonderful. Where did you decide?"

"Moscow."

"Russia? My God. I don't—"

"Not romantic enough for you? Bug-infested hotels with dubious plumbing, gun-toting gangsters roaming the streets, corrupt government officials despoiling the country for their own gain. This isn't your idea of romance?"

Kate shrugged. "I guess it's not what I was thinking."

"It's commerce, my dear, the free market in action. Hans sees dollar signs, rubbles, yen, drachma, whatever. It's going to be a *business* trip, like all our trips. And I'll be stuck in the goddamn hotel while he's partying with his new 'clients.' Except this time I won't even be able to shop unless I want a slightly aged ballistic missile, or a three-ton statue of Lenin." She paused a moment, a sly smile developing. "Now there's an idea! How about a sixty-foot bust of Lenin in my front yard, someone to keep a close and skeptical eye on the good burghers of Los Angeles!"

Kate chuckled, but Lilliana put her cup down with a bang. "You don't know how lucky you are," she said with sudden ferocity. "You have a husband who has some interest in you. I— Oh, Christ, forget it, forget everything. Me and my big mouth. Poor Lilliana, always feeling sorry for herself. I'll bet that's what both of you think." She looked at the wall clock, though it seemed merely perfunctory. "I've got to go. I'm going to be late."

"No, please, Lilliana. Stay a while."

"Can't. Got a dentist appointment. Maybe I'll ask for an extra dose of nitrous oxide. Laughing gas, you know: ha, ha, ha. Something to brighten up the day."

After she was gone Kate picked up Alex and took him out back with his bottle. She sat in a chair, petals of light falling through the bougainvillea to the brick patio, and let the boy down on the ground, where he ignored the bottle and began to crawl toward a toy car, his mind obviously engaged. Kate's eyes went to the fence that separated her yard from Lilliana's, and for some reason a sudden anger at her neighbor rose in her, a feeling so unexpected and intense it frightened her, and an iciness rippled along the back of her neck and made her shiver. She hugged herself in the dappled sunshine.

"Anyway, she's wrong," Kate said to Alex. Her voice was almost angry. "I do know how lucky I am." She looked at her child as he crawled along the brick floor. "We all are. All three of us."

9

Kate jumped up from the kitchen table when the alarm on the stove began buzzing. She had finally gotten around to reading the *Times* and had set the alarm to remind her of Alex's medication. Pushing to her feet, she walked upstairs to the nursery, where he was sleeping. Paul had painted the room a cheery red and blue and yellow last year, and constructed a built-in bookcase that took up one complete wall. "He can put his law books on it when he's older," Paul joked. Now, though, it held a vase full of the roses Paul had brought her this week, and an assortment of Paddington bears in various sizes that Kate had collected over the years. Paddington was a favorite of hers, a reminder of her own childhood, when kids found entertainment in the gentle antics of bears and raccoons and ducks, rather than hideous robotic figures that kickboxed each other to death, or who had "powers" to turn themselves into machines or wild animals. Dominating the room from one corner was a six-foot-high stuffed rabbit Paul's parents had bought at FAO Schwarz at Christmas. It had cost more than Kate and Paul's monthly rent had been out in the Valley, but Paul was Tom and Helen's only child, and Alex their only grandchild, so a little spoiling was to be expected. And so far the grandparents didn't interfere in their marriage or tell them how to raise Alex, so, she knew from listening to friends, she ought to be thankful for her good fortune.

Kate stared at Alex sleeping in his crib. *So what happened to you last night, kiddo? Did you get bitten by something? Get your hands and legs caught on the side of the crib? What was it?*

Sensing his mother's presence the boy stirred slightly. *Time for your medicine, son.*

Kate went to the changing table, thinking again of Alex's lost-and-found jumpsuit, and started to measure out a dosage of Tylenol when a wave of dizziness hit her. *My God, I've got to sit down.* Lowering herself into the rocking chair, she thought, *That settles it: I've got to find out what's happening to me. Tomorrow I'll check with one of the doctors. . . .*

Suddenly Alex was crying. Jerking up, Kate looked at the crib. She must have dozed off, though it couldn't have been for more than a minute. How did her body clock get so messed up?

"All right, come here, honey." She picked the boy up and began to walk around the room, comforting him. "What's wrong, hon? Want some milk, or is your diaper wet? Both, probably." The soft words and the movement seemed to calm him, and a minute later he was relaxed enough for Kate to put the dropper of medicine in his mouth. She smiled at his predictably sour face. Why didn't they make this stuff taste like fruit juice? Or milk? She felt his diaper and smiled ruefully—clearly what Mrs. Alamada called a burrito. "OK, let me change you and then we can go downstairs and eat. We want you in a good mood when Dad gets here."

But it was Paul whose mood was foul when he came home two hours later. "I decided to have my friend Leo picked up today."

Kate was surprised. "Can you do that?"

"Hell yes, I can do it! He's harassing me. It's illegal. But putting out a warrant is not the same as finding him. If you see anyone following you, call me at the office and I'll notify Hollywood station and they can send out a car. But I still think this is just low-level annoyance. He isn't going to try anything." He opened the refrigerator and took out a Corona. "How's Alex doing?"

"Fine. No fever. The redness is going away but the black-and-blue marks are still there."

"Did the hospital call? They were going to do some tests."

"No. I'll check tomorrow when I go in."

"You're going to work tomorrow?"

"Alex is fine, Paul. And the work doesn't go away when I'm not there. It just means more for me the next day." She threw him a glance. "You didn't have any problems because of . . . ?"

"No. There was no police report on the abusive McDonalds yet. I was going to tell Ferguson about it, then decided to forget it. Maybe the hospital won't file the report after all."

"It's normally my job, you know. Filing the report."

"That irony hasn't escaped me." He swallowed the remainder of the beer and reached over to the refrigerator for another.

"Someone will do it for me this time, obviously. Probably the night person. I'll check the log, though, and tell you when it goes in. Maybe you can soften up Ferguson before he hears of it from someone else. Probably no one will figure out which McDonald it is, anyway. It's a common enough name." She stood up and went over to the sink.

"Someone at Hollywood division will notice. Bet on it. So how was the rest of your day? It had to be an improvement on last night."

But Kate was no longer listening. Her body had gone rigid and she was staring out the kitchen window.

Paul put down his beer and came over to her. "You all right, honey?"

She spun around, startled. "Of course. I'm fine. Just worried, I guess."

He slipped his arm around her waist and squeezed. "Well, it's understandable. Moms and kids. It's normal to be concerned."

But that's not what I'm worried about, Kate thought. She turned again to the window. *Someone's watching me. I feel it.*

Who are you?

What are you hiding for?

10

Patty was taking her break in Kate's office the next morning when Joel Symonds came by carrying an armload of patient files and balancing a chipped ceramic cup with *Symonds* written in red on the side. "So how's Superboy doing?" he asked as he sat down. "Packard told me he had another problem."

"Problem?" Patty said, raising her eyebrows. "Is that a medical term, like ow-ee and boo-boo?"

"He's doing fine," Kate told him. "His temperature is back to normal."

"I read the file. I guess those marks are still a mystery. Unless the lab results came back with something."

"I don't think the lab's finished," Kate said. "I probably would have heard."

He stared at her over the rim of his coffee cup. "How are you holding up? It's got to be difficult. I know how moms of only children worry."

Kate shrugged, trying not to show too much emotion. "I am worried. Naturally."

His eyes narrowed as he gazed at her with professional curiosity. "You sure you're OK, though? You've been looking a little pale lately."

"How would anyone feel knowing they had been reported to the police for possible child abuse?"

"I'm sorry about that. A bunch of nonsense. But Packard feels she doesn't have a choice. I'm sure it's not something she wanted to do."

"Who wrote up the report?" Kate had looked for the report

when she came in but hadn't found it, and it hadn't been entered on the log kept in the computer system.

"Packard did it herself. I haven't seen it. She wrote it and faxed it to Hollywood station last night."

"Efficient," Patty said with obvious sarcasm.

Symonds gazed into his coffee as if looking for something that shouldn't be there. "Your husband watches Alex sometimes, doesn't he?"

"What do you mean?"

He lifted the cup, draining it quickly and putting it down. "Just thinking about the abrasions. Sometimes men are a little rough with kids."

"Alex is eight months old. Paul doesn't play football with him."

"Yeah, I guess you're right. You're sure *you're* feeling OK, though? No aches or pains for the ol' country doc to check out? Why don't you let us run a complete blood test? You might have come down with something. At the least you ought to take a few days off, stay home and relax. I'll run interference with Kamel, if that's what's worrying you."

"No, I'm fine. Really." His concern was making her uneasy. She didn't want anyone at Midtown doing tests on her. And she definitely didn't want Symonds or anyone else developing a romantic interest in her.

Symonds abruptly shifted in his chair so he was facing Patty. "Did you ever get any feedback from the police about your cat?"

She grimaced. "I'll never hear anything. This is small potatoes to them. Jesus—" She halted as an ambulance pulled into the parking lot, its siren grinding down as it neared the hospital, then reluctantly came to her feet. "I guess we'd better get out there, Doc, and submit the new admits to twenty minutes of bureaucratic bullshit. What do you think it'll be this time? A liquor store owner shot with an AK-47, or a homeless woman beat half to death for three bucks? Sometimes I think they ought to play the music from 'M*A*S*H' over the loudspeakers. Korea couldn't have been any worse than Hollywood Boulevard."

As soon as Patty and Symonds left, Kate turned back to her computer, which was displaying a screen saver of odd geometric shapes that morphed into other odd geometric shapes. She moved the mouse, and the hospital form she had been completing reappeared, but when she hit a key it dissolved and the dime-size smiling face of a girl about five years old flashed suddenly on the screen, then magnified instantly, rushing toward her and taking up the entire monitor. The girl's mouth stretched open and a harsh scream shot from the speakers. The whole thing was over in two seconds.

Kate's hand slammed down on the off switch.

She felt her eyes close and her body stiffen. *Turn the monitor back on; it's not there! You imagined it.*

Her finger went to the button, hesitated for a long moment, then slowly pushed it. The monitor came alive with a swish of electronic noises. *It's not there, it's not! I imagined it.*

Again her eyes went to the screen. The half-completed hospital form stared benignly back at her. Broken hip, she remembered now. What was the patient's name? She glanced down on the desk where scraps of paper lay. Daniel Michaels, age ninety-one, fell in the bathroom of his nursing home. He had been brought in late last night, and now was up on three recuperating.

Daniel Michaels, age ninety-one. *Forget the picture.* Daniel Michaels. Broken hip. *But I know that girl. I've seen her face. Where? Why did she scream? And why does it make me tremble so? Damn it, who's doing this to me?*

Ten minutes later the telephone rang.

"Katie, Jesus, you gotta come out here at once. Hurry!"

"Patty?" Kate's heart sank. She wasn't in the mood for more of Patty's enthusiasms. "What are you talking about? Come why?"

"Just do it!"

"No. I—" But Patty had hung up.

A minute later Kate was staring at Patty's computer monitor.

"A hunk, isn't he?" Patty said excitedly. "Jesus, look at that stomach. Flat as a chopping board and hard enough to make Jell-

O bounce. I wish he wasn't wearing those stupid swim trunks. Let's see the merchandise!''

It was a photo of a swarthy, muscular young man in a bodybuilder pose: tanned and oiled, hands clamped together over his head, muscles rippling. The picture revolved completely around like a turntable, so his muscular backside came into view.

Kate was mystified. "What's it doing on your computer? Are you on the Internet?" The hospital computer system was set up so that only a few people had Internet access, and Patty wasn't one of them.

"No, of course not. I don't know what it's doing there. Probably someone showing off for me. Let me see if I can zoom in on him a little." She touched the mouse and the picture disappeared at once. "Damn!" She repeatedly clicked the mouse button, trying to recover the picture, but nothing happened. "Lost, I guess. Looked a little like Frankie, didn't it? From the view of that body maybe I shouldn't have turned him down." She glanced over her shoulder and singsonged, "Frankie! All is forgiven!"

Kate stood still, trying to keep her voice calm as a single drop of sweat rolled down her spine. "Has this ever happened before?"

"A hunk staring at me from my computer? Yeah, sure, Kate. Every morning ten men send me their nude photos and I get to choose which one I'm going to spend the night with. No, it's never happened before. That's why I called you." She turned around suddenly. "It hasn't happened to you, has it?"

"No . . ."

"It's Frankie," she said again, a note of finality in her voice. "It's got to be. But, God, what a weirdo. Does he think this is going to convince someone to go out with him? If anything it'd convince me to call mental health up on eight and have them come down with their net and straitjacket." She looked over Kate's shoulder. "Shit, here come some more admits. I'd better get to work. Next time I'll print the picture so I have something to look at during the day besides broken limbs and bloody bodies.''

Back at her desk Kate called down to the lab to see if the results were in on Alex's tests.

Ciji Horne, the lab chief, was evasive. "You'd better ask Dr. Kamel."

Kate felt a moment of panic, followed at once by anger. "Why can't you tell me?"

"It'd just be better to follow protocol," Ciji said. "Call Kamel."

The moment she hung up the outside line rang. "Mrs. McDonald? My name's Nick Cerovic." It was an unusually cheerful voice that made what followed more surprising. "I'm a detective with Hollywood Division. I'd like to set up a time when we could talk to you today. This afternoon, if possible."

Kate's hand tightened on the receiver. "Talk about what?"

"Your child. His injuries. Shouldn't take long."

Kate felt herself go light-headed.

"Mrs. McDonald?"

No, she thought at once. *I won't do it. They can't make me.* Her voice became demanding. "Why do you want to talk to me? Alex is fine. He just had a couple of minor problems, like any child might."

Like any child? . . . Look at the bruises, damn it! Someone hurt him. . . .

"It's just routine, one of those things we have to do. State law, you know. Maybe we could come to your office—"

"No, no. Please!"

"Do you want to come down here this afternoon, then? Maybe around two?" He sounded reasonable, impossible to argue with.

"No, I don't want to talk to you at all. I'm not going to." *Refuse to cooperate, don't let them bully you! They have no right.*

"That's really not one of the alternatives, I'm afraid. You can come here or we go there. Up to you."

"You're a detective? Does that mean you don't wear a uniform?"

"No one need know we're police, if that's what you're concerned about."

She hesitated, fighting a desire to slam the phone down and start running. *Hurry, Kate. Get out. Now!* Finally she asked, "How long will it take?"

"Shouldn't be long. Half hour, maybe."

God, a half hour. How was she going to explain this to Kamel?

"Mrs. McDonald?"

"Come to the cafeteria. It's in the basement. Two o'clock. How will I know you?"

"There'll be two of us. My partner's a woman. She's got short black hair and is wearing a . . . What are you wearing, Annie? It's a brown skirt and white blouse. Very sexy-looking. Are those what you call stiletto heels, Annie? . . . I'll be the handsome dude about forty who gave up a promising career in show business to go into the LAPD." He laughed easily as Kate heard a woman say something obviously sarcastic. "Two o'clock it is."

Kate hung up and thought, *No, I'm not going. I won't talk to them.*

Damn it, I won't let them do this to me. I won't!

Them, she thought, and her mind cleared a moment. *Who do I mean?* She remembered the rattle in the playpen and the blue and red jumpsuit, and shuddered.

Who are they?

11

She saw them at once, a large, square-faced crew-cut man who looked older than forty, and a wiry, thirtyish woman with shoulder-length black hair and small black eyes that followed her from the moment she stepped into the cafeteria. They were sitting side by side at a round table in the rear and, as far as Kate was concerned, could have had the word *police* tattooed on their foreheads. She approached them warily.

The man rose at once, his movements quick and fluid for so large a person, and smiled from a face that was attractive though weathered from too many years of California sun. "Mrs. McDonald? Nick Cerovic." He stuck out a beefy hand that was surprisingly soft to the touch, shook hands with Kate, then introduced his partner. "Annie DeSilva."

The other woman nodded but didn't offer to shake. Kate glanced around to see if people were watching her, briefly imagined everyone in the cafeteria listening to their conversation over the public-address system, then sat gingerly across from them. Cerovic picked up his coffee cup with a sense of wonder. "Cappuccino in a hospital cafeteria. Only in L.A., huh? I bet you got Perrier in the IVs."

Kate wasn't in the mood. "I stayed home from work yesterday. It's going to take me all day to catch up. So if you don't mind—"

"Sure, sure. We won't be long at all. We work in a special Child and Sex Crimes unit—"

"*What?*" Kate had to work to keep her voice down.

"Sounds worse than it is," Cerovic said soothingly. "I told the division they ought to name it something more innocuous, like 'Juvenile Investigations.' But they liked the other name better, has a ring to it the media can grab onto. This is Hollywood, you know. Image is everything. But don't worry about it. There's obviously no question of sexual abuse here, or even a crime, but we need to follow up to keep the paperwork mavens happy. Rat bites! That must have been terrifying for your boy. You, too.''

Cerovic waited for her to reply. When she didn't Annie DeSilva said, as if she had been thinking about it for a long time, ''This report from the hospital lists your husband as Paul McDonald. Is that the same Paul McDonald in the DA's office?''

''Yes,'' Kate told her.

DeSilva looked as if she wanted to say something, then thought better of it. Her expression revealed nothing—not even a nod, just narrow black eyes staring out from a pretty but hard face. An unhappy woman, Kate thought at once, and felt a sudden intense, if probably irrational, dislike for her.

Cerovic asked, ''Did you ever figure out how the rats got in the house?''

Kate shook her head. ''Someone must have left the back door open. We do at night when we're out on the patio. We probably forgot to close it when we went inside.''

''I used to live in Brooklyn. Saw rats all the time. This is the first time since moving to L.A. So Alex is doing OK?''

''Fine.''

''Well, if he cries when you take him to Disneyland you'll know why. Repressed memories of Mickey nibbling on his fingers. Or at least Mickey's cousins.''

Annie DeSilva was staring at the report in front of her with what was supposed to be great interest. It's her interrogation technique, Kate thought. She probably remembered everything that was written there and didn't have to refresh her memory, but wanted to put on the cop act. Image was everything. ''Those marks on the child's arms and legs appear to be caused by ligatures, according to the reporting doctor.''

''That's absurd,'' Kate said. ''It must have been a reaction to his fever.''

"A hundred and four." DeSilva stared at Kate, blank faced. "That's pretty serious if it doesn't come down. He could have gone into seizures, couldn't he?"

"That's why we brought him to the emergency room."

"And it just came on suddenly?" Her tone indicated disbelief.

"You've got the report," Kate snapped. "Is there something about it you don't understand?"

The woman stared at her. "I have a kid myself. She never went from no fever to a hundred and four in two hours."

"And?" Kate continued staring at her. "This is supposed to mean something? You're an expert on fevers? You're a doctor?" *Why am I doing this?* Kate wondered with a stab of panic. *Why am I trying to antagonize them? Just get it over with and get back to work. You don't need them meddling any more than they already are.*

Cerovic tried conciliation. "We're not accusing you of anything, Mrs. McDonald. Our job is to act as advocates for the child until we decide that—"

"Alex doesn't *need* an advocate, Sergeant, Lieutenant, whatever you are." Kate leaned over the table, her voice as angry as his was calm. "Do you know what I do here?"

"Sergeant. Both of us," Cerovic said. "And we know."

Annie DeSilva said, "I remember seeing your name on reports. We've been the investigating officers on some of them. We essentially do the same kind of work you do. That's what makes your attitude so difficult to understand."

"My attitude? What's wrong with my attitude? You walk in here and blame me for what happened to my baby on the basis of a report written by a doctor who saw Alex for a total of, what? Ten minutes? And you don't like my *attitude?*"

"You should be on our side, shouldn't you? The child's side? Rather than arguing with us?"

Kate stared at the woman for a moment before sagging back in her chair. Her eyes closed, then slowly opened, and her hand flopped over on the table in a sign of resignation. "I'm sorry." They were right, of course. If she gave them what they were looking for, they'd disappear out of her life forever. "Look, I don't have any idea how those marks got on Alex's arms and legs. I don't know why he had such a sudden fever. I don't know how rats got into our house, unless it was through the back door. None of this would look bad if it hadn't all happened at the same time.'' She sighed, seemed to sink within herself, and stared over their heads at the blank green wall that evidently hadn't been painted in years. *Green is for cafeterias,* she remembered. *And mental hospitals. And prisons. Color as a sedative.*

Nick Cerovic's tone was calm. ''Like you say, the emergency-room doc gave the boy only a cursory look. I guess it'd be a good idea to have him thoroughly checked out, then. A complete physical exam with blood tests and so on. You don't have any objections to that, do you?''

''He's already had blood tests.''

''I think they were testing for viruses. We'd like a full workup. Just routine things, but it's a hoop we ask parents to hop through. Or their kids, actually. The parents aren't the ones getting poked with needles.'' He smiled good-naturedly.

Kate lowered her head. ''I can have someone besides Dr. Packard, can't I?'' Now she was being really juvenile, blaming the doctor for doing her duty.

''Sure. Whoever you like. What about this . . .'' He glanced down at a paper on the table. ''Dr. Kamel. Is he acceptable?''

Kate said he was, though she felt a momentary doubt she was reluctant to mention. Kamel was fine as a diagnostician and surgeon, but his manner with patients was too brusque for Kate's taste. Or that of most patients.

''How long have you been a hospital social worker?'' DeSilva asked. She, too, seemed to want to defuse things, and offered Kate the ghost of a smile.

''Three years. I was a county social worker before that.''

''Tough job,'' Nick Cerovic commented. ''Lots of tragedy to deal with.''

''You've been married how long?'' DeSilva asked.

Kate stared at her a long moment. ''What are we doing here?''

DeSilva said, ''Answering questions. We can do it at the station house if you want.'' So much for defusing tension.

Kate glared at her. "Four years."

"And you're thirty-four?"

"Yes, I was thirty." She was becoming annoyed again and couldn't help but ask, "Is there a problem with that? Some quaint California law?"

For the first time the policewoman gave a real smile. "Not at all. I was looking for Mr. Right for a long time, too. Too bad when I found him he turned out to be Mr. Pain-in-the-ass."

Nick Cerovic said, "Does your husband ever watch Alex?"

"What do you mean, watch? Of course he does when I go shopping or whatever. I have a sitter when I'm at work." She straightened in the seat and shook her head. Was this a new police interrogation technique, to go from friendliness to insinuation in one minute? She stared from one to the other. "I guess I never thought about what happened after I sent in one of those reports on suspected abuse. Is this normal? You sit around and ask people how old they were when they married, and whether the father ever baby-sits or beats up the baby? This is the police department's way of protecting children?"

Cerovic shook his head in sympathy. "I've been in the department for twenty years and I've never gotten over the rules and bureaucracy. It can't be much different here, Ms. McDonald. You gotta dance the dance and fill out all the forms in triplicate, or some suit in a big office is going to climb all over you. Same thing here, right? Nothing personal, you should know that. We'll write up our report once the results of Alex's physical come through. Don't expect any follow-up. We'll be out of your life forever."

She stirred. "I look forward to it. OK if I get back to work now?"

"One other thing," Cerovic said. "Those rats. Animal Control called the department about them."

"What do you mean?" She was instantly wary. They had deliberately waited until now to bring this up. "Why would they call about the rats? They weren't rabid."

"I guess the lab thought it was odd. The rats weren't wild rats like we have around here, more like laboratory rats."

"I don't follow you."

"Lab rats," DeSilva said. "Like schools or hospitals buy from a supplier to do research. You know, like running through a maze or testing medicine on. Not the kind you find outside in California."

Kate didn't know what to say.

DeSilva's tone hardened. "So I guess it was more than just leaving the back door open. Someone bought those rats, or stole them from a lab, then set them loose in your nursery."

"No."

"Do you have a better explanation?"

"It didn't happen that way. I'm sure."

"Well, it's something to think about, isn't it?" Cerovic said. He slid a card across the table. "If you remember something you think we should know, give us a call."

Kate left the card where it was and stood up so abruptly the chair fell over behind her. "I'll do that," she muttered as she hurried away.

The two cops stopped by Mohammed Kamel's office on the way out to set up Alex's examination. Nick Cerovic said, "We'd like to get a copy of the blood tests you already did on the boy, Doctor. Are the results back yet?"

Sitting behind his desk Kamel hunched his heavy body forward and frowned from beneath bushy eyebrows. His hands were clasped in front of him. "I'm not quite sure what the point of all this is. Do you suspect Mrs. McDonald of purposely abusing her child, or of neglect, or what? This is unclear to me."

DeSilva started to say something, but Cerovic quickly overrode her. "We don't suspect her of anything. It's just a follow-up on the report your Dr. Packard sent us. It's all pretty routine. We wouldn't even be here if it weren't for your doctor's report."

Kamel stared at Cerovic a moment, then flipped open a file on his desk. "I have learned in this country that when people say something is 'just routine' it is always quite the opposite." He glanced down at the report. "The results came back this morning. It's a bit peculiar. I haven't had a chance to talk to her about it. The boy, Alex, has a viral infection. An unusual form of virus, actually. It's a strain of swine flu.''

Annie DeSilva's voice shot up. ''Swine flu? Is that a disease humans get?''

''Oh, yes,'' Kamel replied. ''But it's spread through contact with pigs or hogs. You usually don't see it in an urban area.''

''Would the child have to have been in contact with hogs?''

''No. Not necessarily. But you would expect that someone close to him would have, and probably would have been sick, too.''

''Like a parent or baby-sitter?''

''That's the most likely cause.''

DeSilva asked, ''Is there any other way to contract the disease? Through something he ate, maybe?''

''It could be possible. I am not a virologist, however. You should check with a specialist.''

''Or through an infection?''

''Yes.''

''What about through rat bites?''

''No, no. Couldn't happen.''

''What if someone took something on which the virus was alive and rubbed it on a sore?''

Kamel shook his head. ''That's absurd.''

''But it would cause an infection?''

''Without a doubt. But surely you don't believe that happened?''

Cerovic said, ''Mrs. McDonald is a well-thought-of employee?''

Kamel was insulted by the question. ''Of course she is. Everyone has occasional problems with bosses and coworkers but, certainly, very well thought of. Her husband is on the hospital's board, you know.''

Cerovic seemed interested. ''No. I didn't know. Does that make him her boss?''

''No. Board membership is largely . . . ceremonial, I suppose you would call it. They provide oversight to the hospital, not management.''

DeSilva stood up. "You'll take care of the examination as soon as possible and let us know, then?"

"As soon as Mrs. McDonald brings the baby in."

Cerovic also got to his feet. "Do whatever additional tests you normally do for possible physical or sexual abuse. You'd know what to look for more than we would, so we'll leave it up to you."

Kamel's thick eyebrows rose. "Sexual abuse? And you say this is a routine investigation?"

"We just like to cover all bases. It's for our protection more than anything. We're the ones who might be asked to explain ourselves in court someday. By the way, does your hospital do research?"

"We are a university-affiliated hospital, so of course we do research. Many of our doctors are on UCLA's clinical faculty and are expected to publish."

"Do your research people ever use rats in experiments?"

"Sometimes. I believe it's more common to use mice. Research is not my area, though. I'm more concerned with today's patients than tomorrow's medications."

Cerovic nodded and dropped a card on Kamel's desk. "Our fax number's on the card. As soon as you get the results."

"I want those tests done as soon as possible, Doctor," DeSilva said. "If not sooner."

The annoyance that had been building in Ann DeSilva spilled over on the way to the parking lot. "Come on, Nickie, stop drooling. She's married. To a DA, no less."

"You've got a dirty and devious mind, partner. A little weird considering the most recent date I had was about the time of the last lunar eclipse."

"What then? You were just being all sappy and smiley to her because she's a nice person. Shit!"

"What shit? The woman's as innocent as you or me, Annie, but she's caught in the damn child-abuse industry because some hard-ass doctor says her kid's got some weird marks on his body. Jesus, if they had this law thirty-five years ago my folks woulda spent half their lives in jail. I was always falling down or hurting myself, picking up bruises. Not to speak of getting whacked by my dad when I screwed up. It didn't mean someone was abusing me.''

''This kid's only eight months old, for Christ's sake.''

''So he can't get red wrists?''

''And bites from laboratory rats?''

''Let's talk to someone from Animal Control before jumping to conclusions. Just because that type of rat is used for research doesn't mean they can't be running around wild, too. Look at killer bees. They were imported to Brazil for research, and a few escaped. Now they're everywhere.''

''Nick, she's hurting her baby; she's doing it on purpose!''

''Yeah, for what? For attention? Because she doesn't like the kid? To get back at her husband for some reason? Come on, Annie, she was thirty-three before she even had a child. Women that age tend to be overprotective, not abusive. And look at who she is—a hospital social worker, for God's sake! Someone who *investigates* abuse. Married to a prosecutor. Who's on the hospital board! Does this sound like someone who's going to neglect her baby?''

Ann DeSilva unlocked the driver's-side door of her green Monte Carlo, and stared at Cerovic over the hood as she waited for the heat inside to dissipate. ''Nick, that woman is hurting her kid. I don't know why, but she is. And I'm going to prove it. No matter what you think.''

Kate leaned back in her chair and blew out a long sigh. ''You're kidding.''

''I am afraid not,'' Mohammed Kamel said. His voice was gruff, but Kate knew this was his way of dealing with uncomfortable situations. ''It is an extremely rare virus nowadays. At least in California. Luckily it is not dangerous if caught quickly. And this appears to be a weak strain. I have an antibiotic ready for you.'' He placed a container of liquid on the desktop.

As Kate picked it up, Kamel asked, ''And you don't have any idea how he might have contacted it?''

She shook her head as though in a dream. ''I can't imagine.''

''Are there other children at the baby-sitter's?''

"Just one. A boy about six. He only comes over after school. And doesn't usually even go in the room Alex is in. He plays out in the yard most of the time."

"Well, I'll contact the CDC and—"

"The CDC?"

"Infectious disease. Not that Alex is infectious anymore. That stage has passed. But they keep records to see if there is a recurrence of influenza anywhere in the country. Swine flu is thought to be the cause of the huge epidemic of nineteen eighteen, you know."

That makes the second time Alex has become the subject of a government report, Kate thought.

Kamel stood up, formal and dignified. "You'll bring the child in tomorrow, then?"

Kate was only half paying attention. "Yes, of course."

"Check with Dee to see what time I have available. It will probably have to be early." He seemed on the verge of saying something else but changed his mind and left.

For a long moment Kate sat at her desk without moving. How could Alex have caught something like swine flu? It made no sense. But how did he get those marks on his arms and legs? She felt a dizziness in her head and thought, *I should have asked Dr. Kamel if it's possible I have it, too. Maybe tomorrow.*

Twenty minutes later, when a child's voice seemed to come from the speakers on her computer—*Mommy, Mommy, help me*—Kate was certain it was in her mind.

12
___

"The police interviewed you at work?" Paul's voice filled the room with disbelief. "Why didn't you call me? I could have stopped it. At least kept them away from the hospital. Jesus! Are they trying to get you fired?"

Kate was feeding applesauce to Alex in his high chair. She tried to keep her voice calm. "I thought it better to get it over with. It only took a few minutes."

Paul had already changed into shorts and a knit shirt, and was sitting at the kitchen table with a beer. He was incensed, but Kate wasn't sure whether it was from the fact she had been questioned, or because he—a deputy DA, as well as board member of the hospital—hadn't been informed first. He drank from the bottle, then banged it on the table. "What did they want to know? If you beat your child? If you put rats in his bed?"

Kate smiled and held the spoon high above her son's head. "Here comes a spoonful of applesauce for my friend Alex. Better open up!" As the boy opened his mouth, Kate said evenly, "The rats weren't wild, Paul. They didn't come from palm trees."

He sat back and looked at her. "What do you mean?"

"They're laboratory rats, used for research."

His head was wagging back and forth. "I'm not following you."

"Someone bought those rats, then came in the house and *put* them in the crib."

His face blanched. "Impossible."

Kate used the spoon to wipe applesauce from around Alex's mouth. "Why?"

"Well . . . it just is. People don't sneak into houses and put rats in a bed. The idea is moronic. How could this mythological person have gotten in, anyway?"

"We don't shut all the windows at night this time of year. It wouldn't be hard."

"No. I just can't believe it. It's ridiculous. Why would someone do that? There's no reason."

"I don't know why. The police seem to think one of us did it. For attention." She shot him a look.

"Because of those red marks on Alex's arms and legs? That damn doctor has everyone believing it, doesn't she? Christ!"

He jerked out of his chair and grabbed another beer from the refrigerator. "What about the lab tests? Weren't they due today?"

Her eyes moved away from him. "They came back. Alex has swine flu."

"He has what?"

"He's on medication. Dr. Kamel said he'd get over it without any problems since we caught it so quickly. And he's past the contagious stage."

"But how could—"

Kate lifted another spoonful of applesauce and eased the food into the boy's mouth, but he hadn't completely swallowed the first batch and it oozed onto his chin. He began to giggle. "Who knows how he got it? Babies are incubators for disease. He could even have picked it up from you or me."

"Then why aren't we sick?"

"We could be carriers because we've built up an immunity. Or maybe I did have a mild case. I've been feeling a little sick lately."

"Could he have gotten it from the rats?"

"I don't know. I'll ask Kamel tomorrow."

"But he's going to be OK, isn't he? It isn't going to cause him to be sterile or anything like that?"

Kate shook her head at the maleness of his question. "He'll be fine, Paul." Alex spit out another mouthful of food.

"Here, let me get that," Paul said. He got a paper towel and cleaned the boy's USC T-shirt. "Let me feed him for a while." Paul took the spoon and offered the food to Alex, who automatically opened his mouth. "So what was the outcome of this inquisition about rats and swine flu? Did they say they'd be back with the thumbscrews and cattle prods? Or is this the end of it? What's going on?"

"They want Alex to have a physical examination. They said it was normal in cases like this. Is that true?"

"Yeah, I suppose so. But I still don't like it. If there were any question of abuse I could understand, but you don't consciously go out and expose a child to swine flu to punish him. Or put rats in his crib. What are these people thinking? Do you remember the cops' names?"

Perfectly, she thought. "Annie DeSilva. Nick Cerovic."

"Cerovic I've heard of. Been around a long time. A good guy, but he must have pissed someone off to end up investigating child abuse in Hollyweird. Jesus, what a way to spend your golden years! DeSilva's new to me. Doesn't mean anything—there's fifteen thousand cops on the LAPD. Less than five percent of the known total for street gangs, by the way." He glanced over at Kate. "I think young Alexander McDonald is through with dinner. What do you say, Mom?"

"He did pretty good. Considering." She took the bowl to the sink and washed it out.

Paul took Alex from his high chair and settled the boy on his lap. "How do you feel, sport? Swine flu, huh? That's not going to make you look like a hog, is it? Any urges to go outside and wallow in the mud? A sudden desire to take up politics?" He tickled the boy's stomach under his shirt. "He doesn't even have a temperature, does he?"

"Not since yesterday."

Paul began to pat Alex's back, and the boy immediately burped. "Like a toy, isn't he? Feed-and-Burp Alex, no batteries needed." Kate brought over another paper towel.

"I got another call from my good pal Leo Petrosian today," Paul said, turning Alex toward his mother so she could wipe his shirt. "He said something like, 'It's not over, asshole. You belong to me now.' I just started laughing. I couldn't help it. Finally I said, 'Leo, you're watching the wrong movies. You sound like some forties noir thriller with Robert Mitchum or Sidney Greenstreet. Go down to Blockbuster and get something with Christian Slater or Alec Baldwin so you can see what an up-to-date thug sounds like.' ''

Kate walked over to the sink and threw the paper towel in the trash. ''What did he say?''

''What the newspapers like to call 'a string of expletives.' Most began with *F*. Some were *MF*'s. Some I had never even heard of, maybe variations of ancient Armenian curses.''

Kate began putting dirty dishes in the dishwasher. ''What's this man look like?''

''Now? I don't know. The booking picture in his folder made him look like an Armenian biker, if there is such a thing. Hair to his shoulders, torn T-shirt. Kind of wimpy-looking, though. Maybe five-nine, a hundred and forty pounds. The sort of guy the hard-timers in Tehachipi would turn into a girlfriend, probably pass him around from con to con to pay off debts, or rent out for cigarettes. Maybe that's why he's so pissed at me— he can't sit down anymore without wincing with pain and remembering how he spent his time in the slammer. But don't worry about it. We've got a warrant to pick him up. He'll be out of our lives pretty soon, and everything will revert to its typical humdrum tedium.'' He lifted Alex over his head. ''Won't it, buddy? By next week it'll be boredom in Brentwood.''

Kate felt her intestines tighten. *No, it won't,* she thought. *Things can never return to normal now. Someone's out there, and he knows I'm scared to death because there's no one I can turn to for help.*

No one.

July 15

A tough week, Katie, but you're doing fine. Just fine. Pat yourself on the back for not losing control yet. Many people would have. I know that talking to the police was embarrassing, though. Now everyone at work wonders about you, don't they? But without the police, without the suspicions, there would be no thrill. And for people like us the thrill is all. *Isn't it?*

13

Kate had had to settle for a seven A.M. appointment for Alex's physical, so by the time all the testing and poking and probing was done it was almost nine-thirty. After taking him to Mrs. Alamada's and returning to the hospital parking lot, it was already after ten. Did she have any appointments with clients this morning? She couldn't remember. Usually there was one or two before lunch, so someone was probably waiting in her office right now.

As she hurried out of the Mustang she saw a skinny young man pop like a jack-in-the-box from between two cars twenty feet away. As soon as he saw her looking at him he spun around and disappeared into the rear of the lot, loping with arms askew and head bobbing. Leo Petrosian? From Paul's description it might be. But crazy or not he wouldn't try anything here; there were people all around, and guards fifty yards away in the hospital.

She stared back toward where he had first appeared. A nurse was holding on to the door as she climbed with difficulty into a jacked-up Range Rover, oblivious to Kate's interest. Two men in gray suits were slowly strolling the other way, talking and gesturing with their hands. Doctors, probably. What had happened to Petrosian?

She started walking toward the ER, and was within fifty feet of the entrance when a noise made her jerk around. The man was suddenly just steps behind her, hands jammed in pockets, eyes staring at the ground. When he saw Kate looking at him he quickened his pace. Heart pounding, she started to walk faster, heard footsteps slapping rapidly against the asphalt, and began to run. The ER door swung open and a security guard stepped out and smiled with bad teeth. "Not so hectic today, Kate. No dead cats, anyway."

She glanced over her shoulder. The man wasn't there. The guard held the door for her.

"Thanks, Chuck." She started to go into the waiting room, then halted. "Did you see that man behind me?"

The guard shifted so he could look beyond her, into the sea of cars. "Nope. Was he giving you trouble or something?"

"No." She felt the breath rush out of her. Turning back to the guard she tried to smile. "I'm just being stupid, I guess. Thanks."

The moment she sat at her desk she dialed Patty's extension, but someone she didn't recognize answered. "Patty called to say she'd be late. No, I don't know what the problem is, but she sounded upset. Sorry."

Kate found out an hour later when her friend phoned in. "I was up with the goddamn cops until three A.M. Someone trashed my house last night when I was out with my doctor friend." Kate could tell from her voice it was all she could do not to start crying.

"Trashed how? Do you mean vandalized? What happened?"

"What happened is that someone got inside my house and tore it apart." She forced her voice into something approaching normalcy, but Kate could sense the effort it took her not to break down in sobs. "Tammy came home from a friend's about nine and beeped me at once. The front door was open, furniture turned over, drawers emptied, the refrigerator pushed on the floor, shit spread on the walls. . . ."

"My God," Kate whispered.

"They were very thorough. They even ripped up the carpet. It was like they were looking for something. I guess the worst thing they did is smash all the toilets. Why would someone do something like that? Can you imagine two people, one of them a ten-year-old girl, living without toilets? The health department won't let us back in until they're replaced, and the shit cleaned off the walls. I have a plumber out here now. Luckily it's covered by homeowner's insurance. There's got to be fifteen thousand dollars' worth of damage.''

"Do the police have any idea who did it? Were there finger-prints?''

"Fingerprints?'' Her sarcasm was obvious. "Like maybe Columbo came out and spent three hours with his little find-a-crook kit? Not a chance. They didn't even look! This is small potatoes to the LAPD. They figure it's teenagers because of what they wrote on the walls—stupid kid stuff like 'You can't hide' and 'Teddy's dead.' There's a group of punk devil wor-shipers living in abandoned buildings in east Hollywood who get a kick out of scaring people, this cop said. So why me, I asked him, and what the hell is this 'Teddy's dead' supposed to mean? He said it probably has something to do with a punk-rock song. Or it could even be a band. Sex, drugs, and rock 'n' roll, that's all these kids care about. That and violence. That's when I told them about the cat.''

Kate's body had gone cold. She thought she was going to be sick, and put her hand on the desk to steady herself.

Patty's voice rose with emotion. "The cat! I should have kept my damn mouth shut. But the cops were as happy as two pigs in shit when I told them about it, because they could wrap up their investigation. *Got* to be punks, they said. They just *love* to skin cats and use them in their ceremonies. OK, I said, but this cat was taken from my home and brought to my job in a hospital. Does that sound like stoned-out teenagers?''

Joel Symonds came through the door, hair askew and smiling as usual. "What's today's disaster?'' he asked, then saw Kate's face. "Sorry. Another Symonds foot-in-mouth?''

Kate hushed him with a wave.

Patty said, "Ah, shit, the plumber wants to talk to me. I promised to be in by noon. I know the department's falling behind on the paperwork again. I'll see you then.''

When Kate told Symonds what had happened, he shook his head. "Maybe I'll move back to New Hampshire and get myself a place out in the woods. Where there's no punks with pierced nipples and .45s. And no cats killed or houses trashed for amusement.''

Kate bent forward at the waist. God, I'm going to be sick, she thought.

Symonds looked at her with concern but tried to keep his tone light. "I know I've mentioned this before, young lady, but you don't look so good. The technical medical term is *crappy*."

Kate shook her head and tried to gain control over herself. "I'm just upset about Patty. I feel fine." *Go away,* she thought. *Damn it, just leave me alone!* And her mind began to repeat, *Teddy's dead, Teddy's dead,* like the endless clacking of a train over the rails. Her eyes went to Symonds, pleading. "Really. I'm fine."

"Really, you're not."

Kate forced a laugh, and let her hands drop to her sides so he couldn't see her clenched fists. "Don't argue with your patient."

"You're not my patient. But I'm going to keep annoying you until you weaken and let me run some tests. You're not feeling well. Period. Don't argue with someone who got an A minus in diagnosis."

Kate felt herself warm with resentment. "Come on, leave me alone. I'm OK."

Symonds turned serious. "All right. Then it's not something physical. I don't want to butt in where I'm not wanted, but I'd still like to help if I can, Kate. And if I can't, I can at least refer you to someone else." He smiled. "No charge, professional courtesy."

A loudspeaker in the hallway began blaring a code blue just as Frankie Yorba appeared in the doorway. "Possible suicide coming in, Doc. Rescue's two minutes out at most." His eyes went to Kate, and lingered on her face. "The wife's with him in the ambulance. They might need you later. She's pretty shook up."

Symonds came to his feet. "I mean it, Kate. If there's something you don't want to talk about at work I can see you at my practice. Or refer you. Or we can have lunch away from here someday and just talk. Please think about it. I don't like to see people suffer. That's why I chose ER work."

* * *

Patty showed up just before noon. She stood anxiously at the open door. "I've got to get to my desk. They're swamped out there. Just wanted you to know I'm OK. Tammy's more upset than I am."

"I can't imagine why people do things like that," Kate said. "It's so senseless." But it wasn't, she knew, which made it all the worse.

"It's a sick goddamn world," Patty said angrily. "We ought to know that better than most people, given what we do here."

"Are you going to see the police again?"

Patty took a step inside. "The often imitated but never duplicated, highly trained Los Angeles Police Department professionals? Yeah, sure, I'll see them when they arrest these assholes and hold a trial. That'll be in my dreams, though. But you can't come to the trial, if that's what you're thinking. No women but me allowed in my dreams."

"But if they do catch them . . ."

"Yeah, yeah. And if Jupiter crashes into Venus." Her gaze suddenly went to Kate's desk and the monitor of her computer. "Does that say what I think it says?"

Kate turned to look. Scrolling across the screen was the message:

KATE KATE DON'T DIE YET KATE KATE DON'T DIE YET. . . .

Patty said, "What the hell?"

Kate's head sank to her chest. She gritted her teeth to keep the tears away.

"What the hell is it?" Patty demanded.

Kate shook her head. "I don't know. Someone's been sending stupid messages, making the screen go blank. This one . . ." She looked at the screen and waved a hand weakly. The message had already disappeared. "That was a new one. But I've been getting one almost every day." She held her body rigid so Patty wouldn't see her starting to shake.

"Every day? For how long?"

Kate shrugged. "A week maybe."

"A week! Why didn't you say something? Go to the computer department, for Christ's sake. They should be able to stop it. Go to goddamn Zamora if you have to! Find out who's doing it. Have you just been sitting here like a marshmallow while some creep's threatening you? Jesus, Kate! What's wrong with you?"

"I didn't know what to do."

"Do? You get someone looking into it. It's got to be someone here in the hospital. Right? Probably someone with access to the computer department. Shit, call the police. This is illegal. You can't just sit back and close your eyes when someone is bothering you like this. Is this why you look like shit—are you scared of this guy?"

"It's nothing, Patty. Just someone getting a kick out of trying to scare me. If I complain it'll just encourage him. Then maybe he will do something."

"Oh, for Christ's sake! You sound like Dear Abby. So you're just going to let him do it?" She threw her arms up and began to pace around the small office.

"It'll stop. Believe me." *Damn it, why doesn't everyone just leave me alone?*

Patty halted. "Do you know Dennis Flagstad?" Her voice was demanding, like a parent to a child who had just done something to disappoint.

Kate shook her head.

"He works in Computing with all the other technowienies down in the basement. Kind of fat, with limp hair, a goatee, and Coke-bottle glasses. Probably hasn't seen the light of day in a decade. He told me he set up our e-mail system a couple of years ago. He claims he's the only one who really understands it. I'll ask him how someone could be harassing you. There's got to be a way to track it down."

Kate said nothing.

"You'll talk to him if I get him to come up here? You won't fink out and say, 'Oh, it's nothing'? This isn't going to be cheap, you know. I'll probably have to bribe him with a box of Skittles and a dozen comic books. It's the only way to get these guys out of their burrow."

"I'll talk to him." There wasn't much force in her voice.

Patty looked at her. "Why do I get the feeling you're not real interested in finding out who this is?"

"I said I'd do it," Kate snapped.

"Damn right, you will. I'll lock you in here with Dennis if I have to. But you *are* going to talk to him."

Half an hour later Kate picked up the ringing phone and heard a man's soft, wondering voice. It was so low she had to strain to hear as he asked, "Still alive after all these years, Kate? I didn't believe it when I found out. I told them they had to be wrong. But you're still making a go of it, aren't you? Good for you!"

Kate's mouth opened. She tried to form the words getting through her brain but couldn't.

"Thanks for loaning us that jumpsuit. I put it back for you. See, it wasn't lost at all."

Her whole body shook as she slammed the phone down.

14

Mrs. Alamada was saying into the phone, "Sure, sure, honey, Alex is just fine, no fever," when Joel Symonds hurriedly stuck his head in Kate's office and said, "The wife of the suicide you were going to—"

"Oh, God." Kate had forgotten all about it. She was supposed to be comforting this woman whose husband had just inexplicably cut his throat in their bedroom, and instead had become wrapped up in her own problems, all of which suddenly paled in importance. She hung up and hurried out of her office. "I'm so sorry," she said to Symonds, who patted her on the back and said, "She's in the chapel. I told her you'd be along."

When she returned to her office an hour later, Judith Zamora and Matthew Dotson, the vice president of Human Resources, were waiting for her. Kate halted at the open doorway and looked at them in surprise. Zamora, in a stark black dress and high heels, was seated, flipping through a file in her lap, but Dotson was standing with his back to her, looking at a framed picture on the wall. "Your child?" he said when he noticed her. "Alexander, isn't it? Handsome boy. You and Paul must be proud."

Kate jerked out the chair behind her desk and tried not to look annoyed. Dotson, an elegantly dressed fifty-year-old with a droning voice, was as superficial and nonsensical as his title suggested. Zamora was unsmiling and silent, as likable as a cobra, whose smooth triangular face, Kate thought, she resembled. She felt her intestines clench as they both stared at her.

Dotson took the available chair, his perfectly coiffed gray

head wagging with gentle sympathy. "Terrible thing, suicide. Is the widow doing OK?"

"Her husband cut his throat with a straight razor in their bedroom while she was in the shower. She came out and found him gurgling in pain and bleeding to death on their bed. Do you think she ought to be doing OK?"

Dotson's eyes went to Zamora as if to say, "Ah, well, I tried; now it's up to you." Without missing a beat the woman flipped through the file on her lap, eager to take the initiative. "Candace Deane," she said without preamble. "Age fourteen, severe fracture of the radius, numerous abrasions on her legs and buttocks . . ."

"I remember her," Kate said, seeing in her mind a pathetic, underweight blond girl whose parents, taking out their frustration at society for their own lack of success, regularly beat with a child's baseball bat.

Zamora wasn't through. "One of her toes was fractured, she evidently hadn't attended school for eighteen months, and there were scars on her wrists where she may once have attempted suicide."

Kate didn't see where this was headed. "I told you, I remember."

Matthew Dotson crossed his legs, exposing brown calf-length socks decorated with tiny embroidered golf clubs. "Sometimes in your role you have to make a judgment call, something I or Judith may disagree with. That's just part of the job, of course, like calling faults in tennis. It's to be expected that people might disagree, saying you were too lenient or too harsh. But in this case—"

Kate was feeling the exhaustion of the day and didn't want to go on with this. "Can you tell me what you're talking about? Or do you want me to guess?"

Judith Zamora's Gypsy face jerked up as though struck from below, long silver earrings jangling with contempt. "You sent them home without any action. You didn't report the parents to Child Protective Services or notify the police that this girl was living with two probably psychotic people, both of whom were certainly capable of killing her when they got drunk. Which was practically every night.''

Kate's anger flared. ''That's not true. I notified both agencies at once. Any idiot could see that the parents were abusing her.''

Zamora held up the file she had been looking at, facing it toward Kate. ''That's your signature and NFA, no further action, checked off.''

''That's ridiculous! I typed up the report myself and had it faxed to the police that same day.''

Zamora tossed the report on the desk with a note of triumph. Kate picked it up and felt a flutter of confusion as she saw her name signed in ink on the bottom. She shook her head, trying to make sense of it. ''That can't be my signature. Someone forged it.''

Matthew Dotson's eyes narrowed. ''Are you saying there's a conspiracy here, that someone set out to . . . to what? To send that poor child home in order to protect those vile parents?''

Kate's voice rose angrily. ''To make me look bad! Someone's trying to embarrass me!''

Dotson's face closed and his eyes darkened in the way that people's do when faced with a mentally deranged panhandler. His voice strained with disbelief, he asked, ''Do you really think someone here at Midtown dislikes you enough to go the extreme of forging your signature, and putting a young girl's life at risk, just to make you look bad? That's absurd, paranoid, as well as being grossly egotistical. Who do you think this *person* is, this anonymous conspirator?''

Kate's eyes went at once to Zamora, but she said nothing. The woman didn't like her for reasons Kate could never understand, though she wouldn't have gone this far to make her look bad. But now Kate was certain that whoever was harassing her was employed at the hospital. Someone she knew. Not Leo Petrosian. She looked back at Dotson, her right hand closing around a metal ruler. ''I don't know who would do it. All I know is that this isn't my signature.''

Zamora lifted a handful of files she had been going through. Again that note of triumph came into her voice. ''I thought you might say that. So I went through some other reports you've filled out. The signatures match. Perfectly.''

''It's not my signature,'' Kate repeated, biting off each word. ''Someone *copied* it. Is that so difficult to understand?''

Zamora took the file off Kate's desk and added it to the pile in her lap. ''Candace Deane was brought into the ER an hour ago. Dr. Kamel had the file brought down and saw your recommendation. That's when he called me.''

''Candace is on life support,'' Dotson said. ''Her father was high on methamphetamines and beat her almost to death. She's not going to make it. Even if she somehow did she'd have permanent brain damage.''

''God!'' Kate felt sick.

''You can see the difficulty this puts us in,'' Dotson went on. ''Our failure to notify the proper authorities places us in serious potential legal liability. As well as perhaps making us the defendants in a wrongful-death suit that could reach into the millions, assuming the girl has relatives who would bring such an action. It also puts our accreditation as a hospital at risk.''

Kate glared at him in disbelief. ''You're worried about accreditation and lawsuits while this girl is dying out there?''

''That attitude,'' Zamora went on, ''is another reason we're here. I'm fed up with the way you strut around here with this air of moral superiority, looking down your nose at everybody.''

''What?'' Kate was nonplussed. Was Zamora talking about *her?*

''You obviously think you can get away with anything because your husband is on the board. It's time for a little reality check.''

Kate was beside herself with fury. ''What does that mean, other than that you're up on last year's clichés?''

''That *means,*'' Zamora said, her anger showing for the first time, ''that Mr. Dotson and I are scheduling you for a personnel hearing. It's the first step in the hospital's progressive discipline policy, and documents the steps taken if it becomes necessary to fire you.''

''And protects *you* from lawsuits by showing you took

immediate action when informed of the problem employee who overlooked Candace's home situation.'' Kate laughed harshly and sank back in her chair.

"I wish you wouldn't look at it like that," Dotson said sincerely. "I like this as little as you do—"

Again Kate laughed. "Sure you do. As little as I do."

"But," Dotson went on as if he hadn't been interrupted, "we need to set up a hearing where you'll formally hear the charges concerning your performance, and be able to respond to your accusers. Isn't this really to your benefit?"

"Of course it is. And black is white and up is down." She shook her head dejectedly.

Zamora smiled. "Today is Friday. How about Monday afternoon? That good for you? We'll set up a time and be in touch. Check your e-mail."

July 17

Death is the ultimate mystery, isn't it, Katie, especially that final micromoment of life? Even medical science can't tell us what goes through a person's mind as the brain accepts the fact that this one second, this briefest tick of the clock, is the final one that it will ever experience. Does pain disappear at that point, and hope spring up as eternal bliss beckons? Or is the famous "white light" a fantasy and what awaits us only a black nullity?

Is there some way you can tell me?

Will your sins pass, one by one, through your mind? Will you panic and think, No, no! I'm sorry, I didn't mean to . . . ?

Have a nice weekend, Kate. Take the time to relax.

Because it gets better.

For all of us.

I promise.

15

Kate knew it wasn't going to be a good day as soon as she got to work Monday morning. Mohammed Kamel, never the most gregarious of men, threw a hostile look at her from under unruly black eyebrows as she walked through the waiting room, and Patty Mars, already at her desk, glanced up miserably, muttered, "Hangover," and let her head drop down on her arms. Two nurses, skinny young women who had worked in the ER for a year, walked by as Kate turned into the short hallway leading to her office; as soon as they saw her they dropped their gazes and stopped talking. Kate felt a stab of anger—What was going on?—then halted at her open office door. Her body went warm as she saw Nick Cerovic and Ann DeSilva sitting comfortably in the two visitor's chairs, looking up at her. Cerovic came to his feet, smiled pleasantly, and said, "Hey, good morning."

Kate stomped inside and dropped into the chair behind her desk. "What do you want?"

DeSilva looked at her blankly. "The lab tests on your child came back."

Kate could feel her stomach sink. If the tests had been negative the two cops wouldn't be sitting here now, staring at her with their smug, tough-guy looks. She held her body rigid, giving away nothing, and clasped her hands together on the desktop. "OK." She knew she was supposed to ask what the results were but wouldn't give them the pleasure.

Ann DeSilva, watching from angry black eyes, said, "We'd rather have a medical doctor explain what was found."

Cerovic nodded. "Dr. Symonds from the ER will be here in a minute."

But he wasn't, and they sat in silence for at least ten minutes, Kate keeping her body from shaking, and forcing her mind to go blank. *Don't let them upset you,* she remembered someone telling her years ago. *It's all part of their technique; they push and push and push, and wait for you to crack. Never admit to anything, not even what day it is.*

Finally Symonds appeared in the doorway. He was wearing his white clinic coat and holding a manila folder with a metal clasp at the top, and appeared reluctant to come in.

"Ah, Doc," Cerovic said with a big smile, and waved him inside. There was no place to sit, and Symonds stood uncomfortably in the middle of the office, between the police officers and the desk. "I didn't ask to do this," he told Kate as if the cops weren't there. "None of it's any of my business."

Cerovic agreed at once. "The doc's a little pissed at being here. He thinks he's being put in the middle of a criminal matter. But we thought it best in case you have questions. Medical questions."

Kate stared at the middle-aged detective but didn't reply. Her mouth had gone dry and she wasn't able to slow the racing of her heart. Still she refused to play their game. *Never show fear. Never show emotion. Be stronger than they are.*

DeSilva fingered some papers in her lap. "Dr. Symonds . . ." She was clearly anxious to get it out where they'd have to talk about it.

Symonds's eyes dropped to the lab report. His neck muscles tensed and his voice was tight, as though the words wouldn't form in his mouth. Finally he said, "Alex has herpes."

"*What?*" Kate bolted from her chair.

"There's no telling how long he's been infected. But it doesn't seem to be a particularly severe case." He paused. "It's type two. Genital."

Kate's body was shaking uncontrollably. "That's impossible! It can't be. The test is wrong."

Symonds looked at her sympathetically. "That's what I thought. So I had them run it again." He indicated the two blue-and-white pieces of paper with their computer-generated numbers. "Virtually identical."

"No. They're not. It's not possible." She could hardly make her mind calm down enough to form the questions screaming at her. "You got the lab samples mixed up. They didn't come from Alex."

Symonds shook his head. "It wasn't a blood test, Kate. It was a genital swab. It's the only sample in the lab."

"Oh, God, no. No. No." Her eyes lost their focus, and she had to brace her hands on the desktop to keep from collapsing.

Symonds glared at the police officers. "There could be a logical answer here, you know. You're jumping to conclusions without an investigation."

"You're the investigation," DeSilva said. Her tone was cold, as though telling him not to butt into things he didn't understand.

"It *can't* be herpes!" Kate said loudly. "It's impossible. There's no penetration."

"Doc?" Cerovic said.

Symonds looked miserable. "There needn't be penetration. It's a virus. Usually it comes from direct contact with an infected person. I suppose in some cases it could also be passed by body fluids, for example—"

"*Semen?*" Kate screamed. "Is that what you mean? He came into contact with semen?" Her legs were so rubbery she couldn't remain standing, and she dropped into the chair with a thud.

Symonds closed the file, and his hand dropped to his side. "Look, I'm an ER doc. Herpes isn't my area. I'm not even sure fluids—"

DeSilva looked at him with contempt. "It could be mother's milk. Right?"

Kate screamed at her, "I don't have herpes!"

"How do you know?"

"Get out of my office! I'm not going to talk to you anymore. Get out of here." Kate was on the verge of hysteria. She came to her feet, steadied her knees against the desk, and screamed at DeSilva, "Get the hell out of here!"

Nick Cerovic turned calmly to Symonds. "Thanks for your help, Doc. You can leave now." Just then Mohammed Kamel walked by the open door, glancing in and frowning, demonstrating his displeasure at the loud bickering.

Symonds seemed uncertain what to do.

With a slow, fluid movement, Cerovic rose to his feet. He was as tall as Symonds, but thirty pounds heavier, and had the manner of someone unused to being ignored. "This isn't something you need to be involved in anymore. Go mend some broken arms. We'll be in touch if we need you."

Symonds stared at him for a long moment, then turned and looked at Kate. "I think you ought to check with a specialist on sexual diseases. You need some expert advice. I can give you some names, if you want."

When he was gone Cerovic eased the door shut. "He likes you. I guess you knew that, huh?"

"Goddamn you!" Kate said. "Who the hell are you to come in here and claim my baby's gotten sick, been harmed, by his parents." But she didn't know what they were accusing her—or was it Paul?—of. She just knew her family was being attacked. Were they going to claim that Paul had somehow abused Alex, giving him herpes? Or that she did it? She dropped again into her chair and propped her forehead in her hand.

DeSilva, acting as though she faced this sort of scene every day, opened a file on her lap. "We need to ask you some questions."

Kate glared at the woman gazing at her without emotion. *She's enjoying this,* Kate saw. It was in her eyes, the slight curl to her lips, the way she was sitting there in quiet triumph. *She likes going after women who don't measure up to whatever standard she holds them to. She wants to see me hurt. But I'm not going to give her the pleasure. I'm stronger than she is.* Focusing on the policewoman's face, she made her voice emphatic. "I'm through answering questions. I want you to leave."

DeSilva acted as though she hadn't spoken. "Have you ever heard of Munchausen syndrome by proxy?"

Kate's defenses collapsed. "My God, you think I'm deliberately harming my baby. You think I'm mentally ill." The horror of it stunned her.

"Most cases of Munchausen's have been mothers of young children. Often they don't even realize they're doing it. But the attention *they* receive from their child's illnesses or accidents provides a thrill they get nowhere else. . . ."

"Good God, no . . ."

Nick Cerovic's voice, surprisingly calm in the turmoil her mind had become, suddenly registered. "We're not accusing you, Kate. We're just investigating a possibility. Help us rule it out. Then we'll look at something else."

"What else?" she demanded. "If you can't blame something on me, are you going to go after my husband? And if he's in the clear do you try the baby-sitter next? No one did anything to Alex. Those were just accidents!"

"An eight-month-old with herpes is an accident?" Ann DeSilva asked belligerently. She looked as though she wanted to strangle Kate.

"I didn't give my son herpes! It's a virus. He might have picked it up anywhere. Including here. Hospitals are full of germs."

"It's a sexually transmitted disease." DeSilva's sarcasm was meant to enrage. "It doesn't float through the air like pollen. You don't pick it up off toilet seats, or by using someone's coffee cup. You get it from sexual contact."

"No one had . . ." The words died in her throat. "No one did anything to Alex. My God, he's only eight months old; you don't have sex with a baby."

"Some people do," DeSilva said.

Cerovic nodded. "There's a lot of sick people out there."

"But not me or my husband."

Cerovic eased back in his chair. "Has your husband . . ." He checked his notes. "Paul. Has Paul ever shown any unusual interest in children? I don't mean sexual necessarily, just *interest*. Or maybe he mentioned things in passing. Like, 'Gosh that's a cute little girl.' "

"Jesus—"

DeSilva put her hands in her lap. "Have you ever had a herpes infection? Once you contract it you can have it for life."

"I don't have herpes. Goddamn you!"

"Then your husband."

"If my husband had it I'd have it, too. Right?"

"We want the two of you to be tested."

"I'm not going to talk to you anymore." Kate stood up, steadied herself, and forced her face to go blank.

"You didn't have a driver's license until five years ago," Nick Cerovic said. He was smiling amiably. "Why is that?"

"Get the hell out of here!"

DeSilva sat back in her chair. "Anything in your background we should know about? We'll find out, you know. There aren't any secrets anymore."

Kate stared at her hatefully. "What does that mean?"

"We want you to come down to the station and get fingerprinted. This afternoon. And we have some more questions for you. You can bring an attorney if you want. But we're going to find out who's doing these things to your child."

"No," Kate said at once. "I'm not going to. My husband's a prosecutor; I know my rights. You can't make me. If I did something wrong, arrest me."

DeSilva rose to her feet. She looked as if this was the outcome she expected; she also seemed not to be disappointed. "We'll be back with a warrant for your arrest. I guess that's what you want."

Kate looked wildly at the desk as if searching for something to throw at her.

"It'd be better to come willingly," Cerovic agreed. "You don't want to have an arrest on your record, do you? Even if you are innocent. It'd probably make it difficult to get a job when people find out you might have injured your own child."

"*Get out.*" Kate couldn't think now, couldn't stop yelling. All she knew was that she needed them to go away. And when she didn't stop screaming they did.

Annie DeSilva had trouble waiting until they were in the parking lot before unloading on Cerovic. "Jesus, Nickie, she's dirty as dog shit. She's hurting her eight-month-old baby to get attention from all the doctors around here, and maybe her husband, and the orderlies and the guy who does the floors, and God knows who else. Don't tell me you don't see it. All I had to do was mention Munchausen's and she fell apart. Kinda proves she's heard about it, doesn't it?''

Only nine-thirty in the morning and already close to ninety degrees, Cerovic thought, and wiped a line of perspiration from his forehead. He wondered if he had set the thermostat when he left home this morning. If not it was going to be unbearable when he got back. Probably have to go up to the mall for a couple of hours while the house cooled down. Or better yet, see if he could talk Howard next door into going to Dodger Stadium. The Phillies were in town tonight. *Let's see, who'd be pitching?*

"Nickie! You listening to me?"

"Yeah, yeah, Annie. The woman's a world-class criminal, probably a serial killer who moved to L.A. and is going after babies now. Likes to stab them in the heart and make them bleed to death on their little Winnie-the-Pooh blankets.''

"Jesus!'' DeSilva threw up her hands, falling into an angry silence as they strode out to Cerovic's eight-year-old Ford Explorer with 126,000 miles on it. But as he unlocked the door for her she couldn't hold back any longer. "Are you telling me you think she *didn't* do it?''

Chan Ho Park, Cerovic thought. Park was pitching tonight. That meant a longer game by what? Maybe twenty minutes while the guy starts to go into his windup, then stops while he thinks about some girl in Seoul, then finally throws the damn ball? That's OK, though; it'd give him time for one more beer on a hot night. Last week when he'd forked over four dollars for a Bud, he asked the attendant how he managed to pour a whole six-pack into that little cup. The guy gave him a look and said, "You know how many times I hear that every night?''

"No,'' Cerovic said. "How many?''

"Nickie, damn it!'' Annie, muted, shouted from inside the car.

He unlocked his door, settled behind the wheel, and smiled at her. "Annie, what you and me think about this don't mean diddly. We've got to go to the DA with enough proof to get an indictment. We don't want to screw up here. Do you remember where the hubby works?''

"I don't care if he's the Pope. That woman—''

"Prove it, Annie. Prove she did anything.''

"The kid's got herpes, for God's sake.'' She started furiously picking at her slacks. "Damn it, Nickie, you got dog hair all over your car. Don't you ever clean it?''

Nick started the engine and backed out of the parking space. "And where do you think the kid got it from? Some sort of physical contact? Mother's milk?''

"Why the hell not?''

"Is that intentional, then? Can you prove she knew she had herpes, and knew she would transmit it to her child? What if she had an itch, scratched it, then touched the kid? Is that a crime? Come on, use your brain. You're letting your Sicilian blood run away with you.''

"Me? What about you?'' She began to imitate his guttural voice. "How are you, *Kate?* Is everything all right, *Kate?* Would you like to spend the night at my house, *Kate?*''

Cerovic grunted as he swung the Explorer onto the street. "Maybe you exaggerate just a bit.''

Annie slumped in her seat. "Never, never, never send a man to investigate a crime committed by a good-looking woman. They should inscribe that in foot-high letters on the wall of every police station in America. Christ, men are stupid!''

"You think so, Annie? Twenty years of police work tells me you're right. Men are stupid. And so are women. And everything in between. It's just the human condition.''

"The human condition!'' She slapped her forehead and sank down in the seat. "I can't believe you said that. I'm riding in a car with a *cop* who wants to tell me about the human fucking condition!''

Patty came bustling into Kate's office, talking rapidly, needing to get back to her desk before anyone noticed she was gone. "My computer friend's coming up here right after lunch. Hey, what are you—''

Only vaguely aware of Patty's presence, Kate grabbed her

purse and headed for the door. *Goddamn them,* she thought. *Goddamn them. Why are they doing this to me? They aren't going to get away with it.*

"Where are you going?" Patty yelled as Kate took off down the hallway. "Are you going home? Your computer's on. Hey—"

16

Kate remembered none of it, getting Alex from Mrs. Alamada, driving home, warming a bottle while he lay in the playpen in the family room. She was sure she didn't answer the doorbell when it rang, but a minute later Lilliana, looking as if she had already started drinking, was sitting across from her saying, "What's going on? Did you quit your job? Why are you home so early?"

And then it all rushed out in a torrent of sobs and angry words. Lilliana stared in disbelief as Kate told her the police were convinced she was purposely harming her child.

"*What* by proxy?" Lilliana asked, and blinked several times. "What kind of disease is that?"

Kate shook her head. She didn't want to go into it, didn't even want this woman in her house.

Lilliana reached over, grabbed Kate's knee, and tried to shake an answer out of her. "What are you talking about? I've never heard of this."

"It means you're lying about your child to get attention. I guess sometimes parents consciously hurt a child, then rush him to the hospital."

"Like with rats?" She fell back against the couch. "They think you put rats in the house for attention? That's crazy."

Kate stood up suddenly, and the words tumbled out despite herself, without thought, though talking about it frightened her to death. "There were some marks on Alex's body. They think I did it to him. And he has swine flu. Today they said he has herpes."

"Herpes?" Lilliana said in a loud voice.

"God, I can't believe any of this is happening," Kate muttered. She looked in the playpen, where Alex was sucking on a pacifier, and thought, Make this stop, please. . . .

Lilliana said, "Does that mean you or Paul . . . ?"

Kate was only half listening and didn't respond.

"Does Paul have herpes?" Lilliana repeated. Her words rushed into one another, a drinker's hurried questioning, the unnecessary emotion grabbing Kate's attention.

"I don't know! I don't even know if Alex does. It's not possible." But it was not only possible, Kate knew, it was certain. Her knees gave way, and she sank into the couch again.

Lilliana's tone turned bitter. "What did I tell you? Men are the same everywhere. Bastards!" Her body was wound with emotion. "What's the treatment for herpes? They can cure it, can't they?"

"I don't know. . . . I think they can slow it down, control it. I don't know if they can cure it. Especially in a baby."

Lilliana shook her head. "You have it, too, then?"

Kate nodded silently, trying not to think about it. "Probably." Just then Alex started crying, and she remembered the bottle warming on the stove. After going into the kitchen, she came back to find Lilliana on her knees, playing with Alex on the floor. Kate hurriedly put the bottle in the boy's hands and he began to suck, then immediately started screaming and flung the bottle away.

Lilliana picked it up. "Good Lord." She squirted some milk on her wrist and flinched. "This is practically boiling. What were you thinking?"

Kate's whole body stiffened. Her face went red, and she looked as if it was all she could do not to start screaming.

Lilliana's gaze locked on her face. Her voice was unaccustomedly sympathetic. "My God, Kate. What's happening to you?"

Paul was disbelieving and outraged when he got home. Holding Alex to his chest with one arm, he raged around the kitchen. "He can't have herpes! Christ, it's insane. It's a sexual disease. Alex can't have a sexual disease."

Kate sat at the table, her head propped in her hand, and said nothing.

"Can he?" Paul demanded. He stopped in front of her, his lower lip quivering with emotion. "Goddamn it, can he?"

"Paul . . ." Why was she always called upon to explain things? Especially things she had no answer for.

"I'm asking a question," he shouted. "Did you see the lab results?"

"I didn't actually read the report, if that's what you mean. It probably wouldn't mean anything to me anyway. It's just numbers."

Alex, reacting to Paul's loud voice and tense movements, started crying. Kate went to the refrigerator and took out a bottle of juice.

"Then maybe it's not true! Maybe he doesn't have herpes."

"Why would they lie, Paul? And who do you think is lying, Dr. Symonds or the lab?"

"Why does this Symonds keep getting involved? He was the doctor when Alex had the rat bites. Is he the one who's claiming Alex has herpes?"

"He's on staff in the ER. That's why he's involved. And all he did was interpret the results, not run the test."

Paul began walking with Alex, trying to calm him down. "Then you believe it? You believe he really does have herpes?"

Kate said nothing.

"Then where the hell did he get it from?" He moved abruptly in front of her, where she had to look at him. "Where did it come from?"

"I don't know, Paul. I don't have herpes."

"And I do? Is that what you're saying?"

"Before we start accusing each other, let's talk to Dr. Symonds. Maybe there's another answer."

"Is Symonds the only doctor in the whole goddamn hospital? Why can't we talk to Kamel about this? Or even Glazier? I'm on the damn board; I should be able to talk to any doctor I want."

Alex started screaming now. Paul shifted the boy from his shoulder to his hands and held him out in front of his face.

"Hey, relax, little man. Mommy's getting your dinner. She's just a little slow tonight."

"You're scaring him with your yelling."

"Yelling? Jesus, Kate, I'm asking questions. About my son with a sexual disease. Is that all right?"

"Give him to me."

"Now what? I'm too emotional to hold my own child? Or are you afraid I'll give him some new disease by holding him?"

"He wants to eat. Put him in the high chair."

Kate poured juice into a baby bottle, then gave it to Alex. He began to suck noisily.

Paul yanked out a chair and sat down at the kitchen table. "All right, let's assume neither of us has herpes." It was clear from his tone that he wasn't ready to concede that Kate was free of the disease, but wanted to move on to his next question. "How could Alex have gotten it?"

Kate leaned back against the sink. "He could have picked it up in the hospital, I suppose. I don't know about these things! I never had any medical training. Maybe a nurse didn't wash properly after treating someone. Or *she* has herpes. Or an instrument wasn't sterilized."

Paul seemed to sink within his body, though he didn't move. "God!" He brooded for a moment, then said, "I started an investigation of the ER doctors this morning."

"You did what?"

"They're obviously inept. And overstepped their authority by notifying the police."

"I don't believe this. So you're going to . . . to what? Look into their backgrounds to see if they really went to medical school? God, Paul, what's gotten into you?"

"Not all of them," he said with annoyance. "Just Symonds and Packard. I've contacted the medical society and the State Board of Medical Examiners in Sacramento. I want to find out who these people are, and if there've been complaints about them before."

Kate shook her head. "You're paranoid. How dare anyone question Paul McDonald! Or I guess the real point is, how dare anyone question this deputy district attorney who only has to pick up a phone to call Sacramento and harass two doctors who were just doing their job.''

"You're awfully protective of the people who are causing you trouble.''

Kate glared at him, then went into the living room. She was staring out the window toward Lilliana's house when Paul came up behind her. "Do you remember Rick Hazlitt?''

"Of course I remember him,'' she said without turning around. Hazlitt had been in Paul's class at law school. A better student, with a far more aggressive instinct for the jugular, he had been hired at once by one of the city's largest criminal-law firms, and spent his time now defending white-collar thugs masquerading as legitimate businessmen. Paul had always had contempt for him—"Going for the gold,'' he'd said of Hazlitt's career choice, implying that he was a man who had defiled the sanctity of the law for filthy lucre.

"I made an appointment with him for tomorrow at two o'clock. At his office, of course. I don't want people downtown talking about this. We both need to be there.''

Kate spun around. "Why do we need an attorney? We didn't do anything wrong.''

"You don't have to do anything wrong to need an attorney. You only have to be accused. I can pick you up at work or you can drive yourself. It's at Wilshire and Western.''

"I'll drive.'' She turned back to the window.

Paul lifted his briefcase from where he'd dropped it minutes before, and put it on the couch. "I don't want you to get upset, but I thought I needed to do this.'' His voice had taken on a tone Kate had never heard before, causing her to spin around and see what he was doing. Flipping open the briefcase, he removed a box about nine inches square. "I applied for a permit when Petrosian started harassing me. Us. Just in case.'' He took the top off the box and lifted out a new .45 automatic. With its light sheen of protective oil it glistened like a black pearl.

Kate's eyes squeezed closed as though she could make everything go away if she wished hard enough. "I don't believe this. It's not happening.''

"I'm not going to carry it around like Clint Eastwood, Kate. I bought it to keep here in the house. Just in case."

"In case what?" she demanded. "In case Petrosian tries to kill us? You said he'd never try anything, since he already has two strikes. One more and it's life in prison."

"And I still believe that. But criminals don't always think rationally. That's why they're criminals."

Kate thought of the man she had seen hanging around the hospital parking lot. Had that been Petrosian? This wasn't the time to ask Paul. Not in the mood he was in now.

"I'll keep it in the nightstand," he said. "On my side of the bed. But you have to learn how to use it."

"I don't want to know."

"I'm not asking you to go out in the backyard and assassinate squirrels. I'll show you how to take off the safety and how to hold it steady with both hands and squeeze the trigger. It's going to be loaded, so you'd better find out how to handle it. You don't want to accidentally kill someone."

Later, when Paul was in the shower, the weight of the last few days began to fall on Kate like a huge stone pressing her into the earth. Suddenly an overwhelming need to call her mother took hold, and she began to feel like a child craving the comfort of someone whom she knew loved her unconditionally. Hurrying to the kitchen she grabbed the phone and dialed. "It's not too late to call, is it?" she asked when it was picked up, hoping her breathlessness didn't sound as clear to her mother as it did to her.

"Oh, no, honey. I always stay up for Leno now."

Just hearing her mother's voice always had a calming effect on Kate, conjuring up memories of a childhood happy beyond anyone's right to expect. Her mom had been a stay-at-home, always there for her two little girls, both before school and after. Later she went to work for McDonald-Douglas in the purchasing department, but for years she had volunteered in the girls' classrooms and driven them to soccer, and taken carloads of kids on Girl Scout trips, or to ballet practice, or even fishing in the summer.

"How's Alex doing?" her mother asked. "Getting fat and sassy and smart as his parents?"

Kate could feel herself starting to break down. Suppressing her tears with difficulty, she closed her eyes, and the years fell away. She was six years old and had scraped her knee and wanted her mother to make it all better. Her throat swollen almost shut, she managed to say, "Alex is fine, Mom. He's doing beautifully."

"Going to be a big boy, like his grandpa, isn't he?"

"Looks like it. And handsome as Brad Pitt."

"Well, I kinda like that Leonardo fellow. You know the one—in that *Titanic* movie. Pretty as a flower, isn't he?"

Kate smiled. "Alex has them all beat, Mom."

"And his health. He's not . . ." She was stumbling for the right words and trying desperately not to bring up the past. Kate felt her heart sink.

"He's doing all right, isn't he?" her mother added quickly, then said, "I'm sorry, Kate. You know what I mean."

She closed her eyes. "He's doing fine, Mom." *Fine, wonderfully: he has swine flu and herpes, he's been bitten by rats, and has unexplained marks on his arms and legs. Like any eight-month-old kid.*

Her mother's voice turned apologetic. "It's always difficult for me, honey. . . . I'm sorry."

"It's OK. Really. How are you doing?"

There was a pause before her mother said, "Oh, about the same."

"Mom . . ."

"A little difficulty sleeping, maybe."

"Those dogs next door?"

"No. Just some silly man who calls and says stupid things when I'm ready to go to bed."

Kate felt an iciness on the back of her neck. "What kind of stupid things?"

"Oh, you know—nonsense. I just hang up."

"Mom!"

The older woman sighed. "Says he's going to kill me. Not very creative, is he? He doesn't think I have a right to live. A *right!* Pretty silly, huh? Like *he* decides who gets to live and who doesn't.''

"Mom, call the police. Do it. Tomorrow morning. They can trace the calls and tell who's doing this.''

"Kate—''

"Mother, do it! Promise right now or I'm going to do it for you.''

The woman sighed again, a parent who had learned when to give in to her child. "I'll call, Katie. But I don't think they'll actually do anything.''

"First thing!''

Her mother agreed. First thing tomorrow.

Ten minutes later when Kate put the phone down, she thought, *They know I'll find out about the phone calls. That's why they're doing it. They're going after my mother and my son to get at me.*

Still standing next to the phone, she pictured the .45 Paul had brought home. It was already in the night table next to their bed.

He had no idea that she already knew how to use it.

But it was like an omen, a sign or a talisman that gave a sudden terrifying glimpse into the future. *It wouldn't be entering my life at this time if there were no reason for it.*

17

But another omen awaited her as she arrived at work the following morning. The first item on her e-mail was a notice that her personnel hearing would be that afternoon at two o'clock in the office of the VP of Human Resources. At once she called Paul, who agreed to reschedule their meeting with Rick Hazlitt for dinner. "We'll meet him somewhere, probably about seven. Can you get Mrs. Alamada to baby-sit?"

"She said she was going to be at her daughter's tonight."

"How about the Queen of Clean, then?"

"Lilliana? I'll ask. I think she'll do it. Alex will be asleep most of the evening."

When Patty came by at break time, Kate told her about the hearing. Patty immediately began fuming. "So what's it all about? Are they going to claim that you've suddenly become incompetent? Christ, Kate, go up there with your last performance review. Didn't they have you in the top category?"

Kate could feel her control beginning to slip. The burden of everything that had happened over the past few days was smothering her, like a huge wave pulling her deeper and deeper beneath the sea. *Don't cry,* she angrily warned herself. *Damn it. . . . Don't!* But tears began to build behind her eyes. She desperately needed to confide in someone or she'd lose her mind. Still she held back. It was madness to trust anyone, she knew from before. *Don't do it.* But if she didn't tell her friend about Alex she'd crumble under the weight of despair that had built up since yesterday. Finally it all spilled out.

The other woman was devastated. "My God, no wonder you left so upset. Poor Alex. I hate to see children suffer. It's so unfair.'' Her hand had gone to her chest as though to slow her heart. Then she leaned forward aggressively. ''Does Zamora know what you've been going through?''

Kate shook her head. ''I'm not going to use Alex's condition to save my job. And I'm not going in there to argue. I don't want to embarrass Paul.''

''Paul? You're the one being dumped on. Go in there with your claws bared and rip that bitch's heart out. She's just jealous of you. She and Symonds used to be an item, you know. Or so the rumor goes.''

No, Kate said, she didn't know. And she didn't care. Though she felt a strange disappointment in Symonds. She thought he had better taste than that.

''So now she sees him coming by your office all the time, with his tongue hanging out, and she goes after you.'' Patty took a breath. ''Oh, hell, don't mind me; you have to do what you think is best. So what's next with Alex? Is there a cure?''

Kate shook her head. ''I don't know. I'll take him to his pediatrician. I don't want anyone here involved.''

''Involved with what?'' Joel Symonds said. He was sipping a cup of coffee and holding a burrito he had warmed in a microwave; he smiled and offered it to Kate. ''Would madam care for some haute cuisine, hospital-style?''

She shook her head, tears still not far from her eyes.

''Sorry about yesterday,'' he said, sensing her mood. ''I didn't want to get involved, but that woman cop with the pit-bull eyes kept pressuring me, said you might have a question about the test, and how I'd be doing you a favor. Afterward I decided she was trying to embarrass you.''

Kate's body sagged. ''There isn't any doubt about the results? You're certain?''

Symonds nodded, glancing at Patty, then Kate. ''I'm sorry.''

Kate's eyes closed and her head hung.

''Who's your ped?'' he asked.

Kate didn't look up. ''Broward.''

''I know her. Good doctor. You ought to get Alex in as soon as possible. I don't know what the protocol is for an eight-month-old. Maybe nothing at this point. It's not life threatening.

Or even dangerous in the conventional sense, as far as I know. And there're some new drugs on the market.''

"But how could he even have it?" Kate demanded.

Symonds again glanced at Patty and didn't say anything.

"It's all right," Kate told him. "We don't keep things from each other." Her voice was steady, the lie easily told after so many years.

Symonds's eyes moved again toward Kate. "The most likely way would be to come into contact with the virus during birth, if you had an eruption at that time. Or he may have gotten it through nursing. Or he could have had physical contact with someone outside the family who somehow passed the virus along.''

"You mean through sexual contact, don't you?" She sagged forward, her elbows on the desk, holding her forehead.

"Whatever the cause, don't blame yourself. It's not like you set out to infect him. It just happened.''

She looked up abruptly. "You didn't hear what the cops think, then.''

"What do you mean?"

Kate just shook her head. She couldn't go through it again. But Patty told him, and Symonds was stunned. "They actually think you did it on purpose? That's crazy.''

"Not to them," Kate said.

"But they don't have any medical reason for implying that. What's their rationale?''

"Munchausen's syndrome by proxy.''

"Jesus." He sat back, then came quickly to his feet as he heard his and Kamel's names being paged to the ER. "Next time the cops come in, give me a call. There's no reason for that sort of accusation. It's idiotic.''

When Symonds was gone Kate said, "No reason except being bitten by rats, getting infected with swine flu and herpes, and having unexplained marks on his body.''

Patty sat back in her chair. "Pardon me for bringing it up at a time like this, but can't you see that that gorgeous hunk of medical doctor is dying to get in your pants?''

"Patty, please—"

"Yeah, yeah. You've got morals. Well, *he's* got a Porsche. Wouldn't you like to trade? Then you could afford to tell Zamora to go to hell." All of a sudden Patty sensed that she had overstepped herself. She reached out and caught Kate's hand, then let it go. "Sorry. Guess I always tend to think like Patty. You've got enough to worry about with Alex. You don't need to add an affair to it. Have you made an appointment with your pediatrician yet?"

Kate shook her head. "I'll do it today." The phone rang and she grabbed it automatically. "Kate McDonald."

"Did you like the picture on your computer?" the now familiar voice whispered softly in her ear. "That poor girl! You must have recognized the scream. It was death, the exact moment life stopped."

Kate began to tremble.

"What?" Patty asked at once.

"I know you're upset about Alex's herpes," the voice continued. "Sufficient to harm but not to kill. Isn't that right? Everything at its proper time, Kate. First Alex. Then you. But you knew that years ago, didn't you? You knew it had to happen or the circle wouldn't close."

Kate slammed the phone down. She couldn't stop shaking.

"Goddamn it, what?" Patty demanded.

Kate put her hands on the desktop to steady herself. But fear was quickly swept away by anger. "Someone's trying to scare me." She told Patty what the caller had said.

"It has to be someone you know, someone who knew about Alex. So . . . someone here at the hospital. Did you recognize the voice?"

Kate shook her head. "He might have had an accent. He was whispering."

"Hispanic?"

She shook her head. "It was hard to tell."

"Frankie Yorba? Zamora?"

"It was a man."

"Frankie!"

"I don't know. Maybe it wasn't Hispanic. He was whispering."

"Kamel?" Patty didn't seem to think it possible, then said, "Hell, half the hospital was born somewhere else."

Kate put her head in her hands. "Someone threatened my mother, too. It's got to be the same person." But why would they be after her mother, a woman who had hardly left St. Louis in her sixty-seven years?

"My God, Kate, call the police. Now." When she saw Kate's reluctance her tone became demanding. "Pick up the damn phone. Do it."

Kate saw herself in Patty's sudden demand. She had said the same thing to her mother just last night. A sigh escaped her lips and she sank back. "I can't."

"Why—"

"Because they already don't believe me. They think I do these things on purpose. They think I'm looking for attention."

Patty stared at her, her mind working. After a moment she said, "Has anyone else heard one of these phone calls?"

"Just you."

"I didn't hear it. I only heard you. Next time get someone in here so they can hear it. Or go down to Radio Shack and get a tape recorder and tape it."

"And then what? The police will say I made the recording myself. First I harmed my baby; then I started threatening myself. All part of the syndrome, they'll say."

"So you'll do nothing?" There was a note of irritation in her voice.

"I don't know. I'll tell Paul."

"Oh, hell, that'll solve everything. What's he going to do? Go look for the guy on the golf course?"

"Patty, lay off him. Please. I have enough to worry about. Don't make me get upset with you, too."

The other woman shook her head as though to clear it. "I'm sorry. You've got enough problems without Patty butting in. Poor little Alex." She came to her feet. "Guess I'd better get back to work. Sorry to go on about Symonds like that. I just want to see you happy."

When Patty was gone Kate looked at the clock. Three hours until she had to face the inquisition in Matthew Dotson's office. *Why do I think that's not the worst thing that's going to happen to me today?*

18

There were four of them behind a polished mahogany table, like judges at a military tribunal: Judith Zamora, Matthew Dotson, Mohammed Kamel, and Elton Glazier, the hospital director. *Kafka,* Kate thought as she sat dully in the armless straight-backed chair in front of them. *You will not be allowed to hear the charges against you; you will not be allowed to make a defense.*

". . . difficult for all of us," Dotson was saying in his mild, trance-inducing voice, but Kate's mind was elsewhere. *None of this is important,* she told herself over and over, hoping to make it true. *None of* you *are important. The only thing I care about is the health of my baby.* She gave a start when she realized she was expected to make a reply. "I'm sorry. Could you repeat that, please?"

Elton Glazier, MD, tall and thin, a onetime blond now mostly bald, leaned his patrician face slightly forward, catching the light from overhead, and frowning from bloodless lips as he took her in. "I said, we don't want to take that step, especially since your husband has been such a valuable addition to our board. Perhaps there are extenuating circumstances that resulted in your suddenly erratic job behavior."

Yes, Kate said in her mind as she looked at Judith Zamora: *Joel Symonds has broken off his relationship with my boss, and she thinks it's my fault. Is that extenuating enough?* Zamora glared back at her. *She knows what I'm thinking,* Kate thought, and could see the woman's eyes darken with hostility. None of the others sensed it, however. *Why go after me?* Kate wondered. *Symonds might have dropped you, but I didn't have anything to do with it.*

"Mrs. McDonald." Dotson, the human in charge of Human Resources.

Kate set her jaw and stared at Elton Glazier with sudden loathing. *Jesus, just say the right words and get it over with. It's what they want to hear.* She bent forward at the waist, her voice weak as she sought to explain without giving too much away. "I've had some problems with my baby. As you know. He's been sick, and I'm worried about him. But I don't think it's interfered with my job at all."

Judith Zamora allowed her head to jerk up with feigned amazement. "Hasn't affected your job?" She flipped open a file in front of her. "Let me refresh your memory. Perhaps that, too, has been affected by your baby's problems."

I want an attorney, Kate thought with a dull sense of having gone through this before. *I know my rights. I refuse to talk to you anymore.*

Zamora was gazing at the file, her finger tracing down the list of indictments. "You sent home a fourteen-year-old girl who had been severely abused by her father without—"

Kate's cheeks burned with sudden fire, and she forgot her resolve to be contrite. "That's not true! My signature was forged."

Matthew Dotson's large body stirred with discomfort. "Do you really expect us to believe someone threw out the original form and wrote up a new one, forging your signature?" His voice bordered on the incredulous, as though he couldn't fathom such a ludicrous allegation.

"I remember the girl very well," Kate shot back. "I remember what I wrote. That's not my form or my signature."

"The girl is in a coma," Elton Glazier said flatly. "She's going to die."

"I know she's going to die!" Kate snapped. She wanted to scream and throw things; she wanted to jump up, overturn the table they were hiding behind, and storm out of there. Part of her—the irrational part, the psychologist had called it—wanted to get Paul's gun and start shooting, kill them all.

"But how could this happen?" Glazier went on, as though seriously trying to get to the bottom of things. "And why would someone want to? Do you think someone here is trying to frame you for something? Are they trying to get you fired?''

"Obviously!"

"But"—Matthew Dotson leaned forward, eager to rejoin the fray—"thirty years I've been in Human Resources—"

"As opposed to what?"

"Pardon?"

Kate shook her head. "Nothing. Make your point." If there is one, she said to herself.

"My point," Dotson declared, a tincture of emotion unexpectedly enlivening his voice, "is that this claim of forgery borders on paranoia. Isn't that right, Doctor?" He glanced at Mohammed Kamel, who had been silent until now.

"Only if untrue." The man's dark eyes burrowed into Kate's as though he was trying to make up his mind about her mental state.

"Well, of course it's untrue," Dotson continued, as if that settled it.

"Then you're calling me a liar as well as incompetent?" Kate said, and thought once again, *Don't do this. Don't make them angry. Just get it over with and get back to work.*

Zamora was unmoved by Kate's anger, seemed even to welcome it. Still looking at the folder, she said, "You received pornography at work—"

"Received, not ordered. I didn't ask for it."

"Someone else again," Matthew Dotson said. His pale lips formed a bleak smile. "This . . . person who forged your signature."

"Obviously."

"And," Zamora continued, "the computer department has been asked to investigate threatening—or was it obscene?—messages and pictures on your computer."

"That makes it pretty obvious someone's harassing me, doesn't it?"

Elton Glazier said, "I looked into that myself. I won't countenance one employee bothering another. But no one in Data Processing knows anything about this. I can't find anyone who's ever *seen* these messages."

"You didn't ask me!"

"Well, I guess we're doing that now."

"Patty Mars saw one a few days ago. This has been going on for a week or so. Every day I get one or two threats. Things like 'Don't die, Kate, not yet.'"

"*Don't* die? Is that a threat?"

"And the sound of a child screaming. And a picture of a girl." Kate tried to hold her voice steady, but they were provoking her.

"Still," Glazier went on. "That's not exactly in the realm of threatening messages."

"What realm is it in, then?" she snapped.

Zamora was miffed at not being able to continue her list, and bulled ahead. "The police suspect you of deliberately harming your child. Munchausen syndrome by proxy is the technical name. I looked it up in the *Diagnostic and Statistical Manual*. It's a severe mental illness, and people afflicted with it are unable to stop or help themselves. They're essentially out of control. Given your position of trust here, it would be irresponsible of us to continue to—"

"The police don't know what they're talking about. I didn't hurt my baby. You can't fire me for something I didn't do."

Zamora looked at Dotson, who said, "We can't fire you for being accused of something, naturally. Accusation and proof are two different things. The question is, are you carrying out your job in the manner our patients and clients properly expect it to be done?"

Kate's voice shot up. "Show me where I didn't. Give me one example. Just one!"

"This report on the fourteen—"

"Damn it, how many times do I have to repeat myself? I did not write that report!"

Elton Glazier tried quickly to defuse things. "I think we've gotten pretty far afield here. We didn't call you in to fire you or humiliate you, Kate. We want to give you every benefit of the doubt. At this point we are merely going to ask you to talk to someone of our choosing who can give an assurance that your personal problems won't interfere with your ability to do your job.''

"What kind of someone?" Her guard immediately went up.

"Dr. Marcia Egerman," Judith Zamora said. "She's a psychologist, very well known in—"

"No."

Glazier's bald head gave a surprised jerk. "I beg your pardon?"

Angry at herself for losing her temper, Kate lowered her voice. "How many times am I going to have to see her?"

"That depends on Dr. Egerman."

Kate could feel the icy sweat of panic moving on her ribs. She closed her eyes and said nothing.

Glazier clasped his hands prayerfully. "I've known Marcia—Dr. Egerman—for years. You'll like her. She's a lot like you."

"Meaning what?" Kate's eyes shot open, focusing on the man's narrow, polished face.

"Well, I guess I mean she's a younger woman, someone you can feel confident talking to. Better than an old duffer like me or Matthew or Dr. Kamel. And she's familiar with what I guess you could call women's problems."

Kate stared at him, more sweat swimming along her torso now.

Judith Zamora closed the folder in front of her with a decisive slap. "Your appointment with Dr. Egerman is for tomorrow at two-thirty. I'll e-mail her address to you. It's on Wilshire in Beverly Hills."

"Two-thirty," repeated Kate. "Will I be reprimanded for missing work?"

Zamora smiled without showing her teeth. "It depends how long you're gone."

"You're a classic, Judith. A jewel. We all think so."

"Getting personal doesn't help things."

"Interesting. Is that what you told Joel?"

Zamora glared but the other three on the panel seemed not to know what was going on. Dotson said, "We also want you to have a physical exam."

"Mind and body. Of course. They work together. Nature's wonder."

Glazier seemed unsure whether she was being sarcastic. "Just a precaution. I notice from your son's file he has swine flu. We wouldn't want that going around the hospital."

"Maybe they'll find a strain of paranoia, too," Kate said. "We wouldn't want that going around the hospital either."

Glazier was getting annoyed. "Dr. Kamel has agreed to do your physical. This, naturally, is acceptable to you."

It wasn't a question. Kate looked at Kamel, who merely stared back at her. "Naturally."

"You two can arrange a mutually convenient time. And don't forget your appointment with Dr. Egerman. Tomorrow at two-thirty. I'm sure that will put an end to everyone's concerns, yours and ours."

I won't do it, Kate told herself as she walked out of the office. *They can't make me talk to a psychologist. Never again.*

19

A vaguely familiar young man with a ponytail was sitting in the client's chair as Joel Symonds walked up to Patty Mars's admitting desk. When he turned around, Symonds could see his name tag: *Ramsey*. A respiratory therapist, Symonds recalled, though he didn't know him more than to say hello. The man smiled pleasantly. "Howdy, Doc."

Symonds nodded a greeting.

"Time to get back to work, Miles," Patty said without looking up from her computer. "I'm busy; you're busy."

Miles Ramsey came to his feet and grinned at her. "And Admissions is the nerve center of the hospital, the heart and soul of patient care."

She still didn't look up. "No. *I'm* the nerve center of the hospital. That's why I'm surrounded by people all day."

"You're surrounded by people because you're so lovely."

"Miles!" This time she did look up. "Damn it!"

"All right, all right." He raised his hands in mock surrender. "Hey, I'm out of here. Catch you later."

Ramsey squeezed past Symonds, who took his chair. "Seems like a nice guy."

"Too nice to be real. You know what I mean? Anyway, these sweeter-than-sugar 'new men' aren't my type. I'm into muscles and net worth." She went back to her typing.

"Are the flowers his?" He indicated the bouquet on the desk.

"He's persistent."

"So are you." He nodded at the computer she was diligently working at. "So what is it? Myst? Riven? An old Mario Brothers?" He laughed softly at her furious typing. "If you ever want to find out how to break into one of those games so you can beat it, let me know. I spent one summer working for a software company in Boston."

Patty didn't even glance up from her keyboard as she gave an amused grunt. "What kind of happy-pills are you taking, Doc? You're the only person around here who's constantly in an up mood. Most of us get depressed working with death and tragedy all the time, but you always act like it's the first day of summer camp and you can't wait to get to the canoes."

"I learned to block out negative vibes in med school. If you start getting wrapped up in the lives of patients you'll end up psycho or committing suicide. So what game has you so fascinated?"

Patty kept on typing. "You really think I could play games with Mohammed the Camel sneaking around here like a vice cop trying to catch me doing something nasty in the rest room? Only in your dreams, pal."

"You don't report to Kamel, do you? He's only got medical personnel under him." He put the coffee cup he was holding on her desk and poured a small container of cream into it.

"That doesn't stop him from watching everyone in this part of the building." She hit the Save button and swiveled around to face him. "He thinks anything involving the ER is his concern. I caught him going through my hard drive last week when I came back from lunch. He claimed it was an emergency and he was looking for a patient file because his computer was down. Hell, if his computer was down there were a dozen others he could use in the ER. He was probably looking to see if I've stored any pornographic videos." She glanced at the clock and frowned. "If you're taking your break here it must mean Kate's still being grilled upstairs by our local witch-hunters."

"I noticed she wasn't in her office. What's going on upstairs?"

"Thumbscrews and the rack, administered by Zamora, the Bitch of Floor Six."

Symonds raised his eyebrows. "I'm lost."

''A personnel hearing,'' Patty explained. ''Discipline! To show Katie what a bad girl she's been, while insisting on a complete change of behavior.''

''I'm still in the dark, Patty. Care to try it in plain English?''

''They're claiming Kate's screwing up her job.'' She explained about Zamora and Dotson. ''But who wouldn't be a little distracted with all the crap that's happened to her?''

Symonds paused, unsure what to say. He didn't feel comfortable discussing the medical aspects of Kate's problems. But Patty waved a dismissive hand. ''Hey, I know it all, Doc. Like Kate said, she and I don't have any secrets.''

Symonds sat back in his chair, relieved at being able to discuss it with someone. Everything about Kate's problems had been bothering him for days. ''It has to be tough for her, for any mom. Unless she's doing it herself.''

''You don't believe that.''

''But none of it makes sense, does it? Especially the herpes. Not unless—''

''She's screwing around? Come on, you know better than that. Look how unlucky you've been, and you're practically panting every time you're around her.''

''Is it that obvious?'' He began to feel foolish. He thought he had been more circumspect than that.

''Well, the bulge throbbing in your pants when you're talking to her kind of gives you away. It's fun to watch, though. Reminds me of a jack-in-the-box I used to have. You can even hear the *boinnnng!*''

He laughed and reached forward to pick up his coffee. ''Who can explain the mysteries of attraction? There's something special about her. For me, anyway. And she's a nice person, something I haven't seen a lot of in my life.''

Patty frowned at him. ''It's not good to fixate, Doc.''

''I guess I sound a little single-minded, don't I?'' He squirmed in his chair.

''You're probably the real reason she's in trouble around here, you know. Our Gypsy queen is pissed because you dropped her and started lusting after Kate. Hell hath no fury . . . as you surely know.''

Symonds put his coffee down. "That's crazy. Judith Zamora? I never went out with her. Hell, I hardly know her."

Patty's eyes widened mischievously. "Not what the rumor mill says, Doctor. They say it was hot and heavy, with the lady doing the chasing. Does that mean she got to be on top most of the time?"

"Me and *Zamora?* That's what people think?" For some reason it annoyed him more than it should have.

Patty nodded. *"Everyone's* talking about it, Doc. Don't play dumb."

His body jerked with dismay. "It's all a crock. So who started it?"

"Probably some nurse you stood up," she said and giggled.

"Uh-uh! I *never* go out with nurses. I've seen too many ERs fall apart because of jealousy when that happens. You know the old saying: Don't get your meat where you get your bread."

Patty shook her head. *"Very* old saying, Dr. Joel. I think most people go to supermarkets now. Where, among other products being featured this month, is the lovely and nicely shaped Patty Mars, star of admitting desks all over America, and the nerve center of Midtown Memorial. Care to try it out? Fresh as tomorrow's bread, soft and warm in all the right places, and available for your very personal inspection."

"Thanks, but—"

"Yeah, yeah, when you get over Kate. Someday, though, OK? I've gone out with an OB, an anesthesiologist, and two GPs. Never an ER doctor, though. What happens if I have an emergency?"

"Call George Clooney."

"I did. He wants me to fly to Paris tomorrow. Unfortunately he's staying in Malibu. What the hell, maybe I'll go after a plastic surgeon instead. That way at least I could get a boob job out of it."

Symonds raised his eyebrows. "You're kidding."

"Not an implant, you goof. A reduction."

"Ah." He sipped his coffee, still annoyed at the rumors about Zamora. Maybe she was having an affair with someone else, and his name was somehow dragged into it. Not that it mattered; he had his sights pointed elsewhere. Trying not to sound too interested, he said, "So tell me about Kate. Is she really as happily married as she claims? Or is this all just a front to keep testosterone-laden doctors at bay?"

"Better not talk like that to other people around here, Doc. Her hubby's on the board, you know. If he thinks you're sniffing around his sweetie he could get you fired in a minute."

"Big deal. I walk down the street and get another job. Or expand my own practice to five days. So what about Kate? Happy or not? I vote for not."

Patty leaned back in her chair and regarded him. "Just wishful thinking? Or do you have a reason?"

"Experience with patients. Something's been bothering her for a while. You can see it in her eyes. Maybe it's not her marriage. But something's not right."

"Like her job? Or the problems with her kid?"

"It started before that. Are you telling me you never suspected anything's wrong with her?"

Patty shrugged. "I don't know. She's been a little moody, but that could be anything. Even I have my bad days, though you could never tell, could you?" She flipped her hair with her fingertips and smiled coquettishly.

Symonds laughed. "You're one of a kind, Patty." He turned and glanced toward the waiting room just behind his chair. An elderly woman was waiting for her grandson to be released after being stitched up for an ugly gash on his leg. No one else was within hearing. He looked back at Patty, getting to what he had really dropped by to find out. "How well do you know the orderlies around here?"

"I hardly ever talk to them. They're always on the move. Why do you ask?"

"I just wondered what the buzz on Frankie Yorba is. Do people around here like him?"

"Frankie? Jeez, you going after boys, too? You like those muscles? Or is it the goatee?"

"Just interested. What do people say about him?"

"There's got to be a reason, Doctor."

Symonds wasn't about to tell her the reason was that he had seen Yorba more than once hanging around the secured drug locker, a place where he wouldn't expect to find an orderly. On the other hand, Kamel, the man responsible for the drug inventory, had not mentioned anything about a shortage. Still, Symonds was curious. "I'm just interested in the ER's dramatis personae," he joked, adding, "in case I want to write a TV script."

"Yeah, you and half the people in the hospital. Would the hero of this epic happen to be a thirty-six-year-old ER doctor with dreamy blue eyes and a receding hairline?"

"Thirty-five. And it's not receding. So what do you hear?"

"About macho Frankie? Mixed messages. Quiet guy, goes about his work, never hassles people. But a little weird, you know, that sneer on his face, like he knows a secret about you and is deciding whether to tell it or not. And then there was the photo on my computer last week."

"What photo?"

Patty explained what happened. "Actually I'm not sure it was Frankie. When I clicked the mouse it disappeared. Kinda looked like him, though. If so, I think his hard body's got you beat, Doc. This guy had muscles where most men have delusions."

Symonds laughed. "He's never acted strange around you? Never looked high or strung out?"

"Frankie *always* acts weird, the way he never looks at you straight on, but kinda over to the side. You ever notice that?"

"Could have an astigmatism. Or maybe he's just shy."

"Frankie, shy? I don't think so."

"All right. No big deal. I was just curious." He stood up. "If you think of anything about him that strikes you as odd, let me know. Let me know if you hear anything more about Kate's problems, too."

Patty looked at him warily. "I think you're a little too interested in Kate for your own good. If you keep chasing married women you're going to end up with your own testosterone imbalance. Or a bullet in the gut. It ain't healthy, Doc. You know how these possessive husbands are."

20

Kate was in the mood for none of this, the rich wood-paneled walls of Chez Cisalpine, the crystal chandeliers and hovering waiters and, most of all, Paul's ill-concealed envy of Rick Hazlitt, which manifested itself in the snappish manner in which he answered all of the other attorney's questions. "How the hell would I know what they're getting at? With me, anyway. With Kate I guess it has something to do with their embarrassment at having an employee who might be deliberately harming her own child. How would you like to be a patient in a hospital that employed someone like that? You'd be afraid to go to sleep at night." He turned quickly to Kate and covered her hand with his. "Not that I believe it, of course. But you can see why they're worried."

Hazlitt, resplendent in a gray Savile Row suit that would have cost Paul two weeks' salary, if he could have afforded to jet to London on a shopping trip, took a leather-covered notebook from an inside coat pocket. "What were the officers' names again?"

"Nick Cerovic and Ann DeSilva," Kate said.

Hazlitt pushed his plate to the side and wrote down the names. "I'll see what I can find out about them." He glanced at Paul. "Anything you can tell me?"

"I don't know a thing about them. I asked around the office, quietly, of course. I don't need any more people to know what's going on. But I couldn't learn anything. Just two cops doing their job." He began to tap his fingers on the tabletop.

Hazlitt turned to Kate. "But they specifically mentioned this Munchausen's?"

"DeSilva, the woman, mentioned it. She's already convicted me. The man hasn't been hostile."

Paul's head snapped in her direction, but the attorney merely shook his head. "I never even heard of it before. Isn't Munchausen a children's book?"

"Baron Munchausen," Kate said dully. "It's a story about someone who was unable to tell the truth. He kept making up stories about his deeds to get attention."

"Munchausen by proxy means—"

"That the person isn't lying about her own illnesses. Only her children's. But to draw attention to herself."

"Why?" Hazlitt seemed perplexed.

"She's supposed to be covering up her inadequacies by making people feel sorry for her. That's what the shrinks say, anyway."

He shook his head. "Typical psychobabble. It all seems a little bizarre to me. But we'll assume this really occurs. What proof do they have that you're responsible?"

"None."

"Your son's been sick, of course. That'd be part of it. And Paul mentioned something about rats."

"Alex was bitten on the hands and toes. They're saying the rats were laboratory rats rather than wild." Kate took a breath. She didn't want to go on with this but had no choice. "He also has swine flu." Briefly she explained. "And . . ." She waved a hand weakly; it was still hard to form the words. "Alex has herpes. They think it came from me—mother's milk, or touch. But they're just guessing."

Hazlitt shook his head and let out a long sigh. "Whew." His gaze seemed to lose focus.

"Right," Paul said. "A lot to explain."

The waiter, smiling preternaturally, swooped down on them with a huge tray. "Trout . . ."

The conversation halted as plates were lowered and glasses filled. After the waiter was gone Hazlitt said, "The police detective actually accused you of this Munchausen's? She used the term?"

"She tried to rattle me. It worked, I guess. I told them I

wasn't going to talk to them anymore. That's when they implied Paul might be guilty.''

"What?" Paul slammed his fork down. "You didn't tell me that.''

"Because I knew how you'd react.'' She suddenly felt bad for lashing out at him. But there were times when he could act like a ten-year-old. "I'm sorry, Paul. It's been tough for both of us. I didn't want to worry you.''

"It's probably a ploy anyway,'' Hazlitt said calmly. "They just wanted to see what you'd say. You did right by not talking to them any more.''

"What do we do now?''

Hazlitt cut a piece of two-inch-thick steak and watched as blood began to circle his plate. "Paul said you had a hearing of some sort at work today. Was that related to any of this?''

Kate nodded. "They claim my work's suffered.'' She briefly ran through what had occurred in the meeting, concluding with their insistence that she see a psychologist tomorrow.

"Jesus Christ!" Paul's explosion was loud enough for half the restaurant to hear. "You didn't tell me this either. How many other secrets do you have?''

Kate felt the energy drain from her as Paul leaned forward suddenly, the candle making shadows dance on his face. "We didn't have time to talk, Paul. You were busy at work.''

"God.'' He slumped back in his chair, looking miserable, and tossed his fork on the table.

Hazlitt immediately jumped in. "Stay away from the psychologist. They have no right to ask that. If they insist, tell them to talk to your attorney. A more important issue, of course, is the herpes. Do either of you have any idea how Alex got it?''

"Well, he didn't get it from me,'' Paul snapped as the waiter approached and then moved away as though from a bomb. "Christ. If I had herpes I'd know about it, wouldn't I?''

Kate felt a stab of anger but kept her mouth shut.

Hazlitt darted a tentative glance in Kate's direction. "Any ideas? Could Alex have picked it up somewhere? Maybe even in the hospital?''

"I don't know. I'm not an expert on viruses." She pushed the uneaten fish away, the thought of food suddenly sickening her, and snatched up the glass of zinfandel, draining it, then waving at a hovering waiter.

"Another glass of wine, madam?"

"Please."

"And two more scotches," Hazlitt said. He put his fork down and wiped his hands on a linen napkin. "I think you both should get tested to prove you don't have herpes. That'll be our starting point."

Paul was incensed. "I goddamn well do not have herpes!"

"Take off your wounded-father's hat and put on your lawyer's hat, Paul. It doesn't matter how long you stand on the parapets proclaiming the decency of your lifestyle or the purity of your blood; you're still going to need lab results."

Kate said, "I'm already scheduled for a physical tomorrow. They can do the test then."

Paul looked at her as if he couldn't imagine anything else going wrong. "What now? Do they think you're a carrier of infectious diseases as well as being crazy? Why do you have to have a physical?"

"It's a hospital, Paul. When something goes wrong they give physicals to people because it's all they know how to do. Just like your office gives lie detectors. It looks like you're doing something. It makes people feel good."

Her attitude obviously annoyed him, and he grabbed his fork and stabbed the steak with a vengeance.

Hazlitt said to Paul, "You'll get tested, too?"

"Hell, yes! Herpes, an upper GI, a rectal. Whatever they want."

"It's not them. It's us. What's best for us. Can you have it done downtown somewhere?"

"I'm damn well not going to do it downtown. I don't want to be anywhere near downtown when I have it done. I'll come in to Midtown on my lunch. I'm not in court tomorrow."

Kate said, "It still won't prove anything. If we don't have herpes the police will say we infected him some other way.

They're convinced one of us is guilty. If they lose interest in me they'll go after Paul.''

"I won't stand for it," Paul said. "I'll call Hollywood Division tomorrow and talk to the commander. They can't treat us like this."

Hazlitt shook his head. "No, you won't. Don't call anybody. Don't discuss this with anybody. We're going to keep it under wraps. With any luck no one outside the police station or hospital will know either of you was ever suspected of a crime. Being a suspect is not a good career move. Especially for a DA."

"It's that goddamn Petrosian," Paul said. "He's laughing at us right now. Hell, he even calls me at my office with his juvenile taunts."

Hazlitt looked up from his steak. "You didn't tell me about this. Who's Petrosian?"

Paul told him about the recently released felon. "It's a side to legal work you west-side lawyers don't get to see. Leo's getting a kick out of harassing me. And doing a damn good job of it. But hell, he's had three years to plan this out."

"Have you actually seen him since his release?"

"I'm not sure. I thought I saw him hanging around the parking lot I use on Spring Street this afternoon. It could have been someone else. I haven't talked to him since the trial."

"So maybe he's not involved in Kate's troubles at all."

"But she's been getting threatening calls at work, too."

He looked at her, and she nodded but said nothing.

"I bought a gun," Paul said, breaking the silence.

Hazlitt sat back. "I'm surprised. I don't see you as the Clint Eastwood type."

"I'm not. I've never owned anything but a .22 when I was a kid. But I'm not going to leave my family unprotected."

"No good ever comes from keeping a gun in the house."

"Save the platitudes for your ethically challenged stockbrokers. It's my family under siege. If Petrosian comes in my house he's not leaving alive."

"It's still possible you're going about this the wrong way. It may not be Petrosian who's behind your problems."

"Count on it," Paul said, clutching his fork as if trying to bend it in half. "Leo's harassing me at work, and he's behind Kate's troubles at Midtown. All this trouble started the day he got out of Tehachipi."

No, Kate thought. *It didn't. It started years ago. But if I only knew why . . .*

21

"Your breathing's a little labored, but there appears to be nothing amiss," Mohammed Kamel said the next morning. "I'm concerned about the elevated blood pressure, though." He walked over to the counter, where Kate's chart was propped open, and made a notation. "Do you have hypertension or blood-pressure problems in your family? No? Heart disease, then . . ." He ran through a list of possibilities.

"Nothing," Kate told him. She hopped off the examination table; the "complete" management-mandated physical exam by the ER head hadn't taken ten minutes. Clearly Kamel wasn't as concerned about this as Zamora and Glazier. She added, "My father died of a heart attack, but he was forty pounds overweight and in his sixties."

"Well—" Kamel seemed to consult his memory. "I don't know what to say, then. Perhaps we should wait to see what the lab tests indicate. In addition to high blood pressure we still have the possibility of herpes to consider, of course. After all, your son got it somewhere. Have you had any skin eruptions? They would be in your genital area."

"None!" There had been some itching lately, which she had put down to nerves. But she wasn't going to tell Kamel.

"No discomfort, no scabs or blisters?"

"No."

"No burning sensation?"

She hesitated.

He looked at her, his tone brisk. "The prodromal symptoms are burning or itching. That usually means something will manifest itself soon."

"Sometimes." The word came unbidden and she repressed a shiver. *God, no, don't tell me I have herpes. Please.*

Kamel leaned against the counter and looked thoughtful. "But no eruptions?"

"No."

"Most people who have herpes don't even know it. Were you aware of that? Then suddenly the genital region erupts in sores. A blood test is merely an indication, by the way. The only definitive way to determine if herpes is present is to take a swab of the blistered area. And since you haven't actually broken out we won't be able to do that. We'll go ahead with the blood test, of course." He picked up her file. "Tell me what you think. Is it possible you have become infected? This is between us, of course. Your husband need not know if you have been active sexually with someone other than him."

Kate shook her head. She was no longer confident she hadn't somehow acquired the disease. But she didn't have a medical background and hadn't considered a virus when the itching began, and certainly never thought of herpes. As it was, all she knew about it was what Kamel had told her. "I don't know. I hope to God I don't." *But if I do,* she thought at once, *where did it come from?*

"Well, it would not be your fault, of course. It is up to your partner to protect himself. But you'll have to go down to the lab and have your blood drawn. Was that Ms. Zamora's idea, too? I don't remember. Dr. Glazier, perhaps. Let's hope there's nothing seriously wrong."

"But you think there is, don't you?" Kate couldn't mask the concern she felt.

Kamel crossed his arms and held her gaze. "I think ... something will be indicated. I don't know what. We will have to wait and see. But as soon as a rash appears come and see me. Then we can test definitively."

Returning to her office after the blood test, Kate felt a wave of exhaustion wash over her as she slumped down in her chair. But it quickly disappeared, replaced by a sense of guilt that seemed to envelop her like a cloak. But guilt over what? She hadn't done anything to be ashamed of! Still, she had felt like a criminal going down to the lab and asking to have her blood drawn. Everyone acted as if this were just another routine request, but it was clear they all knew why—and for what—she was being tested. It was probably all over the hospital by now. The crazy woman who injures her child is suspected of infecting him with herpes. Her stomach clenched and she felt like screaming. *I don't have herpes. I didn't hurt my baby. Someone is doing this to me!*

Someone, Kate? Don't you know who? Surely you must. But I don't, damn it, I don't even have a suspicion.

Her shoulders sagged as she stared at the pile of papers on her desk. Once again she was hours behind on her work. One more thing for Zamora to get on her about. Reflexively she flipped on the computer, momentarily closing her eyes, then opening them in time to see a message scroll across the bottom of her screen: ''. . . extensive abrasions to the vaginal area resulting in massive internal bleeding . . .''

What did that say?

She jerked suddenly forward, staring at the screen, her heart pounding. The message had disappeared. What about the vaginal area? It sounded like something from a patient file. Or a police report. But what did it have to do with her? ''Goddamn it!'' Seized with fury, she hit the monitor with her fist. ''Stop doing this to me! Leave me alone!''

Patty came in at lunch with a sandwich and a Coke, saw Kate with her head on her arms, and said at once, ''Uh-oh, guess you don't want visitors.''

Kate looked up. ''No, no. Come on in. I'm just having a bad day. Again.''

''Bad week is more like it.'' She took a chair and put her drink on the desk. ''So what happened today? Someone blow up your car?''

As Kate was telling her about the physical exam and lab tests, an overweight man of about thirty poked his head in the office and said, ''Hey, is dis da right place?''

''You betcha!'' Patty turned quickly toward the door, waving him inside. "Dennis Flagstad," she said, introducing the man to Kate. "Our resident computer genius. Dennis set up our e-mail system, so he ought to be able to tell who's been sending you these weird messages."

"I can find out where they originate, not necessarily who's sending them," he said. "But tell me what's been going on."

Kate explained. "Sometimes it's a threatening e-mail, more often a message or picture that flits across the screen and disappears before I can capture it."

"I had something weird on my computer, too," Patty told him. "A near-nude hunk rippling his pecs at me. Very impressive."

"That was me," Flagstad said. "I only look like this with my clothes on."

"And I'm a supermodel in my off hours. Get to it, Dennis, or you don't get your Skittles and M&M's."

"Don't threaten me, Patty. A programmer without sugar is a truly ugly thing to see." He turned to Kate. "When did you get the last message?"

"About two hours ago. It said something about abrasions to the vaginal area."

"What the hell does that mean?"

"I don't know. It read like a police report."

"How long was it?"

"One sentence. Maybe five or ten seconds." She explained how the messages moved across the screen and dissolved in a flurry of red dots.

Flagstad was impressed. "Obviously someone who knows what he's doing. And it appears on the screen when you're going about your daily work?"

"Mostly when the computer's been down for a while, I think."

"Well, that's something. Let me play around." He sat at Kate's desk and started hitting keys. Ten minutes later he leaned back and sighed. "There's nothing on your hard drive to cause messages like you've experienced. Let me go down to the Batcave and see what I can find out. It's probably someone on the local area network doing it. That means it could be anywhere in the hospital. Give me a day or so.''

Patty went back to her own office ten minutes later. At two o'clock, when Kate was supposed to be leaving for her appointment with the psychologist, a call came through on her outside line. The same soft, vaguely accented voice she had heard before: ''Are you paying attention to the messages?''

Her body went stiff, and her voice sank to a whisper. ''Why are you doing this to me?''

He sounded upbeat. ''Listen to the message, Kate. The message! Then wait. You have to be patient. We have years to go yet. *Years—*''

''Who are you?'' But the man had already hung up. ''Goddamn it! Goddamn it!'' Furious, she slammed the phone down just as a man and woman appeared at her office door. ''Kate McDonald? We're from Child Protective Services.''

''Get out!'' Kate screamed. She was beside herself with rage. ''I'm not going to talk to you. Get out of here!''

''We have to see you about your son. The police department notified us that you—''

''Go away! Damn you!'' She grabbed her purse and stormed out of the office, running through the emergency room to the parking lot. Once she was in her car, her mind raged as she drove for hours, refusing to stop, as though her past were chasing her.

22

"I went in to have my damn blood test this afternoon," Paul said as he tried to ease a spoonful of pureed carrots into Alex's mouth. The boy was having none of it, though, and pressed his pink lips tightly together as the spoon approached. "Hey, kiddo, the hangar's closed. How am I supposed to get the 747 inside?"

Kate's head was killing her. She went to the kitchen cabinet and shook two Advils into her hand. Twice the amount she was supposed to take, but she didn't care. After washing them down with water, she grabbed a bottle of Cabernet out of the refrigerator and poured an iced-tea glass half-full.

"Bunch of bloodsuckers down there, aren't they?" Paul went on, unaware that she had gotten up from the table. "Goddamn vampires! They must love the sight of blood. Half a dozen lab techs walked by as it was being drawn and stared at me like I was some sort of celebrity." He turned from Alex and stared at the plate of Mexican food that had been delivered from Mario's. "You want some enchilada instead of mushy carrots, kiddo?" He dumped the carrots off the spoon and scooped up some of the soft tortilla and melted cheese.

Kate lowered herself into the chair at the far end of the table and put her head in her hands. Since she had stormed out of the office this afternoon, a blackness had been growing in her mind, an oppressive cloud of doubt and depression that was dragging her down like a drug, making even physical movement difficult. But deep inside, too deep to touch now, she could feel rage again beginning to build, rage and impotence, and a wild, furious hatred that had no focus—*hatred of what?*—or outlet. She hadn't felt this way in . . . years, of course. But she could be more specific. She knew exactly how long it had been. To the day.

She raised her head from the table. Looking at the glass in front of her she was surprised to see that it was empty already. She needed another drink. She should have gone back to work this afternoon after driving around mindlessly for three hours, and gotten some Prozac or Valium. Joel Symonds would have gotten it for her without a prescription. He would have done that; he liked her. And if truth be told, she allowed herself to realize for the first time as Paul made faces at Alex, she was attracted to him, too. He was nice-looking. More than that: he was a nice man, gentle and caring, and without Paul's sudden flights of anger or childish jealousy. Perhaps Patty had been right. She ought not shut him out of her life.

God, I don't need these feelings now. I'm happily married. I am! I don't need Joel; I've got my husband. Who loves me. Doesn't he?

Paul whooped with joy as Alex accepted the spoonful of enchilada. "Hey, *perfecto,* young Alexander. Maybe I'll call you Alejandro now that I know what kind of food you like." He glanced over at Kate, then picked up a spoonful of brown rice. "You'd better eat some of your dinner, hon. You're starting to look like one of those teenage anorexics."

"Maybe I'm not eating to get attention."

Paul put the fork down. "Yeah, Munchausen's. Christ, it's nuts, isn't it?"

"Nuts. Crazy. Insane. The words of the day." *The words of my life. Crazy Kate.*

Paul reached over to Alex and undid his bib.

Kate felt her fingers again clutching the empty glass. "How did Alex get herpes, Paul?" The words startled her, as though someone else had asked, and at once part of her mind wished desperately she could retrieve them. But another part had seized on the question and wouldn't let go, because she wasn't going to have any peace until she had an answer.

"You're asking me? How would I know? I don't even necessarily believe he does have it." He lifted the boy from the high chair and gently set him on the floor. "Don't you think it's time you started walking, kiddo? Go on, get up and walk." Alex began to crawl toward the refrigerator. "Maybe we ought to get one of those television evangelists in here to help the kid get up on his feet." His voice took on a Southern accent. "Go on, bo-yah! Ah command you to *walk!*"

"You don't *believe* he has herpes?" Kate's tone rose with incredulity as she stared at her husband. "You think the doctors are lying to you?"

"Hell, it's possible. Not that they're lying but that they screwed up somewhere. Let's take him to another lab and get him retested. There was something about the people down there I didn't like."

"Bloodsuckers," she remembered. "Vampires."

"Look, don't ever take a medical test at face value. Anyone connected with medicine will tell you that."

"Paul . . ." Why was she doing this now? There had to be a better time, a time when she wasn't so upset. But she couldn't stop herself. "How did Alex get herpes? Do you understand what I'm asking? How did he get infected?" She was almost shouting again, and Alex stopped his crawling and turned back toward his mother's voice.

Paul looked at her with surprise. "Yes. I guess I do." His voice turned angry. "But you're not asking a question, are you? You're implying it somehow came from me."

"Well, I sure as hell never had herpes."

"And I did? Jesus, Kate, are you nuts? Where would I get herpes from?"

"That's what I'm asking. Who was it? Some floozy in your office? One of those clerks who thinks lawyers are just the greatest thing in the world to screw? God, what a fantasy that is."

"Kate, what's gotten into you? Is it the cops? Did they upset you that much?"

"You always change the subject, don't you? Where the hell did you get it, Paul? And why didn't you tell me? At least you could have worn a condom so you wouldn't infect me and your baby."

"Kate!" Paul seemed more confused at her behavior than angry. "From what I've heard, herpes can stay in your system for years before it's observable. Maybe you caught it before we met."

"*Me?* Am I the guilty party here? Are you going to jump on the blame-Kate bandwagon like everyone else?" She pushed out of her chair and jerked open the refrigerator door.

"Well, I don't know anything about your love life before we got married. You're an attractive woman. I always figured you probably had a number of lovers. Probably half the unmarried men in America have herpes. It's nothing to be ashamed of."

"You goddamn well ought to be ashamed if you caused your baby to be infected with a lifelong disease because you weren't honest with your wife!" She splashed more wine in her glass, then banged the bottle down.

"Come on, Kate. You're just striking out at me because you're upset about Alex."

"Alex!" Kate said. "My God." She looked around wildly.

Paul jumped out of his chair. "Calm down, for God's sake. Where can he be? He can't walk out of the house."

Kate ran into the living room. Alex was playing with the cord to a lamp. He had pulled the plug out of the wall socket and stuck it in his mouth. She swooped down and picked him up. She was beginning to cry, and it incensed her. Why couldn't she control her emotions any longer? Alex, frightened at the sudden movement, screamed and grabbed onto her hair, pulling so violently she winced.

"God, Kate. Talk about overreacting. He's not going to be attacked by rats again, if that's what you think."

Kate turned on him angrily. "You betrayed me, Paul. You betrayed our love."

"Betrayed?" He laughed uneasily at the word and stared at the ceiling. "Good Lord, I'm living in a nineteenth-century melodrama. Are you going to 'swoon' now, overcome with grief at my dastardly behavior?" He gave a short, mirthless laugh and wiped the hair from his forehead.

And in that instant she saw it in his face, in the set of his jaw, in the tight white line of his lips and the repeated blinking of his eyes. It had been a guess, made without any proof or even any reason. But she had been right. He was lying to her, and now he was hoping to gloss it over with sarcasm. *Goddamn him! Goddamn him!* What had Lilliana said? All men screw around? *But not my husband,* Kate insisted at the time. *My husband is different.*

The phone rang and Paul answered it. "For you," he said, frowning as he shoved it at her. "Some man with an accent. Your secret lover, perhaps?"

Kate angrily grabbed it from him, still holding a crying Alex. There was nothing but a dial tone. "Damn you, there's no one there!" She slammed it down and turned to see Paul leaving the room. Alex's screaming rose, and he pulled again at her hair. *I can't go on like this,* she thought, and began to tremble as her nerves shrieked. *I can't do it. I'm going mad.*

July 21

You don't like it so far, do you, Katie Kate? But I promised you a living hell, and I always *keep my promises. You should know that by now.*

Such nasty things you're doing to that poor child. Your mother would not be proud. I know she worries about you. But mothers can be so intrusive, can't they? Even when we're adults they want to manage our lives. I suppose they call it love, but we know better, don't we? It's an attempt to extend their control by emotional blackmail, just as the mentally unstable control us with threats of hysteria.

Ah . . . hysteria. We know that one, don't we, Katie Kate? Hysteria . . . madness . . .

23

God, no, Kate thought as she walked into her office the next morning and saw Nick Cerovic sitting in one of her visitor's chairs. *Not today. Please. I can't take any more of this.*

The policeman looked at her with what might have been sympathy. "Good morning."

Kate didn't move from the door, what energy she'd had leaking away like air from a balloon. "Another call from the Storm Troopers. Now what? Are you going to arrest me for attempted murder?"

"No, actually I got so bored impaling babies on my bayonet all day, I thought I'd pop in and mentally brutalize you for a while."

Kate threw him a hostile glance and crossed over to her desk. She flicked on her computer and tried to pretend he wasn't there. "I'm not in the mood for this, and I have a great deal of work to do."

"I believe you started it."

She bit back an angry reply, then recognized the truth of his statement. "Sorry. What can I do for you? More questions?"

"More or less. Along with some advice. And I brought you coffee. It's from the cafeteria. Pretty good, actually." He nodded toward a Styrofoam cup on the edge of her desk. Two small containers of cream sat next to it.

Kate stared at it but made no attempt to pick it up. "What kind of advice?"

Cerovic picked up his own cup. "Child Protective Services called us and said you were rude and uncooperative to them."

"They're right."

"Not a good move on your part. These aren't the people you want to annoy. It's probably better to piss off the entire LAPD than two social services inspectors. Every step a cop takes is scrutinized by a dozen public and private groups. Social services is like the KGB—they pretty much do what they want and no one has the guts to tell them no. Right now they're pretty close to telling us to arrest you for abusing your child."

Kate's head dropped onto her chest.

"I thought you'd want to know," Cerovic went on. "In case there's anything you'd like to tell me."

"Or in case I decide to bolt? Are you tailing me, too? Are you expecting me to grab my son and take off for Buenos Aires? That'd pretty much clinch my guilt, wouldn't it?"

"Truthfully? I don't know what I expect. Hell, I don't even know if you're guilty. I just thought you should know."

"The good cop," she said dully. "Where's the other half of the team? Scowling into a mirror somewhere?"

"She has a court appearance. I didn't tell her I'd be here."

Kate's head lifted as she looked at him. He was gazing at her with concern, not the belligerence she had learned to expect from police officers. She felt a sudden if strange and distant attraction for this large, craggy-looking man, as she might for a stranger who had saved her from drowning. How odd, she thought, considering he was trying to put her in jail. Or was it only his partner who had already convicted her? "She thinks I'm guilty, doesn't she?"

"Annie? I guess she's leaning in that direction."

"She's not leaning at all. She's over the line. Without a shred of evidence."

"Well, it works both ways. She and I are being investigated, too."

"I don't know what you mean."

"The DA's office. One of their junior DAs wants to open an investigation of the meddling cops. I guess he thinks we're not too bright, probably wants us back in Traffic."

"Paul." Kate felt a wave of embarrassment that her husband would be so petty.

"It won't go anywhere. But it'll make the brass wonder

when it comes time for promotion. 'Nick and Annie, weren't they investigated for incompetence?' Like I said, cops work under a microscope most folks can't begin to imagine. And even the hint of so-called 'impropriety' can ruin a career.''

"I'm sorry. Sometimes Paul gets a little emotional and does things he shouldn't. I'll tell him to stop it.''

"Will he listen to you?''

"Probably not. Not about this.'' She sat forward, her elbows on the desktop, and rubbed her forehead. "You'd think working in a hospital I could at least get rid of a headache, wouldn't you?'' Letting out a sigh she turned to her computer and hit a button to call up her e-mail. "Is there something else you need? I've got work to—'' She sighed as the first message appeared, and waved a hand at the monitor. "More your territory than mine, Sergeant.''

"Sorry?'' He leaned toward the computer but was too far away to read the message.

"From M. Kamel, MD. Our resident ex-colonel. Evidently some drugs are missing from the locked cabinet in the ER. How would you like to turn on your e-mail first thing in the morning and be confronted with something like this? 'Any unauthorized person in possession of a key to the narcotics cabinet will be summarily dismissed.' And good morning to you, Doctor! At the end of the month when they do their inventory they'll decide nothing's missing after all. It's happened twice before. But in the meantime we're all suspects. Well, it's better than the e-mail threats I've been getting.'' She turned from the monitor and held his gaze. "Do you think your friend Annie can pin drug thefts on me, too? Or is she only interested in child abuse?''

"Look, Kate, Annie isn't trying to railroad you. She's trying to do what's best for your son. Honestly.'' He leaned toward the computer again. "What did you mean by e-mail threats?''

"My secret correspondent.'' She hit the index of her current e-mails and read through it. "There's nothing now. But wait around; I'll get one—either a weird e-mail or a message that scrolls across the screen and disappears. For variety he sometimes phones his threats to me.''

"Like what? Give me an example."

"Like 'Don't die yet, Kate,' or the sound of a child scream-ing. They're very creative."

"Do you have a record of past e-mails?"

"Sure." She hit a key. "Our system saves everything for two weeks." She glanced at it and began to scroll with her mouse. After a moment she turned to him with a resigned shrug. "The threats aren't listed. He must have erased them. How clever. Now I can't even prove they ever existed."

"How many other people have seen these messages?"

Kate looked at him angrily, but her voice was tired. "You think I made it up, don't you? More fantasies from the crazy woman." Her eyes closed momentarily. "One of the admitting clerks, Patty Mars, saw one last week. And she was here when I got a threatening phone call."

"When was that?"

She shrugged. "A couple of days ago."

"Was that the only phone threat?"

"No. There've been a few."

"You recognize the voice?"

"A man, accented, I think. But he's obviously trying to disguise it. But no, I didn't recognize it."

Cerovic took out his notebook and made a notation. "I've run into threats like this before. With stalkers."

"Stalkers?"

"Usually a guy who's tried to get a date with a woman and was rebuffed. Or it can be more subtle than that. Sometimes she didn't even know the guy was interested but she did some-thing to piss him off. So this is how he gets back at her. The really nutty ones are convinced that this is the way to their true love's heart."

"By threatening them?"

"By getting them all shook up and then offering their assis-tance. There might be something there. Can you think of any-body who might be interested in you like that?"

"No. No one, I'm sure."

"No dewy-eyed, brokenhearted lovers?"

"No."

"All right, let me look into it. A big operation like this would have a computerized phone system. That means there's a record of where calls originated from. Maybe we can run this down. Where's the communications department?"

"In the basement. Next to the lab."

As though on cue the phone rang. Kate picked it up warily and then began to listen with interest. After a moment her voice rose in consternation. "Doxazosin? I don't understand. What's that?" Then her fingers tightened on the receiver, and her eyes closed in pain. "My God," she murmured at last, her body sinking forward and her elbows dropping to the desk. "What about Paul? . . . *I don't care about regulations, damn you! What about him?*"

A moment later the hand holding the phone dropped to the desk, the receiver rolling with a thud onto the metal desktop. Kate's eyes closed for several seconds, then opened onto a spot in space. "I infected Alex with herpes. It's my fault my baby's sick." When Nick said nothing, she added with a dull certainty, "And Paul infected me. How's that for a fourth-anniversary present? My loving, devoted, and never-straying husband."

"I'm sorry," he said, and looked embarrassed for overhearing an obviously private conversation.

"I wonder who Paul got it from?" Kate asked, not expecting an answer. "A typical betrayed wife's question, isn't it? Who's my husband been sleeping with? Not that it matters."

Nick said nothing.

"God, how Lilliana would love this! Time for gloating at her holier-than-thou friend." When Kate saw his baffled face she added, "My nosy neighbor. Who told me all men screw around. I should have listened."

The receiver on her desk began making an annoying buzzing sound, and Kate slammed it down on the console.

"What do I do now, Sergeant Cerovic? Do I go home and say 'Was she prettier than me?' or 'Is she better in bed than I am?' What's the jealous wife's procedure at this point? This is all new to me. What does your wife do?"

Nick's left hand, the one with the wide gold wedding band, flattened on his thigh, but he said nothing.

"Don't be shy," Kate said loudly as two doctors walked by her open door, glancing in at the sound of her angry voice. "What does your wife do when she catches you screwing your little Annie, or some poor woman you pulled in for shoplifting? Does she cry? Or kick you out of the house for two weeks?"

"My wife's dead," Nick said. "Four years ago. And she never had to do anything. Neither of us did."

Kate's throat tightened and she was on the verge of crying. But she was determined not to break down in front of a cop.

Cerovic changed the conversation. "What's Doxazosin?"

Kate sighed. "That, too." She straightened, then glanced at the mess of papers on her desk. It was a moment before she could answer. "I have a blood-pressure medication in my system. It's why I've felt so bad lately. It can cause anxiety and dizziness in people who don't have high blood pressure." She ran a hand through her hair. "Me, in other words."

He wrote the name of the drug in his notebook.

"How do you think you got it?"

"Maybe I gave it to myself," Kate said. "To get attention, you know."

"Would it be locked up in the ER drug cabinet?"

"No. It's not a narcotic. You wouldn't take it to get high. I don't know how I got it. Somebody must have put it in my coffee." She looked at the cup on her desk. "Or maybe it was at home."

"Why would anyone do that?"

"Why is somebody sending me threats?"

"You really don't know? You can't think of any reason someone would be angry with you?" He looked at her skeptically.

"Enough to do this?" Her head shook back and forth.

The notebook balanced on his knee, Nick said evenly, "Where did you work before Midtown?"

Kate's eyes closed. "Suddenly change the topic. Maybe you'll catch her off guard and she'll slip up." She paused a moment. "I didn't work before coming here. I traveled around the world killing babies."

When he didn't respond she opened her eyes. "I wish you would just leave, Sergeant. Please."

"We're almost finished. You were going to tell me about your last job."

Kate tensed her muscles and tried to keep her voice flat. "I worked for a hospital in St. Louis. Do you want the name?"

He nodded without looking up from his notebook.

"St. Luke's. It's on Madison."

Cerovic made a note and thought, *You're lying. You're banking on my not checking, but I always check.*

"What am I supposed to do about my herpes?" she wondered aloud. Her voice shook as she looked at him. "Do I tell one of the doctors here? No reason not to, I suppose. They'll find out sooner or later anyway."

Cerovic came to his feet. "I'm going down to the communications department to check on your phone calls. If I find anything I'll let you know."

Patty Mars froze suddenly in the doorway, her voice dropping dramatically. "Cheese it, the cops."

"I'll be in touch," Nick said to Kate, then, nodding to Patty, left.

Patty smiled and took the just-vacated chair. "Hey, a hunk, isn't he? Stays in shape. Probably spends his nights in one of those twenty-four-hour gyms and obsesses on the Nautilus."

Kate couldn't keep the emotion at bay any longer. Furiously she pushed her chair back from the desk and jumped to her feet.

"My God," Patty said. "What's wrong? What'd he do to you?"

"It wasn't him!" Her face was flushed, and she gave in to the tears. "It's Alex." Haltingly she told Patty about the herpes. "He got it from his mother. Isn't that wonderful?" She sank down in the chair again and put her head in her hands.

Patty looked at her with disbelief. "God. I'm so sorry, Kate. But—" She caught herself and stopped.

Kate looked at her from red-rimmed eyes. "But where did I get it from? What do you think?"

"Are you sure? Herpes is a virus; maybe you got it from—"

"Goddamn it, my husband infected me! Don't give me this toilet-seat shit!"

Patty's mouth clamped shut. She had never seen Kate like this, and didn't know how to react.

"Our fourth anniversary! I wonder how long he's been screwing around. Probably from the first, right? As soon as the honeymoon was over and he got his second wind he started chasing secretaries down at the courthouse."

Patty leaned forward and put her hand on the desk, as though it were a substitute for touching her friend. "I'm really sorry, Kate. I don't know what else to say."

Kate looked at her. "Don't say anything. OK? Just leave me alone."

Patty eased to her feet. "Sure. I'll talk to you later. Maybe we can go out to lunch." But Kate was staring at the wall, wondering what was to become of her family.

24

"What?" Kate shouted as she picked up the phone when it rang just before lunch, only to hear Judith Zamora's angry, "That's not the way to answer the phone. Haven't you ever been trained?"

Kate gritted her teeth. "What do you want?"

"To see you. Now. In my office."

"It's lunch," Kate told her as a pain began to build in her neck.

"Now!" The line went dead.

Kate had not been in this office since the day she was hired, and had forgotten just how precious it was with its dozens of knickknacks displayed on fake walnut shelves: ornate bird cages, tiny wooden laser-carved wolf's and coyote's heads, ceramic raccoons and beavers and other woodland friends. On the walls were plaques from the Sierra Club, Ducks Unlimited, and other do-gooder nature groups attesting to the occupant's concern for the broader community.

Zamora was behind her desk, actually a piece of smoked glass supported by two pieces of rough-hewn pink marble. She was dressed in her typical no-nonsense black, looking, no doubt purposely, like a judge about to pass sentence.

Kate took a chair, pink and armless, without being asked, and said, "What?" She was determined that this woman was not going to upset her.

Zamora flipped open a brown personnel folder as if it held a thousand secrets, and stared across the desk at Kate. "You're being placed on probation as of this moment. I don't care if Paul is on the board or not. He can't protect you any longer."

Kate felt herself come alive. *Paul?* she wondered. *Not "your husband?"*

Zamora waited for a response, and when she didn't get one, said, "Just so you know where we both stand, I've put in writing all the charges we're bringing against you. The purpose of probation is to alert you to the very real probability that you will be terminated. And to give you the chance, if you wish, or are able, to change your behavior."

"OK," said Kate, since Zamora seemed inclined not to go on until she responded.

Annoyed at Kate's seeming lack of concern, the other woman picked up the report and summarized the charges. "Frequent absences and tardiness over the past few weeks, neglect of duty, inability to get your work done on time, refusal to keep an appointment with our staff psychologist—"

"I was ordered not to by my attorney."

Zamora looked up from her desk. "I told them this was all a waste of time."

"Them? Who is *them?*"

"Hospital administrators. There is a widespread consensus that you are unfit to carry out your duties. But they wanted to give you one final chance."

Kate waved a dismissive hand, and felt her anger turn to disgust. *It doesn't matter what you people say,* she thought. *I can't be made to feel any worse than I already do. You are all smoke and mirrors; my son is all that matters now.*

"You were also rude to two investigators from Child Protective Services. That was completely uncalled for. We have to work with these people every day. They're in the same business you are."

"I didn't have time to talk to them. They're not after the truth anyway. They've already convicted me. Like you have."

"You see what I mean about your attitude?"

Kate felt like saying, What would your attitude be if you were being accused of harming your child? Or had just found out your husband had infected you with herpes? Instead she set her face in a blank stare. "Are we finished?"

Zamora handed the typed summary of accusations across

the glass desktop. "This is your copy. If I were you I'd give this a lot of thought. As I said, one more transgression and no one will be able to save you. Even Paul."

And suddenly Zamora's hostility was blindingly clear to Kate. It wasn't the woman's feeling for Joel Symonds after all. It was Paul. Her husband and her boss were having an affair. An empty feeling settled in her, and she thought, *I was wrong. I can be made to feel worse.*

"Our business is concluded," Zamora announced, standing up.

Kate also got to her feet. At the door she turned around. "Have you been tested for herpes yet?"

The woman stared at her, unsure what Kate was getting at.

"Do it," Kate said. "It's something we can share, the three of us."

25

Kate couldn't remember going back to her office. How dull our brains become just when we most need to reason things out, she thought as her eyes settled on her cluttered desktop. The scene in Zamora's office, designed by the other woman to be as hurtful as possible, had been meaningless to Kate— *What do I care about my job when I've just discovered my husband gave me herpes?* Then Zamora—dark-eyed, lithe, lynxlike Judith—let slip the truth about her and Paul (it *had* been accidental, hadn't it?), and the hurt set in, a pain that started somewhere behind her breastbone and radiated throughout her body.

Leaning forward, she rested her head in her hand, and time slowed, then stopped. When her body gave a sudden jerk, she thought, Did I pass out? She looked at the clock. She had been in her office only five minutes. *I'm going crazy. I'm losing my mind. Or it's the doxazosin.*

Her eyes moved to the uneven pile of mail that had arrived during her absence. A dozen brown interoffice envelopes, a magazine on family living, letters from vendors who evidently thought she had the authority to make purchase decisions, and a small paper-wrapped package. *Get to work*, she told herself. *Act as if it's any other day, and stop obsessing on your problems. It's the only way you'll make it to quitting time without breaking into sobs.*

Only half aware of what she was doing, she grabbed the package and ripped it open, taking out a videotape. The label was handlettered: *June 24.* No return address on the package. Now what? More harassment? A joke? One of those training videos on how to interview? After her other problems she couldn't worry about it now.

The interoffice mail would have to wait also; she had to update her files or Zamora would be all over her again. Pushing everything aside, she turned on the computer. Even before today's little drama her ability to keep up with the work had deteriorated. It had to be the doxazosin. How could a blood-pressure drug have gotten in her system? Someone had obviously put it in something she ate or drank. But who? That at least was simple: the person who was harassing her with threatening messages. But how did he manage to get the drug into her food?

Just then loud voices drew her attention to the open door. Mohammed Kamel and Frankie Yorba were walking by with a uniformed security guard who was evidently trying to explain something. Yorba glanced in her direction, then waved and smiled—or was it a smirk?—but Kamel merely shook his head. Go ahead, you bastards, Kate thought—laugh at me, Kate the crazy woman.

She looked again at the computer monitor with its annoying screen saver, and sighed. How far behind was she? Maybe if she came in on the weekend she could catch up. If she still had a job. She called up the first file and began to type. *Make your mind go blank; concentrate on the work.*

Patty came by on her way back from lunch. "Hey, I waited for you, but when you didn't show up I figured you went home."

Kate told her about the meeting in Zamora's office. "No more warnings. The next time I mess up I'm out." She couldn't bring herself to share her suspicions about Zamora and Paul.

Patty shook her head. "Jesus, does she know what you've been through lately?"

"I think she knows everything that goes on around here. About me, anyway."

"But doesn't care."

"I guess."

"Let me see that warning she gave you."

Kate handed it across the desk. Patty became increasingly agitated as she read it. "This is horse shit. Absences . . . Tardiness . . . What? *Rude* to Child Protective Services? Come on, are you working for Miss Manners now? Did she also catch you using the wrong fork at dinner?" She glanced at Kate. "What's really going on here? It can't be jealousy over Symonds. He told me he never went out with her."

"He said that?"

"We were talking about Zamora yesterday while you were being pounded on at the hearing. So why's the bitch after you? Just general envy of anyone prettier than her?"

Kate's lips drew together and she turned toward the computer so Patty wouldn't see the pain in her face. But the other woman's attention was drawn instead to the videotape on the desk. "Hey, what's this?"

Kate began to type, hoping Patty would get the message and leave. "I don't know. It just came in the mail. Look, I've got to get this form done before Kamel or Zamora jump on me again."

"You don't know what it is? Come on, Kate, maybe it's something sexy. Let me take it out to one of the VCRs next door and check it out."

"Just leave it, Patty. Everything doesn't have to involve sex."

Her friend feigned surprise. "Since when? Sex, chocolate, and lobster. What else is worth living for? Not this crummy job, that's for sure."

Kate looked at her watch. She could feel her pulse quicken. More than anything now she wanted to be alone. But since Patty didn't have to get back to her desk for five more minutes, Kate was stuck with her. Rather than let the conversation turn again to herself, she quickly asked, "How's Tammy doing? Is she still enjoying school?" All the time thinking, *Leave me alone. Please. Just go away!*

Patty shook her head in disgust. "She's enjoying it too much. They're this close to expelling her for disruptive behavior. They claim she has ADD. Do you know what that is?"

"Attention deficit disorder."

"That's what they said. I never heard of it. Is it something real or just a nineties name for goofing off?"

"Seems to be real. From what I've read, anyway."

"So what is it? A disease? A mental problem? How do you know someone has it? Do they have some sort of test?"

Kate's mind was wandering. Why had she brought this up? She didn't care about Tammy. Or Patty. All she could think of was Paul. "I don't know," she said abruptly. "I'm not an expert on that sort of thing, Patty. Talk to a doctor."

"Do you think someone around here could test her for it? I mean, I want to know if she's got a problem, if the school's going to make trouble for us. They can't kick her out if it's a medical problem, can they? Isn't there a law against that?"

Kate's eyes had gone to the coffee cup on her desk, and she suddenly began to wonder. *Who has access to the coffee around here? It comes from a coffeemaker in the emergency room, so any number of people could have put the doxazosin in it. But if they had, the whole ER would be affected.* So it would have to have been done after she brought it to her office. It never left her sight once she came in here. She picked up the cup and smelled. Nothing unusual. Then it probably didn't happen at work. Her throat tightened. *My God, it couldn't be Paul. He wouldn't.*

"Are you OK?" Patty was staring at her with concern.

Kate glanced away, biting her lower lip to keep the tears from her eyes. "I'm just not feeling well. Don't you have to get back to work?"

Patty looked at her watch. "Jeez, why didn't you tell me? Call me tonight and we'll talk. OK?"

Kate didn't respond. She looked at her watch. Four more hours until she could get out of here.

And what was she going to do when she got home?

26

"Yeah, yeah, stalkers," Nick Cerovic shouted into the phone as he paced behind his desk. He put his free hand to his ear and tried to block out the rumble of shift-change turmoil in the squad room.

"It's not that simple," said Dr. Leon Brazak, a police department psychologist based at Parker Center downtown. "There's more than one motive at work here."

Cerovic had never met Brazak but already didn't like him. "Well, *make* it simple. You've got three minutes."

The psychologist paused just a moment, the silence intended to show his irritation, which Cerovic didn't give a damn about. "Well, typically, we've dealt with two types in Los Angeles: the celebrity stalker—"

"This isn't a celebrity. It's a hospital worker, female, age thirty-four. Very attractive, but married." *Unfortunately.*

". . . and your type. Do you know the name of the stalker?"

"No."

"Anything at all about him?"

"He leaves messages on her computer. Calls her with threats."

"Ah! The spurned lover."

"She doesn't think she's spurned anyone."

"I've dealt with probably three or four dozen cases like this, Sergeant. Do you want a profile? At least ninety-five percent were male, Caucasian, never married, under thirty-five years of age, socially ill-adroit, if not completely inept. Somehow become convinced the woman is leading them on. Want me to be more specific? Usually they're between eighteen and twenty-eight, in an occupation where they don't have to deal with people very often. Frequently they're bright but have a view of reality we can only term bizarre, ergo the misread signals from the woman involved. Many of them, oddly, are science fiction fans. More and more lately we've found they are heavy Internet users, usually belonging to some on-line pornography service. A number of them are quite knowledgeable about programming and hacking, which might explain her computer messages.''

"And the five percent who don't fit this profile?"

"Are completely unique. They fit no profile, and are therefore extremely dangerous and impossible to pin down. Nothing about them is predictable, including their motives."

"You ever hear of one killing a cat and cutting out its sex organs?" Even though Kate wasn't the target, Cerovic thought there might be a connection.

"No, but it wouldn't be unusual. These people often have a fixation on sex, usually of a sort that involves pain."

"Are they likely to have any sexually related priors?"

"Some do. Peeping, exposing, masturbating in public. Usually nothing of an aggressive nature."

"Thanks, Doc." Cerovic hung up and thought, *Symonds? He doesn't exactly fit the ninety-five-percent mold, does he?* But his interest in Kate McDonald was obvious to Nick even if it didn't seem to be to her. Sometimes women were naive about these things, though. And he'd have the knowledge and skill to remove the sex organs of a cat. But the cat belonged to Patty Mars, and had been left on her desk. So it might not have anything to do with Kate's problem. Still, who besides Symonds was into surgery?

Maybe he should get a listing of all hospital employees and get someone to run their records, looking for anything interesting. In the meantime he wanted to check out the report from social services. They were supposed to fax it to him this afternoon. He rooted around the mess on his desk, not finding it, so went out to the photocopy room, where the fax machine was, and discovered it in the pile of undistributed paperwork. He began reading while walking back to his desk: Upon trying to interview Kate McDonald the two investigators were met with hostility and verbal abuse. Ms. McDonald refused to cooperate and stormed out, leaving them in her office. When she hadn't returned an hour later they left. It was their opinion that Ms. McDonald's attitude was sufficient basis for the police department to follow up by investigating the circumstances surrounding the care and treatment of the child, Alexander Paul McDonald, and in particular certain incidents resulting in harm to the child, to wit, unexplained bruises on his arms and legs, being severely bitten by rats, and becoming infected by a rare strain of influenza.

And they don't even know about the herpes, Cerovic thought. *Not good for the mom, not at all. And worse for the poor kid, of course. God, the misery he's been through.*

He looked over at the wall clock. Half past four. Annie had been gone for an hour, and here he still was, trying to make things fit that probably weren't meant to. But something was keeping him here, wouldn't let him go.

The something being Kate McDonald.

So what is it? he wondered. *You going gaga over the mama? That's what DeSilva thinks.* But hell, that wasn't it at all. Nick hadn't had romantic feelings for anyone since Beth died. He'd just sort of put that part of his life in a drawer and closed it forever because he knew that Beth was an accident that would never be duplicated. No one could even come close. Damn, he thought with a smile, who besides Beth would have put up with his weird enthusiasms—sports, opera, toy banks, and now large hairy dogs? Anyway, cops weren't exactly in the Kate McDonald class. Already married to a hotshot DA, she lived in the sort of Brentwood neighborhood Cerovic could expect only to visit on official business. Add to that a salary that was about $200,000 less than the lowest-paid doctor at Midtown, most of whom probably had their hooks out for Kate McDonald already, and there was no point in even trying to compete.

So you're wrong, Annie. It ain't romance; it's curiosity.

Really! And a sense that this woman is doing a lot of suffering no one but she knows about.

Still standing, he closed the report and picked up the file

he'd started on Kate McDonald. So far there was damn little to look at. That in itself was strange. He'd run her name through the state crime computer and come up blank. So she hadn't been arrested, at least in California, or under that name. Her licensing as a social worker hadn't turned up anything in her past to worry about. On the other hand, he knew she hadn't had a driver's license until five years ago. That bothered him at first, but she said she'd lived in St. Louis before that. OK. He had already faxed the hospital she claimed to work for back there and was awaiting an answer. Which, he felt certain, was that they had no record of her.

What he really wanted to do was run her through the NCIC—the FBI computer back in D.C. that would indicate arrests anywhere in the country. But he'd need her fingerprints and she—as well as her tight-ass DA hubby—wasn't about to agree to that. And he didn't want to try to get the prints from the Department of Motor Vehicles because her hubby would find out about that, too, and Nickie didn't want to go to war with the DA's office right now. *So don't ask anyone. Get the prints some other way and run them without their permission.* Wouldn't be hard; he'd done it any number of times before.

Dropping the file, he walked over to the coffee machine on a stained metal table by the lieutenant's office, poured himself a cup, and went back to his desk. Still standing, he sipped the coffee and looked again at the file. Kate McDonald. Katherine, no doubt. He didn't even know her maiden name. Or where she was born. Or anything else about her. Only that she supposedly had worked in St. Louis, and was married to a low-level grunt in the DA's office. That was a bit too much mystery for someone in this day and age, when files and databases held everyone's history back to conception.

Almost everyone's.

Pulling out the chair, he sat down and moved aside some papers on the desk. He'd started a file on Paul McDonald, too, though he didn't tell Annie. She'd start in on his supposed interest in Kate, and he didn't want to go through all that again. What was it with Annie lately? She acted like a jealous schoolgirl. She couldn't suddenly have been developing a romantic interest in him, could she? No, they'd worked together for two years. If Annie had had some sort of romantic interest she would have shown it before now. Anyway, she was twelve years younger than Nick, though it might as well have been fifty years. She listened to singers Nick had never even heard of, went to movies he wouldn't see on a bet, and thought figure skating was a sport. No, it'd never work. They lived in different worlds.

He flipped open the file on Paul McDonald. Age thirty-two, graduated from UCLA, then went on to a small private law school in the Valley, one of those places for people who don't have the grades or LSAT scores for an established law school. He'd worked as a clerk in a supermarket, and attended school at night, taking five years to do what would have taken three if he'd gone full-time. Lived with mommy and daddy while in law school. Nothing wrong with that, Nick supposed, though a little bit of him wondered if he was a mamma's boy. Those were usually the ones with weird sexual interests.

In McDonald's last year of law school he'd married Kate. She would have been thirty, Paul twenty-eight. He'd passed the bar on the first try. Not bad. And been hired by the city. Which meant he had a noble desire to better the world by putting bad guys in the hoosegow. Or was it because nobody else wanted to hire him? The DA's office didn't attract graduates of big-time law schools, most of whom made five times more than a city job by working for a major law firm. *OK, give McDonald the benefit of the doubt: he's a dedicated crime fighter, the Dick Tracy of the California Criminal Code.*

Nick had never met him.

Then why do I dislike him?

More to the point, how do I check up on a deputy DA without making waves? Probably can't.

He left the file open and opened Kate's next to it. His eyes shifted back and forth from file to file. *One of you is going to be big trouble for me. Paul or Kate. So which one is it?*

He suddenly lifted his head and glanced around the squad room. "Jimmy! Jimmy Soto!" None of the other cops looked up as Cerovic bellowed for the fourteen-year-old Explorer Scout who did odd jobs for the detective bureau each afternoon.

"Hey, Cerovic." It was Sal DeCarlo, a vice dick who grew up in Michigan, yelling from his desk twenty feet away. "Angels are playing the Tigers in Detroit tonight. Wanna go fifty?"

Cerovic tried to remember who was pitching. "Straight up?"

"Sure."

"Make it a hundred."

"Fifty. I'm still in to you for two hundred."

"You lose, I'll take your Lakers-Bulls tickets in December."

Jimmy Soto, a wiry Hispanic kid about five feet tall, appeared out of nowhere.

"Can't do it," DeCarlo said. "I couldn't afford to renew my Lakers tickets. The price keeps going up. If you're not Jack Nicholson you're priced out of the game. I'm buying Clippers tickets instead."

Nick shuddered. "Forget it; I'll take the cash. Fifty it is." He turned to the kid. "What are you up to, Jimmy?"

"Looking at pictures of hookers. They got this book in Vice—"

"You're only fourteen. What the hell kind of job they got you doing?"

He jammed his hands in his back pockets. "No job. I'm looking at pictures of hookers."

Cerovic shook his head. "Well, I want you to do some telephoning for me. Call Midtown Memorial Hospital and get them to fax a list of all their employees, even part-timers. Then I want you to match it against registered sex offenders. You can get that from your buddies in Vice. Got it?"

"Yes, sir."

"Then get moving. And Jimmy."

The kid turned around.

"You call me 'sir' again and I'll take your picture book away."

It's unraveling, Kate thought as she sat at the kitchen table,
staring at a huge crystal vase holding a dozen of Paul's roses.
*My life's coming apart like cobwebs in a storm. Everything
I've built up is going to be taken from me.*

But she was beyond tears now, beyond any emotion except
resignation as a dull numbness hummed in her mind. The afternoon had passed in a blur. After Patty left her office she remembered nothing, not sitting at her desk, not driving to Mrs.
Alamada's, not coming home. But now, with Alex crawling
around her feet and playing with a stuffed Big Bird on the tile
floor, the day came roaring back in a tidal wave of details:
Nick Cerovic asking her about the phone threats . . . learning
she and Paul had herpes . . . Judith Zamora threatening to fire
her, and the joy the woman seemed to take in the prospect . . .
the doxazosin in her system . . .

*Doxazosin! No wonder I've felt like hell for so long! It's
the drug, isn't it? It wasn't me. I'm not going mad! But who
besides Paul could have given it to me without my knowledge?*

She jumped up, almost stepping on Alex, and began to yank
open kitchen cabinets, pulling out pots and pans and dishes
and glasses, letting them drop on the countertop, determined
to find the drug. Paul had to have hidden it nearby so he could
slip it into her coffee at breakfast. Or did he carry it downstairs
in his pocket and then put it in her cup when she wasn't looking?
But wouldn't it take time to dissolve? Maybe he had it in
powdered form, or liquid. She knew nothing of the drug, how
it was formulated, whether it had a taste.

It was nowhere in the cupboards. Leaving the pots and pans

and dishes on the drainboard, she began to pull open drawers, yanking everything out, dropping it on the floor or counter. If it wasn't here she'd go upstairs and check the bedroom and bathrooms. He had to have it close enough to get to without causing her to wonder what he was doing. Maybe it was in the pocket of one of his shirts in the closet. She would never have run across it there.

She got down on her knees and pulled out the larger pans she seldom used, along with electric appliances she hadn't seen since opening their wedding presents. Nothing, nothing, nothing! So it must be upstairs.

She started to push from the floor when the other question hit her, the one she should have considered since the beginning. *Why* would Paul do this? The breath rushed out of her as she sank back against the stove, her mind churning. Why did her husband want her sick and anxious all the time?

Alex began crying and crawled along her leg, pushing aside a set of plastic bowls. Kate pulled him up on her torso, and without thinking undid the buttons on her blouse and pulled it off. She wasn't wearing a nursing bra. She had determined to finish weaning Alex this week. But she didn't have the energy to get up and prepare his bottle. Unclipping her bra, she brought Alex to her breast and he began to nurse. Ten minutes later he started to squirm. He wanted to crawl around the floor some more, and play with the pots and pans. Kate put him down and rose to her feet, the sudden movement making her dizzy. Her purse was on the table, along with silverware pulled from two of the drawers. She saw the videotape she had brought home from work sticking out of it.

Paul came home an hour later. He dropped his briefcase on the floor when he saw Kate sitting on the couch as though dazed, wearing only her slacks. Through the entry to the kitchen he could see open drawers and cupboard doors, dishes and glasses strewn everywhere. "What happened?" he asked. "Are you OK? What's going on?"

Kate picked up the remote to the TV and pushed a button. In an instant the screen came alive with a color video of Paul having sex with a woman whose blond hair—a wig?—had been made into two-foot-long pigtails.

Paul stood frozen.

The camera didn't move. The woman contrived to keep her face hidden, but Paul was unmistakable. She crawled between his legs, took his erection in her hand.

Paul said, "I don't know how . . ." She could barely hear him, his voice strained, as though pulled reluctantly from the deepest reaches of his soul. He couldn't finish, the words dying away. When Kate looked over at him without emotion, he jerked suddenly alive, his body in motion, eyes darting and arms waving. Kate could almost see his mind working, as it did in court when he was caught off guard. Then came the predictable excuses, the whining and the exculpations: "Too many drinks . . . I didn't mean . . . She did it to me. . . ."

"She did it?" Kate shouted, her body turning warm. "Look at the tape, Paul. Is she forcing you to do that?"

Still his feet seemed rooted to the floor. His face colored, but he wouldn't look at the TV. "I mean it wasn't my idea."

Kate's voice lowered. "Who is it?"

"I don't know. I met her at a get-together in a bar after work one day. She started coming on to me, telling me how she admired me. . . ."

"Oh, come on, Paul. You don't know her name? This woman who admires you so much she filmed you?"

"Sheila something. I don't remember."

"So you just started screwing Sheila Something because she thought you were a wonderful prosecuting attorney and obviously deserved the pleasure of her company? Jesus!"

"I was drunk, Kate. Believe me. I don't know what happened. We were talking. The next thing I knew we were in a room at the Hilton."

"Gee, maybe she slipped you some doxazosin."

"What are you talking about?"

"Paul, that isn't the damn Hilton. Look at it. That's her bedroom."

"Kate, for Christ's sake. It was a mistake. I don't know how it happened. I was flattered that this attractive woman was fascinated with me. It was just my ego. It wasn't an ongoing thing.''

"How often?"

He looked at her, his jaw setting as he worked it out. "Twice."

"No good, Paul. Twice times twenty, maybe. Twice times fifty."

"Honestly, Kate. She didn't mean anything to me. I just . . . did it. Something to do."

"What a wonderful thing to tell your wife. Sex is just something to do. With a stranger."

"Kate, it stopped months ago. I only saw her twice. The last time was February."

"There's a date stamp on the video at the beginning. It says June twenty-fourth. That was the night you said you were with your do-gooder friends at a Save the Bay committee meeting. I checked the calendar."

Paul seemed to shrink inside his clothes.

Kate turned her attention to the video. "I don't see where she's any better than me. She's certainly not any better-looking, is she? And what's with the blond pigtails? Is this some sort of German milkmaid fantasy of yours? Or maybe she's a great conversationalist. Is that it? When you weren't screwing you two spent your time talking about tort law, or the buildup of plankton off the coast?"

Paul wouldn't look at her.

"You have herpes, by the way. The lab called today. I guess we know where it came from, don't we? Good ol' Sheila the milkmaid. Unless you got it from Judith Zamora. It must be hard to keep these affairs separated in your mind."

His voice turned ugly. "What's that supposed to mean?"

"Your friend Judith told me you and she have been having an affair."

"No, she didn't. It's not true."

Kate flicked off the television. "I don't think you'd know what's true if it hit you in the face."

"Kate." Paul moved suddenly in her direction, tried to touch her, but she jumped back as though struck. "Let me apologize.

Please. I made a mistake. We all make mistakes. Just let me apologize to you. It won't happen again. I promise.''

"I'm not a priest, Paul. You can't absolve your sins by confessing. You're a shit. You betrayed your wife and you gave your son herpes."

"My God, it was this one woman! How can I make you believe that?"

"No, Paul, it wasn't. Don't treat me like an idiot."

His face closed up; he was getting angry. Always the safe response, Kate thought; when backed into a corner, attack. She came to her feet. "Where do you keep the doxazosin?"

"What are you talking about? I don't even know what that word means."

"When you play stupid you look stupid. Where is it?"

"Jesus, Kate, you're going off the deep end now. You're out of control. Do you want me to get you some Prozac? God knows I've thought about it often enough, the weird moods you get in."

"Exactly. I'm crazy, I think someone is trying to poison me, I think someone's threatening me, and I'm trying to harm my baby. Maybe I ought to be locked up."

Paul suddenly looked worried. "Where is he, Kate? Where's Alex?"

"I killed him. Is that what you think? I drove a stake through his heart and put him in our bed. Along with a dozen rats you got out of the hospital lab."

He kept his voice calm. "Kate, where is Alex?"

"I don't know. After about the twentieth time he got tired of watching his father on the video and left. I don't know where he is."

"Christ!" Paul spun around. "You are crazy, Kate. You're certifiably nuts." He turned toward the kitchen and stopped when he saw all the pots and pans on the counter and table. "What are you doing, taking the house apart?"

"I'm looking for *secrets,* Paul. How many more do you have?"

He hurried into the kitchen. Alex was in his playpen, asleep. Paul came back into the living room and seemed to register for the first time that Kate was wearing nothing but slacks. "Don't you think you ought to get dressed? What if someone comes to the door?"

She paid him no attention. "Aren't you curious why she filmed you? This Sheila Something of yours? Why did she tape your little romp in bed? And why send it to me?"

Paul hesitated. It had evidently not occurred to him before. "I guess she's trying to hurt me. She wanted to make trouble. She succeeded, didn't she?"

"You're a complete bastard, Paul. She didn't do anything but let me find that out. If I knew her name I'd thank her. But in the meantime, we're getting a divorce. Do you understand?"

"Kate, you're upset."

"You're goddamn right I'm upset. And it changes nothing." She went back in the kitchen and sat at the table, where she could see Alex.

That night in bed, Paul in the guest bedroom next door, Kate lay awake and stared at the total darkness of her surroundings. How had her life fallen apart so quickly? Two weeks ago she had been happier than she could recall ever being. A wonderful husband, a beautiful child, a job she enjoyed despite the bureaucracy and office politics of working in a hospital. Maybe this was the penalty for being too happy. *Pride goeth before a fall. And after the fall? An end to happiness, an end to life.*

She could hear Paul moving about out in the hallway. What was he doing out there? Hiding the doxazosin? *I never knew you, did I? Even though I thought I did. I never really knew who you were.*

They had met at a party for a coworker of hers who was moving to Texas. It had been held at the woman's apartment complex in Playa del Rey, and Kate had been standing near the pool with a glass of white wine when Robert Redford walked up and said, "Hi, I'm Paul McDonald, and you're bored stiff." Well, it hadn't been Robert Redford, of course—it was the hair and the smile—but he did see what no one else had noticed or cared about, that she hated being there, where she knew almost no one, and longed to leave but couldn't without being rude.

"Kate Coleman," she said, holding out her free hand, and feeling her heart give a little jump. How long since that had happened?

He took her hand and didn't let go. "I know. I already asked. Amy says you're shy."

Amy was the guest of honor, and had known Kate for only a few months, but evidently considered herself an expert on Kate's mental state. Kate smiled uneasily. "It's not a disease."

"And not unattractive. Come on, we'll make our excuses and go somewhere we want to be."

"Where would that be?"

"I haven't any idea at all. Let me put my psychic powers to work." He closed his eyes and touched his forehead as though in deep thought. "I see you at the beach. You're walking hand in hand with a young man. Your shoes are in your free hand. I think ... I think it's, yes, yes, it must be ... Santa Monica. And there's a wonderful restaurant nearby where you can have dinner and watch the sun sink into the Pacific." His eyes opened. "Correct?"

"No," Kate said, and put her glass down. "It's Malibu, not Santa Monica. I'll show you the restaurant."

And so began their seven-month courtship, ending with an abrupt wedding not even their parents had been invited to, performed in Las Vegas by an odd little man in spats, a permed hairdo, and a lime green tuxedo. "It could have been worse." Paul laughed as they walked out onto the Strip. "At least he wasn't an Elvis impersonator."

Among the congratulations received from friends was a call from Amy in Texas. "So you actually caught our most eligible? Well"—here she paused long enough for Kate to wonder about it—"good luck to you."

Paul had nine more months of law school to complete. They moved into Kate's apartment in Palms, Paul traveling out to the Valley each day, and Kate working for Midtown Hospital on the second shift. Paul had never lived apart from his parents before, and Kate had harbored some secret concern about his ability to share equally in a marriage after having a mother do everything for him for twenty-eight years. But it had worked out from the beginning, Paul taking part in the housework and even the cooking, despite having to study for school, and then the bar. He had a remarkable quality of being able to patch up arguments before they became serious, and he alone of all the men she had known understood how to keep her laughing, with his offbeat and often weird sense of humor. She appreciated how he never probed too deeply about her past, demanding to know, as others had, about her lovers and her life before they met. Mostly she liked that he accepted her as she was, and didn't feel the need to point out shortcomings she was only too aware of. She felt an equal partner in their marriage, and thought herself fortunate to have found him.

Other women must have seen it, too, the magic in their relationship, and sought to duplicate it. *How many other Sheilas or Judiths have there been, Paul? And did they want to marry you, or only take you to bed? Did you resist? Did you ever say no, or did you just ask where to meet them?*

Suddenly she drew up a thousand incidents from the past four years she'd never given a second's thought to: Paul working late on cases ... all the civic groups he belonged to because it would help his career ... even those times when he was supposedly driving Alex around, trying to get him to sleep. When had it all started? She recalled—God, her subconscious was really working on it now—the day they had returned from Las Vegas, and Paul had been summoned to the office to work on a particularly vital case and hadn't returned until past midnight. *How stupid I've been! How many women were there, Paul? Will I ever find out?*

One at least wanted to destroy your marriage. And she succeeded. What will you say to her now? Why does she hate you so to do this? Do you even know?

Again she could hear Paul moving around out in the hallway. *Go back to bed,* she thought as she finally fell asleep. *You'll wake my baby walking around out there.*

July 22

There's something special—unique—about depression. I don't mean unhappiness but real, clinical depression. It's not an illness but almost a living thing that clamps its ugliness onto your heart, and puts your life on a new plane, one I wouldn't wish on anyone. You sit in the same chair for hours, staring out the window, unable to move. And then for no reason you start to cry and you can't stop, and it happens so often and for so long you don't want to live anymore because all you want now is for the pain to go away, just stop! Stop. Please! But only death will do that. And suddenly this wonderful new option opens up: death, nonexistence, nothingness. An end to pain, and an end to suffering. Why not? What difference would it make? The world won't weep. Someone will miss me, sure, perhaps even feel sad for a while, and then put it out of his head. But that huge, dark mass that held us down so long will no longer exist, and its horrible weight will be lifted suddenly from the world.

But if you get past this point, where all that matters is your own death, you move to the next, final, but inevitable, stage, where it isn't your death that now consumes you, but that of the other. It's all we think about, you and I, isn't it—death? One more murder?

But it also made me think: how could I repay you for all the misery you've brought to me? Of course . . . I go after you where you're most vulnerable.

Hang on, Katie Kate. I have a surprise. . . .

28

Kate woke up suddenly when she heard Alex crying. *My God, somethings's happened to him!* She sat up as her heart began to pound. *Not again, please. No!* Then she remembered: *I forgot to feed him!* After refusing to argue any more with Paul, refusing even to talk to him, she had sat on the couch in front of the turned-off TV until close to nine, then taken Alex upstairs to his crib, without thinking that he had missed his dinner. Had he been crying then? She couldn't even remember. A piercing wave of despair accompanied the guilt: *Don't let Alex suffer because of your problems.* Then she thought, *Too late for that. Alex has already suffered more than any child should.*

His crying got louder, and she glanced at the clock as she pushed out of bed. Nine minutes after two. She walked quickly past the guest bedroom where Paul slept, his snoring, like the sputtering of a diesel engine, audible through the closed door, and down to the nursery. Leaving the light off she crossed over to the crib, where Alex was stretched out on his stomach, his voice sounding odd, strained. He must be starved; this was the longest he had ever gone without eating. "Hungry, hon? I'm so sorry I didn't feed you earlier. All right—time for a late-night snack."

She pulled the left side of her nightgown down, exposing her breast. "Last time, little guy. You need to stick to bottles after this."

As she brought the child to her, only half watching in the darkness as his lips went around her nipple, she suddenly started screaming hysterically, and almost dropped him to the floor. *"It's not Alex, my God, this isn't my baby!"*

* * *

Two policemen stood in the living room, taking notes and talking to Paul, while a third wandered around, looking at the books in the bookcase and the pictures on the walls as though he were interested in buying the house. Kate, wearing a bathrobe, was bent over on the couch, hugging her knees and unable to stop crying. A policewoman held the infant Kate had found in the nursery, and was wandering back and forth trying to calm it.

When the police had arrived in response to Paul's call, they found Kate hysterical, screaming that someone had stolen her baby. They calmed her with difficulty, the policewoman forcing her down on the couch and threatening to handcuff her if she didn't stay seated. The officer in charge, a patrol sergeant named Sowers, had tried to question Kate, but she was too overwrought to answer coherently. With his notebook out, he had turned to Paul, who seemed to be in a daze of disbelief.

"I woke up as soon as I heard the screaming and ran to the nursery." Paul closed his eyes and squeezed the bridge of his nose as though he could somehow force everything that had happened tonight to disappear. "I wasn't even sure who it was. It didn't sound like Kate; it sounded . . . I don't know . . . like a madwoman."

Sowers looked at him. "Wasn't it obvious when you got up that your wife wasn't in bed?"

Paul hesitated. "I was sleeping in the guest bedroom. We had a disagreement."

Unable to control herself, Kate leaped up. "We're getting a divorce, you bastard! It's not 'a disagreement'!"

One of the other policemen touched Kate on the arm, trying to urge her down on the couch again, but she angrily pulled away. The policewoman, still holding the baby, came toward her, her tone now threatening. "Mrs. McDonald." Kate slowly sank down, her head in her hands, and her body trembling with cold.

Making a notation on his pad, Sowers said to Paul, "You were arguing tonight?"

Kate's head snapped up and she glared at her husband. He turned from her and said reluctantly, "Yes."

"About . . . ?"

"It's not important." Paul shook his head back and forth. His hair was uncombed, strewn across his forehead like a little boy's, and he was wearing only pajama bottoms. To Sowers, who had seen hundreds of them, he looked like an accident victim, too stunned and disoriented to help, but the questions still had to be asked. Paul brought his palms to his eyes and rubbed. "It's a personal matter. It had nothing to do with Alex."

Kate muttered, "Oh, God," and her head sank down on her chest as she started sobbing again.

Two policemen came down the stairs and approached Sowers. "Nothing out of place in the nursery. Two windows, both locked."

Sowers turned to the patrolman who had been wandering around. "Tony?"

The man turned his palms up. "I checked the back door and garage. No sign of a break-in."

Sowers grimaced. Obviously this was more than normally upsetting to him, and he seemed not quite sure how to proceed. "All right, take Wainright and check outside." His tone indicated he didn't expect them to turn anything up. He looked again at Paul. "And you still don't have any idea how this could have happened, how someone could have gotten inside, taken your baby, and left this one?"

Paul was miserable. He shook his head, and his voice could hardly be heard. "Nothing."

"Or why? Why would someone *leave* a child?"

Again Paul shook his head. "It could have been someone who's been harassing me. A parolee, Leo Petrosian." He explained about the recently released prisoner.

Sowers turned to one of the patrolmen. "Call the lieutenant. See if he wants an APB on Petrosian."

Kate suddenly jumped up and started screaming at her husband. "What did you do to my baby? Where is he?" She was nearly hysterical, her hands gripped into fists at her sides, and her face covered with perspiration.

The baby the policewoman was holding started howling, and she began to rock it back and forth, trying to comfort it.

Paul recoiled at the accusation. "Honey, I didn't—"

"Goddamn you! I heard you walking around during the night."

"No," he said, obviously surprised. "You couldn't have. I was asleep from eleven to when I heard you screaming, two o'clock, something like that."

"You goddamn liar! I was awake most of the night. I heard you walking around out there. I heard you in the hallway."

Paul shook his head as if this latest accusation were more than he could bear, but Sowers seemed interested. "How do you know it was your husband?"

"I've been married to him for four years. I know what he sounds like in the hallway."

Keeping his voice calm, Sowers said to Paul, "Are you sure you weren't up at all? You didn't go to the bathroom?"

Paul shook his head, wincing; *This is too absurd even to comment on,* he seemed to be saying.

Kate lost the scant control she had on her emotions. "What did you do with my baby? I've got to find him!" She started running toward the front door. The policewoman stepped in front of her just as the two patrolmen came in from outside. "No sign of forced entry anywhere," one of them said. "If someone came in they had a key. Or were let in."

"Oh, God," Kate said, and collapsed against the policewoman who handed the baby to one of the patrolmen, then escorted Kate to the couch and sat down next to her.

Sowers turned to Paul. "Maybe you'd better leave us for a few minutes."

"Why?" His guard was suddenly up; he didn't want Kate talking to the police without his being there.

"I'm not really asking," Sowers said evenly.

"Then we refuse to talk without an attorney being present."

"Get out!" Kate screamed at him, coming halfway out of the couch. "Leave! Now! Goddamn you!"

Paul glared at her, his fury obvious. Then he spun around and stalked out of the room. Sowers turned to Kate. His voice was surprisingly sympathetic. "Tell us what you think happened here tonight, Mrs. McDonald."

Kate stared up at him from the couch. "Paul took Alex. To get back at me."

"Get back at you for what?"

"For catching him with his girlfriends. For telling him I'm going to divorce him. For taking Alex out of his life." She bent over, her arms wrapped around her knees again. "Because he hates me!"

The policewoman put her hand on Kate's back. "Tell us what happened when you went to bed."

For a long moment Kate stared at the floor, unable to speak, coughing and sobbing as though she couldn't keep air in her lungs. Glancing at the woman sitting next to her, she noticed a name tag on her uniform: *Edgars.* She remembered someone calling her Lucy. Kate looked away, tried to breathe slowly, finally forcing herself to speak. "I took Alex up to his room about nine. I had forgotten to feed him, but he wasn't crying, just sucking on his pacifier. I put him in the crib, then went to bed. But I couldn't get to sleep. I just lay there."

"Where was your husband?"

"I don't know. He left the house about seven. Maybe earlier. He said he was going for a walk. I didn't ask him where. I didn't care."

"He wasn't here when you went to bed?"

Kate shook her head.

"Did you lock the doors?"

"I didn't care about the doors. I just picked up Alex and took him upstairs. Then I went to bed."

"And didn't sleep at all?" Sowers asked.

Kate's head jerked up. Her face was flushed and covered with tears. "How is this helping to find my baby? You act like I took him. Why aren't you out looking?"

"People *are* looking, Mrs. McDonald. Every hospital in the city has been notified. We'll have Alex's picture on television by the morning news. Someone will recognize him if he's out there.''

"If he's out there? What does that mean?''

The policewoman said, "We'll find him. I promise. We almost always find missing babies.'' She paused a moment. "Do you recognize the child that was in the crib? Have you ever seen him before?''

Kate almost dissolved. "God, no. I've *never* seen him. I never want to see him again.''

"Mrs. McDonald.'' Sowers's tone seemed to have become more official. He looked at her, his pen in his hand, obviously befuddled but ready to record her response. "Can you imagine why someone would do something so unusual like this? It's not like any kidnapping I've ever heard of. What would the person be accomplishing by taking your baby and leaving this baby?''

"I don't know! Unless he's trying to get back at me.''

"Leo Petrosian?'' he asked. His tone indicated skepticism.

She shook her head back and forth and couldn't stop crying. "I don't know. . . . Maybe.'' Her mind wouldn't focus, wouldn't slow down and allow her to think rationally. But she suddenly remembered the threats at work. "Someone's been calling me at the hospital and saying things, trying to scare me. And sending me threats on e-mail. Sergeant Cerovic was looking into it—''

"Cerovic?'' Lucy Edgars said. "He's in a sex-crimes unit. Why were you talking to him?''

"Alex has herpes,'' Kate blurted out, and started shaking again.

Edgars and Sowers looked at each other. Edgars frowned and shook her head. "I'll call him.''

Sowers asked, "Was Cerovic investigating you? Were you suspected of causing Alex's herpes?''

Kate's fury leaped out. "They think I was hurting him. But I wasn't—'' She caught herself using the wrong tense. "I'm *not* abusing him. It was just a series of accidents.''

"What kind of accidents?''

"I'm not going to tell you! It's not important. Why are you

asking me these questions? I didn't take Alex and I didn't hurt him! I want my baby! Why aren't you out looking for him? He might be nearby."

"Sergeant."

Paul was standing in the hallway that led to Kate's little-used sewing room. Sowers glanced at Kate, then went over to him. Paul seemed to be too upset to speak. As Kate's eyes watched him with hatred, he merely motioned for the policeman to follow, then walked past a bedroom to the darkened sewing room and flipped on the light. Alex was asleep in a playpen, a bottle of apple juice next to him.

Paul looked as though he was going to collapse. All he could say was, "I don't know, I don't know. . . ."

Kate appeared suddenly in the doorway. When she saw Alex she began screaming and couldn't stop. A policeman grabbed her from behind as she tried to rush toward the playpen. The baby woke up at once and started crying.

Sowers shook his head and said to Paul, "You don't have any idea how he got here?"

"Jesus," Paul muttered, and looked at Kate as though he wanted to kill her. "Isn't it obvious?"

Officer Edgars came into the room holding the other infant. When Kate saw the two of them her screaming increased. "I want Alex! Let me have him."

Sowers stepped in front of her. "Not now. We'd better take both babies to the hospital for tests. Then we'll decide what to do."

"Tests?" Kate screamed. "What kind of tests? What are you talking about?"

"Let the doctors decide. We'll take them to Cedars Sinai, they do all the medical exams for us. Then I'm afraid the two of you will have to come down to the station house for questioning."

Paul sank into a chair but said nothing. Kate asked loudly, "What kind of questioning? You don't think *we* did this, do you? You don't think I stole my own baby? My God!"

Sowers said, "This is going to take a while to sort out. I'm not the one to do it. We'll let the department decide what to do with you. I'm going to read both of you your rights. Then we'll go to Cedars.''

Five minutes later as they walked out to the police cars, Kate not being allowed to hold Alex, she could see a light on in the living room next door and someone, she couldn't tell who, peering at them through the venetian blinds.

29

They stood in the ER waiting room, Kate and Paul, a half dozen uniformed cops, two howling infants, nurses, doctors, orderlies. A radio in the background was playing rap music, the loud, repetitive sound like a hammer pounding inside Kate's head. The doctor in charge of the ER, a gruff, middle-aged man named Salvi, was making hurried notations on a patient chart. "Is Alex on any kind of medication?"

"For swine flu," Kate said absently. She could barely make her mind calm down from the madness of the past two hours. Why was she here? Why did all these people want to talk to her? She ought to be home, taking care of her baby.

The doctor's round, bald head instantly shot up from his clipboard. He needed a shave, and his massive eyebrows jerked together as his voice rose. "Swine flu?"

Sergeant Sowers's voice turned angry. "You told me he had herpes."

"Both," Kate told them. She started to explain in greater detail, but quickly thought better of it. Everyone was already convinced she was responsible for what had happened; it was better to keep her mouth shut.

The doctor glared at her with undisguised loathing and asked what kind of medication Alex was taking. When Kate didn't respond Paul told him. The doctor said, "What do we know about the other infant?"

No one knew anything.

"Mrs. McDonald?" the doctor said pointedly, expecting her to provide some information.

"Why would I know anything? I never saw him before tonight." She could feel her control evaporating again, and the fingers of her right hand began to tap against her leg.

Dr. Salvi said something to a nurse, who hurriedly took the other child back to the infant ward beyond a pair of green swinging doors. To no one in particular, Salvi asked, "Do we not even know the child's name?"

Sowers said, "On the way over we had a report of a kidnapping from the children's ward at Queen of Angels about eleven last night. There was no other information, but it must be the same child. You could have someone call over."

"Of course." He barked out an order to a young MD standing next to him, and she disappeared toward the back. Then he said, "The kidnapped child was discovered *inside* the McDonalds' house?" He was speaking to the policeman now, evidently not trusting anything Kate or Paul might say. From his manner it seemed he was confused about the chain of events.

Sowers nodded and said, "And *their* child was missing briefly. He was discovered elsewhere in the house."

"*In* the house!" Salvi shook his head, started to write, then asked, "How do you know this *is* their child?"

Paul and Kate exploded at once. Sowers said, "Calm down! I mean it, or I'll have you both booked for disturbing the peace. If not something more serious." When they quieted he said, "You have a birth certificate at home?"

"Of course we do," Paul said. "I'll bring it by today and you can check the footprints. But, my God, don't you think you people are going overboard on the accusations?"

"No one is accusing you of anything," a pleasant voice behind them announced. They turned to see a middle-aged black man in a dark suit approaching; he smiled but didn't offer to shake hands. "Derek Quarles, detective lieutenant with Hollywood homicide."

"Homicide?" Kate said with apprehension.

Paul brushed her concerns aside. "They handle kidnapping, too."

Quarles's smile broadened. "Paul McDonald! My, my, my. I wondered if it was you when I heard the name. Strange place to run into a deputy DA."

Paul looked to be on the verge of exhaustion. "We don't know what's going on, Lieutenant. Someone exchanged babies with Alex—" He halted, unable or unwilling to go on.

"Oh, come now," Quarles said with a friendly smile. His voice was soft but cajoling, tinged with sarcasm. "You must have some idea why this happened. People always have ideas. Try one out on me."

Paul's gaze started to go to Kate, then halted. He said, "It's probably just harassment."

"Probably? That means you must have another explanation, too. The *un*probable one. And what would that be?" He was still smiling, pleased with his reasoning. Paul was angered by the man's smugness, but Kate was beyond caring. She just wanted to take Alex home.

Paul's jaw set. "My family is being harassed by a released felon. Leo Petrosian. You should know that. I filed a report."

"Ah! I do know, in fact. Well, maybe so. I don't know why a seriously disturbed dude like Petrosian would want to play switch-the-baby with you, though. I think his mind is somewhat more basic than that." He consulted his notebook. "The kid who ended up in your house is Angel Hernandez, age nine months, hospitalized for fever, nothing serious. He was scheduled to be released this morning. His mother's having a fit, of course. She's still at Queen of Angels. I guess we should bring her over here." He put his notebook away and smiled at Paul. "So tell me about the harassment."

Once again Paul explained about Petrosian's phone calls.

"We had a be-on-the-lookout for him. That you who ordered it?"

"I talked with the captain. He put out the order."

"I took a look at Petrosian's rap sheet before coming over here. Like I said, this isn't his style. He's a violent guy, likes to use a gun, likes to hurt people. Not the type to play head games. The robbery he went down for wasn't the only time he's been involved in shootings and fights. From his sheet he looks like a complete sociopath. Taking a baby to your house and leaving him in a crib doesn't seem like the kind of crime a guy like that gets involved in, does it?''

Paul threw up his hands in frustration. Sergeant Sowers said, ''There was no sign of a break-in at the house, Lieutenant. If someone came in they were let in or had a key. Or lived there.''

''No kidding?'' *Fascinating,* Quarles seemed to be saying. His eyebrows lifted as he looked at the McDonalds. ''So did one of you guys do it? Just to irritate the other like married folk do? No? Well, shoot, we got a real mystery on our hands, don't we? I guess we ought to go down to the station and talk about things, then. It's all too complex for me. Nickie Cerovic wanted me to tell Mrs. McDonald he'd be there, too. He thought she'd be interested.''

Paul looked at Kate. ''What does that mean?''

Kate glared at him but said nothing.

''Any reason for us to stick around here?'' Quarles asked Dr. Salvi.

''No, please go, the sooner the better. You should be able to take the child home by Saturday noon.''

Kate's voice shot up. ''I'm not leaving without Alex.''

Quarles shook his head. ''Got to keep him here for at least twenty-four hours. You don't know where he was for a while, right? Or who had him, or what this person might have done to him?''

Kate's stomach knotted in pain as her eyes shot to Paul. She tried to keep her voice under control. ''No.''

''Then it's for his own good, isn't it? I'm sure you understand.''

Paul looked impatiently at his watch. It was almost five A.M. ''I have court this morning. Downtown.''

Quarles smiled. ''So you can give us, what? Four hours? That'll be enough, I think. For now.''

Kate said, ''Let me say good-bye to Alex.''

Quarles nodded to the nurse holding the baby. Kate took him, kissed his lips. He was having trouble keeping his eyes open. "I'll see you soon, honey." She felt herself about to lose control again, and quickly handed the child back to the nurse.

"So," Quarles said, and rubbed his hands together in anticipation. "Everyone know how to get to the station house? Good, good, good. I guess we'll meet there in fifteen minutes, then. Don't be late now, you hear?"

30

"I don't see what you expect to gain by pacing back and forth," Nick Cerovic said to Paul McDonald. They were crammed into Lt. Derek Quarles's small, glass-enclosed office, though Quarles had gone home twenty minutes earlier, when the day shift came on. Paul was on his feet, storming around the cluttered room, while Kate sat in a metal chair, her elbows on her knees, propping up her head. Cerovic, behind the desk, was fiddling with a pen. "Why don't you sit down and talk about this rationally?"

"And why don't you explain what the hell you expect to gain by keeping us here? Christ, it's been two hours!"

Kate was staring sightlessly at the floor. Without looking up she said, "Paul . . . please. Sit down."

Cerovic, freshly shaved and looking dapper in a new Harris tweed sportcoat he'd bought at Macy's, relaxed back in Quarles's swivel chair and smiled at the man. "You, more than most people, know we have to jump through the right hoops or we'll look like fools in court. Now why don't you do as your wife asked and sit down." It wasn't a question. Paul darted an angry glance at the detective, then dropped into a visitor's chair that wasn't meant to be comfortable. Cerovic smiled and tried to ease the tension. "Look, we've got every cop in L.A. thinking about Petrosian. We'll pick him up, probably today. Leo's not the type to stay hidden. He's got this weird fantasy life, honestly thinks he's a ladies' man, and every woman in the city is just jumping at the chance to hop in bed with him. If he's in L.A. he'll be struttin' his stuff in some bar or nightclub by nightfall. That's when we'll get him."

Paul glanced at his watch, frowned, but said nothing.

Cerovic continued. "I want you to forget crazy Leo for a while. For all we know he could be in New York or Hawaii, and someone else is behind this. You ever think of that?"

It's all I do think about, Kate thought. She hugged herself and said softly, "Ask Paul where he was last night."

Cerovic's eyebrows rose as he stared at the man.

"Jesus," Paul muttered. "Do you really think I'd kidnap my own kid?"

"I don't know," Cerovic said. "It wasn't really kidnapping. The little guy wasn't hurt, wasn't even taken from the house. There was no danger to him, only to the other kid, and not even any real danger there."

Paul threw an angry glance at the cop. "Do you always start out with the idea that the suspect is guilty?"

"Always," Cerovic said. "It saves time that way. So where were you last night after you left the house?"

Just then Ann DeSilva came in and did a double take when she saw Cerovic already questioning the McDonalds. "Christ, Nickie, you couldn't wait for me? And where'd you get the sport coat? You haven't bought any clothes since Carter was president."

Cerovic said to Paul, "You remember Annie DeSilva, don't you, the famous fashion critic from Culver City? I don't seem to be able to please her, though, even when I dress up. What a life, huh?" He crossed his legs and grinned at his partner. "Couldn't wait, Annie. Paul here's a deputy DA, got to be in court pretty soon. The fate of civilized life in the City of Angels hangs on his being on time, so I thought I'd get a head start. He's about to tell us where he was last night after storming out of the house."

"I didn't storm out. We had an argument. Is there something unusual about that? I went for a walk to cool down. I was back by eleven."

"What'd you argue about?"

Paul's face flushed and his eyes glittered with anger. "That's none of your goddamn business."

Kate's head came up, her elbows still on her knees. "We

argued about who Paul got the herpes from that he gave to me and Alex. I was betting it was some floozy in his office. He said it was a bar girl who liked his courtroom technique.''

"Yeah?" Cerovic said. "So which was it?" He looked at Paul.

Annie DeSilva muttered, "Jesus," ran a hand through her hair, and sat back heavily in her government-issue chair.

Cerovic tried to explain for anyone who wondered. "The usual male response here is that it was some woman who came on to him in a bar or a get-together after work. It didn't mean anything, though. Anyway, he was drunk and not responsible. Was that how it went down?"

Paul said, "Fuck you."

"Well, sure, that, too," he said amiably. "Doesn't answer the question of the hour, though. Where did you go for this relaxing walk of yours while your son was being manhandled by a mysterious stranger?"

"None of this is relevant and you know it. I went for a walk. That's all."

"But you went somewhere!" Cerovic leaned forward and looked at his partner. "That's kind of like a law of physics, isn't it, Annie? I mean you have to be *somewhere.*"

"I walked all the way up to UCLA; then I stopped in at some bar and had a couple of beers before coming home."

"You remember the name of the bar, of course."

"Of course. The Stockade. It's on Barrington."

DeSilva, annoyed at the direction of Cerovic's questioning, grabbed the folder of notes off the desk and began reading. Nick said, "And you got home when?"

"Ask DeSilva. She's got the file. You've only asked that nine times so far."

"This makes ten. What we're looking for here is consistency, right? Just like a courtroom. So you got home at . . . ?"

"Eleven. No, let's make it even more credible to you. It was six minutes after eleven. I let myself in and—"

"Was the door locked?"

"What? Oh." Paul closed his eyes. "No. I turned the handle, walked in, locked it, went upstairs. Then I checked on Alex."

"Why?"

"He's my son, that's why. Do you mean did I expect to find him dead or kidnapped? No, I just looked in on him. It's a habit. It makes me feel good to look at him, touch him. He's the most important person in the world."

"Did you actually look at him? Touch him?"

"No. I didn't want to wake him. I listened, heard him breathing like he was asleep, and went to the guest room. I was asleep in two minutes."

"Must have a clean conscience. It takes me an hour, sometimes two."

"Hey, Mrs. McDonald," DeSilva said, looking abruptly up from the file. "How do you explain the fact that there weren't any signs of a break-in? The report says the only way someone could have gotten in was to walk in the front door. Or been there all the time."

Kate's arms dropped limply to her side, and she sat back in the chair, looking at DeSilva for the first time. "Why do I have to explain anything? That's your job. I'm the victim, or have you forgotten that?"

DeSilva turned to Cerovic, black eyes flashing. "See what I told you? The *victim!* It's textbook Munchausen's. The new little mom isn't getting any attention at home from her big-shot hubby, who's probably got his own fires to kindle. So she starts to do weird things to the kid, lets loose some rats in the nursery, gets a little swine flu culture from someone in the hospital lab, then comes up with this new one—switch Baby A with Baby B, and raise a fuss, maybe do a little hysterical screaming so everyone sees how she's *suffering.* Suddenly she has hubby paying attention to her, the police—one menopausal male cop in particular—pay a *lot* of attention to her because she's a *victim,* the doctors at work get all gaga over their poor little coworker with all the *tragedies* piling up in her life, and mama here gets orgasmic because everyone suddenly *cares* about her. It's like a damn textbook in abnormal psychology, Nickie."

Paul rubbed the back of his head and closed his eyes. "Jesus, instead of good cop–bad cop we've got weird cop–weirder cop. Are we supposed to get mad now and scream out something incriminating? Come on, DeSilva, you and your buddy are making this all up. You haven't any proof at all. Even Judge Ito would throw this out of court.''

DeSilva raised an eyebrow. ''You think? What about it, Mrs. McDonald? Isn't that the way it went down? You stole a kid from Queen of Angels and took him home so you could make a commotion, be a star! It's like the boy who cried wolf, right? No one gave him a second look until he made a fuss. Then suddenly everyone's talking about him. Come on, fess up so we can forget this and get to work on some serious cases. We're up to our keisters in abusers in Hollywood. We don't need any head cases.''

Kate didn't look at her. ''I want a lawyer.''

Paul agreed at once. ''I'm going to call Rick Hazlitt.'' He glanced at the phone on the lieutenant's desk.

''I want my own lawyer!'' Kate shot out, looking at him for the first time. ''Not yours. We're through sharing. Except for your herpes!''

''Trouble in paradise,'' Ann DeSilva said, throwing the file down. ''Lordy, how I hate to see it.''

Paul said, ''I never got involved with cops until cases were filed. I always thought you people were pretty sharp. Are all cops as fucking stupid as you?''

''I don't know,'' Cerovic said. ''What do you think, Annie? Are they all as fucking stupid as us?''

She thought about it a moment. ''Yeah. I guess they are. It can't be much fun for attorneys, can it? I mean, they're all so brainy.''

''And ethical,'' Cerovic added. ''And moral, brave, reverent—''

''I'm going!'' Paul turned toward the door. ''I have to get downtown. I'm filing a report on you two when I'm through in court. Putting people like you in jobs where you have to deal with the public is just looking for trouble.''

''That's what I told the captain,'' DeSilva said at once. ''I wanted a job with the mounted patrol; then I'd only have to work with horses. Closest they could come was to give me a horse's ass as a partner.''

Paul jerked open the office door, letting in the cacophony of the squad room. ''You want a ride home, Kate?''

She didn't answer, and Paul left, slamming the door.

Cerovic said, ''Most kids outgrow that.''

Kate looked up. ''How do I get home?''

Before Annie could say anything, Cerovic had a great idea. ''I'll take you.''

31

Acting as though Kate didn't exist, Annie DeSilva said, "We've got to get to County Hospital in thirty minutes to talk about that beating case, Nick. The doctor won't wait around for us. He's got two surgeries today."

Cerovic was on his feet, hurriedly picking up papers from the lieutenant's desk. "You go, Annie. I'm going to finish up with Mrs. McDonald. I've got a printout from the hospital communications department of the phone calls made to her office. We might be able to pin down who's harassing her."

DeSilva's face froze up. "You're not going out to County? Nickie, you're the one who *made* the appointment with the doctor! You got all official and told him he'd better not be late!"

"Got to prioritize, Annie. You talk to the doc and I'll handle this. Too much work for us to do it together."

"Is that it? Too much work? Whew, I thought maybe there was something personal here. Thanks for reassuring me."

"Think it out, Annie. Since we can't be in two places at once, why don't we act like partners are supposed to act and split the work?"

DeSilva stared at him a moment, then shook her head. "There's no fool like an old fool, is there, Nickie?"

"I'll meet you for lunch. What about eleven-thirty? We can drive down to the Pantry and clog our arteries together." He looked at her expectantly, but DeSilva shot Kate a withering look, then shook her head and left without a word.

Kate had paid attention to none of this. When Cerovic, his arms full of papers and reports, said, "Mrs. McDonald?" her head slowly came up.

"I've got a printout of phone calls to your office. I'd like to go over it with you. Maybe we can find out who's been doing the harassing."

She blinked and shook her head, taking him in for the first time in ten minutes, and wondering why he was standing. "What are they doing to Alex?"

"I'm sure it's nothing more than a few tests. That and twenty-four hours of observation."

"So much has happened to him. He should be with his mother, not with strangers."

"Being in the hospital is probably the best thing for him now. When you pick him up, at least you'll know he's OK."

Kate's eyes moved to the wall of windows that separated the office from the squad room. She could see men and women moving around on the other side, hear the muted rattle and hum of conversation and radios and ringing telephones, the confused and unrestrained excitement that began the day for cops. When she turned back to Cerovic she seemed surprised. "Where's the other one, your partner?"

"Had to run off. We've only got one more thing to do here, and that's go over the phone calls you've gotten."

"Do we have to?"

He managed to open the door without spilling any papers. "Might as well get it out of the way. Then you can go home and get some sleep. What do you say we rustle up some breakfast? I had to run over here without a chance to grab anything."

She looked around, distracted. "I'm not hungry."

"Really? You didn't get any breakfast either. Anyway, let me get the printout from my desk; then we'll go over to IHOP and grab a bite while we talk about it." He smiled, waiting for her.

"Can't we just do it here?"

"This isn't my office. It's Quarles's at night, someone else's on the day shift. He ought to be here any minute. And the squad room's too noisy. Come on, at least have a cup of coffee. After we're done I'll drive you home."

Kate was beyond arguing. She stood up. "Atta girl," he said.

* * *

Cerovic moved the coffee cups and syrup, and spread the printout on the table between them. He had asked for a table away from other patrons, and was given a large corner booth in the mostly empty restaurant. "These are all the calls to your office number for the last month. You must be pretty busy."

Kate stared at the printout with only partial comprehension. "Yes." She couldn't remember what was so important about the calls. The only thing she could think of was Alex. And Paul. What was going to happen to the three of them? She couldn't possibly continue to live with Paul, now that she knew what he had been doing for as long as they had been married.

"Can you remember when you got the calls, the dates and the times?"

"The calls?"

"The threats."

Kate tried to focus her mind, made her eyes go to the printout. "Not exactly. I think last Wednesday, right after lunch, and the day before, in the morning sometime. There were others, but I can't remember."

Cerovic flipped to the relevant dates. "And all the calls lasted less than a minute?"

"Yes, I'm sure. More like half a minute."

"OK." He touched her cup with his finger. "Have some coffee. You look like you need a little boost, a caffeine rush."

Kate looked at the cup but didn't pick it up.

"So we want calls under a minute," Cerovic said, and began running his finger down the list. "On Tuesday morning you had only one call less than a minute. It came from extension 4424. What's that?"

"The admitting desk in Nuclear Medicine. I know because I just sent someone up there."

"OK, that's a start. Someone who works in Nuclear Medicine. Let me look at Wednesday." Again his finger ran down the page. "In the afternoon you had a call at two-oh-two from extension three thousand."

"That's a nurses' station. The third-floor main station is three thousand. The fourth floor is four thousand, and so on."

"Do you know anyone who works there?"

"No one I know closely."

"Could anyone just walk up and use the phone?"

"Not easily. There's someone there all day."

"But doctors use it."

Kate nodded. "Of course."

"All right, let me try some other days." He slowly flipped through the other pages, looking for calls of less than one minute's duration. "I can only find two. One is 566 on Thursday."

"That's the lab." She grimaced unconsciously, thinking of the lab results she had received the same day.

"And 6329."

"Judith Zamora." Kate's lips turned down. "My boss. She's trying to get me fired."

He looked up. "Why's that?"

Kate shook her head but said nothing.

The waitress appeared with three plates for Cerovic. "Eggs, bacon, hotcakes, toast, hash browns." She looked at Kate. "You sure you don't want something? You're going to get hungry watching Godzilla eat Chicago."

"No, nothing."

"OK," she said, and slapped the check on the table. "Enjoy."

Cerovic shoved the plate with two pieces of sourdough toast toward Kate. "Eat, or I'll arrest you."

Kate glanced down at it with distaste.

"Like this," he said, picking up a piece of bacon and chewing it with exaggerated pleasure. "Ummm. Food! Good. Man like; woman like, too. Woman eat."

Kate smiled despite herself. She lifted a piece of toast to her mouth and took a small bite.

"Great," Cerovic said, patting her other hand. "Now, about the phone calls. There were four of them under a minute. How many threats do you think you got?"

"Three, four. About that."

"These calls we just went through are all from different numbers. That would seem to indicate someone who could get around the hospital with ease. Who do you know who has a job like that? Custodian, maybe, or the people who deliver meals, or maintenance workers?''

"I don't know anyone who has one of those jobs. I'm pretty isolated next to the ER all day.''

"An ER doctor?''

"Least of all them. They have to be no farther than the on-call room, where they sleep when they're not needed. Sometimes Dr. Kamel leaves, but that's because he has to go to meetings." Including, she remembered, her own personnel hearing.

"What about an orderly, then? Do they move around a lot?''

"Some of them do, I guess.''

"Or doctors, of course. Those who aren't in the ER.''

"Of course.''

"What about this Judith Zamora?''

"You don't think she'd do it, do you?''

"I'm just asking. She wants to fire you, right? And you say you don't know why. Could be something personal.''

"Like what?" Kate asked, thinking, *Of course it's something personal. It's my husband.*

"I don't know. She must have given you some indication why she wants to get rid of you.''

"She said I've been irresponsible lately, coming in late, missing some days.''

"Does she know the pressures you've been under? The problems with Alex?''

"She knows.''

"Does not sound like a nice person.'' He finished his bacon and started in on the three fried eggs. "Your husband's on the board. I guess that gives him free access anywhere.''

"Paul wouldn't threaten me.''

"You two are having problems. That's obvious. Maybe he's overreacting. People do in this sort of situation. Ask any cop. Domestic disputes are the worst ones to handle.''

She put the toast down. "I'm having problems with Paul, not the other way around. He'd be happy to keep things as they are.''

"And how's that?"

"Me at home, taking care of his kid, while he's running around screwing secretaries and barflies, bringing home sexually transmitted diseases so we'd have something intimate to share."

"You think he has a girlfriend at your work?"

"Why is this important, Sergeant?"

"Look, call me Nick. OK? Sergeant is my title, not my name. Why's it important? Because someone's out to get you. You said you were also getting threats on your computer monitor. So obviously it's someone at the hospital. If Paul has a girlfriend there she could even be doing this without his knowledge. Don't tell me you never thought of this."

Kate sagged back against the Naugahyde booth. "I've thought of it."

"And maybe you thought it might be this Judith Zamora. I'm right, aren't I?"

"It wasn't her. It was a man."

"You're sure?"

"I'm not even sure I'm sitting here. It *sounded* like a man. With an accent."

"What kind of accent?"

"Just an accent."

"So who do you know with an accent?"

"Half the people at the hospital."

"How about elsewhere? Friends, relatives?"

She shook her head. There seemed to be somebody, but she was too upset to think now. She picked up her coffee and gulped it to keep from yawning.

"OK, we'll assume it's a man. With an accent. For now, anyway. So let's follow that road awhile. Has someone been bugging you lately, maybe showing a romantic interest in you, that you gave the cold shoulder to or told to take a hike?"

"No."

"Come on, Kate, you work in a hospital. Doctors are nature's answer to rhesus monkeys; always got a hard-on and ready to reproduce with any female in the area. You're an attractive woman. Someone must have chased after you. Even if you are married. Or *because* you're married—that way you'd be less likely to cause trouble later."

"The voice of experience?"

"No, no. Not me. But I know hospitals."

Kate dropped her head. "It's not like that. Not where I work. It's not like TV."

"But still—someone tried it, right?" His voice was expansive, and at the same time confiding. "Someone thought, Hey, I'd like to tickle that woman's fancy, probably some fat dude with a Rolex and a Porsche who thought, why wouldn't you want to go out with an MD, you crazy?"

"No," she said. "No one. Honestly."

"Not even this Dr. Symonds? He's obviously attracted to you."

She ignored the question. "Can we leave? I still have to go to work today."

"Tell me you're kidding. You're not going into work without any sleep."

"I'm on probation. I don't have a choice."

Cerovic shook his head. "All right. You're the one who's going to be wacko by quitting time. Anyway, we've covered a lot of ground. I'll drive you home. Or to work. Whatever."

Kate sat motionless for a moment. "I want you to believe I didn't take that baby. And I'm not hurting Alex. I don't understand what's going on, but I didn't do anything. I love my son. I'd never hurt him. For attention or any other reason."

"I believe you."

Her expression didn't change. "You do? Or is this the good-cop role?"

"Yeah, actually I do believe you. I think someone's trying to make trouble, and doing a pretty good job of it, too. But I'm on your side. You can trust me." He patted her hand. "Honestly."

Kate muttered, "Thank you," and slipped out of the booth. When Cerovic moved away from the table he grabbed the menu Kate had briefly held and stuck it between the pages of the computer printout. He had a fingerprint kit in his desk.

32

Already ten minutes late, Kate pulled into the hospital parking lot and thought suddenly, God, I can't stand this place. How strange that feeling was: suddenly hating something she had been devoted to for four years, where she'd felt not only that she was useful and liked, but was making a real difference in the lives of people who had been victimized by criminals, or "the system," or even their own family. She had become an advocate and a voice for those who otherwise had none, many of whom, the children especially, would have continued to be victims without her help.

But now . . .

Now she stared at the boxy, dun-colored structure with a sense of despair. *As soon as I walk inside everyone will look at me as though I'm insane. "There goes the crazy woman who's trying to hurt her child. Did you hear they tried to make her see a psychologist and she refused? . . . Did you know she tied her baby up, leaving marks on his arms and legs? . . . That she infected him with swine flu and herpes? . . . That she stole a baby from another hospital? . . . She can't even do her work anymore; she allowed a young girl to return to an abusive father without notifying the police. They had to put her on probation. She's crazy, dangerous, sick . . ."*

So why am I going back?

Because suddenly she *needed* a job, not just *wanted* one. Without Paul's income—and there was no way she was going to stay with him—she couldn't survive, certainly couldn't afford to care for herself and her child, unless she had a job. There was obviously no way she would be able to keep the house on her salary. She didn't care about that. She and Alex could live in a one-bedroom apartment in Hollywood. She didn't even need a car; she could walk to work. But she'd have to find a baby-sitter in the area. That shouldn't be difficult. But if Kate were to lose her job . . . Without the job, then what?

She pulled into a parking space next to a blue Volvo. Killing the engine, she felt a sigh go through her, and her body seemed suddenly drained of energy. Draping both arms on the steering wheel, she stared again at the aging building looming eight stories high on the far side of the ocean of cars, and thought, *I can't do it. I can't face those people anymore.*

But she was beyond the point of having choices in life: no one else was going to hire her with all this hanging over her head. She could imagine what kind of reference Judith Zamora would give if she applied elsewhere. *You want to know about Crazy Kate . . . ?*

Stepping into the early morning sun, she paused and took a deep breath to calm her nerves. *Damn it, just do it, don't let them intimidate you.* How would Lilliana handle a situation like this? She'd put on her best clothes, her most expensive jewelry, grab her Gucci purse, and strut slowly past everyone, high heels clicking with abrasive insolence on the tile floor, and dare them to comment.

But I'm not Lilliana.

She slammed the door and began to walk toward the ER. Men and women were trickling toward various hospital doors; most employees had started an hour earlier, but Kate's schedule, like that of many nonmedical personnel, began later to make her more available to patients and their families.

A car door clanked shut nearby and she spun around to see a woman she recognized as a clerk in Payroll head toward the administrative entrance. *Why am I so nervous out here?* she wondered. *That man, that Petrosian, if that's who it was, isn't going to be hanging around the parking lot again.*

But in that instant she saw his head pop from behind a car: the same smirking, long-haired man who had been in the parking lot last week. Kate quickened her pace. Glancing behind her she saw that he had begun to lope in her direction. It was only fifty feet to the entrance. Kate began to run.

"Hey, Mrs. McDonald, wait up." The man was shouting at her.

Damn it, where was the security guard? Kate was breathing erratically, and running as fast as she could, her purse slapping at her side.

"Mrs. McDonald, I got something to say to you. It's about your husband. It's important." Anger animated the tinny voice.

"No!"

"Damn you!" he yelled. "Damn you! I'll be back!"

Kate burst through the double doors, everyone inside instantly staring up at her as the sounds of the hospital seemed to dissolve. An ER nurse carrying a tray of instruments halted and backed away as though getting ready to flee. Kate stopped suddenly, looked behind her, hearing only the dull hammering of her heart, and the sound of her breath as it caught in her throat. The doors behind her were closed. The man hadn't come inside. Where was the guard? An admitting clerk said, "Everything OK?" in the sort of voice people use with the mentally ill.

Kate put her hand on her chest and forced herself to breathe deeply. The odors of the room—rubbing alcohol, disinfectants, medications, sweat—swirled nauseatingly around her head as though someone were attempting to drive her mad with the stench. I've got to get out of here! she thought suddenly. Not looking at Patty, who was at her desk with a patient, Kate turned abruptly into the hallway and hurried to her office, quickly shutting the door behind her. Going at once to the desk, she collapsed into her chair, then sat up suddenly: why had the door been open? She always locked it when she left for the day.

Her eyes shot to the desktop. Papers and files that had been in her in-box yesterday were strewn around as though someone had been looking for something. But what? There was nothing in her desk anyone would be interested in. *Zamora!* Kate thought. *She probably thinks I keep heroin or cocaine in my desk. Or a gun; like everyone else she's convinced I'm crazy.*

Despairing, she leaned forward, her elbows on the desk. Maybe it wasn't Zamora; maybe it was Frankie. Whoever it was, he didn't try to hide the fact that he'd been there. It would probably take an hour to clean it all up, trying to figure out which forms and documents went with which folders, who needed to be called, who had to come in and talk to her in person.

For the first time she noticed the red light on the phone, indicating that she had voice mail. Picking up the receiver, she dialed her access code. Five messages, the recorded voice said. Four past patients having problems getting their welfare or insurance payments straightened out. And a message from a woman whose voice Kate didn't recognize. She listened to it twice, her heart slowing to a crawl as the clear, calm words pierced her one by one, like the sharp, repetitive stabs of a bayonet. "Did Paul tell you it was a one-night fling? Just some floozy he met who seduced him? Don't believe him. He and I have been together for eight months. I met him at a benefit in Santa Monica, and he took me to the Sheraton later that night. After that it was my place two or three nights a week. All those times he had to work late, of course. Why am I telling you this? Because you should know what a shit he is. It took me a while to find out. Get a good lawyer, doll; you'll need it. He's buddy-buddy with half the judges in town."

Kate slumped forward, her fingers massaging the wall of pain rising like a wave behind her eyes. *Why is this happening to me? What have I done to deserve any of it?*

A timid knock sounded on the door. "What?" she yelled.

The door squeaked open and Joel Symonds peeked in. "Are you receiving visitors, or locking yourself up all day?" He smiled to show he was kidding, at least partially.

Kate moved around in the chair and tried to sound accommodating. "Sure. Come on in. But I'm not much company." At the same time she was happy to see him.

"I can understand," he said. He left the door open as he entered, holding a cup of coffee and a stale doughnut. "More problems with Zamora?"

Kate felt a sudden desire to confide in him. The memory of the horror she had experienced last night when picking up Alex, feeling him begin to suckle at her breast, then realizing it wasn't her child, made her shiver uncontrollably. But she couldn't talk about it to anyone, not even her mother, she was certain. To cover her discomfort, she said, "Insomnia. I only had two hours' sleep last night."

Still standing, Symonds put his cup on her desk and began to eat the doughnut. "I could prescribe a mild sleeping pill, if you want. Nothing that would make you feel groggy the next day, but it would allow you to get some rest."

Kate shook her head. "I don't like sleeping pills. I don't like any kind of pills." Her eyes went to the desk. "I can't believe how the work piles up around here."

"Modern health care," he said with a shrug. "It's more administrative than medical." He swallowed the last of his doughnut, rubbed his hands together, and looked at her with compassion. "I think there's more bothering you than lack of sleep. Do you want to talk about it?"

Kate's eyes stayed on her desk. "No."

"You're going through a lot of difficult times. And I probably only know half of it. It's tough to face problems by yourself, though. You need a friend."

Kate felt the hold she had on her emotions begin to slip. Why did Symonds affect her this way? Why didn't he just go away? She grabbed a ruler from her desk and held it tightly to keep her hand from trembling.

"I don't want to probe where I'm not wanted, but sometimes talking can help."

"And sometimes it can't!" she snapped, then said, "Sorry." She could feel her nerves giving way. If she didn't get a hold on herself she was going to break down. She stood up suddenly.

Symonds took a step toward her. "Whatever it is, I'm here to help, Kate." He put a business card on her desk. "My home number. Any time you want to call. Or we can talk here. I'm not giving you a line. I'm serious; I want to help."

Kate could feel her body begin to tremble. She spun away from him but wasn't able to hold back the tears. As she broke down Symonds put his hands on her shoulders and turned her around. "Go ahead," he said. "It's better than medication any day."

But they were interrupted at once by a voice from behind. "Hey, Doc." Symonds turned to see Frankie Yorba standing loose limbed and bouncing on the balls of his feet at the open door. "Kamel's looking for you. I said you'd probably be here. Good guess, huh?"

Symonds glared at the orderly, then, his voice controlled with difficulty, said, "Tell Dr. Kamel I'll be there in a moment."

Yorba didn't move, his gaze shifting to Kate. "How's it goin', Mrs. McDonald? Hey, how'd your desk get so messy? Not like you, is it? Looks more like Patty's desk."

Kate's voice exploded around the room. "Get the hell out of here. And don't ever come in my office. Don't even talk to me."

"Whoa! What's up with that? What'd I ever do to you?" He looked genuinely upset.

"And don't call me. Ever! Do you hear me? I don't want anything to do with you."

Yorba's gaze went to Symonds. "Hey, what's this shit? What'd I do? I was just trying to be friendly."

"Get out of here, Frankie," Symonds said softly.

Yorba's face turned red, his body jerking up and down and his arms hanging loosely like a damaged marionette's. "Yeah, yeah, pick on the orderlies, right? Everyone else does. Well, up yours, too, Doc."

He disappeared. Symonds turned to Kate. "I'm sorry about that. Has he been giving you trouble?"

"Dr. Symonds!" Neither of them had to look to know it was Kamel. Kate jumped back, bumping into the desk.

The bearded head of the ER seemed as if he were going to explode. "I have been trying to find you. We have work to do. You can attend to romance after work."

"What the hell's that supposed to mean?" Symonds asked. He walked over to the man, staring down into his angry dark eyes.

Kamel assumed a mock-innocent air. "It means your love life will have to take second place to your work life."

"You're out of line—"

"Later, Doctor. You are needed in the ER. Stat!"

Kamel disappeared in a flurry of air and stale cologne. "I'll be back," Symonds said, and hurried away.

Twenty minutes later Paul called from downtown. "Have you been at Cedars to see Alex yet?"

"Paul, I have to work. Anyway, they won't let us see him until tomorrow."

"Maybe I'll stop by on the way home."

"You're not staying tonight, Paul. Not ever. I want you to move out. We'll decide what to do about the house later."

"Kate, you're upset. You don't make good decisions when you're upset."

"And you don't make good decisions when you have an erection. I don't want to see you again. Go to another Sierra Club or Save the Bay meeting instead."

"You can't keep me out of my house."

"If you show up I'll call the police and tell them you hit me. It's domestic battery. The law says they have to arrest you. There's no discretion on their part once you touch me. How's that going to look at work, a DA accused of spousal abuse?"

"You're sick, Kate. You need help."

"Maybe so. Everyone seems to think so." A memory surfaced, and she batted it away. *Subject exhibits irrational anger and an unwillingness to cooperate . . . seems unable to recall relevant incidents of loss of control. . . .*

"The psychologist was a good idea, Kate. Maybe you should go after all."

She started to hang up, but Paul said, "I'll get a room for a couple of days; then we'll talk. I'm going to need some clothes and things, though."

"Get them this afternoon. I don't want you in the house when I'm there."

"Are you afraid I'm going to rape you? Jesus, Kate."

"That's the least I'm afraid of. You'll find an outlet for your sexual urges. You always have."

"Kate, I understand that you're angry with me. You should be. I let you down. It doesn't mean I don't love you."

Kate's mind shifted gears, and the previous night came roaring back as if she were reliving it. Her body began to shake. "Paul, how did you happen to go into my sewing room?"

He hesitated, trying to understand what she meant. "You mean when I found Alex?"

"You know exactly what I mean. You haven't been in that room in months. Why last night?"

"The cops told me to leave the living room. Where was I supposed to go?"

"The kitchen. The family room. Upstairs. Outside. To the bathroom. Why would you go to a room that had nothing to offer you? No radio or TV, nothing to read, no place to relax. What were you going to do? Sew a new jumpsuit for Alex?"

"I don't know." He sounded annoyed. "I just left when they told me to. There's no ulterior motive here, Kate. I walked down the hall, opened the door, and saw Alex."

"You lied to the police. I heard you walking around during the night. You were in the hallway, you had been in the nursery, and then you went downstairs."

"God, Kate, you're delusional."

"Always a safe answer, isn't it, Paul? Blame the victim. Aren't you going to bring up my loss of control?"

She slammed the phone down and saw Judith Zamora standing in the doorway. The other woman smiled her serpent's smile. "Dr. Kamel tells me you were half an hour late this morning."

"I was up all night with the police. Someone tried to steal my baby."

She might as well have said she had had a flat tire. "You knew the consequences when you chose to be late. I have no alternative but recommend your firing to Mr. Dotson. I'm sure he'll concur. Assuming it comes to that we'll give you two weeks' salary and expect you to vacate the premises immediately. You will not be allowed to return. Except as a patient, of course. We're not supposed to turn away the truly ill.''

Zamora left. Kate sank back in her chair. She felt nothing this time. It was as if all life had drained from her soul. Except for Alex there was nothing to live for.

33

How can I eat anything?

As if it had been any other day when she was alone, Kate put a frozen dinner in the microwave when she got home. But when she took out the plastic tray of lasagna minutes later, the mere sight of it repelled her. Like hospital or prison food, she thought. Leaving it on the counter, she filled a tall iced-tea glass with zinfandel and went into the living room, dropping down on the sofa and listening to classical music on KUSC.

When she had gotten home there had been an angry note from Paul on the kitchen table: *Kate—goddamn it . . .* She had stopped reading and left it where she found it. Now as she sipped her wine, Paul vanished from her thoughts and was replaced by a long-buried memory that was suddenly struggling to come alive . . . something from Phoenix, a face, the image she had seen on her computer monitor days ago, peering from the shadows . . . or many faces . . . Or was it the psychologist? *Tell me how you felt that first night. . . . It was hell, all these women, filthy, angry, screaming. Two of them grabbed me, held me down, and ripped off my dress. They were going to . . .* An iciness shuddered through her.

Why did I remember that? Now I'll dream about it for days. She angrily banged the glass down on the end table. *I don't want to remember. I never want to remember.*

It was almost dark when she gave a start and realized she must have fallen asleep. The glass of wine was empty. Twenty-five minutes after eight. God, her body clock had never been right since the doxazosin had gotten into her system. Now she'd have to stay up for a while. She'd never get right back to sleep.

Maybe more zinfandel would help, even though she already had the beginnings of a wine hangover. The worst kind, she knew, the kind that throbbed all the next day.

But first she went upstairs and changed into her nightgown. Almost without thinking she walked down the hall to the nursery and flipped on the light. My God, it was less than twenty hours ago that she had felt the unfamiliar baby at her breast and started screaming hysterically. *How quickly my life has fallen apart!* The huge stuffed rabbit in the corner watched with silent disapproval as she stared down into the empty crib. Poor Alex, he seemed to be saying: what a terrible mother you have. *But I'm not doing these things to you, no matter what people think. I'm not. I'm sure. . . .*

But she wasn't sure. There had been so many empty periods in her days recently, when she wasn't certain what had happened. *You're capable of anything,* they had told her in Phoenix. *You lose control and don't realize what you're doing.* Yet it was far worse now, almost every day, it seemed. *But I'm not hurting you, Alex. I'd never hurt my child.*

Walking over to the window she stared out at the street. At Lilliana's, both cars were in the driveway for once. Hans must be home. Lilliana wouldn't have anything to complain about tomorrow, then. Lights were on downstairs, but upstairs it was dark. She turned away.

Back in the kitchen she took two Excedrin for dizziness, then poured another glass of wine, this time adding ice cubes to it. Paul would have a fit. He was going through his wine-snob stage and had even sneered at her for buying a bottle of zinfandel, as though she had secretly brought home a six-pack of wine coolers. Mozart or Haydn was on the radio; she was too confused or tired or depressed to tell the difference. She went back to the living room, sank down on the couch, and closed her eyes. *How could you have done this to your family, Paul? How could you have betrayed the two people who loved you more than life itself?*

As if in answer the phone rang, and Kate grabbed it at once. "What?"

"You sound drunk," Paul said.

"Goddamn you!"

"My God, listen to yourself, Kate. You're crazy. If you keep this up I'll make sure you never see Alex again."

She slammed the phone down. It started ringing almost at once, and she yanked the cord from the wall. The phone in the kitchen rang and she ran in there, pulling it from the wall. Now the bedroom phone was ringing, and she raced upstairs. "Damn you," she said aloud over and over. "Goddamn you!"

July 23

It happened again. It was all over the local news—a man took a gun out to a mall and started shooting. Why? *everyone asks.* Why . . . why . . . why . . .

I started screaming at the TV. The question is never Why? *it's* Why not? *The man no longer had anything to live for. Wasn't it obvious? Everything he loved was lost. Why should others live? Why should he live?*

Such a quiet person, they always say—no enemies, never made trouble for people—but he snapped—something made him *snap—something made him finally see the futility of life. Something . . .*

After a hundred years, psychology still understands nothing of what goes on in the mind. Any five people picked randomly off the sidewalk know more about human nature than the "experts" because they've been exposed to life, not just thought or read about it.

They understand futility.

34

Her head pounding from a wine hangover and a lack of sleep, Kate arrived at Cedars just before noon on Saturday to pick up Alex. Nick Cerovic was waiting for her. She was embarrassed to discover that his presence pleased her; more than pleased, perhaps, as she was finding herself drawn to this large man and the surprising empathy he seemed to have for her. Empathy! A word Paul knew nothing about. Then she had second thoughts and her voice became panicky. "There's not a problem, is there? I can still take Alex home?"

"No, no, no problem at all." They were standing at the busy nurses' station, just feet from an array of high-tech monitors beeping and humming in the background. Alex had already been cleared for release, and one of the nurses hurried off to retrieve him. "I just wanted you to know we've got a line on whoever took the other child from Queen of Angels."

"You know who it is?" Kate felt her heart miss a beat as she experienced not interest, but an inexplicable alarm.

"Not exactly. But we've got a security tape from the children's ward that shows the woman walking out with the kid."

"Then you haven't identified her?" The PA system above their heads was blaring nonstop—codes, phone calls, people's names—and nurses and doctors were noisily conferring at the nurses' station adjacent to them, making her raise her voice.

Nick took her by the elbow, leading her toward the bank of elevators at the far end of the corridor so they could talk. "Not yet. The film's kind of hazy. You know how those security cameras are. We had to send it to a lab for enhancement. In another day or so we ought to have a pretty good picture of her. Good enough for ID purposes.''

Kate had the sense that he was watching her reaction to his news as they strode past rooms with children in various states of discomfort. All of them seemed to be watching television with a numbed fascination, while their parents sat at the edge of their beds, trying not to appear concerned. "The other baby is OK, isn't he?"

"Sure, he's dandy. His mom already took him home. How are you feeling? When I was in your office you were surprised to find out you had a medication of some sort in your blood."

Kate didn't know what to say. She had forgotten he had heard her side of the telephone conversation with the lab. Something told her she should refuse to talk about it—one more wild accusation by the crazy woman—but Cerovic pushed on. "Kind of strange, isn't it? Blood-pressure medicine? Doxa-something. I was going to ask one of the department docs about it.''

"Doxazosin."

They turned around and began to retrace their steps. "Yeah. So how do you think it ended up in your system? Doesn't sound like an accident."

"Is this a police matter?"

Cerovic smiled. "Hey, I'm on your side. Whatever's going on here, you can't face it alone. You need a friend."

"Mrs. McDonald?"

Kate spun around to see a thin black woman in a nurse's uniform holding Alex. Her heart jumped and she reached at once for him. "Oh, my God, honey, how have you been?" She held him under the arms, smiling into his face, and Alex rewarded her with his own smile as his feet danced in the air.

"Hungry is how he's been," the nurse said with a laugh. "But healthy as an ox. Going to be a big kid, isn't he? Handsome, too. The two of you must be proud." She smiled at Nick.

Cerovic waited on a bench while Kate hurriedly signed some forms and received a clear plastic bag filled with several jars of baby food and powder and disposable diapers, all of which were as alien to him as a foreign language. When she was ready to leave, the nurse appeared with a wheelchair. "But I'm not the patient," Kate protested.

"Hospital rules, honey. Patient's got to be taken to his car in a wheelchair. Even if you hold him."

Cerovic muttered, "Rules," then said, "I'll push," and replaced the nurse at the back of the chair.

"That's fine," the woman said, and bent to kiss Alex on the forehead. "I hope we don't see you soon, sport."

In the elevator Cerovic asked, "You want me to drive you home? I live in Santa Monica, not too far from Brentwood. Except in lifestyle, of course. It's on the way, so it's no problem."

"No, I'll be all right."

"You're looking pale. Effects of the drug?"

"It's from wine, if it's from anything. But really, I'm fine." She dandled Alex on her lap and kissed him on his pink lips, making him sputter.

Cerovic reached over and dropped a business card on her lap. "My home phone's on the back. If you want to call sometime."

"Police business," she said dourly.

"Or just a friend, Kate. Being a cop doesn't make me a bad guy."

She glanced over her shoulder. "Of course. I'm sorry."

The elevator doors swished open, and a half dozen men and women waited with impatience as Cerovic pulled the wheelchair out backward. "Where are you parked?"

"In the emergency lot, I'm afraid. Are you going to give me a ticket? I know it wasn't an emergency. Except to me." Alex began to squirm around on her lap, wanting to sit up instead of being clasped to her bosom as she had done since going outside.

"Hey, it's private property. Park your car in the middle of the OR if you want." He wheeled her out to the Mustang and stood in the midday heat while Kate secured Alex in the baby seat in the back.

When she slid behind the wheel, Kate said, "Thanks," and felt she ought to add something but wasn't sure what. Cerovic seemed to care for her, and care for the truth, too. But she had

had enough experience with the police to distrust anything they did.

"One more thing," he said. "I guess you haven't seen this. I want you to know I didn't have anything to do with it." He handed her the Metro section of the *Times*.

Kate had been expecting something like this. Next to a photo of both babies there was a two-inch headline:

ABDUCTED CHILD FOUND IN WOMAN'S HOUSE

In one of the more bizarre cases Los Angeles police detectives could remember, an eight-month-old boy reported missing by his mother last night was discovered sleeping peacefully elsewhere in the house. Another child, kidnapped from Queen of Angels Hospital several miles away, had earlier been discovered in the missing boy's crib. The mother of the eight-month-old, Mrs. Kate McDonald, wife of a Los Angeles deputy district attorney . . .

Kate let the paper drop to her lap, then snatched it up and read the story through from the beginning, slowing at the words of "an unnamed police source," who stated that this looked like a botched attempt by Mrs. McDonald to get attention, what psychologists called Munchausen syndrome by proxy. "She and her husband have been experiencing marital problems," the source added. . . .

Ann DeSilva, Kate thought, getting her two cents in.

Why not? Everyone was an expert on Kate McDonald.

She looked at Cerovic through the open window. "Is that what you think? I'm after attention?"

He shook his head with regret. "I want to find out what's going on, Kate. I'm trying to help you, not trap you. You're going to have to trust someone sooner or later. I'd like it to be me."

She gripped the steering wheel in both hands, and stared through the windshield without responding.

"Well, like I said," he told her after a moment. "Any time you want to talk, give me a call. That tape ought to be back from the lab by Monday. I'll let you know what we find on it. Maybe you'll want to see it."

Kate thanked him without interest, and turned the key in the ignition. Cerovic stepped aside as she backed out, then watched her head out of the lot toward Sunset. He blew a sigh out of his mouth, and said aloud, "I wish I was wrong about all this, but I don't think you'll want to see that tape at all."

Both hands jammed in the rear pockets of her white tennis shorts, Lilliana hurriedly crossed the cul-de-sac as Kate was unlatching Alex from the car seat. "Hi, guys!"

Kate looked around at the sound of the woman's voice, but said nothing, turning back to the car and removing Alex from the infant seat.

Lilliana was in an unusually upbeat mood. "Hey, Alexander the Great! I haven't seen you for a while. Still conquering little baby worlds?"

Lilliana put her hands out, expecting Kate to pass the child to her. Kate felt a sudden tremor of discomfort, and her arms tightened instinctively around Alex as if an unexpected storm had approached. But Lilliana seemed not to notice and gently took hold of his body. Kate relaxed her grip, handing her son to the woman. Lilliana held Alex under his arms and began to jiggle him up and down like a puppet on a string. "Boy, are you a looker! Going to be a lady-killer, aren't you?" Alex began to cry at the sudden movement. Lilliana laughed. "Hey, your namesake didn't cry until he was thirty, and that was because he had conquered the world and there was nothing left to do for an encore. Don't you think you're a little premature with the boo-hooing?"

Kate said, "I'll take him. He wants to eat. The hospital said he's been hungry." Oh, no, Kate thought with a sinking heart. Now she would have to explain.

"Was Alex in the hospital? What's going on, Kate? I haven't seen you in days. I think you've been ignoring me, haven't you? Between you and Hans, my ego's been taking a beating lately. Don't make it worse than it is or I'll start sending my shrink's bills to you. Anyway, I saw the police out here Thursday night. They must have stayed for three hours. What the heck was going on?''

Kate took a breath. ''Don't you read the newspaper?''

''I gave that up years ago. It's all politics.''

She shook her head. ''Come on in. I've got to feed Alex.''

After putting her son in a high chair with a bottle of juice, Kate made instant coffee for her and Lilliana, and the two of them sat at the kitchen table. Lilliana picked up her cup, holding Kate's gaze. ''There must have been four or five police cars out front, all with their radios blaring. Hans thought you had a break-in. Or did something happen to Alex? Is that why he was in the hospital?''

When Kate explained, Lilliana was stunned. ''Switched babies! That's insane.''

''A word I hear a lot,'' Kate replied.

''What's that mean?''

''I'm nuts. That seems to be the general opinion.''

Her neighbor brushed it off. ''Oh, come on. You're as sane as, I don't know, I won't say 'me.' I'm not sure that would be a compliment. Let's say you're twice as sane as our two husbands combined.'' She gave a little chuckle that sounded both cruel and angry. ''Where's Paul, by the way? I saw him taking his clothes away, and I know he didn't spend last night here, so don't get all wide-eyed and say you just don't know *what* I'm talking about.''

Kate took a silent breath. ''We split up.''

''No!'' Her friend hunched forward suddenly, her voice full of concern. ''Not permanently. You can't! You love each other too much. If you get divorced I won't believe *any* marriage can work.'' She grabbed Kate's hand. ''It's the herpes, isn't it? Paul has a girlfriend and that's where he got it.''

Kate's head dropped. ''I don't know. . . . Maybe.''

''Well, he didn't get herpes out of a bottle! Of course he has a girlfriend. Or he just screws around any chance he can. Maybe he and Hans have the same 'friends.' I guess I should get tested, too, shouldn't I? Hans could be AIDS infected, for all I know.'' She squeezed Kate's hand again. ''So what does Paul say? Does he want a divorce?''

"I don't care what he says. It's not his decision."

The other woman sat back in her chair and frowned. "Maybe you shouldn't be so hard on him. At least your husband loves you. I can't even fall back on that sappy thought."

"Paul was poisoning me!" Kate snapped. "He was putting something in my drink."

Lilliana's jaw dropped open.

Kate pushed to her feet. "Please go, Lilliana. I'm not in the mood for this. I don't feel good. I'm going to take a nap."

Her neighbor looked at the child. "Are you sure you *can* take care of him? Feeling like you do? Maybe I should—"

"Can the crazy mom be trusted with her baby? I don't know. Maybe I'll put insecticide in his food or give him a bath in laundry bleach. You can worry about it while you're polishing your kitchen floor this afternoon. But leave me alone." She grabbed Alex and fled upstairs.

When the phone rang at four o'clock, Kate was sitting stiffly in the living room, watching the local news on TV. Joel Symonds said, "How are you holding up?"

She didn't know what to say—felt like screaming, *How the hell do you think I'm holding up?*—and sensed herself beginning to lose control. She bit her lip to keep from crying. "I'm OK. Fine. Wonderful."

"I saw the article in the paper. I'm sorry about that."

"It wasn't your fault," she said. "It was that woman cop." Then she thought, *Maybe not. Maybe someone from the hospital contacted the newspaper.*

"Still, it's an invasion of privacy," he said. "No one should have their personal problems paraded for every voyeur in the city to gloat over. How's Alex doing?"

"Alex is fine, too." *Damn it, just hang up, leave me alone. Why is my life so important to you?*

"Glad to hear it." He paused, and Kate could hear the chaos of the ER behind him. "I care for you, Kate," he finally said. "I want to help. If you need—"

"Don't!" she said, interrupting. "Just . . . don't." She began to shake. "I have to go."

"Wait," he began, but she hung up. *I'm drowning,* she thought. *I'm being pulled to the bottom of the sea.*

She could feel the familiar pangs of hysteria building in her mind, like the frenzied lashing of a whip, over and over, faster and faster, until she couldn't think anymore.

Her hands clenched at her sides. *Why are you doing this to me?*

35

Sapped of energy, Kate went to bed before nine, hoping to draw a veil over the day and rid her mind, at least temporarily, of worries. But once again sleep eluded her as she lay on top of the sheets watching the room turn from twilight to darkness, and the air become sluggish and foul with the residual stink of midsummer smog. *It's not fair; it's not right. I don't deserve this. Alex doesn't deserve it.*

Sitting up suddenly, she wiped perspiration from her forehead, then sank back down, her eyes wide-open. One question, at least, had been answered. None of what was happening to them had anything to do with Alex's herpes; that was the result of something far simpler, more primal, and as old as sex— her husband's philandering. *How many girlfriends—is that the right word, Paul, or is it* lovers *or* partners?—*have you had in the four years of our marriage? What did you do when you were alone with them, these girlfriend-partner-lovers of yours? Did the two of you lie in bed and tickle and giggle and do all the little things longtime lovers do? Did you whisper endearments to each other at the right times? Were you caring and patient enough to take the time to please each other? Or was it merely hard-and-fast sex, get it over with so the two of you could rush home to your respective spouses, you full of stories about the endless meetings at work, and wondering aloud why you hadn't taken up something simpler, like tax or patent law?*

"The deceived wife's reality," she called it to herself; when things that made no sense before suddenly became vibrantly clear: the woman at a party who looked at her the way one looked at a butterfly in a glass case and said, "So *you're*

Paul's wife!'' The sudden interest Paul developed in exercise—
Tuesday evening was always "racquetball." All the hang-ups
on the phone that Paul said were a result of "deregulation,"
shaking his head at the shortsightedness of the government.

This woman who phoned Kate—his lover-partner-girlfriend
who had sent the film—seemed as angry at Paul as Kate was.
As angry as a deceived wife. Had Paul promised her that he'd
divorce Kate, and was that why she was so upset? Because he
hadn't? *You should know what a shit he is,* the woman said,
the words falling one by one like drops of acid on Kate's heart.
Well, I do know. Now. Thanks to you, whoever you are. Eight
months the two of them had been together, hiding from, and
no doubt laughing at, the foolish wife. Exactly since Alex was
born, in other words. At least he had found time to go to the
hospital for that! *God, Paul, how I hate you!*

This room, hers and Paul's, with its memories and darkness
and rank, stagnant air, began to oppress her, like being wrapped
in a hundred-year-old blanket and shut up in a coffin. Her pulse
began to quicken, and she turned over and buried her head in
the pillow. She hadn't felt this way about nighttime until
recently. All her life she had experienced darkness as warmth
and comfort. As a child, sharing a room with her sister, she
would sometimes retreat to the safety of the closet when something—usually her father, sometimes one of the bigger kids at
school, sometimes a fight between her parents—frightened her.
She'd burrow in among the coats and boots and old shoes and
let oblivion gather around her like a mother's embrace. Now
all it meant was one more night to endure, one more day of
Paul's lies, and threats to herself and "accidents" to Alex that
she would have to explain to the police.

I'm not hurting my baby. I'm not!

I'm not. . . .

Her stomach tightened, and she rolled over and stared into
the darkness. What kind of life could Alex have with his mother
slowly going crazy?

Nick Cerovic's shoulder hurt like hell from where a fourteen-
year-old neighbor boy had given him an elbow after coming

down with a rebound in a neighborhood three-on-three basketball game. The kid couldn't be more than five-nine but rebounded like Dennis Rodman. And he was already multiply tattooed, just like his hero. What next, green hair and wedding gowns? The world was changing, and Nick wasn't sure there was any place for forty-year-olds anymore, certainly not forty-year-olds who thought basketball was supposed to be a noncontact sport.

He showered, being careful not to rub the bruised shoulder, then, wearing only his boxer shorts, took a six-pack of Bud and a bowl of tortilla chips and salsa out to the couch, and flopped down. Popping the top off a beer, he drained half of it in one gulp and stared at the projection TV blaring from ten feet away. Bases loaded in the bottom of the ninth, Dodgers down one run, no one out, and the next two guys struck out. *Jesus!* Eric Karros was up now. The camera zoomed in on his face, and suddenly there were giant ballplayer jowls darkening Cerovic's living room. *How the hell does he always have a two-day beard?* His buddy Piazza had been the same way. *Maybe they own some fancy electric razor that left them mostly unshaved. For the bucks they make you'd think they could get one that actually works. And maybe get a hit about now?*

Two large German Shepherd mixes, unwanted pups rescued from the pound by Nick last year, wandered over and nuzzled the bowl of chips with their wet noses. "Hey, get outta here; you've been fed." He had named them Preston and Bailey, good dog names, not funny "people" names like Tom and Jerry, or Marx and Engels. Names they could be proud of when talking to other neighborhood dogs. They looked at him appealingly. "Forget it. I'm too old to fall for the big dewy eyes. Go chew your bones." The dogs looked at each other, then bounded off together to attack the same large rawhide bone. Establishing dominance; the way of the world, he thought as he watched them.

On a whim he had stopped at the pound several months after Beth had died, and wandered among the foul, noisy cells of the unwanted like a jailer on death row, except that here death was a daily occurrence. And there they were, in the same cage, two ugly mongrels small enough to put in his pocket. He had brought them home not because of any innate love of animals, but for the purely selfish reason that he was lonely. To his surprise the three of them had grown close in a way that seemed almost eerie when he allowed himself to think about it. Preston and Bailey had definitely become the most important things in his life, after his job. Not that they replaced Beth, of course. But, he thought now, looking at them snarl and fight over the bone, filling the air with aggression, they filled a hole that had slowly developed in his soul. *Christ, you're getting maudlin! Think about work.* That always emptied his mind of emotion and forced him to concentrate on facts. Which was what, he knew, made him a good cop.

Karros blasted a foul ball into the stands behind third base. It came off his bat so hard it almost tore through a seat back. *Close but no cigar.* Cerovic frowned at the screen. *Hey, Eric, try to put it* between *the lines. Close only counts in horseshoes and hand grenades. What's the guy make in a year? Six million, something like that? And he gets maybe 175 hits a year. That's . . .* Cerovic took out a pencil and quickly did the math. *Christ, more than $34,000 every time he gets a hit! One lousy hit! Two hits and he makes more than a cop does in a year, even with overtime. And no one's shooting at Karros!* Something was wrong here.

Not that Cerovic's life was particularly demanding. In fact it was easier than most detectives' because of his reputation for closing difficult cases. Hell, age and experience had some privileges. Nick knew he was good at what he did because he was a thinker, not a screamer or pusher, like so many cops. And he had a sixth sense about guilt or innocence. With men, anyway. Annie was right: it kinda fell apart when it came to women. But about men his intuition was almost always dead-on. That he had taken an instant dislike to Paul McDonald had to be paid attention to, then. But he wished Annie would lay off about his being interested in Kate. It wasn't true. Or very true.

Or maybe it was.

Karros pounded another foul ball into the upper deck.

Nick and Annie had always worked well together. Until recently, anyway. His captain had been surprised when Nick told him he wanted to partner with her last year. Most detectives didn't like Annie. She had an edge, an aggressiveness that sometimes made her hard to get along with. Nick didn't always like it either but thought they meshed well together—his dead calm and her tightly controlled fury. Maybe her attitude was just part of a youthful enthusiasm that would dim in time. But that didn't excuse the way she badgered suspects, especially if she was convinced they were guilty.

Moving the chips aside, he pulled out a folder with the results of the computer search he'd just completed. Using a modem and his LAPD password, he was able to run a records check on anyone from home. It would raise a few eyebrows if it was discovered he was throwing a net over everyone involved, and not just suspects. *But hell, the bigger the net the more fish you catch.* If Annie found out what he was doing she'd have a fit. But he figured it was time to turn from looking at Kate to finding out who was harassing her. *Harassing her?* he could imagine Annie saying. *Jesus, Nickie, she's doing it herself. You fucking blind?* Well . . . maybe so.

Jimmy Soto, the Explorer Scout, was only halfway through the employment list Midtown had sent over. Nick was surprised to see twelve hundred people associated with the hospital, part- and full-time. Jimmy had already turned up four registered sex offenders—a male nurse, an orderly, and two administrative workers. None of them had any direct dealings with the ER or Kate's office, not that that meant anything. Nick thought he'd go out and interview everyone on the list once Jimmy was finished.

The sound of cheering exploded from the TV. Nick looked up in time to see Karros, still scowling, round the bases behind two other Dodgers. *Damn!* "All right, Eric!" he bellowed. "All's forgiven! You're worth every penny, kid."

The dogs stopped their playing and bounded at once in his direction. "Hey, neither of you is named Eric. So get outta here." The dogs slunk away, and his eyes went back to the printouts.

Paul McDonald. Nothing. What'd he expect? If the guy had a record he wouldn't be in the DA's office. He'd probably be a friggin' defense attorney instead!

Patty Mars. Three traffic tickets in three years: one for speeding, one for running a red light, and one DUI that had been plea-bargained down to reckless driving. A sign of immaturity, if nothing else. Nick wondered how she got insurance with a record like that. Still, it wasn't exactly what he was looking for.

Lilliana Quinlin. Cerovic had never even seen her, but had heard Kate mention the woman, and living next door she probably had access to the house, so he took a flier and put her name in. But nothing popped out. Was she married?

Using the phone book, he saw a listing for Hans Quinlin, and ran that name. *Surprise, surprise.* Hans Quinlin, arrested once for securities fraud, and barred from stock trading by the SEC. No further criminal charges were brought against him, though he was investigated once for hacking into a competitor's computer system and stealing confidential data. Not a nice guy, it would seem. Something for Cerovic to mentally file away.

He hadn't run any doctors at the hospital. They couldn't have a record and still be licensed. Could they? Of course, half the MDs on the staff of Midtown Memorial came as adults from some other country, so there was no telling what was in their past.

And of course he'd run Kate McDonald, his stomach churning as he typed in her name. But nothing came back. He hadn't gotten the report from the FBI on her prints, though. It wasn't a priority, so it could take several days. But he didn't expect anything. Even if his intuition about women was so often, and so famously, wrong.

He suddenly remembered the last thing Annie had said to him last night before heading for home: "In the back of your mind you know I'm right, Nickie. You can apologize to me after we arrest her. But you damn well *are* going to apologize."

He wondered where Kate was right now, what she was doing.

* * *

Kate rolled onto her back in the overheated darkness of the bedroom and wiped perspiration from her forehead. She had been half-asleep, wandering in and out of a dream state, and thinking of Nick Cerovic. She could feel herself coming under his sway, responding to his obvious interest. *Why is this happening?* she wondered. *It can't be love; it has to be gratitude that someone close to the investigation is on my side. While my husband thinks I'm nuts. You're crazy, Kate. . . .*

She wondered what it would be like being married to a cop. Difficult, she'd heard. They become married to their jobs, and family took second place. But Nick wouldn't be like that. He had a sensitivity, a *caring,* that most cops—and most men she knew—lacked. She liked that, liked how he never seemed to get upset like Paul did. Never raised his voice and yelled or threatened.

Jesus, she thought. *What am I doing? I don't want to get involved with anyone. I have enough to worry about with Alex.*

Go to sleep. It's late.

Rolling over again she suddenly remembered that Paul had brought home a gun last week. It was in the night table on the other side of the bed. Sitting up, she turned on the light, hurriedly took it out, and popped open the magazine. It was loaded. Its weight felt comforting and familiar as she sank back down on the bed, still holding it in her hand. She thought: *Something bad's going to happen. That's why the gun is here. Everything so far has just been preparation.*

36

Sunday mornings had always been special for Kate and Paul. They would sleep in until eight or so and then have a leisurely breakfast outside under the blazing purple of the bougainvillea, and slowly work their way through the massiveness of the *Times*. Increasingly Paul would leave later on in the morning to play golf, and Kate would stay home with Alex. Golf! God, how naive she'd been.

This Sunday morning she skipped breakfast altogether, skipped the *Times*, worrying that there would be another story on her, and while Alex played on the floor, she sat in the living room and watched the video again. And again.

The lighting in the room where it had been shot was poor, and the camera seemed to be shooting from a spot on the wall. Kate had seen advertisements for cameras that were disguised as light fixtures or lamps or almost anything one wanted. That obviously was what was going on here. So poor, hapless Paul didn't realize that this surprisingly energetic performance of his was being preserved for posterity. The drawback to this type of setup was that the lens couldn't move with the actors. One of the actors, though, knew the camera was there, and managed to keep her face and much of her body away from its prying eye. The woman had also edited the tape, probably taking out the spots where she could be identified, giving the film a jerky, amateurish look.

Nothing amateurish about her sexual skills, though. For twenty minutes she and Paul attacked each other like pit bulls in heat. No wonder Paul's sexual appetite had declined lately, a fact he attributed to his busy court calendar. *Well, hell,* she thought; *I'm not the first wife to be surprised by my husband's philandering. Won't be the last, either.* But that didn't make it hurt any less.

Alex was on the floor at her feet. He grabbed her big toe and began to giggle. Kate reached down and pulled him to her lap. "Hi, little guy. Want to see your dada rut like a monkey at the zoo? Here, watch—"

But Alex would rather crawl on her lap and grab her hair. Kate put him in a walker with a plastic seat and wheels, and let him maneuver slowly around the floor.

She hit rewind and again watched her husband and the blonde. Phony blonde, probably. Not that it made any difference. There was something vaguely familiar about her, though, the body reminding her of someone. *Or am I merely hoping, because if I know who it is I know who to hate?*

Though hate seemed redundant at this point. Whoever this woman was, she obviously loathed Paul as much as Kate did, if her telephone message was any indication. And Kate hated them both, while Paul hated . . . *Who do you hate, Paul? Not me, surely, because you think I'm crazy, and you wouldn't waste your hatred on a crazy person, would you?*

Anyway . . .

Anyway, hatred is not really what I feel right now. I wish it were, because I'm frightened to death. For Alex. For myself.

Because I know it's not over. They're not through with me.

She thought of the gun upstairs in the nightstand, next to the bed.

Nick Cerovic called in the evening. Kate found herself warming at the sound of his voice, had almost called him earlier before catching herself as she dialed. *What are you doing? He's a cop. I'm lonely,* she thought; *I just want to talk to someone.* Still, she was aware of a strange but growing attraction to this man. He had a nice face; not handsome necessarily, but pleasant. He was friendly and self-assured, someone she'd want to know. A nice man. Even if he was a cop. And trying to put her in jail.

She was out on the patio with a glass of red wine, watching

the moths that swarmed and flapped noisily around the spotlight that illuminated the backyard, occasionally darting in to land on Alex as he bounced in his walker under the dead coral tree; he laughed and babbled incoherently, certain in the egotism of infancy that they were meant solely for his amusement.

Cerovic was pacing back and forth in his living room with the portable phone while Preston and Bailey took up all six feet of his couch. "I thought you'd want to know. We got the security video back from the lab."

Kate felt a spasm of interest. "Can you identify the woman who took the baby?"

"I can't, but I think someone who knows her would be able to. I'd like you to try. I don't think you want to take off more time from work, so why don't you come over to Hollywood station on your lunch tomorrow? We'll pop some corn and watch the flicks."

"Do I have to? Can't you find someone else?"

"I think you'd better."

"Will Paul be there?"

"Just us. Noon OK with you?"

"I have no choice, do I?"

"No," Cerovic said reluctantly. "I guess you don't."

Kate paused a moment, then asked, "Will your partner be there? The 'anonymous police source'?"

He stopped his wandering. "Look, sometimes Annie gets a little aggressive. Don't let it worry you. But, yeah, she'll be there."

"I think she'd do anything she could to get me convicted of harming Alex. Anything."

He tried a laugh but it came out harshly, making the dogs jerk their heads up. "Come on. She's not like that."

"Sure she is. She's got the single-mindedness of someone who knows she's right, no matter what. And if the evidence doesn't agree, maybe she'll just manipulate things a bit. I guess I'll see you at noon."

When Nick hung up he sank down in a chair and let out a disappointed sigh.

Any way he looked at it, tomorrow was going to be one shitty day.

July 24

I feel my control going today and it makes me so angry. I want to throw my head back and scream: To hell with you, Kate, to hell with everyone, but especially you, and your goddamn child, and your fool of a husband.
But I won't, of course. I want the world to know, but not until the time comes. And on my terms. Until then I'll wait. . . .
And hold my tongue.
But, Lord, how I fear the helplessness *that has clamped itself so tightly on my mind these past few years. I tried seeing a psychologist about it once, this feeling that I was powerless and at the mercy of a hostile universe. After a few weeks he decided that my "problem" was beyond him, and referred me to a psychiatrist. She put me on Prozac, and I tried it for a week, tripping out in Happyland. But then I realized I could regain control over my life by taking over yours. I saw that we could live together, you and I—not multiple personalities, Katie Kate, but* one *personality with me in charge. Me, damn you.*
I think someone saw me coming out of your house today, but it doesn't matter. Things have gone too far for anything to slow us down now, you and I.
Remember: I pull the strings. You dance.

37

Why do I feel so bad about leaving Alex with the sitter? Kate wondered as she came into work Monday morning. His fever was gone, his bites had healed, and the hospital said he would be fine as long as he took his medication.

Still, the guilty feeling grew to fill her conscious thoughts, and as she walked to her office she carried on a debate with herself that she couldn't win no matter which side she took. *Look, the hospital said he was OK! Don't worry about him. I know he's OK, but still . . . Kate, damn it, you need a job; you have to provide for the two of you. You can't expect Paul to do it. I know I can't but . . .*

Everyone's looking at me, she thought as she went through the door. *Everyone heard what happened or read the article in the* Times. She could imagine them all rushing to their reference books and looking up Munchausen syndrome by proxy.

Mohammed Kamel noticed her walking through the ER and frowned but said nothing. None of the nurses or aides spoke either, turning away and pretending not to see her. When she entered her office, however, Kamel was behind her. She turned when she heard a noise, and jumped when she saw him close enough to touch.

Kamel seemed not to notice her nervousness. "I had a disturbing call from Judith Zamora a few minutes ago." His large hands joined and twisted at his chest with unaccustomed tenseness.

Kate stood still, not knowing what he was getting at. "Yes?"

Kamel's eyes narrowed, and he frowned behind his unruly

beard. "She wants to fire you. She has already discussed this with Mr. Dotson."

"Human Resources," Kate said dully.

It wasn't the response he expected. "Yes. Well, I told her to hold off. To wait. At least until the two of us had a chance to talk today."

"I have to leave at lunch," Kate said suddenly. "I have a meeting with someone concerning Alex. I may be late coming back." She was not going to tell him that once again her meeting was with the police.

Kamel was again nonplussed by the sudden change of direction. "Well . . . if it is about your child. And you will be back as soon as you can?"

"Of course."

He folded his arms. "I have no objection, then. But about Ms. Zamora."

Kate felt the energy drain out of her. She wanted to sit down but didn't want Kamel looming over her, so she remained standing.

The doctor's shoulders hunched and his arms dropped to his sides in a display of some emotion that Kate couldn't read. But his voice sounded suddenly more confident, though still raw with tension. "I don't quite understand the reasons for Ms. Zamora's hostility, but it has gotten to the point where you are definitely going to be let go unless you or I can change her mind."

Kate said the only thing she could think to say. "OK." There was no feeling in her voice, not even resignation.

Kamel was obviously uneasy. "I'm sorry. I don't feel comfortable about this. She says it's your work performance that's led to your termination. But I feel as if there are things going on I don't understand. Is there something you can tell me to help me, some reason for Ms. Zamora—"

The phone startled them, and Kate angrily yanked it off the desk. "Yes?"

Paul said hurriedly, "I want to talk, Kate. Don't hang up."

"No."

"Damn it, if you—"

"Paul, I can't. Just leave me alone. Don't you understand? Leave me alone!"

"You're sick, Kate. You need—"

"*Damn you!*" She slammed the phone down. When she looked for Kamel he was gone.

Joel Symonds came by at noon but Kate was gone, so he went out to Patty's carrel, catching her as she also got ready to go to lunch. "Sorry, Doc. I've been busy all day. I don't know where she is."

Symonds glanced around at the waiting room as Frank Sinatra crooned over the public-address system, then looked back at Patty. "How about Yorba? Has he been around?"

Patty stood up and took her purse from under the desk. "He was wandering around earlier. Can't you find him?"

Symonds paused a moment, as if considering how far he ought to go in sharing his concerns. "Has he been bothering Kate?"

"Frankie? Jeez, I don't know. I don't think so. Do you think he's the person sending her those weird computer messages?"

Symonds frowned. "What kind of weird messages?"

"Didn't she tell you about that? Someone's sending her these threatening e-mails. 'I'm going to kill you,' or something like that."

"And she doesn't know who?"

"Someone at the hospital. I've got one of the trolls in the computer department trying to figure out where the messages come from. I haven't talked to him for a while. Maybe I ought to run down there. What are you asking about Frankie for? He wouldn't know a computer from a potato."

"Curious. I've seen him coming out of her office a couple of times. I just wondered why."

"Did you ask him?"

"Of course. He always had some cock-and-bull story."

"We caught him in her office last week. He said he was looking for you."

"Kate's never mentioned anything being taken from her office, has she?"

"I don't think so. She leaves her door open most of the time during the day. But I don't think there's anything worth stealing. If there's a problem with Frankie you should tell Kamel. He's the one to look into it."

"I'm not as concerned about him wandering into offices as I am with his hanging around the drug cabinet. I've seen him in the area a couple of times now when drugs have gone missing. Including today. It's not enough to go to Kamel with, but if you hear anything about him, let me know. Maybe we could start an investigation."

"Yeah, sure." Holding her purse, she came out from the carrel. "I've gotta go to lunch, Doc. I'm already late. How about you? Wanna buy a girl a sandwich?"

Symonds shook his head and got to his feet. "Sorry. I have to stick around today. When Kate comes back have her call me. I want to take care of this as soon as possible." He paused, then added, "They're probably going to fire her this week."

Patty stopped. "It's gone that far, huh? Jeez! What a couple of weeks she's had. I guess the upside of that is at least it can't get any worse."

38

Thrust back in her metal, government-issue chair like a sullen teenager, Annie DeSilva glared at Kate with undisguised hostility, but Nick Cerovic rubbed his hands together and said, "We've got a VCR set up in the training room. That way we can have some privacy."

They were in the large squad room, Kate standing nervously amid the noise and confusion, Cerovic suddenly in motion, coming to his feet, taking her by the elbow, and beginning to move away. "It's over on the other side of the building. You coming, Annie, or do you want to stay here and pout all day?"

"Yeah, yeah, Casanova, I'm coming." With a muttered grunt, DeSilva pushed to her feet and followed as Cerovic escorted Kate through the maze of desks and chairs and filing cabinets that made up the detective bureau.

"Down here," Cerovic's voice boomed as they entered the surprising quiet of the corridor. "Did you have any problem finding a parking space? It can get pretty nasty down there at lunch. Hey, did you get a chance to eat anything? No? You want a sandwich or something out of a machine? How about coffee?"

"Nothing. Please."

"Hey, Nickie," DeSilva said from behind them. "I want a turkey sandwich. And coffee with cream and sugar. You wanna run downstairs and get it for me?"

Cerovic grinned at her. "I'll flip you."

"Come, on, Nickie. I just thought you were so willing to run off for our suspected felon you'd do the same for your pal and partner. Right? Or am I mixed up here?"

"You're mixed up," he said brightly, then to Kate, "Annie's in a mood today."

"You blame it on the time of month and you'll be chewing without teeth. Partner!"

"I'm blaming it on your crummy disposition, DeSilva. Nothing else."

They halted in front of a door. Nick popped it open an inch, glanced inside, and said, "Come on. No one in here."

It was a good-size room, with about fifty chocolate-colored folding chairs set up haphazardly in front of two large tables. The wall behind the tables was lined with whiteboards; one of them had a diagram of a house with an X in one of the back bedrooms, and the scrawled notation, *3 kilos.* To the side of the tables a large-screen TV like the one Nick had at home sat silently. A fluorescent light over their heads hummed and flickered, and the room smelled of sweat and a faint residue of tobacco that had clung to the walls for years.

Nick's tone turned somber as soon as he shut the door. "We can sit up front. The tape still isn't real good, but you might be able to identify the woman. She was pretty good at keeping her face averted from the cameras, though."

Annie smiled without humor. "Like someone who was familiar with hospital security. You know anyone like that, Mrs. McDonald?"

The policewoman was so openly hostile that Kate didn't trust herself to respond, and stared instead at the diagram on the whiteboard: Kate imagined a drug raid, cops busting inside with guns drawn, screaming "Police," everyone's adrenaline pumping. Just like TV.

Cerovic said, "You can sit here," and pulled out a chair directly in front of the television, then took a cassette that had been resting on top of the set. "These labs are pretty good, but the problem is the crappy cameras the hospitals use. Your place probably isn't any better. They put in a surveillance system to keep their liability insurance down, but skimp on equipment, so what's the point? You know what I mean? Go on, sit down."

Perspiration beginning to form on her ribs, Kate sat stiffly in a chair, DeSilva moving behind her. Nick shoved the tape in the VCR on top of the TV, then picked up a remote and sat down next to Kate. He flicked the TV on and waited for it to come to life. "It's kind of jerky because the tape we have is cobbled together from several other tapes. The snatcher was picked up coming into the hospital, then again on the pediatric floor as she walked into the ward and out again. She was only in the room fifteen seconds, so she must have known what—who—she wanted. Then we see her again heading toward the elevator. No film of her leaving, though. So she must have slipped out one of the rear doors, not a patient door."

The TV was ready. He hit a button and the tape jerked on at once with a bright hallway shot, probably the hospital entrance, an orderly walking toward the camera, a woman in a lightweight coat moving away. White letters at the bottom of the screen indicated the date, time, and camera number. The orderly glanced at the woman approaching him without interest. Wasn't he curious why someone was wearing a coat in the summer? Two nurses appeared briefly behind the woman, then veered off. A heavyset man in glasses moved past her, heading directly toward the camera.

"Familiar?" Nick asked.

"I can't tell. It's too blurry. I'd have to see her face."

"Outta luck there," DeSilva said evenly. "No faces in this epic. Doesn't have to be, though."

Another camera picked up the woman walking toward them, but her head was down and she held a hand up next to her face as though she had a headache. The coat was drawn close around her body.

"Anything?" Cerovic asked.

"Nothing."

A camera briefly caught her going into the pediatric ward, then hurriedly out, this time holding a baby to her chest. Her head was behind the baby.

Cerovic said, "We had this part enhanced. See her wrist?"

"Yes," Kate said, not sure of his point.

"Wait. We cut the film here and inserted the enhancement. You can make out the bracelet she's wearing. Watch."

The tape stopped, several seconds of static intervened; then the image sputtered alive again, but this time only the woman's wrist was on the large screen, along with the silver bracelet she was wearing on the arm that held the baby. Cerovic hit pause, and the bracelet seemed to illuminate the entire room as three sets of eyes focused on it, then went to Kate's wrist.

She jerked to her feet, tried to run, then dropped into a hole with no bottom.

39

Dazed and dissociated, like a shipwreck victim pulled from the sea, Kate sat silent and strangely apart from it all, while around her in the small, stifling interrogation room they'd retreated to, voices raged and shouted. Paul, called from court downtown, stormed around the office with his suit coat off, throwing accusations in all directions as though hoping one at least would stick, while Nick Cerovic, unruffled after twenty years of listening to suspects try to deflect blame with noise, kept his voice calm. "We called you as soon as we could, Mr. McDonald. There was no way we could know that bracelet was your wife's." But in fact Annie had recognized it at once, and insisted on bringing Kate in to get her reaction without anyone else there to interrupt or object.

"That bracelet is not proof of anything, damn it. You know that. I bought it for her at Macy's. Anyone could buy one."

Annie DeSilva, seated across from Kate, shook her head and stared at the floor. Capt. Oscar Reddig, looking annoyed, stepped in from the squad room. "Time to use our little voices, boys and girls. Yelling isn't going to solve anything."

"Arresting Kate isn't going to solve anything either," Paul shot back. "For Christ's sake, a bracelet is not identification. Have you had experts measure her body shape and height against the video? That could have been anyone. It could even be a man!"

The captain raised his eyebrows at Cerovic, who said, "Like I told you, Mr. McDonald, there was no reason. We didn't expect—"

Reddig recognized the lie at once, but Paul exploded. "You

didn't *expect!* What the hell did you have her in here for if you didn't *expect?* This was a cheap attempt to trick Kate into breaking down and confessing to something she didn't do. It sounds like a stunt the LAPD would have pulled back in the fifties! Jesus!''

Kate put her head in her hands.

Paul said, ''I want Rick Hazlitt here. We're not going to answer any more questions without our attorney.''

Reddig turned to Cerovic. ''You're not planning to file charges at this time, are you?''

Nick was all innocence. ''Of course not. I was just looking for a little help on our video when Mrs. McDonald recognized the bracelet and almost fainted. That's when I called Mr. McDonald.''

Kate stood up at once. ''Can I go?''

''Of course.'' He smiled.

Paul's face was livid as he grabbed his coat from the back of a chair and headed toward the door. ''I've already contacted Internal Affairs, Reddig. This whole damn division is out of control. It's anarchy; something's got to be done.''

''We'll be in touch,'' Cerovic said.

When the McDonalds were gone Reddig raised his eyebrows at the detective, and Nick said, ''Let me do this my way.''

''Always have,'' the captain said, and went back to his own office.

Annie glared at her partner. ''I'm waiting for your apology.''

Paul followed in his car as Kate drove to Mrs. Alamada's. She was in no mood to go back to work, and wanted only to be with her child now. As she placed Alex in the baby seat in the back of her car, Paul's anger flared up again. ''I don't want you leaving Alex here anymore. I want you to quit your job.'' When Kate didn't answer he jerked the other door open and ducked his head and shoulders in the car, but she paid no attention, fastening the restraint around Alex, who was laughing at the strange antics of his parents.

''Did you hear me?''

Kate touched Alex on the nose. ''Time to go home, funny

face." She kissed him, then backed out of the car and started to slip into the driver's seat.

Paul hurried around the car and grabbed her elbow. "Goddamn it, did you hear me?"

"I heard you, Paul."

"Well, answer me, for Christ's sake." His fingers tightened on her arm.

"It was too stupid to answer. I'm not going to quit my job."

"Damn it, you need to watch Alex. Don't you care about him?"

Kate bristled. "How dare you say that to me."

"But you still intend to leave him with the sitter?"

"It didn't bother you last week."

"Last week he wasn't taken out of his crib by somebody."

Kate yanked her arm free. "That happened at *home*, Paul. Not at the sitter's. Anyway, I'm surprised you trust me so much. Don't you think I might be responsible for what's been happening to him?"

Paul hesitated. "Of course not. That was just my anger talking."

She slid into the driver's seat and slammed the door. "I'm leaving."

"Kate, if you care about Alex you'll quit the hospital and stay home."

"And what do I live on without an income? Your generosity?"

"I talked to Child Protective Services this morning. They're holding off on a hearing to remove Alex from your care, but only because of my position. They don't want to get into a pissing contest with the DA's office."

"What's your point, Paul?"

"Either you quit your job, let me back in the house, and sign up for marriage counseling with me, or I'll tell them to go ahead with their hearing. Without me there's no way you'll be able to keep Alex. Not after everything that's happened. Especially when they hear the testimony from that woman cop."

"Then I *am* responsible for what's happened to Alex."

Paul's face closed up. "You must know something about it. How could all these things happen without your being aware of it? It's just not credible, Kate."

She stared at him a moment, amazed at her calm. Why didn't anything he say bother her? But it didn't; it was like watching a character in a TV drama. Suddenly there was no emotional connection at all to her husband, almost as if their four years together had never happened. She turned the key in the ignition. "And what about *your* testimony? What will you tell them?"

He didn't hesitate a second. "That you're no longer capable of caring for a child by yourself. That you need professional help. I'll see about finding a facility for you while you undergo treatment."

"Good-bye, Paul."

In bed that night, the crib now next to her in the master bedroom, Kate lay uncomfortably on top of the covers. A breeze blew through the window, fluttering the curtains, but it couldn't dissipate the heat that gathered upstairs every night, and she sat up abruptly and peeled off her nightgown. Alex stirred, shifted onto his stomach, and made a gurgling sound.

Kate pushed silently out of bed for the twentieth time tonight and gave him a quick glance. He was fine, of course, she told herself, and returned to bed and the thoughts that had been assailing her for days: *Why is someone torturing us? What did we do to deserve this?*

But of course there was no answer. Only the certainty that didn't become real for her until today, sitting as though alone in the interrogation room at the police department as everyone around her argued and shouted and threatened, that somebody she didn't know hated her. And Alex. And wanted them to suffer more than he wanted them to die. *And I have no idea why.*

Sleep came late, and only with difficulty, and with it the words that had haunted her for two weeks:

Your baby is going to die.... Listen to the message.... The message! ... Teddy's dead. ...

And as she sank deeper into sleep, faces slipped from her

unconscious, moved close and whispered eagerly in her ear, taking the time to torment her:

There was urine in the IV. . . . But I didn't do it; it wasn't me! . . . How do you account for the bruises on his legs? . . . It wasn't me. . . .

Teddy's dead.

I know. I know.

40

Sitting in her office the next morning, Kate stared at her computer as if it were some alien piece of machinery she had never seen before, then sagged forward and propped her forehead on her hand. Maybe Paul was right. Maybe it had been a mistake to return to work. Alex needed her, especially after these last two weeks. And every minute she spent at Midtown was like an hour in hell.

But again, there was no other option open to her. Without a job she couldn't support her son. Of course, that was Paul's real reason for wanting her to quit, so he could force his way back into her life. Although it probably wasn't her life he wanted back into so much as Alex's.

Where had Paul become such an expert at emotional blackmail? *Quit your job. Forget about a divorce. Forget his infidelities. "Without me there's no way you'll be able to keep Alex. . . . You're no longer capable of caring for a child by yourself. . . . I'll see about finding a facility for you while you undergo treatment."*

Thanks, Paul, that's sweet. But I think I'll keep my job for a while. And my son.

She had been surprised to find that she hadn't been fired yet. But with Zamora laboring to get rid of her, it wouldn't be long. Outside the main hospital door she had bought a copy of the *L.A. Times* so she could look at the classifieds at lunch. She checked her watch and almost laughed: *After five minutes I'm already waiting for lunch.*

Get to work, damn it. You're already days behind in your

work. But almost at once Joel Symonds's voice came from the doorway. "You look like you could use a friend."

She didn't trust herself to look at him. "Please don't," she said softly. "I don't want to start crying."

"All right," he said affably. "New topic. How do you think the Lakers will do next season? Don't like that one either? OK, what do you think of Frankie Yorba?"

This time she did turn around. "Frankie?" Warning bells went off in her mind. "I don't know. Why do you ask?"

Symonds sat down. "Has he ever looked strung out to you?"

"On drugs? No."

"Has he given you any indication he might be a user?"

"Does this have something to do with the missing narcotics?"

"I don't know. I've seen him—"

But Mohammed Kamel's voice loudly interrupted them. "Again, Dr. Symonds?"

Symonds looked toward the doorway. "Again what?" Though he knew exactly what the man was implying.

Kamel chose to ignore the question and addressed Kate instead. "I need to see you immediately. In my office."

"Why?" she asked, trying to hide her alarm, and thought, *Not yet. Please. I need a few more days.*

But Kamel had already gone.

Kate's eyes went to her desktop. "He's going to fire me."

"Has he ever given you an explicit reason?"

"Of course. Because I'm incompetent. Because I'm crazy and harming my child. Because I embarrassed the hospital by getting in the newspaper."

"I'll talk to Dr. Glazier. I've been planning to, anyway."

"No, don't risk your job for me. Please. It's not worth it. If he fires me I'll find another job."

"Where?"

"I don't know. . . . I could be a county social worker. I've done that before."

"Let me see what I can do first."

The phone rang and when Kate answered it, Kamel's voice made her shiver. "I said *immediately.*"

Kate smiled at Symonds, and felt suddenly close to him. "You're too late. Thanks anyway."

The ER head's office looked as if it had been removed in toto from a nineteenth-century gentlemen's club: dark walnut paneling, a wall of books (when would an ER doctor have time to read? Kate wondered), rich wine-colored carpet, brass lamps. Kamel was sitting behind a desk so large it managed to make him look almost small and innocent, a varnished and cracked oil painting of one of the hospital's dour-looking founders staring down at him from behind. And, as incongruous as an atheist at communion, skinny Frankie Yorba in his green scrubs sitting in a leather club chair. Vaguely Kate thought, *What now?*

Kamel wanted to get it over with quickly. His fingers began to tap on the polished desktop. "Tell Mrs. McDonald what you saw, Frankie."

Yorba twisted around to see her better. His face was without emotion. "I seen her use a key to take drugs out of the cabinet."

Kate closed her eyes, felt something rise into her throat.

"When was this?" Kamel demanded. His face had darkened under the thick eyebrows and full beard, and his upper body inclined over the desk toward Kate.

"This morning when I came in. No one was in the ER, and Kate—Mrs. McDonald—was putting a key in the cabinet, so I ducked behind a curtain so she wouldn't see me. When I heard the cabinet open I glanced around and saw her put something in her pocket, then lock the door and leave. She was practically running."

Kamel picked up the phone and pushed a button. "Have you checked yet?" he asked the person on the other side, then after a moment snapped, "Now, of course, damn you!"

A moment later the door opened and Chuck, the security guard, stepped in, holding a small bottle. He avoided Kate's gaze, brushing hurriedly past her, and put the bottle on Kamel's desk.

"Where was it?" the doctor asked.

"In her bottom desk drawer. Way back under some papers."

"Thank you." He nodded at the man, dismissing him.

"Morphine," Kamel said softly when Chuck was gone. He shook his head. "We are terminating your employment as of this moment. I've been authorized to offer you free enrollment in Midtown's drug-diversion program. There's no chance that we would ever hire you back, of course, even if you should complete it. You have five minutes to clean out your desk. In the meantime I will call the police about your theft of narcotics. Expect a visit from them." He looked at his watch as he picked up the phone. "Five minutes."

There was a car in front of her house when she drove up with Alex. While Kate removed him from the backseat, a woman got out of the car and approached her. "Marge Simmons of the *Times,* Mrs. McDonald."

Holding Alex, Kate backed out of the Mustang. The sight of the reporter incensed her. She would never go through that sort of mindless badgering again. "I'm not going to talk to you."

"We're doing a follow-up on the kidnapping story. Don't you want your side heard?"

Kate headed toward the door.

"I'm going to interview the police again. Shall I write that you refused to cooperate?"

Kate spun around. "How did you know I'd be home at this time of day?"

The woman's face closed up. "I didn't—"

"Someone called from the hospital, didn't they? Who was it?"

"No, really. I just took a chance."

Kate put her key in the lock.

"You were fired today, weren't you?" the woman, suddenly belligerent, asked. "Was it because you're a danger to the patients? Are they really calling you the Angel of Death?"

Kate went inside and slammed the door.

Again that night sleep eluded her, insomnia becoming the condition her mind and body had come to expect. But rather than toss and turn for hours, she walked up and down the second-floor hallway while Alex slept, her brain raging with plans: *I'll look for a job in the morning. I'll go to every hospital in L.A. No, that doesn't make sense. They'll want to know what I have been doing the past three years, and I'd have to tell them about Midtown. I'll leave town, then. Go to . . . to where? Go north. I've never been north. Go to Seattle. Or Portland. Portland! Tell them, tell them I've, I've been working . . . as what, damn it? Working . . . Tell them the last place I worked burned down and there weren't any records of my employment. No, that's ridiculous. Who would believe that? Tell them I haven't worked since . . .*

The phone rang in the kitchen. It was the only one plugged in now. Kate halted. *Don't answer it. It's bad news, something terrible. Portland!* It rained all the time, people said. That didn't matter. It never rained in Phoenix, and what did that get you? *Portland . . .*

She shuddered. The phone kept ringing. *Damn it, leave me alone!* Alex, in the bedroom, made a noise like a gurgle, then settled down.

The phone rang . . . rang . . . rang. *It's Joel Symonds. How do I know that? But I won't talk to him; I'm not going to talk to anybody.*

Maybe I'll look for a county job in Portland. Government departments don't always check references.

Still the phone rang. Her hands flew to her face; she wanted to scream.

Damn it! Damn it! Damn it! Sweat covered her body. The phone rang. . . .

July 27

Just think: for five years it was only us, Katie, playing our two-person game of tit for tat. The world neither knew nor cared what was happening to us. It's strange how lives are lived today—alone amid hundreds of millions who care not at all what happens to us. How many similar tragedies are played out every day, how many millions of other lives are turned to madness and misery, like ours, without anyone else being aware?

But it's not as fun as it was, Katie Kate. I'm angry all the time now. At you, at your mother, and Alex. Mostly Alex. He should never have been born. The mere fact that he lives makes me want to kill.

But you know that feeling from before, don't you—the sense that life is piling too many burdens on us? It's not fair, Kate. We don't deserve this, our lives the two sides of a single coin. My handwriting is getting bad. Holding a pen like a knife, I scratch out the words as hard as I can, ripping the paper like skin.

41

How much sleep did I get last night? Two hours? Three? Insomnia had become a habit, and she knew from experience that once the brain began to expect sleeplessness, that was what it ensured.

Pacing in the kitchen Kate swallowed her third cup of coffee and felt her stomach clench in revolt; she needed food, not more caffeine. Alex was moving slowly about in his walker, holding the plastic Big Bird and giggling with a sort of manic glee. *Got to get Alex to Mrs. Alamada, and go out and look for a job. Get my best clothes on. A dress. No, a suit. A résumé? Do I have a résumé? Maybe there's one on the computer.* She came to a stop. *Concentrate: a suit, a résumé, take Alex to the sitter.*

Write it down or you'll forget.

Who had called last night? Symonds? Why had she immediately thought it had been him? Whoever, it had to be bad news. There was never good news at night. Hadn't been good news in weeks.

Alex banged his toe and started crying. "It's OK, honey. Stop crying." She glanced at him but kept pacing. She ought to eat something. Then she'd feel better before looking for a job. But what she really wanted was to crawl back into bed and get eight hours' sleep. This insomnia was making it impossible to think rationally. She sat at the table and looked at her empty coffee cup.

God, she loathed the idea of job hunting. It was demeaning. *Please hire me, please, please, please.* Why? *Because I need a job. Why else would I be begging you?* Last employer . . . ?

Take it easy, she told herself. *You're getting panicky. Relax, relax. You can handle this. You're stronger than last time. Stronger . . .*

Portland! She'd go to Portland. No, a small town. Grant's Pass, Ashland, Bend. One of those.

Alex kept crying. She picked him up and continued pacing. *I'm not hurting my child. Damn it, I'm not!*

Her gaze darted around the house. *What should we take? Nothing. Just leave, get out before Paul can do anything about it.* The fingers of her free hand clenched, unclenched, clenched again so tightly against her palm she winced. *Run, Kate. Hurry! You've got that down pretty well by now.*

The doorbell rang.

Holding the wailing baby to her torso, Kate half ran to the door and flung it open. ''What?''

Cerovic and DeSilva. Cerovic said calmly, ''Put something on. Then we'll talk.''

Kate looked down. She was holding Alex. She was naked. She didn't move.

''Mrs. McDonald,'' Ann DeSilva said. ''Mrs. McDonald.''

Kate looked at her, the cop. The ''unnamed police source.'' *What's happening, what's going on? What are they saying?*

''Give me the baby. Put something on.''

DeSilva took Alex.

My robe! Kate thought. *Where's my robe?*

They sat at the kitchen table, Alex in his playpen, trying to say words. ''Goo. Maa. Ga fa la.'' Laughing at a Barney doll in his hands and dribbling spit on it.

Cerovic could only guess at the strain she had been under the past few days. Trying to be sympathetic, he said, ''Bad night?''

Portland, Kate thought. *As soon as they leave. Or . . . Or what?* Where else had she been thinking? How much money was there in the bank? She'd need money. Max out the credit cards, then throw them away so she couldn't be traced. Couldn't use ATM cards either. They could be traced in just seconds. She knew that.

Ann DeSilva threw Cerovic a look that said, *Get to it*. He darted a hostile look at her in return, then leaned forward and kept his tone neutral. "Mrs. McDonald, we had a call from the hospital yesterday. That ER doctor, Kamel."

Kate came back to the conversation but said nothing, her eyes going to Cerovic's face. She didn't trust herself to speak. But something was happening, something was wrong. *Concentrate! They're trying to trick you.*

"He said they let you go."

"Stealing drugs," DeSilva added, and looked at Kate as though to say, *I'm not surprised.*

"Not our area, of course," Cerovic went on, "but he insisted that someone come out and investigate, so the Narcotics division sent out two guys to take a report. From what I understand they don't have anything except the morphine they claim to have found in your desk."

Kate glared from Nick to Annie. "That's why you two came out here? Because they don't have anything?"

Cerovic shifted restlessly. "I'm afraid not."

DeSilva leaned forward, wanting to get to it. *God! She's enjoying this,* Kate thought. *She can't wait to see me squirm.* "Someone left a message on my voice mail last night that you were having an affair with another doctor at the hospital, Joel Symonds."

Kate shook her head in dismay, feeling a sigh go through her. But she said nothing. Why would the police care, even if it were true? Then she watched in disbelief as Cerovic's mouth formed words that sounded like, "He was found dead this morning."

"I'm sorry . . . ?" She shook her head; she hadn't heard correctly; her mind was wandering again.

"There's a room where the ER doctors sleep at night—"

"The on-call room," she said, feeling the pulse in her temple now, the heavy pounding of her heart.

"He died of an overdose of heroin."

Kate answered immediately. "No! Impossible."

"Why's that?" Cerovic asked evenly.

"It just is. He wasn't a drug addict."

"You and he were close?" DeSilva's eyebrows arched up.

"I hardly knew him. Just at the hospital. He used to take his break in my office sometimes." *My God,* she thought. *I'm already talking about him in the past tense.*

"He was supposed to go off duty at eleven last night. The ER was busy all night, so no one went into the on-call room until four this morning. He was on a bed, a hypodermic on the floor next to him."

Kate felt herself begin to lose control, felt the fragile ties that bound her to the earth break and slip away. *Hang on,* she warned herself as she started to float upward. *Stay calm!* But her voice faltered as she said, "It can't be. . . ."

DeSilva stared at her. "You're pretty upset, considering it's someone you hardly knew."

"I worked with him! He was a friend!"

"Homicide's doing the investigation, of course," Cerovic said. "One of the nurses out there said she saw Symonds using the phone a lot last night. He kept calling someone, but the phone evidently wasn't answered. Maybe the person he was calling wasn't home. It didn't stop him from trying, though. That was from about nine last night to maybe eleven, when he was supposed to go off shift."

"So Homicide checked the communications department," DeSilva said, and Kate thought, They're like an old married couple, finishing each other's sentences. DeSilva continued: "Guess who he was calling?" When Kate said nothing, DeSilva's eyes seemed to impale her. "It was to this number. He was calling you."

Cerovic asked, "Do you know what he wanted?"

"I can't imagine. I went to bed early."

"The phone didn't wake you?" DeSilva obviously didn't believe her.

"I heard it. I didn't want to talk to anyone."

"Lovers' spat?"

"What do you want? Why did you come here?"

"We thought you might want to know your loverboy's dead. Evidence techs are out at Midtown now dusting the room where he died for prints. What do you think they'll find?"

Kate finally made the connection she was supposed to make. "Why is Homicide handling this? Do they think he was murdered? You said it was an overdose."

DeSilva's eyes hadn't left hers. "There was a laceration on the back of his head. He could have bumped it someplace. Maybe that's why he went in to lie down. Or maybe someone whacked him on the head, then injected him with heroin."

Kate shook her head. This was madness. "I don't see what this has to do with me. Why are you here?"

"Whose prints are going to turn up around the bed? Or on the hypodermic that was used? Yours, maybe?"

"Jesus," Kate muttered.

Cerovic, embarrassed by DeSilva's aggressive questioning, said, "Have you given any thought to who might be harassing you?"

Kate shook her head. She couldn't think.

"Your husband's seemed a little overwrought lately."

"What do you mean?" Warning bells went off in Kate's head. *Focus,* she told herself. *They're after something here. There's some point to all this.*

"When he was down at the station house yesterday he was pretty worked up. We know you two aren't living together. Is that why he's so upset about things? Or is there something else?"

"What kind of something else? I don't follow you."

"I don't know. Rumor has it he's been seeing a woman at the hospital. Is that why you two split up?"

Alex began to cry. Kate used the interruption as an excuse not to answer, instead going to the playpen and picking him up, then setting him down on the couch next to her. He glanced without interest at the two strangers, then began to crawl into her lap.

Cerovic pressed on. "Upset husbands can do weird things. Could be he's the one responsible for the trouble you've been having, the rats, the marks on Alex, problems at work. It'd make sense. Who else has access to both your home and work?"

Kate took Alex under the arms and sat him on her lap. "It's OK, honey, relax." The boy reached up and began to touch her lips with his fingertips, as though fascinated by the sounds coming out. "That's ridiculous. Paul wouldn't do that."

"He didn't have any qualms about going out on you. How many girlfriends did he have? Did he ever tell you?"

DeSilva squirmed in her seat and shook her head but said nothing.

Kate said, "He wouldn't try to hurt me. He just wouldn't."

"He's been talking to Child Protective Services. Did you know that?"

"How do you know?"

"They called me. Wanted to know what I think."

"What you *think,*" Kate repeated, as if the words made no sense. "What you think about what?"

"Whether you hurt Alex. Whether you're one of those Munchausen women."

Kate's eyes closed. Alex, full of energy, yanked on her hair, giggled, and tried to crawl over her shoulder.

"So maybe," Cerovic went on, "if he'd go behind your back to Child Protective Services, or he'd have affairs you knew nothing about, he's not quite as trustworthy as you think. It could be he's trying to make you look mentally unstable so he'd get custody of Alex. Maybe he's the one with the mental problems."

"It's not like that! He wouldn't do those things. It's someone from before."

Nick and Annie exchanged a glance. She started to say something, but Nick stopped her with a look. "Before?" His tone was casual, but he could feel his heart begin to speed up.

Holding a giggling Alex at her shoulder, Kate stood.

Nick forced himself to sound only vaguely interested. "What before? Before you were married?"

Kate began to walk around the room, trying to get Alex to relax. "I don't know what I meant. . . . Just that it wasn't Paul. He wouldn't hurt his own child. My God!"

"You're right," Annie DeSilva said. "But I think *you* would."

Still pacing, Kate tried unsuccessfully to keep her voice

calm. "Get out of here. You don't have any right to be in my house."

"Look at you," DeSilva continued. "You can't even sit down. You're a nervous wreck. Look how you're squeezing your baby."

"I'm going to call my attorney." Kate headed toward the phone, then wondered, What attorney? Rick Hazlitt was Paul's attorney. It didn't matter anyway.

Cerovic said, "What is it you're afraid of, Kate? If there's something in your past you're ashamed of or afraid of, you're not going to be able to keep it locked away, you know. We'll find out."

She wouldn't even look at him.

He tried again. "I asked Homicide to check with your communications department to see where that phone call about you and Symonds originated from. Turns out it came from the orderlies' break room on the second floor."

"Frankie Yorba," Kate said at once, turning on him. Alex began crying and she held him closer.

"Why would he do that?"

"I don't know. He's the one who claimed I took drugs from the locker. He lied." Her mind started to work. Why was Frankie doing this to her? Because she yelled at him for going in her office? Of course not; there was something else going on.

DeSilva's face tightened. "To hear you tell it, everyone at the hospital is a liar—this orderly, Dr. Kamel, Ms. Zamora. What a crazy place, huh?"

Kate's eyes locked on the woman. "What are you trying to do to me?"

DeSilva smiled. "It's what we call building a wall. It's what police do. Every day we put another brick in place. Pretty soon you won't be able to get over it."

Kate started to reply, but Cerovic wanted to return to his earlier point. "Is there someone from your past who might have a grudge against you? An old lover, perhaps?"

"No!" Kate said at once.

The response was so sharp that both police officers focused

on Kate's face, which was moist with perspiration. She stopped pacing and shifted Alex, still crying, to the other arm. "No one," she repeated, and sensed that she had just screwed up. *They know!* she thought, beginning to panic, then changed her mind. *No, they suspect. But they'll start probing.* And a voice deep in her brain, much more urgent this time, again whispered, *Run, Kate, while you have time. . . .*

Cerovic leaned forward. "Look, we're not trying to railroad you into confessing to something you didn't do. We want to help. If there's something you're trying to hide, or something in your past you think is going to make people wonder about you, tell us. Trust the system. It works."

Kate stopped pacing, closed her eyes, and swayed on her feet a moment as Alex yanked sharply on her hair. Then her gaze fixed on Cerovic. "Get out of here. Now!" She grabbed a baby bottle from the refrigerator and gave it to Alex who continued to scream as the two detectives left.

Run, Kate!

42

"Goddamn it!"

It was past quitting time when Nick Cerovic threw the case file on the table, then watched as half the papers inside slid to the floor, a slow cascade that stretched all the way to the door. He was alone in the training room, surrounded by fifty empty chairs and the large-screen TV, now turned to the local news, with the sound muted. Getting up with an angry grunt, he collected the loose papers and shoved them back in the folder, then, throwing his head back, rubbed his eyes with the palms of his hands, and again screamed, "Christ!"

This wasn't turning out the way he had expected. Not at all. Maybe Annie had been right and he had let his emotions get in the way here. All right—there was no *maybe* about it—he was attracted to the woman, had been since that first day at the hospital. And for a while there he thought she might be attracted to him, too. Not that he expected someone like that to take a serious interest in a cop, but it was a nice fantasy, along the lines of winning the lottery, he supposed. So all this time he had been wise enough to see it for what it was: a dream, not something that was going to actually happen. In a sense, then, he was properly distanced from it all, hadn't allowed the fantasy to corrupt his progress on the case.

But it annoyed him how it was turning out. Because no matter what the evidence was showing, he was convinced Kate McDonald had done nothing to harm her child. Or had been convinced until five minutes ago.

"Goddamn it!" His gaze shot to the silent TV screen. The weather forecaster was on, a whirlwind of motion as he stalked toward the camera, then away from it, waving his hands at a map. *Weather forecaster, shit!* In L.A. all they said was, "If you liked today . . ." Why did it take eight minutes to say it? "God*damn!*" He tossed the papers on the table again.

"Goddamn what, Nickie? Or who? Or is it the whole world you're angry with today?"

Cerovic turned to see Capt. Oscar Reddig standing in the doorway. At 280 pounds, Oscar was probably the largest and certainly the most out-of-shape cop on the force. Everyone knew he hadn't taken, let alone passed, a department physical in ten years, but his popularity with his subordinates made him virtually immune to pressure from the chief's office.

Cerovic was annoyed at being overheard talking to himself. "Why not the whole world, Oscar? No point in singling out just a few individuals, is there?"

"Too wide a net, Nick. But, hey, I wouldn't mind all of Hollywood being damned, if it hasn't already happened." He came inside, leaving the door open to the babble and madness of the squad room. "So what has brought on this sudden wave of despair? The Munchausen case? I hope you read those articles I left on your desk a few days ago."

"I did."

"Good man. I'd hate to think I did fourteen minutes of rigorous research on the Internet for nothing. I assume you noticed also that the mom is the typical culprit."

"Yeah, yeah, I know."

"Then you also noticed that even good-looking moms can be guilty. You think maybe you got a little too close to this case? Maybe too interested in the suspect?"

"You've been talking to Annie."

"We've chatted from time to time. She's expecting an apology, last I heard. But you're the senior officer here. You make the decisions, and I'll back you up."

"I appreciate that, Oscar. Problem is, I don't like where this is heading."

"Which is?"

"The evidence all points in the same direction. But maybe there's too much of it. Like that bracelet. Who could predict that it would show up on a surveillance video? Or that we could enhance it enough to identify it?''

Reddig was thoughtful. "Someone in law enforcement might. Is that where you're going with this?''

"It did strike me."

Oscar sighed and rubbed his face with a massive hand. "I don't know, Nickie. It's all just a little too fine-tuned, isn't it? Bad guys usually aren't that bright, expecting us to do a video enhancement. Even bad cops."

"Not usually."

"You thinking of the deputy DA?''

Nick nodded, then shot him a glance. "I might be changing my mind, though.''

"What have you got?''

Still standing, Nick picked up the remote to the television and hit Play. "A video cassette came in the afternoon mail. Anonymously, of course. From the TV station logo on the bottom of the screen it looks like it's from Phoenix. I'd guess from the cars in the background it's five or six years old.''

On the large screen they watched a tape of a newscast, a young woman with a microphone standing to the side as another young woman was being hurried into a police station in handcuffs as hundreds of bystanders watched and jeered. "Watch closely," Nick said.

A minute later Oscar was on his feet. He looked at Nick with disappointment. "You're dropping the ball here, bucko. You need to call the FBI. You should have done it as soon as you got this tape. You might want to give Annie a call, too. She's expecting to hear from you.''

43

Glass broke in Kate's dream, a horrible crashing sound as the shards shattered and flew noisily to the kitchen floor. She saw a gloved hand hurriedly reach through the jagged window and flick the lock on the rear door. The handle turned and the door opened. Kate sat up, heart racing beneath her sweaty nightgown.

Got to stop that, got to stop having nightmares. Maybe try a sleeping pill, drug myself to a dreamless sleep.

Next to her Alex rolled over in his crib, moaned softly.

Are you dreaming too, honey?

Kate took a deep breath and lay back down, felt her heart slow to normal, then heard a noise from downstairs.

She froze. Listened.

Nothing.

Then she heard it again.

Someone's in the house! It wasn't a dream. My God!

She swung her feet over the side of the bed.

Someone's in the house.

Again she heard it. A sound like ... what? Almost like something being ripped.

I'm not imagining it. It was like a piece of fabric being slowly pulled apart.

Alex moaned again, blew spittle from his mouth.

God, no. It's not a dream. Someone's here.

She reached on top of the night table, where she'd put the gun Paul had brought home. Careful, she told herself, the safety's off.

Rippppp!

Was it Paul?

No, Paul wouldn't be sneaking around. He'd make as much noise as he wanted and dare her to do something about it.

Moving softly, she crossed to the door, open because of the heat. Her head edged slowly through the opening, but she couldn't see anything.

No sounds.

Nothing. Not even the wind on the curtains.

Wait! Listen.

The night air was warm against her bare skin, but a cold spot, as big as an ice cube, appeared on the back of her neck, making her shudder.

A motorcycle went by outside, its unmuffled engine roaring through the open bedroom window.

Listen!

Nothing.

No, I didn't dream it. I heard something. I did.

The gun at her side, muzzle down, she stepped softly into the hallway, stopped, listened, listened some more. But there was nothing beyond the normal moaning of the house as it cooled down after a hot day.

Ripppp!

It came from the stairs! There's someone on the stairs!

The sound stopped. *He knows I'm out here. He's waiting.*

She took a step, the carpet curling between her toes, halted again. Still nothing. Her head began to spin with confusion. *Maybe I did dream it.*

At least check the stairs or you'll never get back to sleep.

Moving more quietly than she probably had to, Kate walked to the head of the stairway, peered down, and saw the skinny long-haired man from the hospital parking lot smiling at her. He was sitting halfway up the steps, his back against the wall, a machine pistol resting in his lap. "Told you I'd be back." He held up an eight-by-ten photograph that had been in a frame in the living room: Kate, Paul, newborn Alex. The happy family. He was slowly tearing it into shreds.

Kate wheeled around, ran back toward the bedroom. The man let out a shriek and scampered after her. "Hey, bitch lady, you can't outrun Leo."

So it *had* been Petrosian, she thought. Paul had been right. He had been stalking them for weeks. Don't go in the bedroom, she warned herself. She didn't want Alex harmed. The nursery!

She darted inside as Petrosian half yelled, half laughed, "Get ready to die," and put a bullet in the doorway next to her.

Kate slammed the door, hurriedly pushed the dresser in front of it, then realized, *There's no phone in here! Jesus, what do I do now? The window.*

"Your husband's not here, lady bitch. Just us! Let's have some fun. A night of romance you'll never forget." He let out a contemptuous laugh.

The door moved, slammed the dresser, and Petrosian muttered, "Shit!" and pushed again, this time with all his might. The door exploded open, knocking the dresser on its back. He stood in the doorway, peering into the darkness. "Where the hell'd you go?" his heavily accented voice shouted. "Fuck it, where'd you go?"

No answer.

He put his hand on the wall and felt around for the light switch, finally finding it. The room burst into view and Petrosian saw the open window. "Damn you! Damn you! Bitch!"

Muttering, he hurried over to it. There was no balcony, no place for anyone to hide. For a moment he was baffled. Then he turned and stared around the room. A closet! At once he lifted his pistol and put two shots through the door, then pulled it open. Baby clothes, a high chair, a raincoat.

"Fuck, fuck, fuck! Where are you, lady bitch?" Then he saw the huge stuffed rabbit in the corner and gave a laugh. "A rabbit!" His voice became manic, rippling with hilarity. "Hey, Bugs Bunny, you silly wabbit. Time to die."

A bullet tore through Petrosian's side, throwing him back against the wall. Two more knocked him to the floor. He started screaming, his finger clenching the trigger and sending half a dozen slugs into the walls and ceiling.

Behind the rabbit, Kate sank to the floor, sobbing.

44

Lt. Derek Quarles arrived twenty minutes after the patrol officers, and just as the ambulance was about to leave. He sat in his car, Miles Davis on the tape deck, smoking a Newport and looking at the sprawling two-story house, finally muttering, "My, my, my." Life among the savages: the rich, the sort-of rich, and the pretend-to-be rich. It was almost as squalid as the rest of the world imagined. No wonder so many TV writers lived here—every family was a story idea.

Well, hell, he thought, heaving himself out of the car and squashing his cigarette, *let's see what it is today. Lust? Hatred? Revenge? Filthy lucre?* Walking over to the ambulance he glanced at the long-haired man on the gurney, his face obscured by an oxygen mask and his bare torso covered with blood. A female paramedic with red hair past her shoulders was hooking him up to a monitor that communicated with the hospital. Quarles shook his head as he heard the man's labored breathing. "You are one heck of a mess, my man. Y'all look lucky to be alive."

"Three entry wounds," the paramedic said as she heard the lieutenant's voice.

"Going to live?"

"Maybe. Or he might not make it to the hospital. The lady was a pretty good shot. Look here." She pointed to the bandaged wounds. "Can't be even four inches apart."

Quarles stared again, and shook his head as though nothing could surprise him now. "Yeah, I met her before. She's quite a gal. Any man's ideal wife, quick-witted, pretty as all get-out, and handy with a six-shooter." Turning away, he lit another

Newport, then headed toward the house, noticing a downstair light on next door. The neighborhood snoop; seemed like every community had one. *What boring lives they must lead, getting their thrills from other people's tragedies.*

The door to the house was open. Just inside, an evidence tech was coming out of the kitchen with a plastic bag of broken glass, while another was hunched over, taking flash pictures of the stairway. Quarles glanced into the family room, where Kate was slumped in a chair, her back to him, being questioned by a uniformed cop. He motioned to another patrolman who wandered out into the hallway.

"So what do you think, Morley? Should we open a substation in the cul-de-sac, or just respond to calls when they come in?" He flicked ashes onto the Mexican tile floor.

The young cop didn't know if he was supposed to laugh or not. He said, "I guess the lady does have her problems."

"Problems!" Quarles rolled his eyes. "She is the *definition* of problems, Morley. That was the evil Petrosian in the wagon I take it."

"That's what she says."

Quarles's voice was so soft Morley could hardly hear him "Shit . . . shit . . . shit." He glanced at the turmoil in the house cops and techs running around as though hoping to have time to get to the next murder before shift change. Flashbulbs strobe bursts of annoying white light against the ceiling, walls were dusted for fingerprints, and radios crackled nonstop with police calls. The ambulance loudly banged the curb as it pulled out of the driveway, its siren going on as it headed toward Cedars He turned back to the patrolman. "So what's mama's story This time."

"The man broke in and tried to kill her. So she popped him."

"That the way it looks?"

The cop let his eyes wander around. "Broken glass in the kitchen door, bullet holes upstairs, pistol next to his hand. The slugs will probably match his gun. Yeah, I think so."

"And the lady keeps a gun at home! Amazing. Nastier than she looks, isn't she?"

"Seems like."

"So how did this hard-ass Armenian psycho let a wussy little social worker get the drop on him?"

"She was hiding behind a rabbit."

Quarles patted the patrolman on the shoulder. "Don't tell me. OK? Let me work it out for myself. A challenge for the day." He dropped his cigarette to the floor, stepped on it, then put the butt in his suit-coat pocket before going into the family room, where the other officer was still writing down Kate's statement. She looked up, recognized him at once, and dropped her gaze. The cop stopped writing. "Hey, don't let me interfere," Quarles said amiably. "Go right on. Pretend I'm not here."

"We're through," the patrolman said, putting his pen in his shirt pocket. "I told her to come in after she gets some sleep, and give a complete statement. But I think we can wrap things up here as soon as the evidence techs are finished."

Kate hunched over, her arms around her knees. Quarles said, "You OK, Mrs. McDonald?" His tone didn't indicate any real concern. Curiosity maybe.

She didn't reply.

"Another close call, huh? You do seem to specialize in close calls. Luck of the Irish. My family, now, we always seemed to end up with the short end of the stick. Of course we're not Irish. Far as I know, anyway."

Kate's head snapped up, eyes red, moist, and angry.

"Your kid's OK? He wasn't harmed in any way? I heard about the rats you had a while back. I guess you kept a gun around here for them, huh? Weird stuff, those rats. Good thing you got to the kid before they had him for breakfast. Then him being sort of kidnapped . . ."

Kate's voice was drained of emotion. "You think I set this whole thing up, don't you? You think I invited that man over here and then shot him."

The patrolman looked in surprise from Kate to Quarles. The lieutenant shook his head. "Hey, I'm a detective; I'm not paid to think. I hear there's a shooting in Brentwood, so I mosey on out, interrupting some very nice jazz in the process, and it's you again. Twice in one week for me." He crossed his arms. "Pretty handy with a gun, aren't you? Looked like a nice compact pattern. I never can do that out on the range. My hand always pulls to the right after that first shot. But you did Petrosian real nice. Real nice."

Kate glared at him.

"And you hid behind a *rabbit*," he went on in a wondering tone. "I gotta tell you, that's a new one. Wait till the press gets hold of it. Just think of the attention you'll get: a pistol-packin' mama—a compact-pattern pistol-packin' mama—hiding behind Peter Cottontail to blow away a homicidal maniac as he threatens her child and her life. Ought to be a movie-of-the-week in that. Shit, you probably got two producers living within a hundred yards of here. You got an agent? If you don't I'd be happy to handle it for my normal fifteen percent."

"I'm through talking," Kate said, and stood up.

"No, I don't think so," he said easily. "You're through when we tell you." He smiled. "It's the way things work. Right, Morley?"

The patrolman, who had just wandered up, nodded but seemed confused.

"Not until I have an attorney. That's the law."

"Fine, fine, fine. Always happy to learn about the *law* from gun-totin' citizens." He turned again to the patrolman. "Did you read her rights to her in a clear and authoritative voice?"

"What rights? She's the victim, not a suspect."

"Read her her rights, Kenny. Humor me."

"You serious?"

"Kenny, she knows it all by heart. From TV, you know? Or prior experience. But do it anyway, OK? Just to be legal here. Her hubby's a DA, and you know how they are."

The cop looked at Quarles in surprise, then took out his Miranda card and began to recite: "You have the right to . . ."

Kate turned and walked upstairs. Quarles cupped his hand by his mouth and yelled, "We'll be sure to lock up when we leave. Wouldn't want any more bad guys coming in."

* * *

At six-thirty Paul phoned. "Jesus Christ, Kate, why didn't you call me? I learned about it from that asshole Quarles. How do you think that makes me feel?"

"I didn't tell you because I wanted to sleep. I still want to sleep. I was up most of the night." Alex heard her voice and began crying. Kate sighed and sank back against the headboard; now she'd never get any rest. At least she didn't have to go into work today, and had the passing thought, Thank God for small miracles . . . I think.

Paul's voice was taut with barely restrained fury, and Kate imagined him knotting his tie as he hurried to get ready for work, the phone jammed between his cheek and shoulder. "I told you Petrosian was a menace. That's why I wanted to be there."

"You told me he was harmless because everyone knew about the threats. And I thought you wanted to stay here because you loved me. You're having trouble keeping your stories straight, aren't you?"

"Still in a mood!"

"Almost being killed will do that."

He hesitated. "But you're OK? You weren't hurt? Alex wasn't hurt?"

"Thanks for finally asking. We're both fine. Lieutenant Quarles thinks I set it up, invited Petrosian over here and shot him. For attention, you know. Because I'm a Munchausen mother."

Again a pause, a change in tone, wary now. "How'd Petrosian get the address, Kate? Our phone isn't listed; we've only been there a few months. How'd this half-literate sleazebag just out of the penitentiary find out where we live?"

For an instant Kate thought she saw where he was going, then decided, no, he wouldn't. But for her own peace of mind he had to ask anyway. "You don't believe Quarles, do you?"

"Look, Kate, I don't know who to believe. That's why I'm asking."

"Really, Paul? Living with me for four years didn't give

you a clue into my personality? You honestly think I might be like that? That I might somehow trick this violent man into coming over here, and then shoot him?''

Again a pause that was longer than it should be. "No, of course not. I don't believe that."

Kate felt a tightening in her chest, the pain rising up to the hand that held the phone. Her throat swelled with hurt and anger, and she couldn't force herself to speak.

"Look, Kate, I don't know what the hell to believe." There was a break as he seemed to switch the phone to the other hand. "I get a call first thing in the morning saying my wife shot and maybe killed an intruder, and the circumstances are a little strange—"

"Strange how?" She sat up straighter, and her fingers tightened on the receiver.

"Because of the history of events, the baby switching, the swine flu, the rats—"

"The herpes. You forgot the herpes we got from Alex's father."

Paul made a noise in his throat, his anger erupting again. "What the hell did you expect the police to think? They've got this woman who refuses to talk to them without an attorney present, who's had all these things happen to her son, who seems to have had an affair with a doctor who very oddly turns up dead—"

Kate's voice jumped out at him. "Who said we were having an affair?"

"For God's sake, what do you expect people to think? Every time I came into Midtown recently he was hanging around you. And why blame me for the herpes? Maybe your doctor friend gave it to you."

"Good-bye, Paul."

"Don't hang up, Kate. Look, I want you to meet me today at the hospital. I've already arranged things, and it took a lot of time and persuasion, so don't screw things up. Glazier's authorized a seventy-two hour stay in one of their prestige suites, the fancy ones that look like a hotel room. And at no charge. He's having a friend of his, a psychiatrist, come in and—''

Kate put the phone down. She stared at the receiver in the cradle.

''Good-bye, Paul.''

Her eyes moved to the night table, but the gun was gone. Then she remembered the police had taken it.

Where can I get another?

45

No! Kate thought when the doorbell rang just after noon. *I'm not going to answer it. I'm not home.*

She was feeding Alex pureed apricots, and his face was orange from where he'd jerked away just as the spoon approached. He was in a foul mood, and was taking it out on Kate.

The doorbell rang again. She had a strong feeling it was Lilliana. There was no way she could talk to the woman today. "Open wide, Alex. Please." Still the boy refused to cooperate, pressing his lips tightly together and making a gurgling sound in his throat. "Do you want something else? Come on, just try the apricots one more time. If you don't like them I'll get some applesauce." As the spoon approached he raised his arm and hit it, spilling the soupy food to the floor.

Kate put the spoon down and took a paper towel off the counter. As she bent to clean the mess off the floor the doorbell rang again. *Damn it, I'm not home!*

"Kate! Kate, open up. It's Lilliana."

Kate rushed to the door and flung it open. "Damn it, Lilliana, why can't you leave me alone?"

The woman's face went white. But Kate didn't back down, glaring at her while still holding the paper towel, moist with wet fruit.

Lilliana swallowed, recovered herself. "I just wanted to make sure you were OK, hon. I saw the police last night, and the ambulance ... the whole neighborhood woke up. What happened? I didn't hear anything on the news this morning. Who was hurt? Was it Paul?"

Kate gritted her teeth. "Lilliana, can't I live my life without you butting in all the time? How many times have I come over to your house and asked what went on during the night?"

The other woman seemed surprised. "How many times have the police come to my house at two in the morning?"

"Go, Lilliana! I'll talk to you later. I'm not in the mood now. Can't you understand that?"

Lilliana started to reply, but Kate sighed and squeezed her forehead as she saw an ancient Ford Explorer pull into the driveway. Lilliana turned and said, "Oh . . ."

Kate's voice was subdued. "Please, Lilliana. Please! I'll come over and see you when I can. But I can't talk now."

Her neighbor watched as Nick Cerovic and Ann DeSilva began walking toward the front door; then she turned back to Kate. "Jesus, what's happening to you, hon?"

The two police officers halted on the stoop and glared at Lilliana, who said, "Right. Guess I'll be going, then. You'll come over later, won't you? Promise?"

"Good-bye, Lilliana."

When she was gone Cerovic said, "I had a neighbor like that once. She could tell you what everyone on the street had for dinner last night and what they did afterward. And for how long."

"I guess you want to come in," Kate said.

They sat in the living room, Alex, cleaned up now, crawling around his playpen with a plastic car in his hand, and trying out some new noises. Kate was confused. "I thought you didn't investigate shootings."

"Well, we don't," Cerovic said. "Not as a rule. But this time——" He broke off, seemingly uncomfortable, then said, "Petrosian's still alive, by the way. Looks like he'll live. But this is strike three, so he's looking at life. We're all kind of surprised he followed up on his threats. Guys like him usually don't."

DeSilva's fingers were dancing on the arm of the chair. "What do you think he was doing here, Mrs. McDonald? Looking for you? Or your husband?"

"What difference does it make? He tried to kill me."

"It'll make a difference to the trial. What if he only came in intending to steal something and you surprised him with a gun? A jury might go easy on him then."

"He shot at me two or three times before I shot him. I was protecting myself."

"Yeah?" Her face went blank.

Cerovic said, "What's your husband think?"

"Haven't you asked him?"

"Well, I guess maybe we did."

DeSilva held her gaze. "He tells it the way you did. Exactly the way you did: this loser's been harassing you two for weeks, finally decides it's time to walk the walk, comes over, and meets his match with Annie Oakley. Pretty tidy."

Cerovic said, "You're supposed to come down to the station house this afternoon to make a statement. Quarles said you want a lawyer present. You got one yet?"

Kate shook her head.

"You want a public defender?"

Kate stared toward the window. "Paul calls them public disasters."

"Well, that's a prosecutor talking."

Kate considered a moment. "Yes. A public defender would be fine." She stared back at him, then at DeSilva. "Is that it? Is that all you want?"

Cerovic shifted in his chair. He didn't want to ask. But DeSilva leaned forward aggressively, and turned Kate's life upside down. "Tell us about Teddy."

"My God," Kate muttered, and felt her self-control vanish. She began to weep.

"Teddy."

46

"Teddy . . ."

The word reverberated for several seconds before deepening into a silence that threatened not to end.

Then Kate sagged, and her head dropped to her chest. "And Robert. That means you know about Robert also."

Nick Cerovic nodded.

Kate's body gave a shudder. She stood up suddenly. "Where to begin?" Her head jerked nervously to the side. "That's a cliché, isn't it? Where to begin? How about five years ago?"

"Mrs. McDonald," Cerovic said, "Annie's going to take this down. I want you to know that. And you've already been informed of your rights, is that correct?"

She stared at the two of them a moment, taking in what he was saying. "Yes."

DeSilva looked at her blankly, but there was a challenge in the cold deliberateness of her voice. "Anytime . . ."

Kate glared at her. "Five years ago . . ." Then she turned her back and began to pace.

"I was living in Phoenix, but you also know that, don't you?" She crossed and recrossed the room. "I was married. To a wonderful man named Robert Lempke, an engineer. We had a beautiful baby boy. . . ." She paused as something rose into her throat, and had to force herself to go on. "Teddy . . . My little boy. A perfect family—mommy, daddy, baby. Then it all fell apart."

She closed her eyes, hurtling back in time, and Cerovic watched her flesh turn pale as she lived it again. Not remembered it, he thought, but lived it. *What is she feeling? Fear? Hatred? Despair?*

Kate took a sudden step away from them and started pacing again, her eyes on the floor. "I did all the right things when I got pregnant—went to prenatal care, stopped smoking and drinking, never took an aspirin, no matter how bad the swelling in my legs got, or how intense a headache became. Kate Lempke, the perfect pregnant mom. Everybody acted like I was some sort of neurotic, worrying so much. 'What's the big deal about having a baby? It happens millions of times a day.'

"But when he was born it was worth it. He was so beautiful. All his toes and fingers, a big smile that would make your heart break, perfect in every way." She stopped and wiped at her cheeks.

"A perfect mom, perfect child, perfect dad. Like the old song says, 'Who could ask for anything more?'

"It was like that for four months. I stayed home from work and took care of my baby. At six or eight months I planned to go back, but I was having too much fun being a new mom at that point to think about it."

She had come to the window and looked out. Cerovic followed her gaze as best he could, and saw the neighbor's house. *She's probably sitting at a window watching us with binoculars right now, hoping for a tragedy of some sort to enliven her day. That's what keeps people like that going.*

"Then he started getting sick." Kate's voice was so soft they had to strain to hear.

She spun around. "Unexplained fevers. Odd illnesses. Chicken pox at a very early age. Severe colds. But the fevers were the worst. A high fever at that age can be fatal. Or cause brain damage.

"After the second or third unexplained fever he was hospitalized for a week. They ran all sorts of tests, brought in doctors from the university hospital, even called some experts at the Mayo Clinic. No one could figure out what was causing it. But once his fever was down they sent him home. They had me bring him in for tests every week, though. I felt so sorry for him—all the poking and probing, and all the blood work they did.'' She paused abruptly, wincing. ''Excuse me, I have to use the bathroom.''

Kate disappeared and Nick and Annie looked at each other. Annie said, ''She's confessing. You know that, don't you?''

''Let's hear it out,'' Nick said softly.

They heard the toilet flush, then the sound of Kate in the kitchen.

''She's going to offer us tea and cake,'' DeSilva said. ''The perfect suburban hostess. Maybe we can get her recipe for brownies, too.''

But Kate came out of the kitchen with a water glass full of white wine, and offered them nothing.

When she remained standing Nick said, ''Wouldn't you prefer to sit down?''

''I can't sit,'' she snapped, then took a swallow of wine. ''I don't suppose either of you smoke.''

They shook their heads. ''Healthy Californians!'' There was sarcasm to her voice. ''Just like me. For all the good it did.''

DeSilva held her pen over her notebook, and Kate shook her head. ''I know . . .'' A deep breath, taking air far into her lungs. ''Teddy broke his leg one day. He was moving around in his crib, I guess, and came down wrong. I was asleep. My afternoon nap. Try explaining that to some cowboy Arizona cop: 'Yeah, I take naps. You would, too, if you were watching an infant for twenty-four hours a day, seven days a week.'

''I took him back to the ER as soon as I saw what happened. This time they notified the police. Too many problems with this child, they said, too many unexplained illnesses and injuries. Now a broken leg—hey, something tangible, something they could take a picture of and put in a file labeled 'Kate Lempke.' That was the start of the police questioning. You'll be happy to learn that not all the rude and insensitive cops are on the LAPD, Officer DeSilva. Phoenix has a few, too.''

DeSilva glanced up, a slight smile on her lips, but she said nothing.

Kate began to wander again. ''I got to know a few of their cops as well as I know you two. Detective Sherry Blankenship and Detective Ellen Groves. They were the ones in charge of interviewing people, checking my background, and shoving bits and pieces into the 'Kate Lempke' file.''

She dropped heavily into a chair on the other side of the room, and bent over at the waist, her hands falling between her legs. She put the glass on the floor and wrapped her arms around her knees. "I was a *good* mother. One who did all the right things. This shouldn't have happened to me. Or to my baby.''

Abruptly she came out of the chair, swiftly gathering up the wineglass, and started striding back and forth from the hallway door to the windows looking out onto Lilliana's house.

"One day Teddy was hospitalized for a rash that suddenly appeared, and a nurse thought the IV he was being given didn't look right. So she took it down and smelled it and immediately became suspicious. She replaced it with a new IV and sent the original to the lab. They found urine in it. Human urine in Teddy's IV.

"So—Blankenship and Groves again. But this time with a police psychologist, an obese man named Ulrich with a white beard and a blotchy red face. He carried a foot-thick pile of reports on something I'd never heard of before called Munchausen syndrome by proxy.'' She looked at DeSilva. "I understand you're an expert on it. Suddenly.''

DeSilva wouldn't be drawn into an argument.

Kate's voice rose. "Didn't you tell me you had a kid?'' She walked over and stared down at the woman.

"Yeah. A girl.''

"And you still think a mother could hurt her own child?''

"I'm not the only one, Mrs. McDonald. Or the first.''

Kate seemed to shrink within her clothes. "Yeah. Phoenix.''

She stood still a moment, remembering, then said, "Ulrich was a master of the instant diagnosis, just like Detective DeSilva. You notice he came to our meeting with the data on Munchausen's *before* talking to me. He made the diagnosis in his office without even seeing me, then set about proving it.

"I told him he was nuts.'' Kate gave an abrupt laugh. "He was a shrink, so he hears that all day. Just like cops do, right? Everyone says they're innocent, and the cops and shrinks are nuts. But I *was* innocent. It didn't make any difference—Ulrich had made up his mind, Groves and Blankenship had made up their minds, the doctors at the hospital had made up their minds. Only Robert held out. He couldn't believe his wife would do anything to harm their child.

"But the social services people believed it, too, and they convinced a judge that Teddy needed to be placed in a foster home while an investigation was carried out. So they took him away from me while I was subjected to two weeks of testing by Ulrich. 'What do you see in this inkblot? Tell me the first thing that comes into your mind when I read these words to you.' Meanwhile the police were digging through my background to see if they could find any secrets in my past. Maybe I tortured animals as a child or set fires or tried to poison my teachers.

"But they found nothing, and had no evidence I had ever done anything to harm Teddy. Not a damn thing. So back he bounced, our little rubber ball, back with mommy for a while. A week later he died of SIDS—sudden infant death syndrome." She sank into a chair. "That's what you wanted to hear, isn't it. My baby died."

Nick Cerovic waited a minute, watching Kate as she gathered her wits, then said, "You were arrested for murder. Is that right?"

Her eyes glittered at him. "Don't you have their case file? That should tell you whatever you need to know."

"They're sending it."

Kate bent forward at the waist and took another deep breath. "I was a celebrity, I was on TV. Night after night. The evil Kate Lempke who killed her baby for attention was getting more than enough of it. For three weeks I couldn't go anywhere—to the store or a movie, even for a walk. Of course I had been fired by then. The cameras were always with me, reporters shouting, 'How did you feel when your baby died?' or 'Did you kill your son?' They set up camp outside my house, satellite dishes and all. Catering trucks even came by at lunch and dinner, and a man sold 'Kate the Baby Killer' T-shirts, with my picture inside a circle with a red line through it. It was like a local version of the OJ trial. I was in jail a week before

Robert could bail me out, because they set it at half a million dollars, thinking I was going to flee. On what? I asked them. The money I saved as a social worker? But they said, Well, the border is right next door, so . . .

"So I was in jail with hookers and gangbangers and murderers. The other inmates loved having me there because it finally gave them someone they could feel superior to. A baby killer! Practically every night I was beaten, kicked, had food thrown at me in the cafeteria. The guards just stood there and watched, enjoying it. When I got out I looked sixty, not twenty-eight. The first thing I did when I got home was buy a gun and learn how to use it. I was terrified for my life.

"And all this time the DA was preparing a case, the cops were looking for evidence, I'm talking to Ulrich about my childhood, and the newspapers and TV stations are acting like I'm Lizzie Borden."

"The DA must have decided you were innocent," Cerovic said. "He let you go."

"I guess you haven't talked to him."

"Not yet."

"He's as convinced of my guilt as your partner here is. But they didn't have anything. Not *little*—they had *nothing*. He came to see me personally in jail. It was the only time the DA had actually done this, people said. But he had taken a special interest in the case, probably because of all the TV time he got, and because it looked like a slam-dunk conviction when I was arrested. He told me he knew I had killed Teddy and it was just a matter of time until they had enough evidence to go to trial, and they would go easier on me if I confessed. They'd work something out, maybe twenty years in prison. Even my lawyer thought I ought to plead insanity. I wouldn't do it. Finally they let me go because everything they had was circumstantial, and they didn't want to lose in court. This way the case is still open and I can be tried at any time.

"But I had already been convicted by the newspapers and TV stations. And then by Robert. My husband was finally convinced I killed our child. So I just took off one day. I couldn't stand it any longer. I got in my car and started driving out into the desert. . . . I don't even know where I went. I came back a week later, but by then Robert was gone. The next time I heard from him it was a letter from his lawyer informing me that divorce proceedings had begun.''

She slammed the empty glass on a table. "But he didn't divorce me until he told me how much he loathed me. I'm the most evil person he ever met, he told me. Evil! It's the last time we spoke!"

Cerovic was silent a moment, then asked, "And you haven't seen Lempke since then?"

She shook her head. "It's not a part of my life I want to remember."

"You're going to have to get an attorney. Private or public, it doesn't matter. But we'll want you to come down to the station tomorrow morning to give a more complete statement about your past, and to answer some more questions about Alex. They'll probably want to videotape it."

"I'm supposed to talk to the robbery people this afternoon. Can we do both at the same time?"

Nick nodded. "I'll fix it with them." He stood up. "I'm really sorry it's turning out like this, Kate. It's not what I would have wanted."

She stared at the floor.

Ann DeSilva came to her feet and made a point of putting her pen and notebook in her purse. "Off the record, just the three of us, and me and Nickie with our ears officially plugged, did you kill Teddy? Or is it all a little murky in your mind, where you're not quite sure how it went down?"

Cerovic looked as if he wanted to hit her. "Time to go, Annie." He nodded at Kate. "Tomorrow, about ten. That OK?"

When they were gone Kate stood at the door without moving for a long moment. Then she turned suddenly back to her house.

Run, Kate. . . .

47

Run.

If she stayed in Los Angeles she was going to be arrested for harming her child, if not for shooting Leo Petrosian. DeSilva was trying to get her on both. After talking to the Phoenix DA they'd be convinced of her guilt.

Hurry, Kate. Run!

But where could she go? She didn't have enough money to live on. The safe-deposit box! Maybe there was something of value in there. She had always let Paul handle that aspect of their life, thinking there was nothing in it but paperwork. She looked at her watch. Almost three o'clock. She couldn't get to the bank today. Tomorrow, then. She'd go to the bank but not the police station. No, she'd have to. If she didn't show up they'd be looking for her, and she'd never get out of L.A. She'd go to the bank in the morning, close out all her accounts, and run as soon as her interview with the police was over. It'd be at least twenty-four hours before anyone knew she was gone.

Hurrying upstairs, she began to pack. *Don't put anything in the car until tomorrow or you'll have to explain to Lilliana.*

In the morning, then. Get the car packed early, let the police have their interview.

She'd call her mother later, tell her she was leaving, but not tell her where. Not yet. She didn't want her to accidentally let the police know where she was.

Hands flying, she threw the clothes she wanted on the bed.

By six o'clock she had put together three suitcases for herself and one for Alex, along with a box of food, and another of diapers and toys. After feeding Alex dinner she put him to bed in the playpen rather than the nursery because the heat upstairs was worse than ever. Then she sank down in front of the TV. By nine o'clock she was asleep in the chair.

At five after eleven, a ringing woke her. Who could be calling this late? Paul, full of remorse and apologies? No, not in the mood he had been in. Again it rang. Hurrying into the kitchen before it woke Alex, she grabbed the receiver. "Yes?"

"Kate."

The hair all over her body stood up.

"Don't hang up. Please."

A soft, almost loving voice. Seductive, whispering, wooing her.

She had to force herself to speak. "Yes?"

"You don't know why this is happening, do you, Kate?"

She couldn't force herself to speak.

"I thought by now you'd understand. I've kept a diary. I want you to read it. Next week. It'll all be over by then. Just a few more days."

"Please! Who—"

"In your past." Whispering, but animated with emotion now, and so cold and corrosive she could feel the words rubbing against her flesh, making her shiver. "Years ago, Kate."

"Teddy?"

"Before, damn you! Before poor dead Ted. So very long ago . . ."

"I don't know what you mean. How many years?" Panic took hold of her and she began to scream. *"Why?"*

"Stop worrying, Kate. It isn't you I'm after. It never was. It's Alex."

"Oh, God . . ."

"You're safe, Kate. For now, at least. It's always been Alex. I thought I made that clear. I apologize if I didn't."

The flat sound of a dial tone rang in Kate's ear, and she sank to the floor, the phone still in her hand.

Unable to sleep, Kate had moved the suitcases into the car by six A.M., then fed Alex his breakfast. Standing in the kitchen, she went over the day in her mind for the hundredth time: take

Alex to Mrs. Alamada; then get to the police station by ten so they wouldn't suspect anything. After giving her statement she'd pick up Alex, go to the bank, get as much money as she could from their checking and savings accounts, empty the safe-deposit box, max out her credit cards, then leave at once for Oregon. She would have to come up with a new identity when she settled up there. That wouldn't be too difficult.

She shivered as she remembered the way the voice last night had said, "It isn't you I'm after. It's Alex." It was only with an effort that she forced herself not to panic. She desperately needed to be calm now, to be in control and think rationally, and not do anything stupid like before.

My God, I can't take Alex to Mrs. Alamada. They know where she lives.

"It isn't you I'm after. . . ."

The meaninglessness of it was pushing her over the edge. *Why Alex? He's only eight months old! Why would anyone want to hurt a baby?*

She was too panicky to sort it out. But it was obvious that the baby-sitter was out of the question. She couldn't take him to the police station either. There was no telling how long she'd be there. Lilliana? No, she'd want to know too much. *Anyway, she'd figure out what I'm up to. Who—?*

She grabbed the phone and called Patty.

"I was just at the door. What do you need?"

"Patty, I have to ask you a very big favor. . . ."

But the other woman was reluctant. "I have to go to work! Remember? Anyway, what do I know about babies? I haven't watched one for years."

"Please, Patty. Take a day of sick leave. This is important to me. I'll pay you back."

"Hey, I'm not worried about that. Hell . . ." She paused a moment. "OK, why not? I've got a dozen sick days coming anyway. How long do you want me to watch him?"

"Not past noon, I'm sure. He'll sleep most of the time. You won't have to do anything but give him a bottle."

"Do you want to bring him over here?"

"Could you pick him up? I think it would be easier on him

that way." She didn't want Patty to see that the backseat of her car was packed with suitcases.

"Sure, hon. Fifteen minutes OK?"

Alex was asleep when Patty arrived. Kate belted the car seat in Patty's car, then put the Big Bird doll in Alex's hand before kissing him and making him wince. "Be nice for Patty," she whispered, then thanked her friend again.

"Hey, no problem. I could use a day off. Maybe I'll go to the beach this afternoon. I haven't been all year."

"I should be at your place before twelve," Kate promised. "If not I'll call."

As Kate walked back in the house she saw Lilliana staring at her from the kitchen window. She had a vacuum wand in her hand. *No,* Kate thought. *Not today. Not ever again. I'm sick and tired of your butting into my life.*

Back in the kitchen she poured a cup of coffee. Two hours until she had to be at the police station. Jesus, how was she going to make the time pass? She went into the living room and turned on the TV. Anything to keep from thinking.

Today. Then *Live with Regis and Kathie Lee.* All that mindless banter made her want to scream. Halfway through it she stood up suddenly and flicked off the television. Casting a hurried glance around the room, she wondered if there were something else she should take with her. Personal belongings, photo albums, jewelry? *No,* she decided. *There isn't room. Leave it all for Paul.*

And his girlfriends.

The video! Paul and his lover!

The video she would take.

She retrieved it from where she had hidden it in her sewing room, and glanced down at the black plastic cassette. Paul and Judith the bitch.

Zamora? Why did she suddenly think that? Was that who was on the video? No . . .

But why not? Zamora in a blond wig, playing out some fantasy of Paul's.

She hurried into the living room and shoved it into the VCR. Turning on the TV she stepped back and watched with a new intensity, and for the first time without the slightest tinge of emotion, staring at the frantic activity like a zoo visitor watching the monkeys: Paul, hips rising and falling as he drove into the woman again and again . . . now on his back as her lips tweaked his nipple, moved down his body . . . both of them standing and moving in a rush toward the wall . . .

Kate's heart stopped, then began to thud against her breastbone.

She looked wildly for the VCR remote as bile rose to her throat. *Goddamn it, where the hell is it?* Screaming, she grabbed it off the back of the couch and hit reverse, waited, then punched play and watched as light from a window pooled on the floor next to the bed, picking out Paul's underwear, the woman's bra . . . and the silver-spangled shoes she had seen Patty wear to work last week.

The remote tumbled from her hand, hitting the coffee table and falling onto the floor.

48

Kate drove the two miles to Patty's house in a panic, ignoring speed limits and stop signs and oblivious to the horns blaring angrily at her. *Patty!* her mind repeated over and over. Her only real friend at the hospital. *But why? Why do you hate me so? Why are you after my child?*

She had been to Patty's house only twice, the other woman seemingly ashamed of her modest home. Or was there some other reason she didn't want Kate there? She found the house quickly, turning sharply into the driveway and cutting the engine. Reaching for the door, she stopped suddenly, her head jerking forward as she vomited that morning's coffee all over herself.

Only vaguely conscious that vomit clung to her slacks, she hurried up to the front door and began to pound. "Goddamn it, Patty, let me in! Where's Alex?"

Nothing. The house seemed deserted. She ran around to the back and banged on the rear door, shrieking at the top of her voice. "Patty! Let me in! Damn you!"

Coming back to the front of the house, she pushed the doorbell over and over and over, hearing it ring in the hallway. "Patty!" Her throat was raw.

"Hey!" an angry voice said, and Kate spun around, her heart pounding. A man in his seventies was standing several feet behind her, as if he didn't want to get too close. "You looking for the lady who lives here?" He winced as he saw the wild, sweat-stained face, the unkempt hair, and vomit clinging to her clothes.

"Yes," Kate said excitedly. "Do you know where she is?"

"Saw her this morning. Looked like she was moving out one step ahead of the landlord, the way she packed up her old Chevy. She was running like crazy back and forth from the house to the car, throwing all kinds of stuff in there. It hardly left any room for that pretty little baby in the back."

49

When Kate didn't arrive for her ten o'clock meeting at Hollywood station, Nick Cerovic drove out to her house, arriving shortly before noon. The others who had been impatiently waiting for her—Ann DeSilva, Capt. Oscar Reddig, a homicide detective, two social services investigators—wanted to have her arrested. Cerovic persuaded them to let him talk to her first.

He found her Mustang in the driveway, engine off but the driver's door wide open. Aware of being watched by Kate's neighbor, Cerovic rang the doorbell, and when it wasn't answered he went around toward the rear of the house, but the gate was locked. Going back to the front door, he rang once again, then tried the handle. It opened.

"Mrs. McDonald?"

He stepped inside. "Mrs. McDonald?"

Nothing.

Going into the hallway he heard a moaning from the kitchen.

"Mrs. McDonald . . . it's Nick Cerovic. Are you here? Are you OK?"

Following the sound to the kitchen, he found Kate sitting on the floor, her back against the dishwasher, the moaning coming from her lips as she stared sightlessly into space.

"Mrs. McDonald, are you OK?"

He dropped to one knee and looked into her face, but she seemed not to see him. "Mrs. McDonald!" He grabbed her hand. It was limp and without color. The only sign of life in her body was the horrible sound that didn't stop coming from her throat, a low wail that made chills run up and down his back.

"Kate!" he shouted. "Kate! Can you hear me?"

Nothing. He placed a hand on her throat and felt her pulse as it throbbed with the racing of her heart.

"Jesus," he mumbled, and stood up. He was going to have to call for an ambulance.

The phone was behind him on the counter. He picked it up, then saw the flashing red light on the answering machine. He paused, looking back at Kate, then pushed the play button. His stomach knotted as he heard a woman's voice racing with angry emotion.

"I told you it was always Alex I wanted, Kate, not you. There's no point in trying to find us. I disappeared last time—surely you remember the last time, Mrs. Lempke, when your baby died? But this time it will be different. Alex is payback for the hell you've put me through. He has to live until he's five, though. That was Tammy's age when she died, and the dates have to match, don't they? If not, it won't be an eye for an eye; there won't be any justice. So I'll keep Alex with me, my very own child, to bring up as I want, and someone to hate as much as I hate you, Kate. He'll never know I'm not his mommy, will he? It won't be much fun for him, I guess, having a mother who'll be thinking about his death every time she looks at him. But it's only for four more years."

The soft moaning behind Cerovic rose to a terrible roar as Kate sprang off the floor, screaming, "I want my baby. I want Alex!" And on the phone machine the harsh drone of the woman's voice: "You remember Jane Devlin, Kate. Of course . . . Phoenix, Arizona . . . Jane Devlin, damn you!"

In later years he was to remember that even at that moment Kate had no idea what Patty Mars was talking about. She had never heard of Jane Devlin. She had no idea why this was happening to her.

TWO YEARS LATER

1

Three months a lieutenant, and occupying Derek Quarles's old office, Nick Cerovic felt his heart slow to a crawl as he answered the phone and heard a woman say, "This is County Hospital, Sergeant—"

"Lieutenant."

"Sorry. Old information, I guess. I'm calling in reference to a Kate McDonald. Someone thought you knew her or remembered her, or something like that. I'm not quite clear on it."

Nick paused as his heart began to thump. "Is there something wrong? What do you mean 'knew'? Is she dead?"

"No, no, nothing like that. Are you a friend? Or did you know her in some official capacity?"

"A friend. Both, actually. What's going on?"

"One of our new ER doctors, Mohammed Kamel, thought he recognized her as the woman whose baby had been kidnapped after her other baby died in mysterious circumstances. Or did she kill him? I don't remember. That's why I asked about your relationship to her. She's the Munchausen woman who was on the news a couple of years ago, isn't she? Dr. Kamel thought you were handling the case."

"Why was she brought in?"

"She was living in Hollywood, in an apartment in the east end of town, I guess. One of those government projects for people who are having hard times or can't live on their own. Assisted living, I think they call it. Her next-door neighbor hadn't seen her for a while and had the manager open her apartment. They found her on her bed, unable to communicate. Practically catatonic, I guess. It looked like she hadn't eaten for days, so they called an ambulance. The EMTs decided it was largely a mental problem and brought her here.''

"I see," Nick said, because he didn't know what else to say.

"Right now we don't know what to do with her. She'll be OK physically after we get some nourishment into her. But her mental state isn't too good. She won't talk to anyone. We don't even know if she has a job at the present. Her neighbor thought she might be working as a waitress. We want to do some tests, of course, but she can probably be released in a couple of days if she has someone to keep an eye on her. If not, we might have to recommend a state mental hospital.''

"I'll be there in an hour. Don't do anything until then.''

2

And at once it all came back to him from two years earlier: Kate on the floor of her kitchen, mumbling incoherently, then suddenly leaping up and attacking him while the phone machine said, "You remember Jane Devlin, Kate. Of course . . . Phoenix, Arizona . . ."

But she didn't remember. None of it made any sense at all to her. All she knew was that Patty Mars had her baby. And was going to kill him.

After taking Kate to Cedars-Sinai, where they had put her in the mental health ward, Nick had returned to Hollywood station and called the Phoenix police to inquire about Jane Devlin and Patty Mars.

"Jane Devlin," the sergeant he talked to repeated. "Yeah, yeah, sure. Let me check the file and get back to you on it." Which he did an hour later, with the story Nick had thought about almost every day since, just as he thought of Kate McDonald and Patty and Alex every day, wondering what had become of them, and getting no help at all from Paul McDonald.

The day after talking to the Phoenix police, Nick had returned to Cedars and spoken to Kate, now sedated enough to grasp what he was saying and, just barely, able to carry on a conversation. "Jane Devlin," he said. "Doesn't that mean anything at all to you?" No, she told him, nothing, but the nothingness of it made her eyes flash with fear. And all she could do was lie in the bed, her arms in restraints while an IV fed Valium into her bloodstream, and listen to his story.

Five years ago when she'd been working as a social worker in Phoenix, she had reported a mother to social services for possibly abusing her five-year-old daughter. Yes, Kate had said; she did that all the time; it was her job. Well, Nick told her, they investigated, of course, but not until placing the child in a foster home temporarily to keep her from suffering any additional abuse if the mother was indeed guilty. The foster parents who took her in, a middle-aged couple, had been doing this for more than a year. Kate nodded. That was the way most states did things; the child's health and safety were always put first, even above the parents'. It was the way it had to be. It had even happened to Kate and Robert, she reminded him, when Teddy was briefly removed from their home.

Nick pulled his chair closer and rested one large foot on the metal frame of her bed. Looking into Kate's confused face, he took a breath and continued, trying to keep the emotion from his voice: The little girl was raped by the foster father who was supposed to be caring for her. She had been in the home only twenty-four hours when she was raped repeatedly, then thrown off a bridge. Shortly after, evidently overcome with remorse, the man killed himself with a bullet to the head. What made the case all the more heartbreaking was that the girl's mother was later shown not to be guilty of abuse at all. The whole thing had been a tragic mistake.

Kate looked at Nick with dead eyes and said nothing. She still didn't see the connection.

That was Jane Devlin, he told her. Jane Devlin/Patty Mars. The mother of five-year-old Tammy, raped and murdered because of a bureaucratic mix-up. She sued the city and settled out of court for two and a half million dollars. Adding one more layer of tragedy to the story was the fact that Jane Devlin had required a hysterectomy after Tammy was born. She could never again have children. It was one of the factors that encouraged the city to settle without a trial.

Jane Devlin had disappeared at that point. She was not heard of again for years, until she stole Alex. But all that time she had been taking her revenge on the person she blamed for her daughter's death. In her rented house (a house that had never actually been vandalized, he told her) the police found a diary that detailed the woman's thoughts and actions almost from the time Tammy was murdered. Every day she had made some notation, some angry comment about Kate and, after they were born, Kate's children. Teddy, and then Alex, had become obsessions to the woman whose own child had been so tragically and wrongfully taken from her.

Kate moved her drugged head slowly toward the wall, and Cerovic saw her shoulders begin to heave. For at least five minutes he had sat there as the hospital noises swirled around them, wondering if she was going to say anything. Then, without turning around, her whispered voice came to him so softly he had to lean over the bed to make it out: the name Devlin meant nothing to her, she had known none of this, she seldom had any follow-up on cases she referred to social services. But she had just been doing her job. There was no discretion here. The law required that all possible abuse cases be investigated. After social workers reported it, others decided what to do.

Nick waited until she turned to face him before continuing. Seven months after Jane Devlin's child was murdered Kate was still living in Phoenix. Shortly after she gave birth to Teddy, strange things began to happen to him . . . the fevers and so on. That had been Jane. She was trying to establish a pattern of abuse so Kate would be suspected, just as she was. Then, when everyone began to think she must be responsible for her son's illnesses, Jane smothered him. She expected Kate to be arrested for killing him. Which she was. She wanted Kate to suffer as she had suffered, but not just over the death of a child. She needed Kate to be convicted of killing him. Evidently she hadn't considered the possibility that Kate might not be held for trial. So when they didn't file charges she was furious. Her hatred fed on itself, becoming more out of control every day. She would have to do it again, and do it better. There had to be a more blatant trail of evidence tying Kate to the death of her child, Alex this time.

"You have to understand how profoundly mentally ill she is, Kate. For more than five years she's thought of nothing but ensuring your unhappiness. That's why the affair with Paul. She was prepared to do anything to give you pain. But as her hatred grew she evidently decided that even your arrest for murder wouldn't satisfy her need for revenge. So instead of killing your child, she stole him, intending to mimic the death of Tammy. It became her new obsession. An eye for an eye, she said. Everything had to be exactly the same. Everything: her suffering would be duplicated by your suffering. It was only fair, she insisted.''

Kate looked at him. "Tammy died when she was five?"

"Yes," Nick said. "Four more years. That's how long she intends to keep Alex. Then she'll kill him.''

An intense search had been made for Patty, of course, with her and Alex's photos on local television nightly. But she had simply vanished. The ease with which she disappeared indicated she had planned this for a long time and had everything in place when the moment came. An anticrime group offered a reward of $100,000 for the arrest and conviction of the woman who stole the eight-month-old baby. The city council authorized another $50,000.

But the police turned up nothing. Patty and Alex disappeared as effectively as if they had never existed.

And he hadn't seen Kate since.

3

When Nick arrived at County he found they had put Kate in a ward—a pauper's room, though they'd never use that term—with six other indigent and mentally ill women, most of whom were making noises of one sort or another, either of pain or disgust or rage. The loud, discordant sounds made the hair on Nick's neck stand up as he looked for Kate's bed, finding it one removed from the outside wall. There was no chair nearby, so he grabbed one from the bed area on Kate's right. The elderly Asian woman who had been lying on her back talking to herself jerked into a sitting position and shouted something he couldn't understand, though her hatred was blatant, and her voice shook as she grabbed the sheet and pulled it to her waist. Always uneasy around the mentally ill, he tried to block out everything but Kate as he slid the chair next to her bed. As soon as he saw her face he knew the feelings he had tried to deny two years ago were still there, and his throat tightened with emotion. How had he let this happen to her? How had he let her get away without at least trying to help?

At the sound of someone nearby, Kate turned her head, recognition showing briefly in her face, then closed her eyes. The flesh on her cheeks and forehead was wrinkled and pale, her hair had been cut short, by herself evidently, and her fingernails were broken and jagged. She looked as though she didn't weigh ninety pounds, and gave the appearance of someone waiting to die.

"Hi," was all Nick could make himself say.

The woman behind him began to shout angrily in some

Asian language—Chinese, he thought—and he could hear her jerking repeatedly on the sheet.

"Not a pleasant place," he added. "Couldn't your husband—"

"We're divorced." Kate's eyes opened and her head lolled slightly in his direction. Her voice was without emotion. "Aren't you supposed to say 'long time, no see'? Something like that?"

He smiled. "It has been a long time. I tried to look you up several times, but there was no phone number. I had Motor Vehicles check, but you didn't put in a change of address, so they couldn't help. I even had beat cops looking. They remembered seeing you but didn't know where you lived. And when I called your husband he hung up on me. I kinda figured you two split up."

"Of course. Why would he want to be married to a crazy woman? Or vice versa?" Her voice was weak, and she began coughing. Nick poured a glass of water from the plastic pitcher on the end table and offered it to her, but she waved a hand. "I don't suppose you have any gin on you? Or vodka? Something with a mind deadener?"

"Afraid not. I left my mental-health kit at home." Stupid thing to say in the circumstances, he decided, but the words were out.

Kate's lips formed a weak smile. "What difference would it make anyway? It's only temporary." A long pause; then she said, "Yeah, me and Paul are splitsville. So now he chases women and I kill babies."

"I'm not in Sex Crimes anymore. Homicide now. And kidnapping. I had your case assigned to me." He didn't mention that he was required to treat it as closed, Captain Reddig allowing him to work on it as much as he wanted, but only on his own time. Which he tried to do. But with the number of unsolved murders in Hollywood mounting yearly, it had become difficult to justify spending time on a case in which all the legitimate leads had been followed up months ago.

"How about your partner, the one with the fangs?"

"Annie? Still in Sex Crimes, doing a good job."

Kate glanced at him, then looked away.

Nick gazed around at their surroundings. "How did you end up here at the Four Seasons?"

She shrugged, then unexpectedly forced herself into a sitting position and reached for the glass of water he had poured. After swallowing no more than a sip, she said, "It's a little hazy, I'm afraid." She was staring down at the hospital gown she was wearing. "I guess I freaked out. That's what they tell me. It's happened before. It'll happen again." She glanced around at the room. "This is County, isn't it? I was here a couple of years ago. Lovely place."

"Don't you have any medical insurance? You've been working, haven't you?"

She put the glass on the table, and rubbed her eyes with her knuckles, then looked at her hands as if she'd never seen them before. "Pretty bad, huh? I look like a bag lady. I saw my hair this morning. I guess I did that, too. I must have used garden shears. I don't remember, though. Crazy Kate, the baby killer, can't remember cutting her hair."

"No big deal. I wouldn't remember to feed my dogs if they didn't remind me."

She looked at him. "You have dogs? I wouldn't have guessed. Rottweilers or pit bulls?"

"Mutts. Big soft mutts with furry faces, huge feet, and wet noses. The only things they attack are dinner and tennis balls."

Kate shivered suddenly. "I wonder what kind of medication they're loading me up on. I feel like hell. Do I work? you asked. Sure, I'm a breakfast waitress par excellence. What a way to benefit from five years of college. But it was the only job I could get. I've worked in half a dozen places in L.A. and Hollywood. Want to see my technique? 'You folks want coffee with your eggs? Orange juice? Hey, how 'bout them Dodgers!' I was at Denny's until this little fiasco. I guess someone else will have to ask about refills and Grand Slams now."

A heavyset elderly woman in the bed on the other side of Kate raised up on her arm and said, "Hey, mister, you got a quarter?"

Kate smiled uneasily. "She already asked me. I told her if I had a quarter I'd be in a better room."

The woman began to shout in a surprisingly loud voice, and Nick could see that she hadn't more than three or four teeth. "Hey, mister. Give me a fucking quarter!"

A nurse came in and tried to calm the woman, but she kept screaming at Nick as if she knew him. He edged closer to Kate, his knees against her bed. "We still get one or two sightings of Patty every week. Someone yesterday called from Tampa—"

"She's in Hollywood."

"Goddamn you, give me a quarter!" The woman tried to get out of bed. The nurse attempted to hold her down, but she scurried out of bed just as a burly orderly grabbed her from behind and said, "Back to bed, Grandma."

"Patty's here?" Nick asked. "In Hollywood? You're sure?"

"I see her every once in a while. When she wants me to. The last time was two months ago. I was working in a coffee shop on Sunset when she walked by. She was carrying Alex. She smiled and looked right at me through the window when I was putting breakfast on someone's table. I dropped the plates on the floor—hot cakes, syrup, butter, eggs over easy—and rushed out, but they were gone. I ran up the street, onto the cross streets, back down Sunset. I got fired, of course."

"Jesus."

"That's how I ended up here in Happytown. It's a game with her. She times it until she thinks I'm probably doing OK again, then lets me catch a glimpse of Alex. Or calls and tells me what a terrible time Alex is having with her. That's all it takes." Kate looked over at the bed where the woman was being put in restraints and still yelling for a quarter. The Asian woman on the other side jumped out of bed now, ripped off her gown, and started screaming at the woman being restrained. Another orderly burst into the room, and a nurse said to Nick, "You're going to have to leave for a while."

He started to protest, but Kate slipped down in the bed and pulled the sheet to her chin. "I'm living in hell. This is my punishment, isn't it? For causing Tammy's death."

All the patients except Kate were screaming now, along with the nurses and orderlies.

Nick got up and bent near her ear so she'd hear above the bedlam. "I'll come and see you tomorrow." He laid his hand on her shoulder and gave it a squeeze.

Kate didn't answer. With her eyes closed and her arms resting at her sides, she looked as though she were in a coffin.

Nick waited for an hour and a half at the noisy nurses' station until the doctor treating Kate had time to talk to him.

"You're a policeman?" The man's lightly accented voice was almost manic, like that of an old-time rock-and-roll disc jockey, and his hands were constantly in motion, as though he were afflicted with some sort of nervous disorder.

Nick showed him his ID.

"And your interest in her is what exactly?" He picked up a patient chart and began reading it, flaunting his lack of interest in police matters.

"Her child was kidnapped two years ago. That's when she started—when this sort of thing started happening to her." He raised his voice to be heard above the clamor of the hospital. "Is there any physical cause of her problems?"

"Drinking. Drugs. Her physical state is very poor. She doesn't eat much. Look at her, emaciated. Self-abuse. She brings it on herself. What do you expect?"

"What kind of drugs?"

The doctor continued perusing the file, flipping pages rapidly and pretending to read. "Sedatives. Any she can get. Street drugs maybe. Alcohol, certainly."

"Take her out of that ward. I don't want her in a place like that. It's a goddamn zoo."

An irate jerk of his head indicated that the request was ridiculous. "She's a charity patient, policeman! She doesn't have insurance. She stays where she is."

More angry shouting came from the permanently open door to the ward, joining the sound of endless pages coming over the PA system, and the chatter of doctors and nurses and visitors in the hallway. It was exactly what Nick thought a nineteenth-century insane asylum would sound like. He said, "I want her in a private room by six o'clock."

"There is no such thing." The doctor's gaze went back to the file.

Nick snatched it from his hands. "Of course there is. And if you can't find one here take her to University Hospital next door. I'll make up the cost. But if she's not in a private room by six o'clock tonight I'm going to arrest you for obstruction of justice."

The doctor's face tightened with loathing as he yanked the file back. "I came to this country to get away from people like you."

"Too bad. We're everywhere. Six o'clock."

Not ten feet away a woman in a nurse's uniform watched the exchange with a frown. *Damn! Still a hunk. And still getting his way. But who the hell invited you back into our lives, Cerovic?*

As the policeman headed down the hall, his shoulders hunched with irritation, she muttered aloud, "This is between me and Kate. But since you're here why don't we play with her mind some more, the two of us, and see what we can do?"

4

Using his car phone Nick called the DA's office, but Paul McDonald was out. He tried again from his office, this time telling the person he talked to that McDonald had better take the time to return the call or Nick would show up at his office. Finally just before five Paul called. He sounded both annoyed and defensive. "What do you want?" As if Nick were a telemarketer, trying for the hundredth time to get him to change his long-distance phone company.

"It's about your wife." Walking as far from the desk as the cord allowed, Nick stuck his foot out and kicked the door shut, making the window to the squad room rattle in its frame. An eerie silence descended.

"*Ex*-wife," McDonald corrected at once.

"Yeah." Nick could sense his dislike of Paul bubbling up already. He lowered himself to the wooden swivel chair. "Ex-wife. She's in County Hospital. EMTs overreacted, I guess. They thought she wasn't able to take care of herself and brought her in on a seventy-two-hour hold. She's in a mental-health ward with six screaming nutcases."

"I'm sorry to hear that." *No, I don't want to change my phone company.*

"You don't sound too interested in her condition."

"What's the purpose of this call, Sergeant?"

"Lieutenant. The purpose of the call? Well, I thought you might want to visit the woman you lived with for four years and had a son with. It might be good for her to know someone out there cares about her."

There was no response for a moment. Through the office

window Nick could see a young man, his body covered in tattoos, being pushed through the squad room by two detectives. He was yelling at everyone nearby, but Nick couldn't hear him. Finally Paul said, "Look, Cerovic, do you know Kate's history? I mean her recent history."

"She told me she's been working as a waitress for a while."

"That's not what I mean. Her *mental* history."

Nick felt a tightening around his heart. "Why don't you tell me?"

"She's been unstable since Alex disappeared. Depression. Not just unhappy, but massive clinical depression. The first two weeks after ... after Alex disappeared, she was on the streets looking for him. She didn't come home at night, spent all her time showing people his picture, Patty Mars's picture, talking to street people, gang members, store owners. She stopped eating, wouldn't talk to me, wouldn't even talk to her mother. I had to move back in to the house to care for her. But I couldn't help. She was too far gone. Finally I had to have her hospitalized. We had her taken to Metropolitan State Hospital in Norwalk for a psychological evaluation. She ended up staying six weeks. When they sent her home she was better, but only because she was doped up so badly she could hardly function. But at least she wasn't wandering around the streets at two A.M."

Nick planted his elbows on the desk. "She didn't seem all that bad to me."

"You didn't live with her," McDonald snapped; then his tone lightened. "Look, she's never recovered from all that's happened. It was just too much for her, and something snapped. But it's been two years now. It was a terrible tragedy and I think of Alex every damn day. But life goes on, doesn't it? You can't let this be the end of things. She can't see that. She's obsessed, probably because of what happened to her other child. She sees herself as a baby killer, two children, three if you count that five-year-old in Phoenix."

"Is that why you left her? Because she's obsessed with finding her baby?"

"Is that what she said?"

"She didn't say anything." The office door opened, a burst of noise rushing inside, and a man started to come in before Nick angrily waved him away and the door again shut.

"Get the story right before you start moralizing, Lieutenant. I goddamn well did not leave Kate. She had been back from Metropolitan for a week and wouldn't look for a job, wouldn't try to put her life back together, wouldn't eat, watch television, go to a movie or a restaurant. Everything was always Alex with her. Alex, Alex, Alex . . . And Patty. She was still obsessed with the woman. When she came back from the hospital I took a leave from my job, stayed home, and tried to help her get her head straight. But it didn't do any good. One day she just left. No discussion, no note, nothing. Took one suitcase and disappeared. I found her three days later in a flophouse in east Hollywood, living with illegals from El Salvador and spending her time on the streets asking about Alex. I tried to get her to come home and she wouldn't talk to me. Wouldn't even recognize that I was her husband. I gave it six months, then filed for divorce. She ended up with half the assets, what there was; we didn't have much equity in the house and there wasn't much else. God knows what she did with her share—probably gave it to psychics claiming to have information on Alex's whereabouts. There were enough of them—fortune-tellers, informers, street people, prisoners who heard something from their cellmates. Everyone with a story to tell. If they got paid."

Nick pinched the bridge of his nose. "Look, Mr. McDonald . . ." His eyes squeezed shut, then opened onto the pitted desktop with its mass of papers. He felt like going over to the DA's office and strangling the man. "Your—Kate—she needs a visitor, she needs someone to care about her. Are there any relatives locally?"

"Not that I know of. But she wasn't exactly honest with me about her past, was she? I mean, Christ, she didn't tell me she'd been married before. She didn't tell me she'd been arrested for murdering her baby. That's something a prospective spouse might want to know, isn't it? Especially one who works in the district attorney's office. Hell, for all I know she's got a dozen brothers and sisters, or even ex-husbands, lurking nearby. But I don't know anything about it. Ask her mother. She lives in St. Louis.''

"Then there's no one to visit?''

"I would say not.''

"Don't you think you owe that to her? Maybe you could just drop in to the hospital tonight after work, see how she's doing, show her you care.''

"Did she ask me to?''

"She didn't ask for anything.''

"It doesn't matter anyway. I really don't want to be involved in Kate's life. I'm getting married next month, to an attorney in the office here. A very nice, classy woman. Kate is in the past, a mistake I don't want hounding me for the rest of my life. I don't want anything to do with her unless you find Alex. Then I'm going to file for custody because she isn't capable of caring for a child. She can't even take care of herself. Obviously, if you have to do her phone calling.''

"This nice, classy woman you're marrying,'' Nick said. "Did you tell her about your herpes? And that video we all saw? I mean since honesty means so much to you—''

The dial tone sounded in his ear, and Nick slammed the phone down.

5

Kate was standing next to the window in one of the nonexistent private rooms when he visited the next morning.

"Hey," Nick said. "No IV." It felt good being with her again, felt natural.

She turned to look at him. "No crazy bag ladies either. It's almost like a hotel. Except room service won't give me a drink. Are you responsible for this?"

"I think the doctor had a change of heart. How do you feel?"

"Ecstatic. I'm full of happy-drugs. Want to dance?"

"That would really be depressing to you. As well as hard on your feet. What's the view?"

She stared out again. "Three guys with Uzis sticking up a hospital security guard. They've got his wallet and gun. Now he's pleading for his life."

"L.A. Ain't it beautiful?"

She turned toward him. "Have a seat. Only one nervous pacer allowed per private room."

Nick pulled out a chair and sat down. "Want to chat?"

"An official visit from the LAPD?"

"Or not. An official visit from the new lieutenant—you can congratulate me at your leisure—or a friend who wants to see how you're doing."

"Sorry. And congratulations. I'm happy for you." Her hospital gown started to fall away from her body and she clutched it to her neck. "You wouldn't think I had any modesty left after the last two years—living like a street person, or incarcerated in nuthouses where they confiscate everything, including your self-respect." She looked into a small mirror on the wall. "Christ, I look like hell, don't I?"

"Nothing a visit to the beauty shop won't cure."

"The last time I had my hair done was—hell, must be before—"

"You'll be out pretty soon. I'll take you to some chic Beverly Hills salon where the whole staff has names you can't pronounce and everyone will fawn over you as if you were, I don't know, Rosie O'Donnell. My treat."

She glanced at him suspiciously, started to say something, changed her mind, and began to pace the small room. "So let's say you're here as a friend and not as a cop. What's next?"

"Next you tell me the story of your life. Or the last two years."

"Yeah? Is that what friends want to know? OK. You don't mind if I keep stalking around here, do you? Back and forth, back and forth? It doesn't make you nervous, give you the heebie-jeebies to be stuck in here with a crazy woman who won't sit down?"

"I'm tough. I can handle walking women. It's the kickboxers that give me trouble."

"Yeah, I bet in your line of work you get to handle a lot of women." She flailed her arms out as though warding off bugs. "See? For no reason at all I get snippy and smart-assy with you. I wouldn't have done that a couple of years ago. Blame my ex, the Casanova of the DA's office. Never trust a man, I told myself then. But why trust women either?" She halted suddenly and looked at him. "How come you people can't find Patty Mars? It's been two years. You should have her."

"Nothing she does is spur-of-the-moment, Kate. She's a thinker. She'd planned this for a long, long time. She knew how to disappear and stay disappeared. She probably had a new identity and a place to live before she even needed it. At the drop of a hat she was able to go from Jane Devlin to Patty Mars, an identity she invented just for you. So now she's whoever she wants to be. It's Alex who will finally give her away, though. Keep that thought in the front of your mind."

She turned back to the window and didn't respond. After a moment Nick said, "Tell me how you ended up at County."

"Didn't you talk to the ex?"

"Tried to. He wasn't too forthcoming. He did say you walked out on him."

"I did. It had nothing to do with Alex, though. It was his lying and screwing around. I just found out what a shit he is. But this . . ." She turned around and let out a sigh as she crossed her arms. "I never stop looking for Alex. The nut doctor at Metropolitan— Did you know I was—"

Nick nodded.

"The nut doctor said, 'Give it up; move on.' Can you imagine that? Can you see a mother saying something stupid like that? And he was the person who decides if someone is sane or not. Hell, just forget that your baby was stolen by a homicidal maniac. Move on! Move on? *That* would be crazy. Who's looking out for Alex, who's trying to save his life? No one, because they've all *moved on!* Even his father, the one who had all the big plans for him, Harvard and law school and politics, unless he was playing outfield for the Dodgers. Only *me.*"

Again she began to pace. "OK, you know about the state hospital they put me in, along with people who thought they were Madonna or Jesus or George Steinbrenner. You know about my divorce. You know about what they like to call my *obsession* because I want to find my son before he's killed by this lunatic. What else do you want to know because you're a *friend* of mine?" Her voice had gone bitter.

Nick leaned back. "Yesterday you said you've seen Patty."

Kate spun around, furious and despairing. "Every couple of months I see her. On *her* schedule, when she knows I'm just getting over the last time, but when I can't do anything about it. I'll be at work or on a bus, and there they'll be, Patty and Alex waving and smiling and saying hi. Sometimes she sends me pictures or a greeting card, telling me about his illnesses, or how she had to take him to the hospital for broken bones, or whatever. Always some calamity. She's killing him. Slowly, deliberately killing a three-year-old child. That's how she gets to me, by getting to him! And nobody cares; nobody is looking for him but me."

She went again to the window and took a breath as she stared down. "A few months ago she sent me a video of a trip they took to the zoo. Patty and her 'son.' They had a picnic on the grass, and you could see Alex eating out of a box and hear Patty saying, 'I hope you don't mind that I feed him Lucky Charms all day. He likes them so much it's all I give him now."

Nick shook his head. "Did you report these sightings? I haven't heard about any of this."

"Report why? There's nothing you could do about it."

"Still . . . it's information. It might help us."

Kate wasn't paying attention, focusing instead on Patty's attempts to frighten her. "Last week she called to say she hadn't forgotten about me. She and Alex were having a fine time, she said, then reminded me they had another two years together. It was important to her that I understood that Alex had to die when he was five: that's how old Tammy was when she was killed. I'm afraid I got a little freaky. I started drinking again. That's how I ended up here."

Her eyes lost their focus. "Two more years she'll have Alex, two more years to destroy him slowly before—" She put her hand against the wall to steady herself. "Do you know that she honestly believes this is all justified? It isn't just words. She's merely doing to me what I did to her. An eye for an eye. She thinks since I'm a mother I ought to understand."

6

It must have been late at night, long after Cerovic left, when Kate, drifting in and out of sleep, heard the phone, and moaned with displeasure as she rolled over to look at the bedside clock. But there was no clock. I'm in County, she recalled with a sinking feeling, and flopped over on her back as the phone continued ringing. She had been dreaming, she realized with a start—one of those weird, disjointed dreams that made no sense: she and Nick Cerovic had been having a luxurious meal in an expensive restaurant somewhere; then they were both swimming nude in a lake up in the mountains. Nick had just touched her breast with his hand when she abruptly awoke. The memory of it made her warm with embarrassment.

"Are you OK?" A male nurse was standing at the open doorway.

Kate lifted her head to look at him.

"The phone," he said, and raised his eyebrows.

"What time is it?"

"Almost seven-thirty. Breakfast will be here soon."

The ringing continued.

"Want me to unplug it for you?"

Kate shook her head. "No." *Morning? God, the sedatives.* She reached for the phone and the nurse disappeared. "Hello?"

"Kate."

A sick feeling rose at once in her stomach.

"Kate," the voice repeated.

"Don't . . . Please, Patty."

The voice was upbeat, racing with a sort of hyperactive cheer. "Alex says hello, Kate. He'd like to meet you someday,

I'm sure. He thinks you must be a friend. Isn't that wild? He thinks I *like* you. I guess it's because I talk about you a lot. Sometimes I think you're the only thing I do talk about. Poor Kate, I say, poor crazy Kate, lost another baby.''

"Patty—"

"Alex is growing so big. Runs like a rabbit. Of course he falls a lot, but that's to be expected, isn't it? I'm not an expert on little boys and their problems. I had a girl, you know. Remember how pretty she was? How soft her skin was, and what a wonderful smile she had? She was so gentle. That's what I remember most about her, her gentleness and her smile. Do you remember her smile, Kate?''

When Kate said nothing Patty's tone hardened. "Look on the dresser, Kate. Damn you, look at her smile.''

Kate's eyes went to the white lacquered dresser just beyond the foot of the bed. A silver frame held an eight-by-ten photograph of a smiling five-year-old girl, the same face Kate had seen on her computer screen two years earlier, accompanied by a scream. Next to it in a smaller frame was a photograph of a vaguely familiar bridge. Kate's mouth went dry, and she had to force herself not to cry.

"You took her from me, Kate. You took the most wonderful child a mother ever had.''

"Patty, please, I had nothing to do with what happened to your daughter. You have to believe that. I was just doing my job. Those people had been foster parents for over a year; they had cared for a lot of children.''

Patty evidently didn't hear her. "Your son fell last week and cut his knee on an old rake. I washed the wound out but it looks infected. Is that what it means when it turns green? Maybe he needs some aspirin. But he's so adventuresome! Not like I was at that age. Or Tammy. Tammy was quiet. She was in kindergarten, you know. She was learning to read.''

"My God . . . You're sick. You must see that.''

The other woman's tone hardened again. "Because I want justice for my dead child? That makes me sick? Wouldn't you, in my place? Wouldn't any mother?''

"Because of what you're doing to Alex. He's innocent,

Patty. *Alex* didn't do anything. If you want revenge go after me. But leave my baby alone.''

"What I'm doing to Alex is what is called *abuse*. You're the expert on the term. It's what you accused me of seven years ago. You accused me of abusing my own daughter, and took her from me so she could be raped and murdered by someone who *didn't* abuse children. Isn't that what I'm doing to Alex? Isn't it the same thing? Why is it wrong for me if it wasn't wrong for you?''

"Patty, listen! I did not accuse you of abuse. I reported a possible *case* of abuse. It's the law. I had no choice. If you have an argument it's with the state, not me. I didn't accuse anybody.''

"Goddamn it, don't tell me who my argument is with. You're the one who stole my baby; you're the *only* one who can redress it. An eye for an eye, Kate, a death for a death. It's the way of the world, the only way to right a wrong.''

When Kate started crying softly, Patty seemed to get even angrier. "Maybe you're right. Maybe Alex has taken up enough of our time. I think I'll kill him tonight.''

When Kate heard the dial tone she jumped out of bed, pushed her finger down on the phone cradle, and hurriedly called directory assistance for the number of Hollywood station. A minute later she was talking to Nick Cerovic.

"I'll see if we can get a location on the call. It won't do any good, though. She wouldn't be dumb enough to call from home.''

"But she's going to kill Alex tonight. She said so.''

"No," Nick said at once. "That's the last thing she'll do. If she kills Alex the game's over. Like she said, she doesn't want your suffering to end. She wants you miserable, and she knows exactly what to say to ensure it.''

Nick could hear Kate's heavy breathing on the other end of the line, but she said nothing.

"I know this is a stupid thing to say," he told her, "but try not to worry about it. Patty's in this for the long run. Don't forget, she got a huge settlement out of the state of Arizona. She doesn't have to work; she can live wherever she wants, hire people to do her dirty work for her. That might be how she keeps tabs on you. But the one thing she doesn't want is for this to end. She needs Alex alive and well. Otherwise there's no point to her life.''

Kate was trying to stop her sobbing. After a moment she said, ''I don't know. . . .''

''I do know,'' he told her. ''I've worked with people like this before. I know how they think.'' A lie; he had never met anyone like Patty before, and was certain he never would again.

''Maybe . . .''

''Not maybe. It's the way it is.''

Kate's breathing was becoming steadier, but she said nothing. Nick's tone eased. ''Take some time to pretty up. I'm taking you out of there today. You'll want to look nice for the world.''

''Taking me where?'' She was suddenly wary, then angry at herself for feeling that way—the result of spending two years with people trying only to get something out of her.

''Where would you like to go? The Hilton? The Ritz?''

''I want to go home.''

''You are. My home. Until we take care of Patty once and for all. The two of us are going to go after her, just like Batman and Robin. We're going to get your baby back. We can talk about it in the morning. In the meantime Bailey and Preston are expecting you.''

''Who are they?''

''My roommates. You'll love them.''

She paused a long time. Finally he said, ''You still there?''

''Are you sure people like her don't just lose control and do terrible things?''

Nick took a breath and tried to sound convincing. ''Trust me, Kate. I've dealt with a hundred like her.'' He added, ''Try to relax. I'll be there by noon.''

He arrived before noon, but the particulars of checking out a patient, the questions and forms and bureaucratic nonsense, delayed their actual departure until two o'clock. Kate spent the time sitting in the room, or waiting in a wheelchair, as Nick dealt with a succession of clerks and administrators. She felt an odd sort of pride in him as he refused to be intimidated by the unfamiliar process, or the often rude people he had to deal with.

"You acted like you enjoyed it," she said as he wheeled her toward the elevator.

"Hell, I hate hospitals! Worst place in the world for sick people, and not much better for those who aren't. But I got used to the runaround when my wife was in. Everyone here thinks the future of the world depends on filling out one more form, or following some idiotic rule even if it doesn't make any sense—like using a wheelchair for someone who doesn't need it. The doctors are the worst, but I'll defer to them at least part of the time—when I think they know what they're talking about. But the damn pencil pushers—hell, they're career bureaucrats, could just as well be working at Motor Vehicles telling people to stand on the white line and smile for their license photo. They all have the same snotty, to-hell-with-everyone attitude. I learned a long time ago that the best way to get what you want is to dig your heels in and raise your voice. Act a little crazy if you have to. They're not ready for that; they're used to people nodding and saying 'yes, sir, no, sir.'"

"How did she die?"

"Huh?"

"Your wife."

"Oh." He was caught off guard for a moment. "Beth. She had a melanoma on her arm. California girl, you know. Always out in the sun. Got this mole, thought nothing about it; finally a doctor said, 'You'd better get it biopsied.' So she did. It was cancerous. She died four months later."

"Were you married long?"

"Ten years, just a month short, actually."

"Any kids?"

"No. That was the idea, just like dying at eighty-five had been, but that didn't happen either. The best-laid plans, huh?" He stopped for a moment. "Are you a cripple?"

"What?"

"You can walk?"

"Of course."

"Well, do it. Jesus, pushing a wheelchair makes sense if you got a broken—"

"Hey!" A young MD hurrying toward them halted suddenly as Kate started to stand up. "You can't do that. Hospital rules."

"Watch," Nick told him, as if it indeed were worth watching. He took Kate's hand and glanced back at the doctor as she rose gracefully from the chair. "You've never seen a rule broken before? You're a virgin?"

"Don't worry," Kate said over her shoulder as they headed for the elevators. "I wasn't in for anything physical. They had me in the nut ward—paranoid schizophrenia and an inability to control my violent behavior."

"Hey, pretty good, McDonald," Nick said as he put his hand on her back. "I always figured self-diagnoses were the most accurate."

Nick drove, the long freeway trip lightened by the CD he was listening to. "Opera," Kate mused. "I never would have guessed it."

"Yeah? What'd you think? Fifties rock? Country and western? Sinatra?"

"Muzak." She closed her eyes to the passing scenery—abandoned factories, eighty-year-old houses in various states of disrepair, graffiti-covered freeway walls. Urban America. Half an hour later Nick pulled into the driveway of his three-bedroom tract house. "Hey, wake up, Goldilocks. You're home."

Kate opened her eyes. "You live here all alone?"

"Me and the kids."

When she looked at him he said, "The dogs. My roommates."

She stared out the window. "You didn't have to do this."

"I know." He paused a moment. "So how do you feel? Emotionally, I mean."

"How am I supposed to feel?"

"Better than a week ago. Worse than two years ago."

She tried a smile that hovered for a second, then died. "I guess that's exactly how I feel."

"I don't want to get melodramatic, but if we go about things the way I think we should, it's going to get nasty. I want to make sure you're up to it."

She shrugged. "I guess we won't know until we start, will we? How long will that be?"

"It's started already." He pointed toward the front porch. "Someone left a nice bouquet of flowers for us. Probably a get-well card with it."

She glanced where he indicated. "Who would—"

"Only one person knows you're being released. And where to."

"How would anyone know?"

"The first thing I did at County this morning was leave my name and address, and I told them if anyone called for you to tell them where you are. It's how we're doing things now. We're not resting and we're not hiding. We're taking the war to the enemy. And you can be General Patton, standing in the front lines and kicking ass."

Her head sank to her chest.

"Want to read the card? It ought to be something to get our blood going, motivate us a little."

Without saying anything Kate opened the door and stepped out.

"Go ahead," he told her. "I'll be along." He needed her to do this herself, to take the first step on her own.

Kate walked up to the cement steps and looked at the inexpensive basket of carnations and roses. A small card was perched on a plastic stick. Willing her fingers not to tremble, she picked it up.

A moment later Nick took it out of her hand. "Happy homecoming, from the two of us." There was a cheap photo of the sort taken in one of those two-dollar booths—Patty laughing, holding a child with a big, innocent smile.

Kate said calmly, "I'm going to kill her."

"Good," Nick told her, and put his arm around her shoulder. "We're on our way, General."

7

The dogs were barking from the backyard as they looked through the rear door and saw Nick inside. "Let me get you settled first; then I'll introduce you."

He put her in the bedroom next to his. The bed was made and a new floral bedspread was in place. Her clothes were already in the closet. "How did you get those?"

"I went to your apartment, waved my badge, and said it was all evidence."

She smiled appreciatively.

"Your toiletries are in the bathroom. Along with a bathrobe. It used to belong to Beth. Never threw it out, for some reason. You're going to need some new clothes, though. And underwear. The stuff I brought over didn't look in very good shape. We can go out to the mall later."

Kate stared around the room in a sort of semidaze. "Why are you doing this for me?"

"Because no one else is. Because you need someone on your side. Because I like you." He looked at her awkwardly. "Just because."

Kate ran a hand through her short hair. "Thanks." The mirror over the dresser caught her attention, and she gazed at her image, her hand still in her hair. "God. What a mess, huh?"

"You want to see the rest of the house?" The dogs were still barking and banging the door with their noses.

"Please."

Nick took her around. "We bought it two years before Beth got sick. Bigger than I need. We expected to have kids, of course. . . ."

She stopped in the living room and looked at a collection of mechanical banks he had displayed in a bookcase. "Are these old?"

"Nineteenth century. I used to be able to find them at garage sales and swap meets. Now you've got to buy from dealers. They probably cost a dollar or less when new. Now they're usually four or five hundred. Some a lot more."

She turned to the extensive stereo system. "And a CD collection as big as a teenager's. Is it all opera?"

"Mostly. Opera and jazz."

"You're a strange fellow, Cerovic." Her gaze moved around the living room, but she seemed not to be taking it in. "She's out there, isn't she? She's watching us."

"Oh, yeah. Patty or someone she's paying. They'll watch everything we do from now on. I guess we ought to give them something to think about."

"Like what?" She looked concerned.

"Wait till after dinner. Now it's time to meet the kids. Brace yourself."

He walked to the rear door and let Bailey and Preston in. Within seconds they had nuzzled Kate back to the couch. She sank down and one of the dogs put his paws on her shoulders and began to slobber on her face. She said, "Quite a reception. How come Paul was never this happy to see me?"

Later they sat in the kitchen eating takeout pizza while Nick outlined his plan. "We're going to change the game for Patty and take away the fun. We're not going to let her call the shots like she's been doing for years. We're not going to sit back and worry and wait. We're not going to get all sobby when she calls. From now on, we attack, we go after her. Every time she phones, you're going to argue with her, call her names, fight with whatever comes to mind. Tell her what you think of her. Call her crazy. Tell her you talked to a shrink and he says Patty belongs in an asylum for the criminally insane. Whatever. Look for her weak spots, the places that make her mad, and use them against her. But don't ever back down. You're not wimpy Kate anymore. We're Batman and Robin, going after the Riddler." He took a cell phone off his belt and handed it to her. "The Batphone. Keep it in your purse. We're not going to be together twenty-four hours a day and I may want to get in touch with you. Or vice versa."

Kate stared toward the window. "She's watching us. Right now. I always know; I can feel it."

"Let her watch. It makes things easier for us." He dropped another piece of pizza on his plate, and patted her hand. "Number one rule: from now on you don't let her use Alex as a pawn. When she says Alex had an accident, tell her you don't believe her, or you don't care, or whatever. If she says it's Monday, you say it's Thursday. She says up, you say sideways. But never play victim. Disagree, argue, needle her, fight her, tell her you don't give a damn about Alex any longer."

He grabbed a handful of napkins from a holder and dropped them on the table. "You ever think about who might have been helping her at the hospital? She had to have someone doing the computer threats. And calling you on the phone. Patty couldn't have done it all. Can you remember anything about the person's voice?"

"I couldn't even tell if it was a man. I thought so. But it could have been a woman. Sometimes I thought he had an accent."

"The orderly?"

"Frankie lied about my stealing drugs. But I'm sure he did it to cover his own drug thefts. I don't think he had anything to do with Patty." Suddenly she remembered something. "Did the police ever arrest anyone for Dr. Symonds's death?"

Nick shook his head. "The coroner wasn't even sure it was murder. But no, it's still an open case. We'll never close it now." He swallowed half the can of beer he was drinking. "There was a woman there you were having problems with."

"Judith Zamora. She and Paul were having an affair. It didn't last long, though. He moved on to someone else a month after I quit."

"It's probably too late to work that angle, anyway. We're going to have to focus on Patty."

Kate took a deep breath and turned toward the window. She said nothing for several seconds, then shifted back and caught

Nick staring at her. He colored at once. Kate took his hand and held it. "I'm not sure I'm strong enough to do this."

"Sure you are." He nodded toward the uneaten pizza. "Eat! Tomorrow you'll be a different woman. You have to be. It's the day we start to find your baby."

Nick was in bed, waiting, when the phone rang shortly after midnight. Right about on schedule, he thought. Rather than pick it up he swung his feet to the floor and walked softly down to Kate's room. Standing outside the door, he heard her say, "I don't believe you. . . ."

A long pause ensued; then Kate's voice shot up. "Damn you! You're not smart enough for that. . . ."

Nick moved to where he could see her. Kate was sitting on the side of the bed with the lights off, her bare feet pressing against the floor, the phone clutched in her hand. She suddenly exploded. "Alex is dead! You can't do anything else to me! So go to hell."

Nick flicked on the overhead light. His voice was calm. "Good girl."

Kate was trembling, the phone on the bed where she had dropped it. After a second she snatched it up and slammed it in the cradle.

Nick sat next to her, the bed sinking under his weight, and put his arm around her. She was bathed in sweat. "I can't believe I told her Alex is dead. I can't believe I said that."

He held her tight, feeling her body tremble inside the nightgown he'd given her.

"It's not true, is it? Alex isn't dead."

"Of course not. She needs him. Alex is fine."

"God!" He felt her go rigid. She seemed suddenly not to recognize that he was next to her, and for a moment said nothing. Then a huge sigh shuddered through her body.

"Tomorrow," he told her with a reassuring squeeze. "Tomorrow we turn things around and take the war to Patty. Tomorrow everything changes."

The phone rang and Kate lunged at it. "No, you listen to

me! You're out of my life forever as of now!'' She slammed the receiver down and pulled the plug from the wall.

The phone in Nick's room began to ring, and he said, "I'll unplug them all. Then we can get some sleep.''

Later, alone in his room, Nick could hear Kate weeping next door, and knew there was nothing he could do for her. It was going to get worse tomorrow. Maybe he should have told her what he'd done. But it was too late now.

8

Kate was startled to see that the sun was up when she awoke, and rolled over to look at the clock: already after nine. She stared in confusion at the unfamiliar room for a moment; then last night's phone call roared back into memory, and a chill went through her. How had she managed to say those things to Patty about Alex? He wasn't dead! She mustn't ever say it again because it might make it true. She pulled the covers over her head as she had done when she was six, hoping to blot out everything that had happened. But there was no comfort in the darkness now, only terrors she couldn't see.

Vaguely she heard voices coming from somewhere. The living room? Or was it from the television? Slipping out of bed, she put the robe on over her nightgown and walked out of the bedroom, stopping suddenly as the voices became clearer. No, she thought in a panic, it can't be. Feeling her knees go weak she stepped into the living room and said, "Oh, my God."

Robert Lempke, her first husband, was sitting on the couch talking to Nick, a cup of coffee in front of him on the table.

Nick hurried over and took her by the elbow. "I thought it would be a good idea to talk to Robert about Patty. He might be able to help us find her." After a second he added, "Maybe I should have warned you."

Kate didn't hear him for all the roaring in her head. She had forgotten how handsome Robert was. No, that wasn't right: she had tried to convince herself over the years that she could barely remember how he looked, and the effect it always had on her. But it wasn't true; she could never forget. Sinking into the nearest chair, she stared at her ex-husband as her heart rose to her throat. "You're looking good, Robert," she managed, recognizing the banality of her comment but not caring. She couldn't help her stupidity: she was still in love with him, and always would be.

Lempke was clearly uneasy. "You're looking good yourself, Kate."

"No," she said. "I'm not. And I'm feeling even worse." Her hand went to her head as though to brush away imaginary cobwebs. "God, I can't believe this."

"I shouldn't have surprised you," Nick said, feeling now that he had made a mistake. "I was afraid you might have objected, so I just sort of arranged things myself."

Kate couldn't keep her eyes from Robert. "When did you get in?"

"A couple of hours ago. Nick called me yesterday. I told him I'd do anything to help, of course."

Kate felt a moment of alarm. "Do you know about . . . everything? I mean Alex, Paul . . ."

"Kate," Nick said calmly, "I told him what you've been through. I think he knows everything he needs to know to help us."

"My God," she murmured. "My heart won't slow down. I can't believe it." She bent over at the waist, her voice a whisper.

"Do you want some milk? Something to eat, maybe?"

She shook her head. "I guess I still don't understand. How can Robert help with Patty? He doesn't even know her."

Nick leaned forward, his hands clasped between his knees. "This all started back in Phoenix. Right? That's when you reported Patty—Jane Devlin—for possible abuse, and where her child was murdered. And where your own child started to suffer from a series of strange ailments."

Kate's intestines knotted. She didn't want to live through this again.

Nick continued. "I think one or both of you must have run into Patty back then, or even become acquainted with her in some distant way. She was familiar with your family. She had to have actually come into your house to do the things she did. I think you might have seen her posing as a house cleaner, a flower-delivery person, or something like that. Or Robert might have met her at work, or socially. Which means you might know something about her—how she thinks, who her friends are, or where she might be living now. Something you've forgotten about, perhaps. Anything.''

"I'm sure I never met her," Robert told Kate. "I'd remember."

"You met her," Nick said with confidence. "You had to. Either then or later. We just need to make you remember. She could even be someone you knew fairly well, a social acquaintance, or someone at work. We know how far Patty went to get close to Kate." He turned to her. "You never actually saw her when you reported her daughter's possible abuse, did you?"

"No! I told you, I just reported it to the state and forgot about it. I did that a dozen times a month. I seldom saw the parents. That was someone else's job."

Nick said, "I've set up some interviews for Robert with people down at the station house—a couple of detectives, a psychologist—"

"Why a psychologist?" Robert wanted to know.

"If you do remember her maybe you can give us a clue into her behavior. Perhaps you'll recall some relatives or friends of hers. Or where she lived or worked. Anything like that. You could have a lot of information stored away and just not be aware of it. So far all we know about her is that she's consumed with revenge, an eye for an eye. Talking to the shrink might shake something loose in your memory."

Kate had been staring silently at her ex-husband. Almost shyly she asked, "Have you remarried? I haven't heard anything for—since I left Phoenix. I always wondered."

Lempke seemed uneasy. His shoulders hunched and he spread his hands, a gesture that could have indicated embarrassment or resignation, or even anger. "I've been married for almost five years. Actually I don't live in Phoenix anymore. I moved to Albuquerque."

Kate's throat swelled as she managed to ask, "Kids?"

"Two—two girls."

Her eyes closed, the pain in her heart growing. "Why didn't you ever—I mean not a phone call, or a postcard." Her head buzzed with confusion. "All these years, all that's happened to us both . . ."

Lempke's face flushed and his voice hardened. "I couldn't, Kate. Because of what you did to Teddy!"

"My God, Robert! You still don't understand? I didn't . . . Patty . . ."

"I know!" He took a breath, and his tone relaxed. *"Now* I know. I didn't. Not until—" He glanced at Nick, obviously embarrassed.

"But you must have heard about Alex being kidnapped. It was on television. People all over the country heard. And you never called? You didn't care?"

"Goddamn it, don't you understand? I wanted to *hurt* you! My boy was dead. I held you responsible, and I wanted to hurt you in the worst way I could. Not to *help!"*

She sank back in the chair, seeming to sink within the robe. "All these years you believed I killed our baby?" She closed her eyes. "My God."

Lempke shrugged his shoulders, moved his hands uncomfortably in his lap. "I don't know if I actually believed it or not. I—it just seemed easier not to have any contact. Especially after I got married."

"I wrote to you! After I moved here. I wrote. There was never any response. The last one came back with no forwarding address."

"I know." He leaned back and rubbed a hand over his face. "I just couldn't stay in Phoenix anymore. I had to get out."

"Because your ex-wife was a suspected child murderer?"

"Of course not. Because I'd be reminded of Teddy every day. I didn't want that. I didn't want to be constantly agonizing over what I had lost. I wanted to begin all over. Without the memories."

Kate shook her head; her voice dropped as though she was

talking to herself. "I think of Teddy every day, even now, Robert. And Alex. I've had two babies taken from me."

"I know, Kate. I can't tell you how sorry I am that I never contacted you. It was stupid, childish. But it was the only way I could deal with my hurt. I just drew a curtain across the past—it never happened; I didn't know you."

Kate ran a hand through her cropped hair. "Does your wife know you're here? Does she know you're helping me?"

Lempke stared briefly at Nick. "She doesn't know I was married before."

Kate's head dropped.

"Cerovic promised I'd be back before six tonight. That way she won't suspect anything. I don't want to have to explain."

Kate's voice was pleading. "We had a *baby*, Robert, a beautiful child. Don't you want to keep that, remember that? You were his father. He deserves to be alive in your heart. He *deserves* that."

"I can't, Kate. I can't live in the past. It's not healthy."

Concerned that Kate was getting upset, Nick got to his feet. "Robert's got a two-forty-five flight home, so I'd better drop him at the station house. I'll be right back."

Lempke stood up. He didn't seem to know what to do. Should he offer to shake hands? Kiss her on the cheek? Kate remained seated. Her eyes were on the floor. "God, Robert. We lost so much."

9

Kate stood at the kitchen window, watching as Nick backed his Explorer out of the driveway and headed toward Hollywood station with Robert. For ten minutes she didn't move, staring at the empty street. Her knees were still weak, and perspiration covered her torso. How many years had it been? More than seven? And still she wasn't able to forget him. But she could feel an internal anger start to replace the longing still alive in her heart. *Seven years, and he never tried to contact you. Even when he heard about Alex being kidnapped. And you still love him? I can't help how I feel,* she screamed inwardly. *I can't help it. Even if I know it's stupid!*

"Hey, Mrs. McDonald! Been a long time."

Kate jumped and wheeled around. Her hand flew to her heart. "My God, Frankie!"

Frankie Yorba, in a sleeveless black muscle shirt and tight pants, bounced on the balls of his feet. "Hey, you remember me, huh? Bet you remember my phone calls, too. 'Still alive after all these years, Kate?'" He laughed as he saw the look on her face. "Yeah, shit, you remember. Pretty good, wasn't it? I'd walk by your office and see you ready to pee your pants." His eyes were darting everywhere, as though he was high on speed, and he couldn't seem to stand still, bouncing, moving his arms around, talking.

Kate's surprise was edged aside by the sudden realization of the precariousness of her position. She cinched the robe tighter around her waist. "What are you doing here?"

Yorba's gaze traveled up and down her body. "Still pretty good-looking, ain't you? For your age, I mean. Didn't surprise me, though. I been watching you off and on for years. Had some bad times, didn't you? Been down on your luck.''

"What do you want?" Kate's eyes shot around the kitchen, looking for a way out, but Frankie was between her and the door. Where did Nick keep knives? She saw a wooden knife holder on the wall next to the stove, but there was only one small knife in it. Maybe she should just start screaming and hope a neighbor would hear and call the police.

Frankie didn't take his eyes from her. "No sense looking around, babe. It's just you and me. Your cop friend took off. He won't be back until we've done what we're supposed to do.''

"What do you mean?" Her breathing stopped as his gaze settled on her face. Jesus, she thought, he's so wired he can't stop moving.

Frankie grinned at her. "Patty thought maybe you'd want to see your kid.''

Kate's heart leaped. "Where is he? Please!" She unconsciously took a step in his direction.

"Getting excited, huh?''

"Where? Please!''

"Heart going all pitter-patter? Getting wet between your legs? Hey, I do that for all the girls.''

"Please, Frankie.''

He jerked his head. "Take a look out the window.''

Kate ran the three paces to the window over the sink. Across the street a woman was kneeling and talking to a little boy. When they saw Kate looking at them, the woman said something and the boy slowly raised his hand, the fingers opening and closing in a childish wave. His mouth formed words but she couldn't hear them. He looked frightened to death, and his body began to shake.

Kate spun around and exploded toward the front door, but was caught from behind by Frankie.

"Uh-uh. Patty said you can look but not touch. When you're done looking you become my payment for sneaking in the cop's house here.''

Kate tried to twist out of his grip. "Let go, damn it." She started screaming at him. "Let me go!"

He was grinning at her resistance. "Got an attitude, don't you? I remember that."

Kate broke free, but he reached from behind and ripped off her robe, grabbing her wrist in the process. "Goddamn you," she yelled, then raised her voice. "Alex! Alex!"

Frankie said, "You don't gotta cooperate; it's all the same to me. A little tussle is OK." He yanked sharply on her nightgown, tearing it down the side. Holding one wrist, he pulled the nightgown all the way off.

Kate was hyperventilating, sobbing and shouting, trying to get to the door, but Frankie jerked her roughly toward him, pulling her off her feet, then screamed as he was thrown into the wall. Nick Cerovic held him from behind and rammed his face into the wall, blood splattering onto the plaster. Frankie wailed, tried to break away. Nick kneed him in the small of the back, and when Frankie bent over, he hit him with both hands on the neck and watched him land spread-eagled on the floor.

Kate was running naked toward the door. "Alex, Alex!"

"*Kate!*" he yelled. "They're not there. They're gone."

She halted, tried to catch her breath. "A woman and a child. Across the street—"

"I know," he said, and tried to make his voice calm. "I saw them as I drove up. They were getting into a car and leaving. I didn't make the connection until I saw this scum." He hauled Frankie to his feet.

"They're gone?" Kate couldn't seem to make sense of that. "They *left?*"

"I'm sorry. I wish I'd known."

Kate rushed back into the kitchen and grabbed the knife off the wall. Before Nick realized what she was doing, she lunged at Frankie, screaming. The knife creased his shoulder, blood jumping out over his arm and onto the floor.

Nick grabbed her wrist and twisted until the knife fell. "Kate," he screamed. "For God's sake, no!"

Frankie howled and grabbed his shoulder, then scrambled

to his feet and tried to run out of the kitchen, but Cerovic was on him in a second, throwing him to the floor. He jerked a pair of handcuffs from his belt and snapped them on Frankie's wrists. He could hear Kate in the kitchen, sobbing. Nick rolled Frankie over and looked at the wound. "Not that bad. Let's stop the bleeding and you'll be OK. Looks kinda like something you did breaking in." He put a finger in the warm blood. "I'll leave a little on the window in case anyone wants to do a DNA test. Just like TV, isn't it?"

10

Kate remembered the small interrogation room from two years ago. The same table, the same mismatched chairs, the same foul, oxygen-deprived air. Even Oscar Reddig was there, once again lending a disheveled and distanced supervision to the questioning. Only this time Frankie was the focus of attention, rather than her or Paul.

Reddig said, "You ought to have Weems or Wheaton here if you're going to charge him with attempted burglary or rape, Nickie."

Cerovic was sitting on the table, looking down at Frankie in the chair in front of him. "I haven't decided what I'm going to charge this piece of shit with. So far it's just breaking and entering. We'll jack it up to attempted rape if he doesn't cooperate, though. Let's see how it plays out."

Reddig said, "How'd he get inside?"

"Broke a window in back. He probably thought I was leaving for the day, but I dropped Lempke off and came right back. I heard Kate screaming as I drove up."

"Looks like he cut himself on broken glass."

"It's not serious. Is it, Frankie?"

"Fuck you."

Reddig nodded. "Another product of our Los Angeles schools."

Cerovic moved off the table. "I might call for a video camera later, Oscar. In case you want to review the questioning."

"Good idea," Reddig said, seeing that Nickie wanted to be alone with Yorba. "Take your time, though. We don't want to be too hasty. I guess I'd better get back to work. I've got some new pencils that need sharpening.''

Frankie looked up in alarm. "You're not leaving me alone with him, are you?"

"Not to worry, Frankie. Nickie's a gentleman. Sometimes. Aren't you, Nickie?"

"See you later, Oscar."

Reddig smiled and disappeared out the door.

Frankie was suddenly belligerent. "I want a lawyer."

"We'll get you one. But first we talk."

"About what?" He looked at Cerovic with wary eyes.

"Rape."

"Shit. My word against hers."

"Frankie, *I'm* a witness. And we have a broken window with your blood on it, and the lady's torn clothes, and Polaroid photos of marks on her arm where you held her. What's a jury going to say? I think they'd say twenty to thirty years in Pelican Bay State Prison."

Frankie's face froze up.

"Unless Mrs. McDonald decides not to press charges."

Yorba's eyes shot up, hope returning. "You shitting me?"

"Sound OK to you?" Nick asked her.

Kate nodded tightly. "If he cooperates."

"Yeah," the man said quickly. "I mean, look, I wanna help you. I wanna see you get the kid back, too. I didn't have nothing to do with that." He tilted his chair back against the wall on two legs, and looked up at them with concern.

"Start with Patty Mars. Where is she?"

"I don't know—"

Cerovic kicked the chair so violently Frankie crashed to the floor.

"Hey, goddamn it, I'm telling you the truth." He got up and straightened the chair, careful to keep all four legs on the floor when he sat in it. "I hadn't seen her in a year. Then she pops up at my apartment last night and tells me she'll give me a thousand bucks if I sneak into your house when you're gone and have Kate here look out the window at her and the kid.

That's it. I never even been to her house; I don't know her that well.''

Kate's cheeks glowed red as she leaned suddenly forward. "You're lying. You know where she is. You know where my baby is. You told me you were watching me.''

"I'm telling you, I don't know where the lady *lives*. She just showed up last night, didn't even call. She does this every once in a while, wants me to do something for her. Like I used to do the phone calls. Hell, it was a thousand bucks.''

Nick said, "How'd she know I'd be gone?''

He wagged his head in disgust. "She didn't. We sat up the block in her car for four hours this morning, eating doughnuts and drinking coffee. It was fucking boring, especially with that kid in the backseat whining all the time.''

Kate jumped out of her chair. "Damn you, where did she take him?''

"I don't know nothin' about that. Honest. I was doing a job for her, is all. I just sat there and smoked some weed and ate doughnuts and waited. She hardly said anything, just stared at the house and banged her fingers on the steering wheel, bang, bang, bang, like she's whacked-out. Sometimes she'd get out of the car and walk up and down the sidewalk. She couldn't stand still, couldn't stop moving. Then she'd get back in the car. Bang, bang, bang on the steering wheel again. If me or the kid tried to talk to her, she'd get pissed and yell at us. She's getting bad head-crazy, not like she used to be. She acts like she don't even like the kid, hardly talks to him.''

Cerovic moved behind Frankie, making the skinny young man squirm in his seat. He twisted around to see the detective. "Shit, if we'd known you was only going to be gone a few minutes we never woulda tried it. I thought, you know, I'd have a little fun. It was Patty's idea. She said, 'Take your time, enjoy it, do what you do.' ''

Kate, still standing, struck out at him, but he raised his arm and deflected the blow. "Goddamn you," she said. "Goddamn you! You know where they are.''

Nick, behind Frankie, put his large hands on the man's shoulders, moving them slowly up to cup his head. "Frankie, you were in the car with her for four hours. She must have said something to give you a clue as to where she's staying."

"She didn't, man. She talked to herself more than she talked to me. She wasn't like she used to be. She was always fun to be around, you know. Now she's just weird, mumbling to herself, pounding on the steering wheel, acting antsy. I asked her if she wanted to screw and she laughed at me."

"And she didn't talk to Alex?"

He shrugged. "I got the impression she might not have been living with him. Or maybe she just didn't like him."

"Why do you say that?"

"Hell, the only time she looked at him was to scream at him to shut up. And the kid acted sick all the time, anyway."

"Jesus!" Kate started pacing around the room.

Nick remained where he was, his palms moving back and forth on Frankie's neck. "When did you first start working for Patty? At the hospital?"

Frankie tried to slump down in the chair, out of Cerovic's grasp, but Nick held him immobile, his hands closing just under the man's jaw. "She had me call Kate a few times, is all."

"Did she tell you what to say?"

"Shit, she always acted like I was some kind of moron. She'd make me repeat it a dozen times until she liked the sound of it. 'Make it spooky, Frankie, make her shake.'"

"What'd she pay you to do this?"

He gave a sly grin. "She'd do me, you know. Down in the supply room. She never gave me money. But we were like friends."

Cerovic's hands tightened on the man's head, and he gave a painful twist. "Weird friend, Frankie."

"Jesus, let me go. You fuck—"

"Tell me about Dr. Symonds."

Kate spun around to Cerovic. "He killed Joel, didn't he?"

"Looks like it. Doesn't it, Frankie? Did Patty want to do away with him for some reason? Did he find out she was behind the phone calls?"

Yorba twisted his head out of Cerovic's grasp and slid his chair forward. "Shit, fuckin' Symonds thought I was stealing dope. I told the dumb fuck I don't do the kind of stuff they keep around there. Just a little weed, sometimes some blow if I can afford it. I don't want that medical shit. I gotta keep my body in shape, and that crap'll ruin you. Kamel was the one getting stoned all the time. He was stealing anything he could get his hands on. He'd take it home to his girlfriends and get high before screwing.''

Cerovic grabbed the chair and pulled it and Frankie back, his hands again going to the man's head, as though testing a melon for ripeness. "Did you tell this to Symonds?''

"Hell, no. Why should I help that asshole, always watching me like I'm some kind of scum? I told Kamel that Symonds thought I was taking drugs but I talked my way out of it.''

"Did you talk your way out of it? Symonds believed you?''

"I don't know if he believed me or not. Symonds said if it wasn't me, who was doing it? I told him, How the hell should I know? Maybe he figured out it was Kamel. Who knows, man? He died that night.''

"Kamel," Kate said. She shook her head in disgust. "Kamel killed him.''

Nick nodded over Yorba's head. "Looks like it.'' Then to Frankie: "Why did you accuse Kate of taking drugs?''

"Hell, Kamel wanted me to say that. Told me he'd protect me from Symonds if I did. And he got some weed for me from a patient of his. He was scared shitless Symonds was going to figure out he was the one stealing out of the drug cabinet. He thought he'd lose his job and get deported back to Pakistan if Symonds made a fuss.''

Kate looked at him with loathing. Frankie turned suddenly aggressive. "Look, I never did nothing you can hold me for. A few phone calls two years ago. DA's not going to file on that. Shit, you got nothing on me. I cooperated. Whyn't you let me go? I gotta get my shoulder looked at.''

"I don't know, Frankie," Cerovic said. "I don't think so.'' He turned to Kate. "What do you think?''

"He tried to rape me," she said.

"No way!" Frankie shouted. "You told me if I cooperated you'd drop that.''

Kate flared at him. "I lied. We both lied. Tough luck, Frankie. It's the way of the world.''

11

As she hurried down the rear stairs with Nick at Hollywood Division, Kate's voice was tense. "Patty's cracking, isn't she? She's losing it. That's what Frankie's telling us."

"She couldn't keep this up forever," Cerovic said, nodding to half a dozen detectives coming noisily up the stairs with two handcuffed juveniles between them. "She's under pressure, too. She's been torturing you for what? Seven years? It keeps getting harder and harder for her to get the thrill she needs. She's at the end of her tether now; she's getting bolder all the time. I think she knew Frankie was going to get caught in my house. That was part of the fun. She doesn't care what Frankie tells us. She knows he can't give her away, but she wants you to get your hopes up so she can knock you down again. And again. And again." He was about to hit the back door when Kate stopped suddenly. "Robert's here, isn't he? He's in this building somewhere."

Nick nodded. "Yeah. Probably with the shrink. He can't stay much longer. They have to get him to LAX." He started to move away, but Kate seemed rooted to the floor. Cerovic's voice turned tentative. "Look, Kate, I'm sorry about springing him on you like that. I didn't think after all these years—"

Her head snapped in his direction. "That I'd still be in love with him? Pretty pathetic, isn't it? Me and Robert . . . And all this time he's blamed me for Teddy, carrying that hatred with him." She paused a moment. "He didn't used to be like that. When we got married he was the most loving man I'd ever met. I don't think we had a single fight, not a real fight anyway, all the time we were married. Then when Teddy was born—

it was like magic to Robert. I never saw a father more attached to his son. He spent more time with Teddy than he did with me. He couldn't go anywhere without packing up his boy and taking him along, even if it was just down to the store for a minute. For a while I was actually jealous. It was almost as if he had a mistress, the way I had suddenly become number two in his life. But I loved him for it, too, because it meant Teddy wouldn't grow up distanced from his father like so many boys do. And of course he had all the proud-papa plans for the future. He was already setting up a college account when—''

Her body stiffened. ''God, no wonder he hates me so. He thinks I took all that away from him.''

Cerovic touched her elbow, hoping to comfort her, and she gave a little shudder. ''But I still get tingly just looking at him. Like a teenager on a first date. It's amazing how stupid people can be.'' She hit the rear door with both hands, and a blast of hot, dry air enveloped them as they stepped into the parking lot. ''I don't want to go back to your place yet,'' she suddenly decided.

''OK.''

''Let's go for a walk.'' She took his arm, surprising Cerovic, and they headed over to Ivar, then east on Sunset, Kate saying nothing for a long while. Passing a bookstore, she halted and stared at the books displayed in the window, but seemed not to be taking them in. Then she turned suddenly in his direction. ''We'll never find her, will we? She's too smart for us.''

Nick disagreed. ''She's not thinking real well right now, Kate. Going out to my house this morning was just plain stupid.''

''Or bold. She's fearless. Nothing bothers her.''

''Not so. She's getting edgy. And reckless. So we'll jack things up another notch and see how she handles it. We're going to do something she'd never expect you to do—go public with your story, all of it, including Teddy.''

He could feel her tense. ''This was all in the news two years ago when she took Alex. How is it going to help us now?''

''Two years ago people were fascinated by *your* role—the mother who lost two children. This time we'll focus on Patty and her mental health. I've set it up already with a guy I know on the *Times*. I got him an interview with a police shrink who'll imply that Patty's nuts, that she's dangerously paranoid. The article will play up how she's tortured you for years, how she's endangered Alex and murdered Teddy. A million people are going to see this, and I want them angry, I want them thinking this woman is the epitome of evil. Then we'll announce a hundred-thousand dollar reward for her capture.''

Kate's head swung in his direction. ''Who's going to put up the money?''

''It'll come from the equity in my house. Don't worry; we won't have to pay it out. As soon as Patty sees what we're doing, she'll contact us. That's the beginning of the end. I'll have all of L.A. looking for her. I'll have one of our media guys contact *America's Most Wanted* to see if they can do an episode on the case. We'll put out pictures of Patty—we can use that photo she left with the flowers, of her and Alex.''

Kate swallowed hard. ''This morning at your house—it was the first time I've seen him in three months. He's so big.'' Her throat swelled. ''I still talk to him every day. Can you believe that? I tell him how much I love him, or talk about places we'll visit when he's back with me. Last month I told him he'd be starting preschool soon, and he ought to know his numbers and letters by then, so I went out and bought these little books to use to teach him. Matt and Sis, a monkey and a snake. Alex's first books.''

Her arm unconsciously tightened on his. ''A few months ago when I was walking home from work, I saw two women get out of a cab on the other side of the street. I noticed them because they were arguing with the driver over the fare. Each of the women had a child about eighteen months or two years old. One of the little boys was standing on the sidewalk, and he did a double take when he saw me. I couldn't move. I stood frozen while the women argued, just staring at the child as my heart shot up to my throat. The little boy looked right at me and his eyes lit up and I could see his lips form ''Mommy.'' I started running across the street when one of the women said, ''What, darling?'' He pointed in my direction and the woman said, "Kitty, Jason." And I saw this cat moving off to my side. He hadn't been looking at me after all. In fact, neither of them was even aware I was there. The same sort of thing has happened a hundred times. I see some little boy, rush up, and . . . nothing. After a while you get used to the disappointment, but you never give up." She darted a glance at him, an uneasy smile. "Even when I was crazy I never gave up."

"There's a difference between crazy and determined. Let's say you were very determined to find your son."

"I wonder what I'm going to say to him. How do I explain it all? Do I tell him he was stolen and that the woman who raised him was not really his mother? Do I just say I was lost for a while? Don't you think it'll upset him to suddenly change mothers like this?"

Nick put his arm around her, and she moved closer to him, the movement as instinctive as a married couple's. "I think when the time comes, whatever you say will be right."

Kate stepped away from him so she could take his hand, then continued down the street, grasping him tightly. They were silent for a moment, then she said, "I think I was falling in love with you back then—two years ago. I didn't want to, but I was." She gave him a shy smile. "About the time I was going crazy."

"Well, maybe they go together."

"But I was afraid to say anything. Even to myself. I guess I wanted you to make the first move."

"It wasn't right for you. Or me. You had enough problems."

"Is it right now?" She was aware of the sudden wetness under her arms, the ratcheting of her pulse.

"Let's take care of Alex first. Then I guess we'll have to see." They fell silent again before Nick said, "I think we'd better get back to my place. The reporter's going to call sometime tonight. And your mother is going to call in an hour."

Kate's eyes went to his. "My mother? How do you know?"

"I phoned her yesterday. She's been worried about you. She and I talk every few weeks. Have for two years."

"You and my mother? Why?"

"A couple of years ago she called the station house, worried about you. She said she hadn't heard from you in a long time."

Kate felt terrible. "I just couldn't. . . . She was so broken-hearted when Teddy died. Then to have Alex taken . . ."

"She lost more than you have, Kate. She lost two grandchildren and a daughter. You need to talk to her."

Kate squeezed his hand.

An hour later she heard her mother's voice for the first time since Alex had disappeared. "I've been so worried about you, hon."

"I know, Mom. I'm so sorry. . . ."

They talked for twenty minutes, Kate's spirits gently lifting as she and her mother reestablished the comfortable relationship that had always existed between them. As they were getting ready to hang up, her mother said, "You have some good friends, Kate, people who love you. Especially Nick."

"I know."

"And that woman who came to see me last week. I could tell she really cared about you."

Kate stopped breathing. "What woman?"

"Jane or June something. Jane, that was it! I don't remember the last name. About your age. Don't you know who I mean? She said she was a friend of yours."

"Yes, Mom. I know who you mean."

"She said you'd have wanted her to stop by when she was in St. Louis. She had her little boy with her. Not a very active child, I thought. So quiet. But she said he'd been sick a lot."

The phone dropped from Kate's hand.

Nick picked up the receiver. "Mrs. Coleman, you'd better tell me what you just said to your daughter."

While Kate jumped up and began pacing, Nick listened to everything her mother remembered about being visited by Patty. "If she shows up again, call the police, Mrs. Coleman. Call nine-one-one and get them there as soon as possible." When he explained why, the woman was devastated. "My Lord, I had no idea."

Nick reassured her that she had done nothing wrong, that there was no way she could have known who it was. When he asked Kate if she wanted to say anything else to her mother, she merely shook her head, unable to stop her pacing.

12

The *Times* article was more prominently featured than either Nick or Kate had expected, taking up half the first page of Sunday's Life and Style section. A MOTHER'S MADNESS, it was headlined in huge type, with the picture of Patty and Alex that had been attached to Patty's bouquet of flowers.

Sitting at the kitchen table with a cup of coffee, Kate took a breath and quickly read the entire story, then read it again, slowly. But this time—reliving one by one the events of the past few years—there was none of the emotion, none of the sadness and pain that had been such a part of her life since Teddy had died so mysteriously. Instead she felt an icy numbness that went through to her bones as the reporter retold the story much as Kate and Nick had told it to him: Jane Devlin/Patty Mars admitting two years ago on the phone tape that she had been relentlessly stalking Kate in revenge for Kate's role in her daughter Tammy's death; the nationwide search for Alex and the kidnapper; the excited TV coverage (along with pictures of Kate's previous arrest in Phoenix, reporters screaming questions and thrusting microphones at her); the reward that had been offered; and most of all the feeding frenzy in the local media (special reports, interviews with childhood friends, newsbreaks that interrupted normal programming), and the way it suddenly came to an end only two weeks later as new crimes grabbed people's attention. And finally Kate's lonely two-year search for her baby, and her descent into mental illness, which she was only now working her way out of with the help of friends.

How far could revenge be taken? the article asked. For seven years Patty Mars had meticulously, slowly ruined Kate's life—abusing and murdering her first child, stealing the second, and indirectly breaking up her two marriages. Now she was bringing up a baby she had every intention of killing by his fifth birthday.

For years Patty had been wanted by the police in both California and Arizona, and yet there hadn't been a solid clue as to her whereabouts. How could someone as well known as she had become through the media, with a child she obviously wasn't hiding from view, have been able to disappear as she had? That, the reporter wrote, was what had prompted the article—the need to find Patty Mars—now, according to a police psychologist, completely out of control—before she killed another baby. To that end there was a renewed reward for her capture: a hundred thousand dollars—put up by an anonymous donor. Someone, the article concluded, must have seen this woman recently. She had been spotted in southern California within the past few days. Someone knew where she was and had an obligation to come forward, to prevent another murder if not for the reward.

While Nick made her a breakfast of eggs and bacon, Kate finished the article for the second time. She was surprised at how calm she felt. Or was dead how she felt? She looked up as he slipped two pieces of toast onto her plate. "What do you think she'll do?"

"I guess we wait and see."

Shortly after eleven they knew.

When the phone rang Nick told her to wait until he got the cordless phone for himself. As he held it, ready to push the on button, Kate lifted the receiver in the kitchen. Patty was giggling. "Was that supposed to make me go nuts and do something stupid?"

Kate felt her heart sink.

"The part about the police calling me Crazy Patty was Nick's idea, right? Hey, Nickie-the-cop, you listening in? You got the recorder going? Why don't you play this tape on TV tonight? Crazy Patty *relentlessly* stalking poor old Kate. Jesus, get out the violins!"

"Patty—"

"Look, Kate, I don't do stupid things! Ever! I'm just not the type to get mad and say, 'How dare they call me crazy?' " They could hear her swallowing noisily, as if drinking from a bottle. "What was I supposed to do? Come running over to Nick's house and yell at you? Christ, give me credit for intelligence if nothing else. You haven't been able to get a handle on me for years; how did you think a dumb stunt like this would do it? All I see is that it made me famous. Someday they'll write books about me, maybe even do a movie. Hey, Cerovic, who do you think should play you? Maybe an aging Sly Stallone? I'm going to get Kim Basinger to play me. Any old dead baby could play Alex." She laughed loudly, and again they could hear her taking a drink.

Nick said nothing, but Kate could feel sobs building in her throat. She put a hand over the mouthpiece, not wanting Patty to hear, but it was too late. "Hey, Katie Kate, I know how you feel. You're upset about your kid, right? Just like I'm upset about Tammy. Even seven years later I'm upset." Her voice rose, full of contempt now. "You hear what I'm saying? It's not going to get any better. Take it from someone who knows: the pain never stops. So don't get your hopes up."

Kate's voice, suddenly angry, burst in. "How's your friend Frankie, Patty? Is he still helping you try to scare me?"

There was a brief pause. "I suppose the cops have him, huh? I wondered about that. Doesn't surprise me. Frankie's none too bright, as you know. Well, shit, it's no loss. Frankies are a dime a bunch down at the beach, gal. And thanks to you I have a bundle of money to buy them with. Everything's for sale around here, isn't it? Well, say good-bye for me to your stud muffin. I know you folks are tracing this call. I'll save you the time and trouble. Alex and I are across the street right now with a cell phone I stole out of a car last night. Hey, Cerovic, isn't that the same piece of shit car you had two years ago? Christ, are you spending all your money on those stupid little toy banks I saw in your living room last night? And the two of you are still sleeping in separate beds! Isn't that just a little weird?" She hung up.

Kate put the phone down and said, "She's out front."

"Not anymore. No point in running after her." He glanced at the banks. They had all been turned around so their backs faced out.

"She was in here," Kate said. "While we slept. Walking around and looking at us."

"She's a resourceful woman."

Kate put her head on the kitchen table. "I need a drink."

Nick put his arm around her. "We'll go out and have lunch someplace later. And don't let Patty fool you. She's rattled. It's why she called. It's the first step. Let's see what the second one is."

13

It took four days to find out.

Nick and Kate had gone to a movie, returning home at ten, and she was changing into her nightgown when the phone rang. In the bedroom next door Nick glanced at the caller-ID display he had just added to his phone, and didn't recognize the number. "You'd better get it," he yelled toward the bedroom.

Kate picked it up. "Hello?"

Her stomach cramped when she heard, "It's been a while."

"Please, Patty—"

"Sorry I've been out of touch. I had things to do."

"Patty, this is pointless. I told you I'm not responsible for Tammy. You must understand that."

The woman sounded strange, her voice taut with some emotion Kate hadn't heard before, but so low, almost whispered, that it was difficult to make out the words. "Pointless? Is that what it is? What would you do if someone killed *your* child?"

"Someone did."

"That was justice!"

"Patty, I did not—"

"Kate, stop, take a breath, and think carefully about this question: What would I do if the person who killed my child wasn't punished? Do you understand? *That* is the key to both of our lives for the past seven years. It's the only thing that gives meaning to our existence. How do you think people feel when someone who killed a loved one is set free on a technicality? They want revenge, Kate; they want to balance the scales of justice. It's the only way they can make sense out of the ugliness of life."

Kate could feel her throat swell, but said nothing.

"If someone killed your child and got away with it, I hope you'd do what the legal system was incapable of doing. If you didn't it would mean your child had died for nothing, that nobody cared enough to seek justice. You'd act, Kate. I know you would; any mother would."

"Patty . . . people just don't do that. We have laws—"

"Which no longer work. We live in a barbarous world, a world in which people get away with murder every day. Thirty thousand people are murdered in this country every year, and thousands of those killers go unpunished. The government's broken down, civilized life is disappearing, we have to look out for ourselves."

Kate was beginning to lose her hard-won control. "I want my baby! You have no right—"

Patty interrupted, once again taking the conversation in a new direction, as though linearity of thought were no longer possible. "Did I ever tell you what happened to my mother after Tammy was murdered? She went into a shell; she wouldn't talk to anyone, including me. Not even on the phone. Finally she stopped eating. That's how much it affected her to lose her only grandchild to a rapist and murderer. We had to have her put in a county care facility so someone would make sure she was taking care of herself. But it didn't help. She still wouldn't communicate, had to be force-fed. Two years after my daughter was murdered my mother died, just went to sleep one night and didn't wake up. That's one more death you're responsible for."

Kate sighed with genuine regret. "Patty, you can't carry this much hate forever. You're not well. You're so obsessed with the past that you can't think clearly."

"Yes. Of course. Crazy Patty. And Crazy Kate. Two years after my baby was taken and murdered, my mother died in her bed. It's amazing how much our lives are alike, isn't it? But that's the point. They have to be *exact.*"

It took a moment for Kate to realize what Patty was getting at. "No . . ."

"It had to be, hon. Without matching lives one side of the

scales is always out of balance.'' Patty hung up, and Kate began to scream.

Nick hurried inside from where he had waited in the hallway. ''What?''

Kate forced herself to speak. ''She's going to kill my mother.''

''How do you know?''

''She blames me for her mother's death. She said our lives have to be the same, exact.'' She began punching out the number for her mother in St. Louis.

Nick put his hand on her shoulder as Kate listened to the phone on the other end ring and ring. Kate slammed it down. ''I misdialed.'' As carefully as she could Kate made her finger punch the correct buttons. Again it rang and rang.

Nick said, ''Let me try. What's the number?''

She told him and he dialed, listened to the ringing, and started to hang up when he suddenly heard a male voice say, ''Hello?'' Nick recognized the tone at once. He said, ''This is Lt. Nick Cerovic of the Los Angeles Police Department. Who am I speaking to?''

There was a hesitation; then the voice said, ''Sergeant Walbeck, St. Louis homicide. What can I do for you, Lieutenant?''

''We're investigating a kidnapping and murder case. This number is the home of the mother of one of the victims, Kate McDonald. We're afraid something might happen to her.''

''Something like murder?''

Nick sat on the bed. ''You might as well tell me.''

As he listened, Kate said, ''What? Tell me.'' But he waited until he was off the phone, then stood and lowered her to the bed. ''Your mother was strangled as she slept. It happened two nights ago. Whoever did it called the police this morning and told them. It was a woman.''

Kate's hands flew to her face.

Nick put his arm around her and let her cry.

When the phone rang an hour later, Nick picked it up and Patty said, ''Let me talk to her.''

''Goddamn you,'' he said softly.

"Let me talk to her!"

"Go to hell." He started to hang up, but Kate's voice came on the line.

"What do you want?"

"Hang on, Katie. We have two more years to go. Don't give up now."

"I have given up." Her voice was soft. "I don't care."

"But Katie, it's not over; we have to carry on. Your mother's dead, just like mine is. But your child—Alex *lives!* Keep hoping, Kate. Keep the flame burning. We still have a long way to go. Two whole years. Think of all the things that can happen in that time."

"Hang up on her," Nick said into the phone.

"Katie, my lass, do ye want to hear him?" Patty had suddenly gone into a comic Irish accent. "Do ye want to talk to the wee fella?" There was the sound of a scuffle, Patty saying something they couldn't make out, but it sounded as if she was angry. Then a soft, hesitant voice said, "Hello . . ."

Kate thought she was going to start crying.

"Go on with ye," Patty urged. "Be polite, Katie Kate McDonald. Answer the lad."

"Alex? Honey?" Her voice was tentative.

"My name is Alex," the child said. He sounded frightened to death, his voice little more than a whisper.

"Oh, God—"

"Enough!" Patty announced, her mood again changing. "I just wanted you to know he's still alive. Maybe I'll walk by your house soon so you can see him again. Stick by the window and watch for us. Getting big, isn't he? Too bad he's had so many problems. His right foot's deformed, you know, so he has trouble walking. It started when a hammer broke his ankle."

"My God, Patty."

"I was aiming at his leg and he moved. It didn't make any difference, I guess. Still, the other kids make fun of him, call him peg leg."

"You're insane," Nick said before he could stop himself.

"Hey, Kate, tell your boyfriend to butt out, OK? At least

your kid's alive. Right? Mine's dead, goddamn it. But you knew that already.''

"*Patty!*" Kate screamed at her.

"Two more years, Katie. Hang on, hang on. There's so much that needs to happen. And I've planned it for so long.''

14

When the phone rang half an hour later, Nick stared at the caller-ID readout. "I don't recognize it."

Kate was lying on her bed, not paying any attention to Nick or the music he had on the stereo. Opera, she vaguely sensed. Italian. She didn't care.

Nick picked it up in the bedroom. "You don't know me," the woman's voice said. "I used to live next door to Kate."

Nick's interest stirred. "I remember. Lilli-something."

"Lilliana." She paused. "Look, I don't know if this is a good idea or not, but I want to talk to Kate."

"I don't think so." He looked up. Kate was standing at the open doorway. "Wait a minute," he said into the phone. Holding the mouthpiece he told her who it was. Kate stared at him a moment, then went back to her bedroom and picked up the receiver. "Hello, Lilliana."

"Hi, Katie. Been a while, hasn't it?" The other woman's voice was hesitant, as if she was not certain she should be doing this. "I didn't mean to lose touch with you, but after—"

"It's all right, Lilliana." Kate closed her eyes against the apologies she didn't want to hear, the excuses people made for not wanting to be around a crazy woman. To make it easier for Lilliana she tried a neutral topic. "Are you still living in the same place?"

"Oh, yes. Just me now. Hans took his Jaguar and left to revel in the hay with one of his young ladies, a ballet dancer this time. I lie in bed and fantasize about him burying the poor thing's dainty ninety pounds under his folds of fat during their lovemaking. How awkward it must be for them both."

"It was nice of you to call, Lilliana."

"Hey, don't hang up. I wanted to tell you something. I saw that story in the paper Sunday and phoned your ex to see how I could get in touch with you. I'm afraid it took me this long to work up the courage to call. I felt bad about not seeing you for so long. It's my fault, of course. I could have called Paul earlier and gotten your address."

"Lilliana, I told you, it's OK. Don't worry about it. I went away because I *didn't* want to see people. I could have contacted you if I had wanted company."

"You could, couldn't you? I never thought of that." She paused again. "Well, anyway, this all sounds a little foolish, I guess, but someone bought your house. Did you know that?"

"It's not my house. We sold it before the divorce."

"You know what I mean. Someone bought your *old* house. They've never come over to introduce themselves, though. This is going to sound stupid, I guess, and I might be wrong. I've only seen pictures of her, but I think it's that Patty. I've been watching them, and I can see a woman and a child—"

Nick, on the other phone, started screaming for Kate to hang up. Disconnecting with his finger, his hand shook as he punched out Oscar Reddig's office number.

Two blocks from the Orchard Drive address, Nick slowed to show his badge to the SWAT officer in charge of setting up a perimeter and evacuating nearby houses. Her heart pounding wildly, Kate looked out the passenger window and saw Lilliana talking to a policeman in the back of a squad car. Yellow crime-scene tape and sawhorses crisscrossed the street, blocking off an area for neighbors to wait, and rerouting traffic away from the cul-de-sac.

A specially equipped travel trailer waited up the street, just beyond the view of the house. Nick parked beside it, in the middle of the road. Inside, the black-clad SWAT team leader, a fortyish man named Connors, discussed the plan he and Cerovic had worked out by phone. "We've got two people in the house on the left. That's the reporting party's residence." He checked his notes. "A woman named Quinlin. There's two on the other side, and four in the yard behind. So far no one reports seeing or hearing anyone.''

''Oh, God, they have to be there.'' Kate couldn't stand still, but there was no place for her to pace in the crowded trailer, so she sat down in front of three TV screens showing views of the house. There was no movement of any sort, and no indication of police anywhere.

Connors said, ''I think we ought to try the phone first, tell her we're out here and give her a chance to give up.''

''No!'' Nick said at once. ''She's obsessed with the death of the child she has in there. If we let her know we're out here, she'll kill him, then probably kill herself. We have to take her by surprise. As soon as we're inside we bring her down, bang, bang, bang. We use any way we can, but it has to be over within five seconds. And remember, there's a child wandering around somewhere, so everyone has to be careful. No tear gas and no explosives. And no shooting unless you have to.''

Kate started moaning. Connors nodded in her direction. ''I don't think she ought to be here, Nickie.''

''It's her child, damn it. She stays.''

The man shrugged uneasily. ''OK, it's your plan. So what's next?''

''Did you bring a woman cop?''

''Bobbi Weir. You know her?''

Nick shook his head. ''It doesn't matter. Where is she?''

''I have her getting a floor plan of the house from the RP. I didn't figure on the homeowner being here. Want me to call her back?''

''Let her finish. As soon as she gets here, she and I will start working the neighborhood like real-estate agents, ringing doorbells and pretending to leave literature. When we get to the hostage house we'll start talking about real estate the second the door's opened—Hey, the market's really cooking, do you want to sell your house?—that sort of thing. If it's who we think it is I'll recognize her at once and grab her before she has a chance to react. If it's not, we'll play it by ear. Do you have a mike for me?''

Connors took a nickel-size microphone and an earpiece from a plastic bag and handed them to Cerovic.

"I'll let your people know what I'm up to every few seconds. If I yell 'Now!' I want them coming in from the back. They can take out a door, can't they?"

"They've got a battering ram."

"OK. If you don't hear from me, just hang loose out there."

"You have to stay in contact with me, Nick. Sixty seconds without hearing your voice and they're coming in."

Just then the door opened and a young, short-haired woman entered. They were introduced—Bobbi Weir—and Kate said, "Please don't use your guns inside the house. My baby's there."

Both Connors and Weir said they understood. "But," Connors added, "that doesn't mean the crazy lady won't start shooting. And we don't know if she has confederates. So both of you have to wear vests. Captain's orders." He pulled out two Kevlar vests and handed one to Nick, who hurriedly stripped off his shirt. Bobbi Weir said, "I hope no one's embarrassed," and took off her blouse, putting the vest over her bra, then buttoning up. She grabbed a blazer off the back of a chair. "My cunning disguise," she said with a laugh, and pulled it on. "Do I look like Century 21 to you?"

"You look wonderful," Nick said, and hurriedly adjusted his sport coat so the holster on the left side of his hip didn't show. Then he attached the microphone to the underside of his tie. "Let's look at the layout."

Kate stood behind them. "I had a nursery upstairs. Patty knew that; she'd been there. I think that's where she'd have Alex."

Nick said to Bobbi, "As soon as we cuff whoever answers the door, I'll yell for SWAT to come in through the back. You check the first floor; I'll head upstairs and get Alex." He jabbed his finger on the drawing.

Kate's legs wouldn't let her remain upright. She lowered herself to the chair in front of the TVs again, and thought, *Please hurry. I can't stand this any longer.*

Connors shook his head as he looked at the house layout.

"I don't like it. I'd rather use flash-bangs. That's SOP here." These were grenades that exploded in a deafening noise and a burst of smoke and light, but did no damage, other than disorient whomever was nearby.

Nick looked at his watch. He was anxious to get going; they'd already wasted too much time. "Not here. We don't know what room she's in. If she's upstairs she'd go after the kid before we got inside. He's our priority. I really don't give a damn about her." He smoothed out his sport coat. "Let's get moving before she wonders why the neighborhood is so quiet."

Kate's fingers tightened on the arm of her chair, but she said nothing.

Connors looked at Weir. "Ready?"

She smiled and nodded at Nick. "We've got buyers from all over America looking for houses just like this one."

Nick said to the SWAT officer, "I hope your people know what we look like. I'd hate to be killed by a cop."

While Connors sat next to her, speaking rapidly and loudly into a headset microphone, Kate hunched forward in her chair, watching the three video screens. For a longer time than she expected, there was no movement. Connors sensed her unease. "They're going to your neighbors' houses first in case someone's watching. They're supposed to be canvassing the neighborhood."

A moment later one screen showed Nick and Bobbi Weir coming from the left of Kate's house. She could see them only from behind, but they were moving their arms, obviously talking, like two people working the street would. Another screen showed them approaching the front door. Kate thought, *My God, Alex is in there, just feet from me, just feet!* Every organ within her seemed to cramp at once. She could hear the tension in Connors's voice as he told the SWAT team, "They're at the door."

Bobbi Weir raised her arm and pushed the bell.

Connors said into his headset microphone, "Get your flash-bangs ready, Two."

"No!" Kate jumped up. "Nick said—"

Connors grabbed her wrist without taking his eyes from the screen. "Only if we need them. Relax." Then into the microphone. "One and Three, we're counting."

Again they watched Bobbi ring the bell.

Nothing.

Kate thought she was going to be sick. "Be there," she muttered under her breath. "Please be there!"

Connors put a hand to his earpiece. "Nick says no answer."

They watched as Bobbi tried a third time.

Again Connors put a hand to his ear. Kate heard him say, "No. Try again."

This time Nick banged on the door with his fist.

Connors said, "Anything, Two?" Then to Nick: "No sign of life in back."

Bobbi turned as if to leave, but Nick said something and she stopped. Connors yelled in alarm, "Nickie, no! Let the team do it. You don't know what's going on in there. She could be sitting right there with a shotgun waiting for you."

But they watched helplessly as Cerovic tried the door, standing back as it swung open. Connors shouted, "No, damn it!" But Cerovic and Weir suddenly yanked their guns from their holsters. Connors jumped up, screaming, "Jesus Christ! Two, go, go, go! Use your ram and flash-bangs. Remember, our people are in there."

At once the house was lit up with deafening explosions, windows blew out, and light shot through the broken glass.

Kate was on her feet. "What's happening?"

"Goddamn it!" Connors yelled above the noise. The house seemed to be exploding, smoke coming through the broken windows, and bright flashes of white light pop, pop, popping every few seconds. "Damn it, Cerovic!" But Nick and Bobbi Weir had disappeared inside.

Kate bolted for the door, but Connors whirled around and grabbed her shoulder. "Not yet! Let them go through the house. If you go running in, someone's going to get killed." Then into the microphone, "Cerovic, damn you, what the hell's going on?"

Weak with panic Kate stared at the TV screens, but there was no movement now, only smoke drifting in huge clouds through the windows and the open front door. Connors turned to her, one finger holding his earpiece, another hand still on Kate's arm. "Nick's upstairs . . . my people are searching the first floor."

They waited, Connors still on his feet, barking angrily into the microphone, Kate swaying back and forth, her head buzzing with noise. After three or four minutes a black-clad SWAT member appeared on the TV screen in front of the house and removed his gas mask. Connors was listening to him on his headset. "Oh, shit!" He struck the table with his fist. "Shit, shit, shit!"

Kate spun on him. "What? Oh, my God, Alex is dead." She thought she was going to faint.

"No," Connors said. "Patty Mars is dead. They can't find your boy. He's not there."

There were half a dozen police cars and an ambulance in the cul-de-sac, cops standing around a perimeter of yellow tape to keep reporters and bystanders away. Kate waited in the small downstairs sewing room and looked at the body on the floor as a photographer took dozens of flash pictures. Connors said, "It is her, isn't it? Patty Mars?" Police radios and walkie-talkies buzzed in the background. Outside they could hear four or five helicopters from television stations, their rotors making the window frames rattle with broken glass.

Kate was in a state of shock. One of the ambulance attendants was taking her pulse while she stood. All she could do was nod.

"No mistake?"

Nick came into the room, obviously upset. "Jesus, leave her alone. That's the woman."

"So where's the child?" Connors asked for the hundredth time.

Nick shook his head. "We've looked everywhere. Even in her car." He stared at the body. "Poison?"

A medical examiner was on her knees next to Patty's face-down body. She looked up at Nick. "Who knows? No exterior marks or injuries. Someone said there was a note."

Connors nodded. "It was in her hand. It said, 'I still win.'"

The ME frowned. "What does that mean?"

Kate began sobbing. Nick put his arm around her and led her to a chair. She sat without an argument.

Connors said, "It means we don't know what happened to the child. The mother doesn't get him back. The crazy lady kills herself, but she still wins."

The ME said, "Do you think the kid's—" then stopped when she saw Kate's face.

Connors grimaced and turned away from Kate. "We're digging up the backyard. I don't like it, but it's got to be done."

"He's alive!" Kate said, staring without expression at the SWAT officer.

Connors nodded at once, still not looking at Kate. "Of course. Now we've just got to find him. There has to be some clue in this mess." He glanced toward the hallway. The house was in a state of disarray: almost no furniture except two beds, clothes dropped on the floor, little food in the refrigerator.

A detective came in from the hallway holding a photograph. "Is this the missing kid?"

Kate bolted to her feet. "Where'd you find it?"

"There're a lot of pictures upstairs, the woman and the kid. Is it—"

"That's Alex, yes!"

"They're in a dresser in the kid's room, pictures of Big Bird and Bert and Ernie on the wall, some toys, kids' clothing all over the place. There was blood on one of the sheets, so I ordered a team of dogs. Maybe we can get a scent." He paused a moment, his eyes going to Cerovic and his voice dropping. "I thought I'd better ask for a cadaver dog, too, Nickie." Meaning one trained to look for bodies.

Kate put a hand to her mouth, holding her breath so her stomach wouldn't empty right there.

"'I still win,'" the SWAT chief repeated, looking at the note again. It was already in a clear plastic evidence envelope.

"It was the newspaper article," Nick said softly, feeling

that this was all his fault. "I never should have done it. It pushed her over the edge."

"Alex is alive!" Kate shouted at all of them, her face wet with tears. "She didn't kill him. He's alive! If he was dead he'd be here with Patty."

Nick put his arms around her, holding her close as she cried into his sport coat.

Connors looked again at the body. "She must have had a hell of a lot of hate to keep this up for what? Six or seven years? And keeping it going even now after she's dead. I guess she really wanted to hurt you."

"Oh, my God!" Kate moaned, moving away from Nick. She could sense her knees giving way, and fell into the chair as if her bones had turned to jelly. "I know where Alex is."

Everyone spun in her direction. " 'I wanted to hurt you in the worst way I could.' That's what he said to me. My God, no!"

"Who?" Nick said. "Who said that to you?"

She flew out of the chair. "At your house! Don't you remember? He said he hated me all these years. He hated me and wanted to hurt me. He was *looking* for a way to hurt me."

"Robert." Nick grabbed the kitchen phone as he glanced at Connors. "I'll call the Albuquerque PD and have him picked up for questioning. He might even have Alex with him. We can be there in the morning." Then he shook his head, still looking at Connors. "Jesus, what a bastard."

15

"We found some kids' clothing at his house," the Albuquerque cop who picked them up at the airport twenty minutes earlier had said. "But we're going to need something more. Either that or let him go."

They were walking rapidly through the basement of the jail building, their footsteps echoing in the long empty hallway, to an interrogation room where Robert Lempke had been brought after a night in custody. Kate was still in a daze, but Nick seemed energized by the plane trip. Or maybe it was their closeness to finding Alex. This is it, he knew. Either Lempke had him or he knew where he was. But they'd have him back by the end of the day. He said to the cop, "One way or the other Lempke's dirty. Until we talk to him we won't know how bad. But he's not walking."

They stopped outside a door with a small window at eye level. The cop unlocked it, and Lempke glanced up from the table he was sitting at by himself. There was no expression on his face. Kate looked at him and held back tears as a sense of both resignation and rage raced through her. Nick said to the cop, "I'd rather do this by myself."

"No problem," the man said. "Just knock when you want to leave."

The second the door shut Kate said, "Robert, how could you?"

Nick wasn't interested in explanations or excuses. "Sit down," he said to Kate, indicating a chair across from her ex-husband, then grabbed the chair next to her. Without preamble he said, "Look, Lempke, I don't give a rat's ass *why* you did it. I just want to know how involved you are and where Alex is. And no more bullshit. We've got to find that boy before something worse happens to him.''

Lempke's face flushed red and his voice shot up with fury. "I want him found just as much as you do. He's my son!"

"Your . . . ?" Kate gasped, her body falling back in the chair. "What are you talking about?"

His eyes bored into hers. "Who do you think's been bringing him up for the past two years?"

Kate stared at him, stunned, her heart seeming to stop beating. "He's been living with you for two . . . You mean ever since he was stolen?"

Robert glared at her, but he was so angry he seemed unable to trust himself to speak.

Nick, too, was startled but tried not to show it, or to show how little he knew. "We're not taping any of this, Lempke. There's no notes, no one sitting behind two-way glass watching you. We just want to find Alex. You're one minute away from a kidnapping charge that will keep you in prison for the rest of your life. So talk, and keep it short."

The man glared at him as if he was going to argue. Then he changed his mind. "I wanted a child. . . . After Kate killed our son." His tone eased, but only slightly, when Kate's eyes filled with tears. Then he sounded like a kid caught stealing, angrily justifying himself and hoping his rage proved his innocence. "I wanted my boy back. If I couldn't have him—"

Nick shook his head. "This doesn't make any sense. Did you take Alex? What about Patty? Or were you the one harassing Kate all that time?"

"Don't be an idiot. Jane Devlin—Patty—came to see me a couple of years ago. I guess she knew how much I hated Kate for what happened to Teddy."

"Robert!" Kate yelled, half coming to her feet. "We've been through this. I didn't do anything! *Patty* did. Patty killed Teddy! She admitted it!"

"How was I to know that? All I knew was that my son was dead and everyone in Phoenix was convinced you did it. The DA told me there was no question about it. But they weren't sure they could get a unanimous verdict without more tangible proof, so they were going to hold off on the trial until something turned up. Or you confessed.'' He took a breath and tried to relax, but his tone stayed accusatory. "Jane told me what you did to her—reporting an innocent woman for child abuse when you didn't have any reason to do so. It was just stupid! None of this would have happened, Kate—no babies would have died, we wouldn't have gotten divorced, there would have been no kidnapping, if you hadn't given her child to a rapist.''

"God.'' Kate sank toward the table, putting her head in her hands. "You won't understand. You're so full of hate you won't let yourself see the truth.'' Her eyes jerked up and she stared furiously across the table at him. "Are you really that damn stupid?''

Nick said, "Let's stop yelling at each other and get to the point. Why did Patty come to see you?''

Robert took a breath. "I didn't even know her as Patty. That's what you call her. Her name is Jane Devlin. She told me who she was, told me about Tammy, her daughter, being raped and murdered because of . . .''

Nick could hear Kate next to him tense angrily, but he didn't want to interrupt the flow of the tale. Robert paused a moment, then said, "She told me Kate had married again and had a child. She knew how much I missed Teddy, and that I'd never remarried.''

"You told us you were!'' Kate said accusingly. "You told us you had two girls.''

He brushed a hand across the table. "What was I going to say? That I'd had Alex for two years?''

Kate jumped up, consumed with fury, and tried to attack Robert across the table. "And all this time Alex has been at your house? All the hell I went through—''

Nick grabbed Kate, forcing her back into the chair. Keeping his voice level he asked, "Is Alex at your home now? Or is someone watching him?''

"I don't know where he is. Truthfully.''

"*Liar!*'' Kate screamed. "Goddamn you, you have him!''

Nick said, "After Patty—Jane Devlin—took Alex from Kate, she brought him to you?"

"Not right away. Maybe two or three weeks later."

"But why?" Kate screamed. "Why would you do that?"

"Damn you, do you think mothers are the only ones who care about children? I wanted my boy. If I couldn't make my son come back to life, at least I could have this one." He halted, staring directly at her. "And because I hated you more than I've ever hated anyone. I wanted to *hurt* you. Like you hurt me."

Kate slumped forward, her forehead propped in her hand.

Nick tried to stay on track. "Didn't Jane want Alex?"

"Of course not. All she cared about was Kate, getting back at Kate. *Justice,* she called it. An eye for an eye, a tooth for a tooth. Christ, it was a mantra to her. I heard it enough. This was about Tammy, not Alex. And payback."

"Did you know she planned to kill him?"

He looked miserable and his voice drained away. "Not until you told me. I don't believe it even now. She never acted as if she liked or disliked him. He was just there, a thing, a chess piece. It's always been Kate she was after. Alex was just a part of the puzzle."

Kate began to whimper.

"So you passed Alex off as your child?"

He nodded. "That's why I moved to Albuquerque."

"How often after that did you see Patty—Jane?"

"She'd come down here every two or three months and stay with me a while. Alex thought she was his mother."

"You were lovers," Kate said, suddenly looking up.

"You have no right to ask a question like that."

"Where is he now?" Nick asked once again. "Even if you don't have him you must know where he is."

"Am I going to be charged with kidnapping?"

"You're not in a position to make deals. Let's get the boy back; then we'll decide about you."

Lempke slumped forward. "I don't know where he is. Jane came down to see me a couple of weeks ago. She spent the night. The next morning she was gone, along with Alex."

"And you didn't tell the police?" Kate shouted.

"Tell them the baby I kidnapped had been kidnapped from me? I don't think so! I thought she'd bring him back, anyway. You know how weird she could be. She's so goddamn obsessive, the way she fixates on something. I figured maybe she just decided to spend time with Alex and would bring him home in a few days."

Kate jumped up. "I don't believe you. You have him someplace! You're hiding him."

Lempke said, "I'm sorry, Kate. But I stopped caring what you think a long time ago."

"Patty's dead," Nick told him. "Suicide."

"I know." He sank back in his chair. "The cops told me last night."

"Before she killed herself she did something with Alex. You're the only person who knew her well. You must have some idea. He could be alone in a motel room, starving. Or out on the streets somewhere. Without you we aren't going to find him."

He shook his head. "Look, I've been thinking about it all night. I want Alex found, too. When you do find him I'm suing for custody. I'm the only parent he's had for two years."

Kate's head shook back and forth. She couldn't believe what she was hearing.

Lempke glared at her. "He loves me, Kate. He doesn't even know who the hell you are."

After Kate and Cerovic left, Lempke was in an agitated state as a guard escorted him back to his cell. It had suddenly struck him that no one, including himself, grasped what Jane Devlin had been planning for the past two years. "Take me to the pay phones," he told the guard. "I need to call someone right away." And he knew that he, too, had been made a fool of. They all had.

16

Kate and Nick had no more than walked in the door of his house after their return flight the next morning when the phone rang. Kate picked it up, and went cold when a woman's voice said, "It's still not over."

Kate couldn't speak. Nick, holding a suitcase, said, "What?"

"It didn't die with Patty, Katie Kate. It goes on. And on. Until the circle is closed."

Nick went into the bedroom and picked up the extension.

"It has to be *exact,* Kate. Otherwise it doesn't count."

Kate forced herself to speak, her voice no more than a whisper. "Who are you?"

"Tammy's mother, Katie. The woman you accused of abuse."

"But—"

"It doesn't matter. This phase of our life is over. An eye for an eye. Sixty more minutes. That should be sufficient. Then you'll be free until next time."

"No—"

"Don't beg," the voice said sharply. "I just wanted you to know this isn't the end. You can have more children. But even if you don't I'll be around. I'll always be around." The line went dead.

"She's going to kill him," Kate said as Nick came in from the bedroom. "Sixty minutes."

He had already picked up the phone and begun dialing Hollywood station. "What does she mean by it's having to be exact? Tammy died when—" He spoke suddenly into the phone. "Captain Reddig, please. This is Nick Cerovic." Then to Kate: "She died when she was raped."

Kate was pacing rapidly back and forth in the living room. "Not exactly. After she was raped she was thrown off a bridge. She actually died by drowning. Oh, my God—"

"What? Hold on, Oscar. It's Nick."

"There was a picture of a bridge in my hospital room, right next to Tammy's picture. It didn't make any sense to me at the time."

"What bridge? Any bridge?" Nick's voice had become demanding.

"I don't know!" She shook her head, feeling frantic. "I don't know! A bridge!"

"But you've seen it before. You must have. She said sixty minutes, Kate. There aren't that many bridges around here." He spoke into the phone again. "No, just hang on, Oscar." Then again to Kate: "A freeway bridge? Maybe over one of the arroyos in Pasadena?"

"No, no." She was trying to think. "It was near water. Anyway, Tammy drowned."

"Water? The ocean?"

"No. Yes. There were ships in the picture, cargo ships."

"Jesus," Nick said. "The Vincent Thomas." Then into the phone: "Notify Harbor Division, Oscar. Someone's going to try to throw a kid off the Vincent Thomas Bridge. We'll meet you there."

He grabbed Kate's hand. "It's going to take us fifteen minutes to get there. We've got to hurry."

17

But they couldn't hurry.

"Jesus Christ, move it! *Move it!*" Nick exploded in obscenities as he pounded the horn while craning his head to stare at two police helicopters circling a mile or so away. Even with the suction-cup light attached to the roof, the car hardly advanced through the massive congestion of vehicles on the freeway off-ramp caused by the sudden closing of the Vincent Thomas Bridge. The top of the bridge, a turquoise arching of steel supports that connected the mainland to Terminal Island, with its federal prison and abandoned shipyards, glistened in the sun. Kate was hunched forward, staring out the windshield, when the garbled report on the police radio made her blood run cold. "What did that say? Who were they talking about?"

"It was one of the copters. They were too late. They can see a woman on the bridge with a child. She's evidently disoriented, wandering back and forth. They don't know how long she's been there."

"Oh, God." She sank back, biting her lip to keep from breaking down in sobs.

"The SWAT team and a negotiator just arrived," Nick said as calmly as he could. He reached over and patted her thigh reassuringly while steering with one hand around a pickup truck at the end of the off-ramp. "They'll be able to talk her out of it. They're pretty good at that. It's what they do." He darted a glance in her direction. "We couldn't have made a mistake about Patty, could we? That *was* her body . . . ?"

"Of course it was her!"

Then Patty gave Alex to this other woman before committing

suicide? he wondered. But why would this woman want to kill him? He couldn't think, and didn't want to talk about it to Kate in the state she was in.

"How much longer?" she suddenly asked.

"Depends on whether I can make it through these goddamn cars. I can see the barricade up ahead. Shouldn't be more than two or three minutes." He started pounding on his horn when another burst came from the radio. Unable to make sense of it, Kate said, "What about Harbor Patrol?"

He took a breath, wondering how to keep it from her, then realized it was impossible. "They're putting two boats under the bridge."

"In case she jumps?" Kate felt bile rise into her throat. "Or throws him?"

"It's just a precaution," he said quickly, then swore loudly and jerked the car onto the sidewalk to make it around a knot of immobile vehicles, most with their engines off. People were getting out now, standing on the roadway, trying to see what the obstruction was. Screaming at the civilians, Nick gunned the car forward, two of its wheels on the sidewalk, two in the street. "Anytime someone threatens to jump they put out the boats. Damn it, get out of the way." Someone had opened a passenger door, missing the car by an inch.

"They'd be dead as soon as they hit the water," Kate whispered. "Especially a child."

Nick had no response to that.

In another minute they were at the barricade of police cars and orange cones at the base of the bridge. Nick shot past, pulling up behind a parked SWAT van. They could see the copters circling above them like huge gray birds of prey, hear a disembodied voice from a loudspeaker asking the woman to leave the bridge, as police waited uneasily just beyond her view. The amplified voice boomed all around them: "Walk toward me. . . ." was drowned out as the copters neared; then the loudspeaker blared again: ". . . help you . . ." as they moved away.

Jumping from the car before the engine was killed, Kate started running, but was unable to see anything because of the steep arch of the bridge. Racing after her as fast as he could, Nick instinctively glanced over the side. Far below, a huge white cruise ship was trying to disembark passengers, but several hundred people stood on the decks, watching the helicopters and the activity on the bridge just above them. There was something surreal about it, the merrymaking, the white ship, the dead calm of the blue sea.

Racing ahead, Kate came to the group of police officers near where the bridge leveled out. A man in a suit was speaking into a handheld megaphone. ''. . . will happen to you. I promise.'' His words sounded both urgent and gently pleading as the amplifier sent them toward the center of the bridge a hundred yards away.

Out of breath, Kate almost collapsed. ''My God, there she is.'' Oscar Reddig suddenly appeared, out of breath from the short run from his patrol car.

They could barely make out the woman. She was striding back and forth, upset or frightened, and holding Alex to her breast as though suckling him.

Kate screamed and started to run, but Nick grabbed her. ''Don't be stupid. You don't know what she'll do if she sees you.''

The man with the megaphone wheeled around. ''Is this the mother?''

Both helicopters swooped low over the highest arch of the bridge, then circled toward the police barricade, their engines drowning out conversation. Fifty feet farther up they could see four or five men holding sharpshooter's rifles with scopes attached, crouching behind the hoods of two squad cars that had been parked sideways in the roadway, keeping the woman in their sights as she continued her frantic pacing.

''It's her child,'' Nick told the man.

He angrily jerked the microphone away from his face. ''Get her out of here, Cerovic. If that woman sees her, both she and the kid might go over the side. Look at her; she's ready to jump now.''

''*No!*'' Kate screamed. ''You can't make me.'' She wrenched free of Nick's grip. ''I'm not leaving.''

"She can stay back here," Nick told the man. "She can't be seen."

Reddig agreed. "Leave her alone. She's far enough away." The man shook his head in disapproval, but brought the megaphone to his mouth again; then he said suddenly, "My God, she's going to throw him off the bridge."

"No!" a dozen people yelled.

Discipline among the police broke down, and everyone was shouting now, including the cops at the barricade—"No, don't!" "Stop her!" "Please ..." Hundreds of frightened spectators on the cruise ship were also yelling, the terrible sound rising toward those on the bridge like an amplified organ chord from beneath their feet.

Screams, shrieks, demands ...

"Don't do it. . . . Stop!"

But the woman seemed incensed, moving suddenly to the side of the bridge and lifting the child over her head. A ten-foot chain-link fence ran along the length of the walkway, and she began to push Alex to the top of it, working furiously, as if she had just seconds left to accomplish her purpose. Two patrolmen, screaming loudly, rushed onto the center span, but they were obviously going to be too late.

"Fire!" the frantic SWAT commander yelled. "Jesus Christ, stop her!" All five sharpshooters opened up at once, the gunfire like explosions in Kate's ears, drowning out the shouts and cries. But it was too late. As the passengers on the ship below screamed in horror, the child was flung over the fence, arching upward for a foot or so, then falling to the water more than a hundred feet below, and instantly disappearing from sight. At the same time, the woman was hit, her body spinning, twisting violently this way and that from the force of the bullets tearing into her. She sank forward and slipped from sight onto the surface of the bridge.

Kate screamed and screamed, and couldn't stop screaming.

Nick had to carry her back to his car. He opened the passenger door and put her in the front seat. "He might be all right, Kate. Babies are resilient. And the boat was right there. I'm going out on the bridge and see if I can yell down to Harbor Patrol. Are you going to be OK if I leave you? It'll only be a minute.''

Kate was sobbing so loudly she didn't hear him. He said softly, ''Hang on. Please, Kate. We don't know yet. . . .'' But he did know. There was no way Alex could have survived.

Around them everything was chaos, people running, weeping, waving their arms. Reporters had arrived en masse and swarmed around the area, the police not even trying to keep them back now. Nick patted Kate's arm, then said, ''I won't be long,'' and began to race toward the center of the bridge.

Kate was sobbing so uncontrollably, her body racked with convulsions, that she didn't hear the rear door open. But when a voice said, ''He's still a stud, isn't he?'' she spun around. ''Lilliana!''

''No,'' the woman said. ''Jane Devlin.''

18

Nick stared at the body on the bridge. "I don't know who it is." The woman was Hispanic, probably fifty years old. Half of her teeth were missing and she was dressed in rags.

The cop with the megaphone was yelling angrily at uniformed officers to keep the press thirty feet from the body. At almost the same time four TV news helicopters appeared overhead as though flying in tandem, their rotors thumping the air. Someone hurriedly put a blue plastic tarp over the body before the zoom cameras on the choppers focused in on it.

Reddig said, "But the child. Alex—"

"I don't know. I can't figure it." He was feeling sick. He had just fucked up badly. But how?

A patrolman raced up to them, out of breath. He stopped, bent over at the waist, tried to catch his breath. "Harbor Patrol just fished out that package that went off the bridge. They said it's a bundle of clothes, not a baby."

Nick whirled back to where he left Kate. "Oh, shit!" He began to run.

19

Kate was driving Nick's car while Lilliana sat in the back, watching out the rear window to make sure no one was following. But the confusion at the bridge was so great no one had paid the slightest attention to their leaving. "You said something about my flair for the dramatic once. Remember? If only you knew *then*, huh?" When she turned back Kate caught a glimpse of her face in the rearview mirror; her forehead and cheeks glistened with perspiration, and her hair, usually so neatly set, was in disarray.

Kate could hardly maneuver the car, her heart was beating so wildly. "Alex . . ." She forced herself to stop crying, forced the words out. "Lilliana, where is Alex? Did he, did someone drop him from—"

But the woman was too wound up to reply. "Turn right at the next light. And don't break any traffic laws, not that I expect the cops around here are concerned about that today. They're all hanging out at the bridge hoping to get on the six o'clock news."

"Lilliana, please! Alex—"

"Not now! Here, damn it! Turn!"

Kate swung so sharply to the right that the steering wheel slipped from her sweaty hands. The car swerved, spun out, and slammed headfirst into the side of a parked Volvo. Lilliana was flung forward, half falling over the front seat, where Kate was screaming and trying to extricate herself from the air bag, which had inflated upon impact and was now deflating.

"Damn you!" Lilliana screamed. "Damn you. You did that on purpose."

"No, please!" Kate pushed frantically at the deflated air bag with both hands, clearing her vision. The windshield was cracked and the radiator was emitting a cloud of steam. The Volvo's door was crushed, and the burglar alarm was screaming.

"Get out of here!" Lilliana screamed. "Move it!"

Kate threw the gearshift into reverse and the car jumped back.

"Go, go, go!" Lilliana screamed as two men rushed from a nearby house and raced toward them, waving their fists and yelling angrily. Kate rammed the car into drive and slammed her foot on the accelerator, tearing off down the street, and a minute later they were three blocks away, the men gone from their sight. Lilliana sank back against the rear seat.

Kate's heart was beating so fast she thought she was going to hyperventilate. She took three deep breaths through her mouth and tried to calm herself. She needed to think. Looking suddenly in the rearview mirror, she caught Lilliana staring at her. Still breathing rapidly, she said, "I don't understand. Wasn't Patty . . ." She shook her head. She couldn't make any sense of it. "Are you the one who called me? What are you doing?"

"Doing?" Lilliana said with sarcasm. "Exactly what I said I was—closing the circle. With you." She turned to the rear, staring out the window, then spun back, her voice racing with so much rage and contempt that Kate could barely make out the words. "Robert called yesterday after you talked to him. Very upset. Pissed. At me, you, himself. Hard to understand, but it was obvious everything was moving too quickly for me to control. Thanks to you and your boyfriend. So I decided this phase of our life had to come to an end even though you couldn't take the role I had sketched out for you. But I long ago decided that if I can't be in charge, I don't want to play. That's why I came down here, to at least send Alex off the way I had always planned. We've been here a hundred times, Alex and I." Her voice slowed, became almost calm. "We stare at the bridge and talk about life. And Tammy. We always talk about Tammy. Turn here."

Kate pulled into a residential area of eighty-year-old wooden clapboard homes. From the children on the sidewalk it looked like a Hispanic neighborhood. Farther up an elderly man with a pushcart was selling ice-cream novelties to a group of parents and kids.

Lilliana wiped a layer of sweat from her brow as she continued looking from window to window to make sure no one was watching them. She hunched forward suddenly, hair askew and smelling of perspiration, her voice racing again as she stared out the cracked windshield. "It never occurred to me you'd show up out here, Katie Kate. Never entered my mind that you'd know what I was talking about! But when I was parking the van I saw a police helicopter arrive and start to circle over the bay. Then as I started onto the bridge two Harbor Patrol boats positioned themselves right underneath. There weren't any police on the bridge yet, but it was obvious every cop in L.A. knew what I was up to. I could still have pulled it off, but I had a wonderful idea, one of those rare, sudden, transforming moments in one's life: why not give the police something to think about while you and I went about our business? That way I could resurrect my original plan, the one with Kate as Best Supporting Actress. Without Katie there was no closure, no *justice!* Alex wasn't enough. I needed Alex's mother, too. So I hurried back to the van."

"But the woman!"

"Slow down, we're almost there. The woman was my simple diversion, one of San Pedro's many homeless. They're everywhere, like locusts, except locusts don't harass you for money. By the time I told her what I wanted, another helicopter had showed up. I knew the cops would be there any minute, so I sent her *pronto, pronto,* out onto the bridge. I had to practically push her, because she could hear sirens and started to panic. 'Immigration, immigration,' she yelled, and I told her, 'No, no, dear, a parade, a fiesta! For you!' So . . ." Lilliana's voice eased. She was suddenly enjoying herself as she watched Kate's neck redden with tension. "I thought, just hang around a bit and see what happens. Maybe we could make a piece of performance art out of this, something for the world to remember all of us by, certainly more entertaining than anything I taught in English Lit. Lilliana's flair for the dramatic! As things turned out, *you're* what happened, Kate. I couldn't have wished for a better outcome. Won't this be fun? We can play together again. Until I figure out how to bring it all to a happy and equitable conclusion.''

"But that woman, what was she doing? Why did she go out on the bridge?''

"I gave her a hundred dollars to throw a bag of old clothes she had into the sea. I told her if she did it correctly I'd give her another hundred. 'You have to be right in the middle of the bridge,' I said. She was brain-dead, but she understood money. I think all those police yelling at her confused her a bit. Of course, she didn't speak English very well. Unfortunately, there are no other suitable bridges in the area. Believe me, I've looked. It's too bad, because I've thought about this for so long. I so wanted it to be *exact,* you know! Instead we will improvise, make it up as we go along. But at least we'll be together. That's the important thing, isn't it? That three good friends spend their final moments with each other, reliving the past?''

"You mean Alex is alive?'' Her head spun around.

"Turn around! And pull up next to that van near the corner. But keep the engine running. We're in a hurry.''

Kate stopped in the street next to a gray Plymouth van. Lilliana indicated the small boy in the driver's seat. "Say hello to your son. It's been a while, hasn't it?''

20

"She's gone," Nick said, looking at the empty spot where his car used to be. His mind was roaring. How the hell did this happen?

Oscar Reddig stared toward the barricade and the road beyond. "I don't get it. She left on her own?"

"Without knowing how her son is? Not a chance." Nick felt like screaming as his stomach churned painfully.

"Then . . . ?"

Nick shook his head. He had no idea what was going on.

Reddig looked around. "So what do we do?" As a captain he wasn't used to asking advice. But now he gazed at the confused scene surrounding them—reporters, helicopters, police everywhere—as though the answer lay nearby and all he had to do was find it.

Nick continued staring at the space where the car had been. "We fucked up. Bad." He paused, looked at Oscar. "I wish I knew how."

21

Lilliana stepped out of the back of the car. For the first time Kate could see her clearly. She looked spaced-out, hyper, though it could have been the effects of anticipation and adrenaline; this was the moment she had been waiting for for seven years, and she seemed not to know if it was a good thing or not. She turned quickly toward Kate, her voice racing. "Park anywhere. Then come back here. *Hurry.*"

Kate saw Alex smiling and waving from the van, obviously ecstatic to see her.

Lilliana stepped toward the sidewalk, then quickly spun back again. "I can trust you, Kate ... can't I?" It wasn't really a question, and Lilliana had no doubt.

Kate's heart turned over.

"Now, Kate! Park and get back here."

Overcome at the thought of being with her son, Kate put the car in gear and pulled into the first spot she came to. Running back to the van she saw Lilliana fumbling with a key as she tried unsuccessfully to unlock the door. Finally it swung open, and Alex yelled, "Mommy!" Kate's heart was pounding against her ribs as she rushed forward. Then, laughing, Alex jumped from the front seat into Lilliana's arms. "I waited, Mommy. I waited. Like you said."

"Yes!" Lilliana seemed unable to show any emotion to the child, though his love for her was obvious as he threw his arms around her neck.

Kate halted. She couldn't move, but her mind was rushing out of control. *"Alex!"* The word burst from her, and the boy, still in Lilliana's arms, looked back without recognition. She started to scream. "Alex, Alex—"

Lilliana whirled angrily on her. "Don't!"

But Kate couldn't control herself. "Alex, my God—"

"*Stop!*" Lilliana shouted, roughly putting the boy down. Her voice quaked with emotion. "Get in the van. You're going to drive."

Kate couldn't make her body move.

Lilliana's fists jerked into the air, and her voice rose to a scream. "Do it, damn you! Get in the driver's seat!"

Still she didn't move, couldn't take her eyes from her son.

Lilliana muttered something, then yanked a small revolver from the pocket of the blazer she was wearing. Her arm wavered as she pointed it toward Kate. "Don't make me use it."

Kate's mind was screaming at her to do what the woman said—*Get in the van, now, hurry*—but still her legs were frozen. She hadn't been this close to her son in two years; she wanted to reach out and embrace him. Lilliana's eyes flashed with hatred as she twisted suddenly toward Alex. "I know! Let's play Popsicle." The boy giggled and put his head back, opening his mouth wide. Lilliana put the barrel of the gun in his mouth, and he began to suck on it noisily. "What flavor is it today, Alex?"

"Licorice," he said. "I like licorice."

Lilliana's eyes flew to Kate, but she didn't move the gun. "This is fun, isn't it, Alex? Such marvelous fun!" Her voice trembled as she addressed Kate. "We play this game all the time. Especially when we're watching television. Sometimes I pull the trigger, *click click click,* just to see what it will feel like when the moment comes. Want to see?"

Kate couldn't reply, felt her knees weaken, and had to force herself to remain standing. Lilliana eased the hammer back with her thumb, and Kate screamed, "No!"

"Get behind the wheel, Kate. Now!"

Shaking so badly she could hardly walk, Kate moved to the van and climbed inside. Lilliana slid open the side door and got in the rear with Alex. Grunting with exertion, she jerked a seat belt around the boy. "Wouldn't want to be stopped by a policeman, would we? You, too, Kate, buckle up for safety. Hurry, the belt.'' Her voice had none of the dead calm that Kate normally associated with Lilliana; she was out of control, muttering to herself nonstop like a madwoman as she clicked the seat belts, hers and Alex's, into their holders.

Kate pulled her seat belt around her, but her fingers were trembling so badly it took a minute to insert the clasp. Lilliana handed her the keys. ''Start the engine. And stop looking in the mirror at Alex. Keep your eyes on the road and drive very carefully. Do you understand? Very carefully! We don't want another accident!''

''Yes.''

''Pull into the street. *Now,* Kate.''

Alex said, ''Where we go, Mommy?''

Lilliana ignored him, or didn't hear him, twisting around and looking out the rear window to see if they had been observed by anyone.

Kate, aiming down the street, fingers trembling on the steering wheel as she tried to keep the van steady, repeated Alex's question. ''Where do you want me to go?''

''Just drive, don't talk. Get on the Harbor Freeway.''

Kate found the freeway a moment later and headed north. ''Where—''

''Damn it, just keep going—we're improvising. I'll tell you when we get there.''

While Lilliana stayed in the back, swearing to herself and looking constantly out the window for police, they crossed through San Pedro, through the cities of Wilmington and Carson, and finally to Torrance. Without warning Lilliana lurched suddenly forward, raising the gun and jabbing it painfully into the back of Kate's neck. ''I ought to end it right here, all three of us. . . .''

The van swerved into the left lane and a car honked angrily. ''Goddamn you, slow down. And stay in your lane,'' Lilliana shouted.

Kate tried to keep her hands steady. ''The freeway divides up here. Which way do you want to go?''

"Stay on the Harbor. We'll go downtown. No, forget it! Go south on the 405."

Kate eased into the appropriate lane, and a moment later they were heading back again through Carson to Wilmington. "Get off here," Lilliana yelled, and Kate pulled so sharply onto the off-ramp she wasn't able to see what street it was. But she knew she was near the harbor again.

"Just keep going," Lilliana snapped. "Don't stop!"

Staying on surface streets they drove for two hours, moving aimlessly from the grimy industrial city of Wilmington to the housing tracts of Torrance and Gardena, and finally into Hawthorne, as city melted into city. All the time Lilliana remained in the rear, moving restlessly as she stared out the window.

Alex began to squirm in his seat. "I have to go pee."

"Goddamn it, shut up," Lilliana shouted. She didn't even look at him, her eyes fixed on the street, watching, waiting.

Lilliana was so edgy Kate had been afraid to say anything, but finally she asked, "What are you looking for?"

"I'll know when I find it. Turn on Rosecrans."

Kate hesitated, not sure she should mention it, then said, "We're almost out of gas. It's already past the empty mark."

Lilliana spun around. "All right, pull into that Shell station. Pick a self-serve lane. We'll do it together."

Kate drew up to a pump, her eyes quickly taking in the surroundings as she killed the engine. Lilliana bent forward in the seat so she was directly behind Kate, speaking so closely her breath was warm on Kate's neck, making her shiver. "You're wondering how to get away."

"No!"

The woman's lips, cold as dry ice, brushed her flesh as though in a kiss, making the fine hairs all over her body stand up. Then the muzzle of the gun slowly traced a path up Kate's neck to the back of her head. "I'm not worried, Kate. I have Alex. If you want to walk away from here, just do it."

"No, Lilliana. Really."

"Give me the keys." When she had them in her hand, Lilliana slid open the side door and stepped quickly onto the asphalt. "Take the credit card from the console and get out."

Kate's mind was working furiously. *Open the door slowly, slam it as hard as you can into Lilliana, knocking her off balance; then go for the gun.* But as the door clicked Lilliana abruptly stepped back. The hand with the gun was in her slacks pocket. "Don't think, Kate. Just do as I tell you."

A moment later Kate was out of the van, putting the credit card in the gas pump. She could see four other customers, all men. None of them was paying attention to her.

"Hurry it up," Lilliana snapped, her head twisting as she looked from the other customers to the crowded street to Kate. "I don't like this. I want to get out of here." She started pacing rapidly back and forth along the pumps. "Something's wrong. Something's going on here. I don't like it."

Kate took the nozzle from the pump, inserting it into the van's tank and holding the handle to keep the flow of gasoline going. *Move closer,* she prayed as Lilliana paced and muttered to herself. *Come up next to me and I'll drench you with gasoline. Try to use the gun and you'll explode in flames.*

Lilliana threw her a look. "Whatever you're thinking, Kate, it won't work. I'm smarter than you." A car drew in adjacent to them, and an elderly Chinese man got out and began to fill his tank.

The pump in Kate's hand shut off with a loud click. Lilliana said, "Put it back," then suddenly changed her mind. Her eyes glowed with excitement as she realized that she had unexpectedly found what she had been looking for. "No, wait. There's a five-gallon gas can in the back of the van. Get it out and fill it."

Kate stared at her in horror. "No, Lilliana. I won't." Her eyes shot to the Chinese man just six feet away. *Look at me! Look! Don't you see what's happening?*

"Goddamn you, do it!" Lilliana stepped forward suddenly, and Kate jerked the nozzle out of the van and aimed it at her like a gun. Lilliana halted three feet away.

"Something I can help you ladies with?" It was a middle-aged man with a beer gut and a shirt that said *Ralph*. He was looking at them with a mixture of curiosity and concern.

Lilliana's head snapped angrily in his direction. "We don't need any help."

Kate's voice was calm. "Don't move, Lilliana." She stepped forward, the nozzle in her hand, but the other woman paid no attention to the threat and spun around, going rapidly to the rear of the van and flinging open the double doors. Seconds later she had the five-gallon can on the ground and was unscrewing the top.

Kate said, "I know what you're planning. I'm not going to let you do it." Death by fire, she thought—a conflagration. Lilliana's flair for the dramatic. That, and her need to dramatize everything concerning Tammy. *Someday they'll write books about me, maybe even make a movie.*

"Then I'll get in the van and end it right now. It'll take two seconds."

Kate stared at her.

The gas-station attendant was becoming annoyed. "What the hell's going on here?"

Lilliana used her foot to push the empty container closer to Kate. "Fill it. Now!" She had no doubt Kate would do as she asked.

The Chinese man finished pumping gas and climbed into his car.

Still Kate didn't move.

Alex's crying was audible from the open door of the van. He sounded miserable. "I went potty in my pants."

Lilliana spun around and moved toward the van. "I'm going to kill him right now."

"No," Kate screamed. "I'll do it." She stretched the hose to the can and began filling it. Her hand was shaking so badly she wasn't able to keep the nozzle steady, and gas splattered all over the can, pooling on the asphalt.

"Hey, watch it," Ralph yelled. "That's dangerous."

Lilliana whirled furiously on him. "Get the hell out of here."

"What?"

"Get away from me or I'll burn this place down."

His eyes got big. "I'm calling the police." He turned and hurried toward the office.

Lilliana said to Kate, "Put the top on the can and put it in the van. When you're finished get back in the driver's seat. And hurry."

Kate dropped the hose, not bothering to put it on the pump, and began screwing the top onto the can. Lilliana cast a quick glance at her, then followed the attendant to the office, where he was already on the phone. "You're too late," she said, and shot him twice in the head.

Seconds later she was back at the van, throwing the keys at Kate. "Move, move, move!"

22

Once again on the freeway, Lilliana screamed, "Keep it at sixty-five," as she moved quickly from window to window to see if anyone was following. Satisfied no one was interested in them, she reached for her purse, pulled out a box of Remington .38 shells, and hastily reloaded. But when her eyes shot to the back of the van, she started screaming. "Where's that gas can? I told you to put it in the back."

"I left it at the station."

"Damn you!" She struck Kate with the barrel of the gun. "Damn you! Damn you!"

Alex was frightened by his mother's yelling and began to cry. Lilliana spun on him, grabbing his arm and shaking him. "Goddamn it, shut up! Do you understand me? *Shut up!*"

But it only made the crying worse. The woman started screaming at the top of her voice, and shaking the boy in his car seat. Shouts and howls filled the van, and Kate thought her head would explode. She was about to hit the brake when Lilliana tried another tack.

"Do you want to go to Disneyland? You've never been, have you? If you quiet down I'll take you. Today. This afternoon. Won't that be *fun?*" But her voice sounded more threatening than inviting, and she caught Kate's eyes in the rearview mirror. "Don't say anything, damn you. Just drive."

Five minutes later as they approached the airport, Kate saw the flashing red lights of a Highway Patrol car several hundred feet behind her and gaining rapidly. *My God, he's going to pull me over,* she thought in a panic. *What will Lilliana do? She'll think I signaled him.* But what difference did it make?

They were going to die anyway. It might be the only chance she had. Trying to keep Lilliana from looking out the window, Kate said, "The police found Patty's body yesterday. Did you—"

Lilliana hunched quickly forward in her seat and stared at the back of Kate's head. Her hands rose to Kate's neck, roughly caressing the flesh. "Patty's role ran out. It happens to everyone sooner or later. Even us."

"So you killed her—after she helped you all these years?"

"Helped?" Her voice steadied in tone, the topic evidently one she was eager to discuss. "Fat chance. Patty did nothing out of friendship. She was an employee, a hired hand, a blue-collar drudge, just like my gardener or the woman who does my ironing, or that strange Dennis Flagstad Patty paid to send computer messages to you." Her fingers pinched the skin of Kate's neck, leaving splotchy red marks the size of quarters. "I have a great deal of money because of you, and I've spent freely the past seven years to get what I want. Patty ended up with much of it, my reward to her for befriending you at work. I'm surprised you didn't see through her. She was a superficial and avaricious little fool who would have sold her mother for a night on the town."

Kate darted a glance at the side mirror. The Highway Patrol unit was just two cars behind them now. Trying to keep her voice steady, she said, "How did you ever find someone like that?"

Lilliana almost laughed, but it came out like a nervous yelp, her breath a blast of fetid warmth on Kate's ear. "Like *what?* Money hungry? Hell, look around. We're in southern California, the home of the greedy rich and greedy poor. What difference does it make where I found her? I don't even remember what her real name was. She was from Canada somewhere, which was just what I needed. She had no identity in the US, no fingerprints, no history. So, we made a deal. I said, 'Hey, how'd you like to be rich?' and she jumped at the chance. Most people would. After all, she didn't know what I really had in mind for young Alex. After she brought me the kid she moved to San Francisco and lived like minor royalty on the half million—tax free, of course—she made off me. Every once in a while I'd bring her down here to give you a little thrill, seeing her and Alex on the street.

"But she was getting bored and undependable, and taking more chances than I liked. Then she told me the money I gave her was gone. Drugs, I suppose. She'd developed quite a habit recently. She wanted another half a million to go on. So I said, Let's talk about it over a few drinks. Which we did. Until I dropped a smidgen of sodium cyanide into her margarita. You remember how I used to dope your wine, don't you? Three minutes later it was over, a frivolous life coming to an unlamented end. *Hey, goddamn you—''* Her voice exploded through the air as she saw the Highway Patrol car. Without a second's hesitation she spun toward Alex, the gun jabbing him painfully between his eyes. "You first."

Alex screamed, and Kate yelled, "No!" But the CHP car passed them in a blur of flashing lights, and disappeared up ahead. "Slow down, damn you," Lilliana shouted; then, so trembling with rage that she could hardly control her movements, she struck Kate on the back of the head with the barrel of the revolver. "You both would have been dead before you pulled over."

"Please, Lilliana. I didn't see him until you did."

"Don't lie, damn you. Turn around and look at me."

Taking her eyes from the road, Kate twisted in the seat and saw Lilliana holding the barrel of the revolver hard against Alex's cheek. The boy's face was white with fear, his eyes fixed on the weapon.

"Now drive, Kate. And don't fuck up."

As always traffic thickened at the airport, and they had to crawl up to the Santa Monica Freeway. Past the interchange the congestion lightened, and Kate sped up again as they neared Westwood and the UCLA campus. "Turn off on Sunset," Lilliana suddenly decided, her voice rising almost to a scream. "Here, here, turn! *Now!''*

Kate was in the left lane and had to dart across the freeway, an eighteen-wheeler blaring its horn at her. "Where are we going?"

But Lilliana said nothing as she leaned forward, staring out the windshield.

Kate drew onto the short off-ramp, then into the left lane, and headed west on Sunset, traveling half a mile through the upscale residential area that she had come to know so well during her marriage, before Lilliana ordered her to turn north on Kenter. But the moment she was off Sunset a siren blared briefly, not more than three seconds, like an overloud mechanized belch that made everyone in the car jump. Kate's heart hammered as she looked in the rearview mirror and saw the spinning red and blue lights of an LAPD motorcycle immediately behind her. "Oh, my God, no. Lilliana, please. *Please!* I didn't see him. I promise you."

"What did you do?"

"Nothing. I—"

"Forget it, damn you! Pull over and do nice for the man. I trust your judgment, Kate. Otherwise Alex will play Popsicle for real."

Kate drew onto the gravel shoulder at the side of the road, her heart beating wildly as her hands gripped the steering wheel. The policeman sat on his cycle a moment, running the plate. "Don't worry, it's not stolen," Lilliana told her. Her voice was shaking with emotion as she sat back and pulled the seat belt around her waist; but instead of snapping it shut she shoved the end under her thigh.

Kate's eyes locked onto the side mirror as the policeman swung off his cycle and began to approach. *I have to tell him,* she thought at once. *I have to let him know what's happening.* As she buzzed the window down, Lilliana seemed to sense what she was thinking. "The gun is pressing into your son's back right now, Katie, dear. He goes first. *Pop, pop.* Blood and brains all over the car. Do you understand? It doesn't matter what happens next."

The cop's face suddenly appeared, seeming to take up the entire open window. Large square head, trim mustache, about forty years old. Scowling. "Can I see your license, please?" No emotion to his voice, doing something he did a dozen times a day.

Kate grabbed her purse. "Oh, my God." She spun around to Lilliana. "I don't have my wallet. It must have fallen out in Nick's car."

The cop put his head through the window so he could see in the rear.

"It's my van, Officer," Lilliana said with a tense voice and an unconvincing smile. "I wasn't feeling well, so I asked my friend to drive." She hesitated just an instant before her tone became demanding, a mother scolding a child. "The registration's in the glove compartment, Kate. Get it for him."

The man's gaze went from Lilliana to Kate. She stared into his face, pleading with her eyes. *Please please please* . . . He looked at her for a long moment without moving, working something out in his mind. *He knows,* Kate thought, and felt a sudden rising of hope. *He knows there's something wrong. Maybe he heard about us on his radio.* The policeman's body shifted so he could look in the back again, his gaze coming to rest on Lilliana. Kate's eyes shot to the rearview mirror and Lilliana, her face frozen, holding the man's look without blinking. No one said a word for at least ten seconds. Then she saw Lilliana's right hand slide down from behind Alex's car seat. Kate's body jerked and she started to scream at the policeman, but Alex suddenly said, "We're going to Disneyland!"

The policeman's eyebrows contracted, and his head moved back to Kate. "Heading the wrong way, aren't you?"

Lilliana again tried a smile, but her lips were bloodless and stretched thin with tension. "We have to stop by my house first to get some money." But the spell was broken. Turning again to Kate, the policeman straightened up. "Take the registration out of the glove compartment, please."

She handed him the registration slip. "What name's on here?" he asked Lilliana.

"Lilliana Elizabeth Quinlin. Do you want to see my license?"

"What's your address?"

She told him.

He turned to Kate. "What's your name?"

"Kate McDonald." Her body felt as though it were going to explode any second from tension.

"You wouldn't happen to know your driver's license number, would you?"

She shook her head, beginning to cry, and furious at herself for not being able to stop. "It starts with an *N*, I think...." Damn it, she'd given it enough times when writing a check, but she couldn't think. *"N!"* she almost shouted. "Then a zero. *N* ... zero ... five ..." She stared into his face, her eyes wet with tears, unable to go on. *Please please please.*

"Wait right here."

He went back to his motorcycle. "Don't, damn you!" Lilliana whispered harshly into Kate's ear. She leaned forward, again painfully pinching Kate's neck. "Whatever you're thinking, *don't.* Stay cool, stay cool." But Lilliana didn't sound cool at all, and even Alex was beginning to cry.

A few minutes later the policeman returned. Kate's torso was swimming in perspiration. "You were right about the first three digits. I filled in the rest for you. Carry your license from now on, though. You won't always get someone as accommodating as me." He handed her the ticket pad. "Sign at the *X.* You crossed the yellow line three times back there on Sunset. You've got a kid in the back. You ought to be more careful. You're endangering his life, you know. Nothing's more important than our children."

Kate took the pad and pen. Lilliana put her foot on the back of Kate's seat and pressed hard. Hands trembling, Kate wrote on the signature line, *Help Me,* and handed it to him.

The cop ignored the signature as he ripped out a copy of the citation and gave it to Kate. Then his eyes went from her trembling hands to her face. His voice was suddenly wary. "Are you all right?"

Kate again felt the pressure at her back. "Yes ... fine," she whispered. Then, breaking down in sobs, she said, "Officer, please help us—"

Lilliana's foot slammed into the back of the front seat.

"What?" Not certain what he'd heard, the policeman bent again and stared into Kate's face, then craned his neck through the window, looking back at Lilliana. "What's going on here?" His hand went to his holster and carefully slipped the gun out, holding it muzzle down against his leg. His face started to redden as understanding slowly dawned.

"Nothing," Kate told him, fighting back tears. "It's OK. We need to get going." She began to weep, and her head sagged on her chest. But Lilliana said, "Maybe I should explain," and moved the revolver from behind Alex, shooting the policeman in the face. "Get out of here!" she yelled as blood flew into the car, and both Kate and Alex started screaming. "Now, damn it! Go! Go! Go!"

23

"Get back on Sunset!" Lilliana screamed. "Move, damn you! *Now!*"

Trying to steer while Lilliana was screaming in her ear, Kate attempted to U-turn, fishtailing wildly on the gravel as she slammed into reverse, banging into the motorcycle and knocking it over, then shoving the van in drive and leaping forward. "Where—"

"I don't know where." Lilliana was frantic, staring out the rear window, then wheeling around to the front again. "I haven't decided. Just keep going. I'll think of something. Up there! Turn right on Sunset. Go to the ocean."

Kate spun the van toward the west, merging into the flow of traffic on Sunset, and heading through the hills of Brentwood toward the community of Pacific Palisades and, minutes later, down to the Pacific Coast Highway and the ocean.

"Go left on PCH," Lilliana shouted, then twisted toward Alex, who hadn't stopped crying since the policeman had been shot. "Shut up, damn you. I mean it."

When the boy couldn't stop his crying, Lilliana slapped him with the back of her hand, and he exploded in wails. Without thinking, Kate jerked around, her arm raised as though to strike Lilliana. "Damn you, don't hit him. Don't touch him. Ever!"

The other woman sank back in her seat and almost laughed. "Don't touch him! Ever! *Ever?*" She lurched forward. "Or what, Katie Kate? What terrible fate will befall me if I touch the sacred form of dull little Alexander Lempke? Will my fingers fall off, or my heart turn to stone, or will I simply die of shame?" Her face flushed a sudden violent crimson. "Don't tell me what to do. Don't even talk! Anyway . . .'' She eased back again. ''I'm Alex's mother. I'd never do anything to hurt him. I *wuv* my wittle boy, don't I, Alexander?''

She turned toward the child, who was trying desperately to stop crying. ''You're Mommy's darling, and you love Mommy, don't you?'' she asked harshly.

The child nodded his head up and down, up and down, up and down. But he didn't say anything, and couldn't stop crying.

''Oh, God.'' The air went out of Kate.

Then, unexpectedly, Alex lifted his head and looked appealingly at Lilliana. ''Are we at Disneyland, Mommy?''

''Disneyland? Venice Beach? Los Angeles? I don't know, Alex. It's all the same big California amusement park. Just hang on and enjoy the ride.'' She directed her attention to Kate. ''Don't stop again until I tell you. The next time you try thinking for yourself, Alex is the price you'll pay. Now *go!*''

24

Concentrate! Nick told himself as he waited alone in the back of a patrol car at the Vincent Thomas Bridge. *Stay calm. And work it out. Any problem can be solved with enough thought.*

But he'd been sitting in the car for twenty minutes and was no closer to understanding what had happened today than when he began. He turned back to the bridge. Everyone he could see—there must have been thirty cops in and out of uniform—seemed to be moving with a glacial, cover-your-ass deliberateness, knowing there would be a detailed departmental investigation, since an unarmed civilian had been killed by police officers, even if responsibility clearly lay elsewhere. He sank back in the seat and pressed his palms against his eyes. Goddamn it, why was everyone worrying about this bureaucratic bullshit when the lives of two innocent people were at risk? It was idiotic.

So much for calm, rational thinking.

But the policeman's part of his mind, the part that had governed his conscious thoughts for twenty years, said, *What else can we do? There's no telling where Kate is. Or who she's with, especially since our only suspect is dead.* He twisted suddenly around as he heard the sound of running feet, and saw Oscar Reddig racing in his direction. "A traffic officer was shot in west L.A.," Oscar said, jumping into the driver's seat. "By a woman in a van with another woman and a child."

Nick sat up. "Is he dead?"

Oscar slammed the door and cranked the ignition. "He's still alive, but barely." He rammed the car into reverse and spun around, turning on the siren. ''He told the EMTs the kid said they were going to Disneyland.''

''Disneyland?'' Why the hell would they be going to Disneyland? That was nuts. But all Nick could think to say was, ''Did someone contact Orange County?''

Oscar nodded. ''And the CHP. They'll never get to Anaheim. Even if they do, the area will be swarming with cops in two minutes.''

''Where are you going?''

''West L.A. We have people interviewing homeowners in the area. They might have seen something.''

''No,'' Nick said at once. His mind was working on it, gratified finally to have something tangible to grab on to. He climbed over the front seat as the car bounced over a dip in the road where the bridge access ramp hit the street. ''We've finally found her. We know where she's heading. We need to be there.''

''Nothing we can do in Orange County, Nick. Not our territory. We'd just get in the way.''

''Damn it, what use are we in west L.A.?'' He hesitated and added, ''I want to be there when they're freed.''

Reddig looked at Nick's face as he considered for a moment. ''OK. Orange County it is.''

Nick sat back and strapped on his seat belt. But his mind wouldn't focus, couldn't sort out what was happening. Disneyland!

Then his instincts began to speak up, too. *No,* he heard from somewhere deep inside the policeman's part of his brain again. *That can't be right. . . .*

But he said nothing.

25

"There!" Lilliana shouted. "Pull into that lot."

They were in Venice, on Washington Boulevard, an area of aging strip malls, fast-food joints, and gas stations. Kate spun into the lot Lilliana had indicated. There was a video rental store, a bakery, and a liquor store, all with the dreary, hopeless look of the near-bankrupt.

"Get as close to the gas station as you can."

A foot-high concrete barrier separated the strip mall from a large Mobil station with a convenience store attached. Kate parked adjacent to it.

Lilliana stared out the side window. "I trust you, Kate. Completely. Because you know as long as you do exactly as I say Alex remains alive."

Kate's head moved in a slight nod.

"Hold on to the dream, Kate. You and Alex! Pray for the impossible."

"What are we—"

"Not now. I'm looking." For ten minutes she stared out the side window at the gas station. People came, bought gas, food, left. More people came. "A busy place," Lilliana muttered. "You'll have at least three minutes."

"What do you want me to do?"

"Wait! Just . . . wait."

Five minutes later there were eight vehicles at the gas pumps. Another half dozen cars stopped in at the convenience store. Lilliana seemed to be expecting something. Then her voice rose excitedly. "There, Kate. See it? The white Toyota. There must be a million of them in L.A. Let's see how she pays."

The car stopped at a pump, and a young woman got out and began to look in her purse.

"She's going inside to pay. The keys will be in the ignition. You have three minutes. Don't screw up." Lilliana jumped out of the back of the van and pulled open the driver's door. "Hurry, Kate. Get in the car, drive up to the first light, and turn left. I'll be right behind you."

Kate stepped out, her purse in her hand. There must be something she could do. She could start screaming and hope someone came to her aid. But Lilliana hurried into the van's driver's seat and started the engine. "Pull into the first apartment parking lot you come to, and Alex and I will join you." She started to back out. "Run, Kate. Now!"

26

Five minutes later both vehicles were parked in the alleyway of an aging apartment complex just off Washington.

"Don't talk," Lilliana ordered as she hurriedly transferred Alex from the van to the Toyota's backseat, then got in after him. "Don't look at us. Don't think. Just drive!"

And drive they did, first heading east to the 405 Freeway, then north through west L.A., and finally over the mountains and into the San Fernando Valley, where they got off and traveled on surface streets for hours—through Van Nuys, Reseda, and Northridge, west to Chatsworth and Canoga Park, south to Woodland Hills—as Lilliana seemed to be looking for something. When she couldn't find it her mood darkened from frenzy to despair, and she sank back in the seat and began to talk of Tammy. "She'd be twelve now, almost thirteen, in the seventh grade. Thinking about boys." She leaned toward Kate, speaking softly, two mothers sharing confidences. "Thirteen. Do you remember thirteen, Kate? Boys! It's all we thought about, isn't it? But Tammy's a good student, too. She gets *A*'s in all her subjects. Like her mom did. We're a lot alike, Tammy and I. Good students, popular with the boys." Her voice fell to a whisper. "Maybe I wasn't that popular. I don't remember. But everyone likes Tammy. Especially the teachers. She joined the science club—"

On and on. Tammy's charmed life, Lilliana's dark, obsessive telling.

For hours.

In Tarzana they went through the drive-in window of a Jack

in the Box and bought tacos and Cokes, then headed back onto the freeway and toward downtown Los Angeles.

It was dark when they stopped in east L.A. and filled the car with gas at a full-serve station on Whittier Boulevard. Lilliana started to pay with cash, then gave the man her bank card. "They'll have Visa monitoring my account," she told Kate as Alex slept next to her. "Let's give them something to get excited about." But there was no excitement in her voice, no emotion at all.

Kate put her head on the steering wheel. "I can't go much farther, Lilliana. I'm going to fall asleep."

"No, Kate. Falling asleep is the last thing you'll do."

27

"Christ, I can't believe this," Oscar Reddig said, storming back into his office and slamming the door. "I've been talking to Anaheim PD. They went through the Disneyland parking lot three times and found sixty-two different gray vans. But none was the one we're looking for. They're keeping at it, but—"

"But it was a stupid idea," Nick said. "My fault! We never should have wasted time going down there."

Oscar dropped into his chair. "I don't understand it. We've had Kate's and Alex's pictures on TV all night. Every station in L.A. is showing them. Someone must have seen them!" He glanced at the wall clock. "Almost ten o'clock. I talked to channels five, nine, eleven, and thirteen. They're all going to lead their newscasts with the story." He pushed his chair away from the desk. "Cops on the street are looking; we've contacted motels, hotels—" The phone rang and he yanked it off the desk. "Reddig." He listened a moment, his eyes shooting to Nick. "No, no. Get an evidence team down there now. We can't wait until tomorrow. I want the prints in D.C. tonight." He slammed the receiver down. "Pacific division found a gray van in Venice that'd been stripped—seats, air bag, stereo. A resident said she saw a woman and a child leave it and get in a white foreign car with another woman, then take off."

Nick wasn't listening, staring instead at the phone.

"What?" Reddig asked.

Nick stood up. "I gave Kate my cell phone. It's in her purse."

Reddig wasn't sure what the point was. "Are you going to call her?"

"Why not?" He felt a sudden excitement. "Can cell phones be traced?"

"I know 911 calls can. They can pinpoint the cell and narrow the phone location to about a hundred yards. I suppose they can do it for other calls."

Nick handed him the phone. "Get hold of L.A. Cellular."

28

Shortly after midnight Lilliana ordered Kate to turn into an all-night market in Pasadena. "Just wait for us, Kate. Don't put the window down, don't talk to anyone, don't even think. Alex and I will be right back."

There was one customer at the counter, paying for a six-pack of beer. Lilliana, holding a just-woken Alex by the hand, took a bottle of gin off the shelf, then crossed to the next aisle, grabbing a prepared sandwich without looking to see what kind it was, and walked to the counter. A middle-aged man was sitting on a stool, ignoring them as he watched television. Lilliana put the two items on the counter, then stared dully at Kate's and Alex's faces staring back at her from the television.

". . . authorities think they're still in the southern California area and are likely to . . ."

Lilliana felt her heart skip a beat.

The clerk grunted, swiveled on his stool, and stood up. "That going to be all for you?"

Lilliana was still staring at the TV.

"Ma'am?"

When Lilliana didn't respond the man turned in the direction of her gaze and saw the picture on the screen. "Oh, yeah. Weird, ain't it? Cops have been searching for them all day and haven't turned up diddly yet."

Lilliana's gaze moved at once to the man's face. "You mean this has been on TV *all day?*"

"Hell, you living in a closet? Every hour or so, when the shows end. And on the news, of course. Cops had a big deal

news conference earlier tonight. Some dipshit named Krovack
or something.''

Lilliana's eyes narrowed. ''News conference? About what?''

''I guess the cops fucked up traffic in Orange County for
hours today. People was really pissed. They got some weird idea
this lady and the kid were kidnapped and taken to Disneyland, so
they sent a jillion cops down there, closing freeways, stopping
cars, looking inside vans, and the like. Can you imagine all
those cops inside Disneyland looking for a *kid*? Jesus! So they
had this Krovack saying he's sorry, blah, blah, blah. But they're
still missing.'' He began to ring up the items on the cash
register. ''That'll be fifteen twenty-three.'' He put the bottle
and sandwich in a bag, then glanced at the TV again. ''Pretty
good picture, ain't it?''

Lilliana was getting increasingly agitated. The fact that the
cops were looking for her was nothing to get worried about.
But Cerovic's turning her and Kate's personal conflict into a
public spectacle for half-wits to follow on television incensed
her. He had no right to intervene; this was Jane Devlin's story
to tell, not Cerovic's or Kate's or anyone else's. *She* was the
one who had had her daughter taken from her. *She* was the one
who had suffered.

''Fifteen twenty-three,'' the clerk repeated.

Lilliana's head gave a furious jerk, and she shoved her hand
in her purse, yanking out all the money she had and throwing
it on the counter. ''Keep it.'' Grabbing the bag, she half ran
to the car.

As Alex squirmed next to her in the backseat, Lilliana twisted
the top off the bottle and took a drink. ''You're a star, Kate.
All southern California is looking for you.'' Her voice was
sharp with anger and contempt.

''What do you mean?''

''You're on TV—tragic Kate and Alex. Can they be saved
from some madwoman who kidnapped them?''

Kate didn't say anything. But she thought, Nick.

Just then a Pasadena PD car pulled into the lot, and Lilliana
started screaming. ''Get out of here. Now.''

"Where—"

"Just get out. Drive!"

As Kate pulled out of the lot, Lilliana sank back against the seat. Why the hell was the world getting in an uproar about Kate and Alex, when Tammy's death had caused so little interest? Just another dead kid, everyone seemed to imply. Another dead kid. No news coverage, no TV alerts. Another dead kid.

A beeping noise came from somewhere, and all three of them jumped. "What was that?" Lilliana leaped forward, and Alex started crying.

"I don't know." Kate was as shaken as Lilliana. Then she said, "Nick gave me his cell phone. I forgot I had it." She reached for her purse on the passenger seat, but Lilliana lunged at her, snatching it from her hand. The phone tumbled out. Lilliana hit the on button. "You bastards. Where were you seven years ago?"

Nick was standing in the small Hollywood station communications room with Oscar Reddig. The call was on a speakerphone, and an operator was on another line with L.A. Cellular, trying to trace the transmission as the car passed from cell to cell. Unable to keep his voice from racing, Nick said, "Whoever you are, I want to talk to you. Name a place. I'll show up by myself, unarmed. I want to help you."

"Bastards," he heard again. "Damn you! Damn you!" And then a dial tone.

Nick looked at the dispatch operator. "Pasadena," she said, putting her headset down. "On Colorado, near Orange Grove. That's all we can tell you."

Lilliana was screaming as she bent forward, staring out the windshield. "Get on the freeway up here. And don't talk. I have to think."

She sank back again, but her mind was churning. How dare they interfere! This was her story, and she would decide how it turned out.

29

Kate had been driving for more than an hour when the low-fuel light flickered on. She half turned toward the rear. "We're out of gas again."

Lilliana hadn't spoken ten words since the phone had rung. Sitting stiffly behind Kate she gazed straight ahead with empty eyes, while Alex slept next to her. Hearing Kate's voice, she jumped, coming abruptly back to life. "Get off the freeway. I'll tell you what to do."

They were just north of the airport on the San Diego Freeway. Kate pulled off on Manchester, heading east into Inglewood, near Hollywood Park and the Forum. Gang territory, no-man's-land, she thought vaguely as she glanced at the dashboard clock: 1:06 A.M.

"Here!" Lilliana ordered, and Kate pulled into an aging 7-Eleven with two graffiti-covered gas pumps out front.

"This time I'll do it. Hand me the keys and stay in the car." She threw a glance at Alex, still asleep, then climbed out the rear door with a credit card she'd taken from her purse.

Kate sat frozen, watching in the mirror as Lilliana walked to the rear of the car and slowly unscrewed the gas tank. Something had happened to her, her mood sinking deeper into despondency since stopping at the market in Pasadena. Even Kate and Alex seemed to have slipped from her thoughts as she sat in the back and silently brooded. Kate shifted in her seat, keeping Lilliana in sight with the rearview mirror. "Alex, wake up! Wake up!"

The boy stirred.

"Sit up! Now."

"Huh?" Alex was groggy, as well as frightened and confused. He sat up and rubbed his puffy eyes with his fists.

Kate watched Lilliana step to the gas pump and glance at the display of accepted credit cards. Keeping her voice down, she asked, "Can you see the telephone your mother was using? It's on the seat, next to you, isn't it?"

"Yeah." A soft voice—scared, sleepy, not wanting to talk.

She tried to sound cheery. "Can you hand it to me? Not over the seat but through the seat here." She carefully twisted her right arm around and slipped her fingers between the two front seats.

Alex didn't say anything.

A loud clanking came from behind them as the nozzle was jammed into the gas tank.

"The phone, honey. Hurry, pick it up and hand it to me. It's right next to you on the seat."

The boy looked at it a moment, then shifted so he could pick it up.

"Put it in my hand, Alex. Hurry."

"I want to play with it."

"You can play with it in a minute. Give it to me now."

Alex dropped the phone on the seat and said nothing. He looked as though he was going to fall asleep again.

Kate looked at him in the rearview mirror. "This is very important to me, honey. I need to have that phone. Please."

Lilliana appeared suddenly in the passenger window. She stared at Kate a moment, then walked slowly around the front of the car and came to a stop next to Kate's window. Her eyes went from Kate to Alex. "What are you two doing?"

"Just talking, Lilliana. He's frightened."

The woman stared at her a minute, then stepped back to the pump.

Kate kept her eyes on the mirror. "Give me the phone. Hurry, Alex. Give it to me."

The boy picked it up again. Moving forward, he started to hand it over the seat. Noticing movement in the car, Lilliana glared through the rear window.

"No!" Kate said hurriedly. "Put your hand down. Give it to me between the seats."

But Alex sat back, confused or angry at the strange requests.

The gas pump shut off. When Lilliana removed the nozzle and placed it back on the pump, Kate spun around and grabbed the phone from the boy's hand. As Alex began to whimper she glanced down quickly, hit the power button, and punched 911. The phone beeped and lit up. Kate put it under her thigh just as the back door opened and Lilliana climbed in. "Go, Kate." She turned angrily to Alex. "What are you whimpering about?"

"She—"

Kate hurriedly said, "I don't know where to go."

"Shut up, Alex! Just drive, Kate. Get us out of here."

Kate lifted her thigh and maneuvered the phone between her legs. "But where do you want me—"

Lilliana made a hasty decision. Her voice eased, lost its anger and despair, sounded almost relieved. "Let's go home, Kate. Where the heart is. Let's close the circle."

"Please, Lilliana—"

"No, Kate. We're going home."

30

Nick was pacing back and forth in Reddig's office when the phone rang. He lunged at it, but Oscar grabbed it first, coming to his feet as he picked it up. His eyes went to Nick. "That's all? . . . Where's the cell?"

He slammed the receiver down a minute later. "She made contact again. A nine-eleven call. They heard a woman's voice tell someone they were going to go home. Then another voice said the word 'Lilliana' before it became garbled. But the phone's still on; they're tracking it."

Nick felt his legs go weak and he sank into a chair. "Lilliana?"

"Her neighbor, isn't it?"

Nick's head shook back and forth as he tried to make sense of it. "But Patty . . . Is *Lilliana* Jane Devlin?"

"Does it matter now?" Oscar moved out from behind the desk.

"Jesus," Nick said. He sat still a moment. "Where was the cell?"

"Inglewood. The first one was just off the 405. So the car could have either been on a surface street or on the freeway. Now they're heading north, probably along the freeway."

"But no way of telling what kind of car they're in."

"We can flood the area, look for any car with two women, or a woman and a child. Or even a single woman. As long as the phone's on we can keep the area to search pretty small."

"Lilliana," Nick said again. "My God!" He tried to recall what he had learned of Jane Devlin from the Phoenix police. He remembered that there had been no booking photo in the file because Jane Devlin had never been arrested. It hadn't seemed to matter. Even when the FBI crime computer had come up blank on Patty Mars no one was concerned. Everyone *knew* Jane Devlin and Patty Mars were one in the same. But Lilliana . . .

There wasn't time to worry about it now. He came suddenly to his feet. "We can't risk her spotting cops, Oscar. Anyway, what would they do if they see her? She's not going to pull over, not until Kate and Alex are dead." He turned toward a map on the wall. "She lives on Orchard in Brentwood. It'll take them at least twenty minutes to get there. We can beat them."

Oscar's brow contracted as he stared at the map. "I don't get it. Why would she want to go to her house?"

"Maybe it has some symbolic meaning—where she lived next to Kate for two years. Maybe she feels it's the only place she'll be alone. I don't think she's real rational now anyway." He turned from the map. "She's not stupid, Oscar. If we saturate the neighborhood with police she'll spot something out of place and start running again. We need to surprise her. That means being inside when she gets home."

Reddig put his finger on the map. "Can't do it with just the two of us. We ought to use SWAT, block off the cul-de-sac as soon as she enters it."

"Goddamn it, no! SWAT's about as subtle as an aircraft carrier. Anyway, they can't deploy that fast this time of night." He glanced out at the empty squad room. "How many people have you got here?"

"Just two guys from Vice in the locker room, if they haven't left already."

"Get them. We'll use them inside with us. I'll call Parker Center and have them send two unmarked civilian vans, not SWAT vans, and half a dozen officers in each." He turned back to the map. "One can park three blocks away on Adais here, and the other out on Harding. But not on an access road. We'll be inside Lilliana's house and keep everyone in radio contact. As soon as we see her pull into the driveway they can move in and block the cul-de-sac. But that's *all* they do. I don't want them taking action unless they hear gunfire. Have you got some passkeys? If not we'll have to break a window to get in.''

''There's keys out in the squad room.''

Nick was already at the door. ''We've got to get there before they do.''

31

Kate had no sooner pulled onto the San Diego Freeway than Lilliana grabbed her hair from behind. "Where's the phone?" Her voice was racing and she had difficulty breathing, as though she had just completed a long run.

"I think you threw it somewhere."

"I didn't throw it. Where the hell is it?"

Alex tried to say something, but Kate quickly drowned him out. "Maybe it's on the floor. Or under Alex."

As Lilliana frantically looked, Kate pushed the power button, turning the phone off.

"Damn you, move!" Lilliana said to Alex, shoving him aside and feeling along the edge of the seat.

Kate lurched suddenly forward, swooping down and coming up with the phone. "It rolled under the seat. Here it is."

Lilliana snatched it from her hand.

Alex said, "Why can't I play with it?"

"Shut up, both of you. Just shut up!" She put down her window and hurled the phone onto the freeway.

32

Though there was little traffic this time of night, they used the suction-cup light to clear a path down Sunset, putting it back inside the unmarked car on the other side of the San Diego Freeway, but not lessening their speed. Two minutes later they swung north, and in another two minutes they were on Orchard Drive.

"Park on the corner," Nick said. "I don't want the car anywhere near the house."

They sat a moment—Nick, Reddig, and the two Vice cops Nick had met for the first time tonight, Rich Santiago and Walt Mears—and stared at the house a hundred yards away at the end of the cul-de-sac. There were no lights on in Lilliana's and no lights next door in Kate's old house, where Patty's body had been found.

Reddig said, "Maybe they didn't mean Lilliana's. Could have been Kate's. There should still be a department lockbox on it."

Nick was in a hurry to get moving. "Have you got any walkie-talkies?"

"In the trunk."

"We'll split up. You and me in Lilliana's, Santiago and Mears in Kate's. We'll keep in contact."

Oscar said, "We'd better hurry. They'll be here any minute."

"Remember," Nick told the others as he opened the door. "We have to take Lilliana out before she can react. Don't take time to talk to her, don't yell 'Police!' Just bring her down."

Reddig said to them, "You're sure you'll recognize her? Don't take out the wrong person."

No problem, they said. They'd studied Kate's photograph, as well as the description of Lilliana that Nick had given them.

Nick pushed the door all the way open. "Let's do it."

They hurried to Kate's old house. Oscar took the key from the lockbox the evidence techs had left and unlocked the door. "She might pull into the garage and come in through the kitchen instead of the front door. Either way, stay out of sight until you see where the kid is. If she's alone, take her down right away." He handed them the walkie-talkie. "Keep in touch until she gets out of the car. Then we go silent."

Nick and Oscar went next door to Lilliana's house. As Oscar fiddled with the door lock, Nick squinted impatiently at his watch. "They'll be here any minute."

"Moving as fast as I can."

A moment later they were inside. Oscar picked up the phone. "I'm going to check on the vans Downtown sent."

While Oscar was on the phone, Nick flipped on the walkie-talkie. "One of you guys had better keep an eye on the backyard. It's not likely she'd come in that way, but we're dealing with an unpredictable woman." Then he looked at his watch again. Twenty after one. "We forgot to do something," he told Oscar, still on the phone.

"What?"

"I don't know." He felt a pain in the pit of his stomach. "I guess we'll find out in a minute."

33

The Toyota pulled into the driveway at 1:22, and idled for a moment before Kate cut the engine.

Lilliana strained forward, staring at the darkened house, then turned quickly to look at the nearby homes as though worried that someone might be watching. "Pull out," she said hurriedly.

"What?"

"You heard me. Get out of here. We're leaving."

"But—"

"Do it, damn you. Move!"

Kate reversed out of the driveway, and headed back the way they had come. Two blocks later Lilliana shouted, "Slow down." She turned and looked out the rear window of the Toyota for another block, then said, "Pull over. Here!"

Kate drew up to the curb and waited, the engine idling.

"Go back to the house now."

Kate twisted around and looked at her.

"Just being careful," Lilliana said. "I wanted to see if anyone was expecting us."

Kate turned the car around. A minute later she was again in the driveway. Lilliana said, "Inside, Kate. And you . . ." She whirled on Alex, who had been whimpering since they stopped for gas. "Be quiet. Do you hear me? I don't want any neighbors waking up." Opening the door, she took Alex roughly by the wrist as she stepped out, the gun in her free hand. "*Now,* Kate. And no noise."

Feeling as if her legs wouldn't carry her, Kate climbed out of the car, the late-night breeze from the sea cold against her skin. Lilliana stood aside, letting Kate lead the way to the front door. Keeping her voice to a whisper, she spoke like a parent to a child. "You have the key, Kate. Open the door. I don't want to stand out here."

Kate's fingers shook as she tried to insert the key in the lock. But she couldn't hold her hand steady, and the key dropped to the stoop with a hard, metallic clunk.

"Get it, damn you."

Kate bent, picked it off the cement, and straightened slowly. *Do something! Do something, damn it! Once you're in the house it's all over.*

Lilliana stepped suddenly forward and snatched the key from her hand. Briefly letting Alex loose, she unlocked the door and kicked it open. "Inside, both of you." She pushed Kate harshly on the back, and suddenly all three were in the house, and the door locked behind them.

Kate steadied herself on her feet, took a breath, and went into the living room, Alex and Lilliana behind her. Lilliana turned on a table lamp, only partially lighting the room.

"I tired," Alex mumbled softly. "I want to go to sleep."

"You will," Lilliana said. "Just wait. We want this to be perfect, don't we?"

Kate took a sudden step forward. "Let him go, Lilliana. He didn't do anything. Let Alex go and I'll do whatever you want."

Lilliana's fury erupted. "Goddamn you. Alex isn't leaving. He's why we're here." She jerked on the neck of the boy's shirt, almost lifting him from the floor. "Alex and Tammy, Kate. It's only just. Eye for eye, tooth for tooth, hand for hand, foot for foot, burning for burning, wound for wound, stripe for stripe."

Kate forced her voice to go calm. "Alex did nothing to you, Lilliana. *I* did. *I* killed Tammy. I did it on purpose. You should punish me, not an innocent child."

"Goddamn it, don't patronize me. I know what you did, and I know exactly what *I'm* doing."

Kate started to say something, but Lilliana yelled, "No! No more talk." She loosened her grip on the boy and he fell to his knees. He began to cry at once, but Lilliana ignored him, taking a step back and glancing rapidly around the room as though looking for something. "Not here. In the kitchen!"

Alex understood none of what was going on. Pushing to his feet he went to Lilliana and hugged her leg. "I scared, Mommy. I want to go."

For what seemed the fiftieth time today, Lilliana's mood suddenly shifted. Sounding as if she had just had the most wonderful idea, she said, "I know what, Alex. Let's play a game. Do you want to play a game? That'll make you happy."

He rubbed his tears on her slacks. "I want to go. Where's Daddy?"

But Lilliana's manic mood had returned. "Let's go in the kitchen; then we'll have fun!" She was practically dancing as she waved the gun at Kate. "You first." Lilliana grabbed Alex's arm and dragged him along as she followed Kate to the kitchen. She started to turn the light on, then changed her mind. "We don't want to alert any nosy neighbors, do we?"

"Now what?" Kate asked, her mind working as she sought a way to overpower Lilliana. But the woman never came close enough. And Kate was too weakened with terror anyway.

Lilliana was triumphant. "Götterdämmerung! How proud my Hans would be!" She offered a small, hateful smile. "We really were married, by the way. I didn't in the slightest care about his romances, tawdry as they were. It was enough that I lived next to my lovely Katie Kate and had a credible story. I felt a single woman in such a large house would raise such *troubling* questions. Hans could, and damn well did, do whatever he wanted. The silly man actually thought I loved him. Until I set him free unexpectedly, with everything except the house, of course. But now . . ." She turned the lock in a door next to the refrigerator, opened it, and said, "Let's go in the garage, shall we?" She stepped back. "You first, Kate."

Moving slowly Kate crossed in front of Lilliana, who smiled brightly. "Easy does it, Katie, my girl. Don't trip and hurt yourself. We're so close now; we don't want anything to interfere with our success." As Kate went down the two steps, Lilliana said, "Turn on the light. No one will see it in here."

Dragging Alex with her, Lilliana followed, going at once

to a shelf over a workbench. Grabbing a small can of lighter fluid, she smiled and handed it to Alex. "Take this into the kitchen and I'll show you how to play with interesting things you find around the house. That ought to be fun, shouldn't it? Now go!" As the boy scurried away Lilliana picked up a cardboard box of twelve quarts of motor oil and hurriedly dropped it on the kitchen floor just inside the door. Back in the garage she lifted two large plastic containers of liquid fertilizer and grinned happily. "Fertilizer! Do you remember the federal building in Oklahoma City, Kate?" She tossed both containers in the kitchen, then grabbed several gallon cans of paint from a shelf and threw them one by one into the kitchen. Picking up a laundry basket, she filled it with aerosol cans of insecticide, spray starch, paint, and WD-40, and shoved it at Kate. Then, hurrying over to the workbench, she grabbed a can of shellac thinner and a two-gallon container of gasoline meant for the lawn mower. "Into the kitchen, Kate. We're going to play a game."

Back in the house Lilliana opened a door beneath the sink and grunted with approval as she removed a container of liquid bleach. "Don't worry. I'm not going to do the wash." She turned to Alex. "Fun time. A new game called Spread the Bleach. Do you want to play?"

Alex stepped away from her, pouting. "I don't want to."

Kate saw what she was planning and almost fainted. "My God, Lilliana."

"Shall I put Wagner on the stereo—The 'Entrance of the Gods into Valhalla,' perhaps? I've been thinking about this since we were at the gas station this afternoon. The three of us can go boom together, and watch the sky burn at our feet."

"Alex," Kate said very calmly. "Go outside." She heard her voice with a sort of stunned surprise, as though it were a stranger's, completely without emotion and not at all how she felt. Her body shook but the words were clear as she looked into her son's eyes. "Go *outside* and start running, and run as *far* and as *fast* as you can. Now, Alex. Run!"

"Stay where you are, you little bastard!" Lilliana snapped.

The boy looked up at the two women in fear. His lower lip began to quiver.

Kate made herself smile, her heart beating with terror and her face beaming with joy. "Go on, Alex. Run as far away from here as you can. And when you're through running I'll buy you the biggest ice cream you ever saw."

Alex was several feet away from Lilliana. He looked at her in the semidarkness and said, "Mommy," his voice quaking.

"That's right, Alex," Lilliana said, getting angry again. "I'm your mommy. This woman is bad. She's a witch. She wants to hurt you. She wants to make you cry."

"Go, Alex!" Kate screamed, sounding angry now and rushing at the boy, trying to frighten him. "Go! Get out of here. Run, before I hurt you!"

Alex scurried to Lilliana, hiding behind her legs. She offered him a small smile and patted the top of his head. "Good boy. This bad lady should know children always obey their mothers." Her smile grew as she looked at Kate. "Now, let's play Everybody Dies."

34

Alex was clinging to Lilliana's legs and trying not to cry,
though he was frightened to death. "I love you, Mommy. I
love you." He repeated the words over and over, as if they
could make all the scary things in his life go away.

Lilliana ignored him. Bending down, she opened the container of shellac thinner. "Your husband enjoyed making jokes
about my passion for cleaning. Well, we all have our obsessions.
Paul's was bedding women other than his wife. Including me,
I might add. Mine was bringing cleanliness to an ugly world.
Or at least my part of it. But this was only *after*." She tipped the
container over and watched with rapt attention as the contents
quickly spread around the kitchen floor. Her eyes came up to
Kate's. "After . . .

"So I wouldn't have to think. You understand, don't you?
About not wanting to think?"

Her gaze again went to the floor as the thinner pooled around
their feet. "A good start. But not sufficient." She took the
lighter fluid from Alex and flipped up the stopper. "See how
this works, Alex? Just squeeze the container like this." She
demonstrated, sending a spurt of liquid against the wall. "Here.
Won't this be fun! Spray it around the room."

The boy took it uneasily.

"Turn it upside down, Alex, and squeeze."

Alex tried it and smiled when he saw it squirt onto the floor.

"All over the kitchen, Alex. On the floor and on the walls.
Do a good job."

As Alex walked around the room, squirting lighter fluid,
Lilliana opened one of the containers of fertilizer. Holding the

gun on Kate, she spread the liquid on the countertops and splashed it on the walls. "We could have used that gasoline you left at the station, but I've always been good at improvising."

Kate's throat felt as if it had swelled shut. "Alex," she said with difficulty. "I want you to listen very carefully to me. This woman is not your mother. . . . I'm your mother. Do you understand? *I'm* your mother."

"*No!*" He looked at her hatefully.

Lilliana smiled. "You're just confusing him. He's not terribly bright to begin with. Bad genes, you know. Alex!"

The boy looked at her.

"Do you still have some fluid left in the can?"

He nodded.

"Spray that nasty lady who's trying to trick you. Spray it all over her."

He looked uncertain.

"Go ahead, son. Spray it on her clothes. Such a bad lady."

He took a tentative step toward Kate, holding the container in two hands.

"Do it, Alex! Spray her!"

Still he hesitated.

"Damn you!" Lilliana took an angry step in his direction, and almost at once Alex squeezed the can, sending lighter fluid over Kate's shirt and slacks. He squeezed again, but the can was empty, and he let it fall to the floor.

"Alex," Kate said, trying to sound calm as her body began to shake uncontrollably. "This woman is going to do something bad like she did with that gun and the policeman. Your daddy won't like that! He'll be very mad if you stay here with a bad woman."

Lilliana's tone turned contemptuous as she took the top off the two-gallon gas can. "His daddy? Do you mean that half-wit in New Mexico who's been watching him? Or the jerk whose wayward sperm produced him? Two daddies and two mommies. Confusing, isn't it?" Picking the can up— "Don't move, Kate"—she began to splatter gasoline all over the kitchen. When the can was only one-quarter full, she tipped it over Kate's slacks and shoes, then covered her own clothing, beginning with her shoulders. Her voice slowed, became almost restful. "Foot for foot, Kate. Burning for burning . . ."

Kate jerked back at once and began to scream. "Get out of the house, Alex. Leave. Before something terrible happens. Leave the house. *Now! Go!*"

Alex moved away from Kate and came back to Lilliana, clinging to her leg, now soaked with gasoline. She clapped her hands happily. "I know how to make this even more fun, Alex." She picked up a bottle of bleach. "Let's pour this over your head. Does that sound like fun? Like taking a shower!"

The boy looked at her in confusion.

"Just like water, Alex. See?" She took the top off the bottle and poured some on the floor. "Can you hold this over your head or is it too heavy?"

The boy hesitantly took the plastic bottle, but it dropped to the ground. "Damn you!" she screamed, and hurriedly snatched it up. Her tone eased. "Come here, Alex. This won't hurt; it'll be fun."

He took a step in her direction.

"No," Kate whispered. Her voice had deserted her, and her legs were so weak she could hardly stand. "Alex, run! My God, please don't let her do that to you. Run! Get out of here!"

Alex saw what Lilliana was about to do and ducked instinctively just as she poured the bottle of bleach over him, drenching the back of his head and shoulders. The boy was terrified; he began to shake and started to move away. Kate was still begging him to run, but Lilliana suddenly raised her voice. "Come back here. Now!"

He stopped, looked at Kate, then Lilliana. He was trembling so violently he could hardly stand.

"Good boy," Lilliana said soothingly, calm descending now as seven years' effort finally came to a close. "Good boy." She kept the gun on Kate. "If you interfere, he goes first. Then you and me together. Do you understand?"

Kate ignored her, forced herself to speak to her son. "She's trying to hurt you, Alex. Leave the room; leave the house. Go outside and yell for a policeman. Can you do that? Yell for a policeman."

But the boy just stared at her, his body shaking uncontrollably.

Lilliana took two steps to the stove and turned it on. The gas flames shot up from the burners, suddenly illuminating the dark room. Her face had gone blank. "Come here, Alex."

The child stepped slowly in her direction.

Lilliana looked around. Seeing a newspaper on the counter, she rolled it into a tube; then, holding the gun in her other hand, she stuck the end of the tube in the fire. As it caught she said, "Come here, son."

But Alex was terrified beyond words. This was all wrong. "No, Mommy. No! Fire." Seeing his mother in danger he panicked and rushed forward to help her, slipping on the wet floor and falling against her. "Mommy," he yelled, yanking on her leg. "Mommy, no!" But it was too late.

35

Nick squinted at his watch in the darkness of the house. "One-thirty," he said.

Oscar was standing behind the drapes, looking out the window toward the street. "Should be here. Should've been here ten minutes ago."

Nick keyed the walkie-talkie. "Mears," the voice said.

"You keeping an eye out back?"

"Like you said. Not a movement."

"All right. Keep it up." He turned to Reddig. "Maybe they got delayed."

Reddig stepped back from the drapes. "Could be."

"Could have stopped for gas."

Oscar said nothing.

Nick went to the window.

Oscar picked up the phone. "I'm going to check with the guys in the vans."

Nick walked to the rear of the house and stared out a bedroom window. He could see the entire yard in the moonlight, Lilliana's meticulously laid out flower beds, mature trees, a sundial, perfectly shaped arrangements of annuals. When he got back to the living room, Oscar said, "Only one car has passed the vans, a two-seater Miata convertible with a man driving."

Nick sank into a chair. "I don't get it. It can't take this long from Inglewood."

Oscar began to walk around.

Nick asked, "You're sure they said 'home'? They're going home?"

"That's what the operator heard. You don't think she meant Arizona, do you?"

"Not likely." But he thought, *Why not? Who can tell with Lilliana?* She and Kate had both lived in . . . "Oh, Jesus!" He bolted up. "Where's Kate been living? *Whose* home?"

Oscar blinked. "Shit."

Nick began to run.

36

Lilliana's body was knocked off balance by the force of the collision with Alex, and the gun tumbled to the floor. Reaching out desperately with her free hand, she tried to grab onto the counter, but her fingers slipped on the tiles, wet with gasoline and bleach, and she fell to the floor.

Alex, on his knees next to her, picked up the gun.

"Alex!" she screamed.

Holding the gun by the handle, the boy stood and backed away, his entire body trembling violently.

Kate felt a rush of hope. "Give me the gun, Alex. Please. Give it to me."

The counter behind Lilliana began to burn from the gasoline. The flames ran down to the cabinets below, and followed the stream of gasoline to the floor.

"Damn it, Alex!" Lilliana yelled, getting to her feet, the flaming newspaper still in her hand. "Give it to me."

The fire terrified the boy. It raced toward Lilliana, igniting her shoes, but she seemed not to notice. "Damn you," she yelled. "Damn you. Give me the gun."

Kate stepped toward her son, putting her hand out. "Hand it to me, Alex. Let me have it." She could feel the flames against her legs but kept her eyes on Alex, pleading with him. "Hand it to me, please. . . . Hand me the gun."

"No," he shouted to Kate, but his voice quaked with fear, and he began to sob.

The fire had spread to half the kitchen floor and the cabinets behind Lilliana, which were saturated with gasoline and fertilizer. The curtains just behind her head caught a spark and flared up in seconds with a crackling sound. Kate could hear dogs barking from the rear yard—Bailey and Preston, she vaguely recalled—but the sound was drowned out by Alex's whining and the terrible noise of the fire, now all around them. She thought she smelled something like burning flesh.

"Good boy," Lilliana said to Alex in a voice more calm than Kate would have thought possible. "Come here; give it to Mama. Come here."

Kate's eyes were still on Alex. He seemed too frightened to do anything, even to move from the flames spreading in his direction as they traced the trail of liquids on the floor and walls, and moved toward the cans of paint. Kate took a step toward the boy, but it merely galvanized him into abrupt action, and he scurried in Lilliana's direction. Lilliana moaned in triumph, the sound so soft it could barely be heard above the crackling of the flames, and snatched the gun from him.

Alex looked at her and backed away, trembling. The hand she had grabbed the gun with was in flames. His mouth opened but nothing came out.

The phone rang.

Jesus Christ, Kate thought in near-hysteria. *We're burning to death and the goddamn phone is ringing!* Or was it? She couldn't think anymore. The rational part of her brain had shut down, and all she could think of was, Run! A thousand frantic voices were screaming into her ears: *Get out now, before the whole house goes up.*

Lilliana was suddenly exultant, and almost at peace. After seven years everything was finally working out as she had so carefully planned. She had the gun, she had Kate and Alex, and they were dying together. Tammy's death had not been in vain; her short life had not been forgotten; her mother had done what any mother would have. *Eye for eye, foot for foot, burning for burning . . .*

Something exploded from the edge of the kitchen. Kate glanced in that direction and saw the plastic laundry basket going up in flames as the aerosol cans exploded one after another, spewing their contents into the air. She jumped suddenly forward, shouting at Alex, "Get out of here! Go, go go!"

And then it became phantasmagoric, a dream state, unreal. Smoke rose and flowed all around them; one of the paint cans exploded, sending paint and flames into the air, while more flames burned noisily at their feet. *Run,* the voices continued to scream at her. *Hurry . . .*

"No," Lilliana said to Alex as he started to move away. It sounded to Kate as if she had sung the word rather than spoken it, the single syllable drawn out like an extended organ note. Lilliana dropped the flaming newspaper, now burned down to her hand, to the floor at her feet. "Don't go." The flames leaped at once onto her slacks, already soaked through with gasoline. "Not yet. Stay with Mama."

In seconds Lilliana's clothing was on fire, her arms engulfed to the shoulders. But her expression eased, became almost beatific, her voice gently soothing. "Stay with Mama, Tammy. Mama would never let anything bad happen. Mama loves you more than life. Nothing will ever hurt you." Then the gun exploded with a horrible popping and a burst of fractured light, and more flames shot toward the ceiling.

Hysterical, screaming at the top of her voice, Kate grabs Alex—she thinks later she remembers this—grabs him off the floor, her shoes burning as the fire races behind Lilliana and shoots across the kitchen onto the walls and into the living room. And all the time the phone rings and rings as if this were any other night at home. *This isn't happening,* Kate's brain is shouting at her. *None of it's real; you're imagining it. You'll wake up surrounded by water.*

Alex's eyes are closed; he's screaming in fear of the blaze spreading everywhere now, racing even across the ceiling, as Kate holds him like a rolled-up rug and runs toward the front door. She looks back and sees Lilliana's hair on fire. *Medusa,* her fevered brain tells her, and Kate thinks *Yes, the serpent-*

hair turned to flames. But the fiery snakes seem not to bother Lilliana at all, and she stands frozen, a smile on her face, telling Tammy she'd never let anything bad happen to her; mothers always protect their children. Always.

37

When Nick drove up, Kate was in the front yard, screaming and frantically rolling Alex on the ground. His shoes and socks were off and her own shoes were twenty feet away, burning slowly. Satisfied the flames were out on Alex's clothes, she slapped with both hands at her pants, still smoldering from a stream of fire that followed the lighter fluid and gasoline from her ankles to her neck.

Then she passed out from shock. When she woke up the first thing she saw was Oscar Reddig standing over her with a hose, water splashing at her side. The second was Nick, holding her head in his lap.

"Alex, my God." She jolted up.

"He's OK, Kate. Just shook up." The boy's legs were obviously burned, but Nick wasn't going to tell her that now.

Kate sank back, her eyes closed, drifting off. Then her eyes snapped open again. "I was hallucinating. The house was burning all around us and I thought I heard the phone ringing and ringing." She saw his face and said, "Jesus, was that you?"

A fire engine pulled up in front of the house. Others could be heard in the distance. Cerovic shrugged and felt foolish. "I wanted to see if you were home."

38

"This is the calmest I've felt in years," Nick said. "Does that mean love?"

It was six weeks after the fire, and Kate, the bandages off her hands for only the second day, was sitting with him in the backyard, watching Bailey and Preston carefully nose around Alex as he held one of their rawhide bones with both hands. She gave him a look. "A little late to be thinking about that, isn't it?" As Bailey sniffed the boy's neck from behind, she added suddenly, "Hey, where were these supposedly well-trained guard dogs of yours while we were being sprinkled with gasoline?"

Nick sounded hurt. "In the yard, where they were supposed to be at night. I trained them to guard from out back."

"I think you ought to fire them. They were sleeping until the kitchen was in flames. Then all they did was bark."

"What did you expect them to do? They're dogs."

"Lassie always ran over to Mr. Wilkins's farm, or to the general store, and brought back help."

Preston edged toward Alex, who held the bone out, then pulled it back at the last minute.

"Don't tease him," Kate said. "Throw it for him."

Alex appealed to Nick. "Do I have to?"

Nick shrugged. "Mom said."

Alex giggled and threw the bone as far as he could—three feet. Both dogs leaped at it. The boy's legs were still wrapped in bandages, and he was due at the hospital in two hours to see how they were healing. Ironically, the bleach Lilliana had poured on Alex, thinking it flammable, probably protected him from worse burns. The doctors were sure a skin graft wouldn't be necessary but wanted to do some more tests, and were going to keep him overnight. He had so far spent two weeks in the hospital and had come to hate it. The thought of even one more night was dispiriting to him.

Kate and Nick had already planned how to surprise him with a redecorated bedroom when he came home tomorrow afternoon, the room Kate had vacated when she moved in with Nick. But that hadn't been until last week, when they had agreed on a marriage date, September 21 as it turned out, the autumnal equinox (Appropriate for someone in the autumn of his life, Kate had kidded). For now they were learning about each other in the ways of those who trusted their future together: slowly and deeply, but without probing, and careful not to touch the spots that were still painful to each.

Nick had already spent three days running around southern California buying the children's-room furniture he had thought about for years until Beth had been diagnosed with cancer: a headboard shaped like a football helmet, a lamp in the form of a cowboy on a horse, a desk with Winnie-the-Pooh characters painted on it, a huge poster of Mark McGwire hitting a home run to put on the wall. But no giant stuffed rabbits.

Kate took his hand. "Anyway, stop asking stupid questions about love. You're just looking for reassurance like a pimply thirteen-year-old. A macho cop should be more self-confident."

"Yeah, well . . ."

She touched his hand. "Well, nothing!"

"Mommy, he won't give the bone back." Preston was holding it in his mouth, drool running down his chops as he taunted the boy.

"Ask Daddy to get it."

Alex looked at Nick but said nothing. For as long as he could remember, Robert Lempke had been his father, and it was difficult now to shift his affection to this new man. But with Kate he had had no hesitation, the bond instinctive and instant once he had been removed from Lilliana's influence. Kate started to repeat her request, but Nick said softly, "Let me do it."

While Alex still looked at him uneasily, Nick directed his attention to Preston. "Drop it!" he said calmly.

The dog dropped the bone at once. Alex looked from Preston to Nick with big eyes, obviously impressed. He immediately grabbed the bone and threw it. Preston snatched it and came back, the bone held like a cigar in his teeth. Alex said, "Drop it." When nothing happened he was even more impressed.

Nick marveled at how relaxed the boy was. He had been hysterical with fear when taken to the hospital that night. But fortunately, other than her hand, he hadn't seen Lilliana burning. Kate had grabbed him at once and raced out of the house before he grasped what was happening. And now, with the assistance of a counselor from Children's Hospital, they were helping him adjust to all he had been through—the two years with Lempke, the occasional visits with Lilliana, the short jaunts with Patty Mars to Hollywood in order to upset Kate.

The initial hospital stay, along with numerous tests, showed that Lilliana had not been abusing Alex, as she claimed. She had seldom seen him, in fact, and almost never alone; they were usually at Lempke's house. Besides feeding him little except breakfast cereal, she had not had much effect on his development or health. He seemed, in fact, as healthy as most three-year-olds.

His biggest adjustment was being taken from Lempke, who was now facing twenty-plus years in prison for kidnapping. Alex still asked about him, and clearly felt his loss. But children were resilient, Kate knew. They could rebound from almost anything.

Paul's role in the child's life became suddenly problematical when he accepted a new position in the District Attorney's office in Seattle. "A hell of an opportunity," he said; his career was on the rise. "I still want to be involved in Alex's life, Kate, but . . ." But it would have to be on occasional visits to California, and Kate didn't think there would be much of that. Which struck Nick as just dandy.

Kate turned toward the house, where they could hear the sound of conversation from the kitchen, which had been rebuilt after the fire. The painters were there now, finishing up. She said, "Having my own kitchen might take a while to get used to. This morning I wanted to ask you if you wanted coffee with your Grand Slam. And how 'bout them Dodgers?"

Nick laughed. "Maybe we should go to Denny's for dinner, see if they remember you."

"Not a chance. I'm through being the crazy lady. We'll go to some pizza place and pig out on pepperoni and cheese."

Nick glanced at his watch.

"I know. We've got to pack for the hospital. I just hate to give him up again. Even for one night."

"We're not, though. Every time he wakes up he'll see us." Children's Hospital had put two beds in Alex's room so they could sleep over.

"Still . . ."

"Right. Hospitals are terrible places for sick people."

She squeezed his hand. "One more thing we agree on." She rose to her feet. "Come on, Alex. Time to get ready."

The boy threw the bone into the yard and watched as the dogs chased after it. Then he turned to his mother. "Is Nick . . . is Daddy going, too?" His eyes went to this large man who had suddenly become a part of his life.

"Of course, honey. We're a family."

Alex smiled as he tried to run, but his bandaged legs wouldn't let him. Instead he waddled up to Nick and took his hand.

<u>BOOK YOUR PLACE ON OUR WEBSITE</u>
<u>AND MAKE THE</u>
<u>READING CONNECTION!</u>

We've created a customized website just for our very special readers, where you can get the inside scoop on everything that's going on with Zebra, Pinnacle and Kensington books.

When you come online, you'll have the exciting opportunity to:

- View covers of upcoming books
- Read sample chapters
- Learn about our future publishing schedule (listed by publication month *and author*)
- Find out when your favorite authors will be visiting a city near you
- Search for and order backlist books from our online catalog
- Check out author bios and background information
- Send e-mail to your favorite authors
- Meet the Kensington staff online
- Join us in weekly chats with authors, readers and other guests
- Get writing guidelines
- AND MUCH MORE!

**Visit our website at
http://www.pinnaclebooks.com**